DATE DUE

P. S. Wilkinson

C. D. B. BRYAN

HARPER & ROW, PUBLISHERS

NEW YORK, EVANSTON

AND LONDON

P. S. Wilkinson

Portions of this book appeared originally in *The New Yorker*.

To Phoebe

Book One

1

IT WAS COLD OUTSIDE the Bachelor Officers Quarters —too cold to snow. First Lieutenant Philip Sadler Wilkinson 05 001 345, Army Intelligence, stood on the frozen ground in front of his room beneath the bright starry night with his gloved hands tucked deep within the armpits of his Army field jacket. He wore two pairs of woolen socks inside his loosely laced combat boots; but still he had to wriggle his toes to keep them warm. He was watching the Korean prostitutes in their brightly colored robes trot past the barbed-wire fence. Others, already at the front gate, were waiting for the GIs to bring them inside for the party at the NCO Club. The prostitutes, too, were trying to keep warm; and they danced from one rubber-slippered foot to the other, feathery wisps of kimchi-scented breath scooting from their mouths as they laughed happily at themselves. Tonight was P. S. Wilkinson's second Christmas Eve in Korea; and, for him, it was a lonely, homesick, Christless night.

He walked back into the warmth of his room. There was a shallow pool of diesel oil in the pan beneath the stove and he looked around for a rag. He decided to ignore the stench and lay down on his bunk to wait for chow call. He was always waiting now, each day of his tour carefully marked on the FIGMO chart that was taped behind the door of his wall locker. He had only seventeen days to go. On January 10, 1960, he would board a MATS flight out of Kimpo Air Base for Tachikawa, Japan.

3

And from there it was home. He would have completed his six months at the Army Intelligence School, his thirteen months in Korea, and he would be released by the Army at last.

There was a rasping of static, an amplified crunch of a phonograph needle dropping onto a record, then chow call blew across the compound. Wilkinson listened to the men slamming doors and running toward the mess hall, then he stood up and murmured, "Gentlemen, dinner is served."

He ducked into the doorway of the Officers' Mess, slapping the cold out of his hands, and was bumped from behind by Lieutenant Johnson.

"Hey, candles," Johnson said. "Pretty romantic."

"The generator's quit," P.S. said.

There were colored paper napkins and funny hats and antipasto in little glass jars. There were a few strands of frayed and dirty tinsel left over from past years' parties, and there was a cardboard bell or angel or something which P.S. hit his head on as he made his way in.

"It's going to be a pretty lousy Christmas," Johnson said.

"Why's that?" P.S. asked.

"You didn't hear the word? Pyongyang Radio just announced that a MIG-15 shot down Santa Claus for violating Korean People's Party air space."

A Korean waitress brought in trays heaped with turkey, cranberry sauce, peas, and mashed potatoes; but the turkey was dry, the peas were cold, and the reconstituted potatoes were waxy.

"Merry Christmas," P.S. said to the waitress.

"Merry Christmas, Rutena Wirkinson."

"Hey, P.S.?" Johnson said. "What were you doing this time last year?"

P.S. leaned back in his chair and smiled. "If I'm not mistaken I was eating this same piece of turkey." He pushed his tray away half-finished and asked the waitress for some coffee, then, suddenly, the lights came back on.

"My God!" Johnson said, looking down at his tray. "Don't tell me that this is what I've been eating!"

Lieutenant Pratt, the head of the Military Police Detachment, told P.S. that he had been saving a bottle of brandy. P.S. had a bottle of Scotch. And Johnson said he had left a case of beer outside to cool.

"Was that your case of beer?" Wilkinson asked him. "I just found it out there and I gave it to my section."

Johnson looked at him incredulously. "You *what?*"

"There wasn't any name on it," P.S. said.

"You *didn't* . . . you *couldn't* . . ." Johnson was shaking his head.

"Was that the same case I saw out there?" Pratt asked. "I thought it belonged to Blatz."

"Blatz?" Johnson asked.

"His name was on it."

"Now come on, you guys," Johnson said. "You didn't really . . . I mean, you couldn't have given it away, could you?"

"Well," P.S. said, "to tell you the truth I just put it aside until Blatz claims it."

"But Blatz is the name of the beer!" Johnson protested. "It isn't Blatz's beer, it's *my* beer."

"A likely story," Pratt said. "If it had been your beer, you would have had your name on it."

"I guess we'd just better go see if that beer's still there," P.S. said. "I've got a hunch that there ought to be a pretty good reward given to whoever finds it. And since I'm the one who hid it . . ."

"Next to the water tank," Pratt said. "I hid it somewhere else."

"Well, I'd better be the one who finds it," Johnson said.

Much later that evening Pratt, Johnson, and Wilkinson were on the bunks and footlockers which had been pushed together in Pratt's room. The water had been shut off for repairs on a pipe somewhere. The case of cold beer was gone, the empty beer cans were stacked on Pratt's desk. Lieutenant Korkus stopped in to tell everyone he was going to midnight mass. No one offered to go with him.

"I hate that sonuvabitch," Johnson said.

"That's the Christmas spirit," Pratt said.

P. S. Wilkinson sat on the edge of a footlocker looking first at Pratt and then at Johnson. He was trying to imagine them out of the service. He tried to picture the two of them in New York not wearing those ugly olive-green woolen winter fatigue uniforms and he couldn't. He realized that his two friends would never exist, except as two men he had known in the Army. For, to P.S., they were forever enshrined in olive green. P.S. felt the whisky warm in his stomach and he smiled at Pratt and Johnson.

"What are you smiling at, you silly bastard?" Pratt asked.

"We are all brothers," P.S. said.

Johnson burst out laughing. He reached over and patted P.S. on the back and said, "If there's one thing I can't stand it's a maudlin drunk."

"I am NOT muddlin," P.S. said.

"I said *maudlin.*"

"Paddling maudlin home," P.S. sang, and then suddenly he was silent. He was thinking about all his friends who had finished college and by now had good jobs, and the others who had gone on to graduate schools. They were all sitting at home, some with new wives, some with their families, and P.S. envied them. He wished to God he was somewhere with someone he loved. He pushed himself off the footlocker and stood up. "It is traditional—"

"Christ, he's going to sing 'Melancholy Baby.'" Johnson laughed.

"Traditional," P.S. continued, "it is traditional in the Old South on times—on *occasions* such as this to propose a toast . . ." He raised his half-filled glass of warm whisky and stood with his left arm at the small of his back, his feet together and the elbow of his toasting arm locked to his side. "Gentlemen . . . to absent friends."

"To absent friends," Pratt echoed.

"To absent friends," Johnson said. "Wish they were here."

P.S. thought for a moment, and then he smiled. "Yes, wish they were here."

2

WILKINSON had just opened the door to the girl's apartment when he heard the siren. He frowned slightly. He didn't remember hearing a siren before. He tried to get away from the siren but his sheet was caught in her apartment door. He kept pulling on the sheet and all the time the siren was becoming louder and louder and there was someone pounding on a door. And then suddenly Wilkinson was wide awake, still hearing the siren, still hearing the pounding on the door to his room in the BOQ.

"What is it?" he yelled.

His BOQ room door opened and Pak, the Korean houseboy, ran in, his zori shoes slapping against his heels. "Luh! LUH!" Pak shouted.

"Luh? . . . Luh? . . . What the hell's a luh?" Wilkinson pulled the sheet tight around his ears to blank out the sound of the siren. " 'A-luh!' JESUS, an ALERT! *An alert!*" Wilkinson swung out of bed and turned on his light. "Okay, Pak, I'm up now." The Korean houseboy slapped in his zori shoes out of P.S.'s room and hurried down the hallway to awaken the other officers.

Wilkinson dressed quickly. He sat back down on the bed and began lacing his combat boots. As he was trying to thread the raveled ends of the laces through the eyelets he glanced at his wristwatch. *Three in the morning! And on Christmas Day! Jesus Christ what a time to call an alert! . . . What kind of gung-ho*

7

chickenshit is this now? Goddam Army! . . . *Goddam regulations* . . . There was a knock on his door.

"Come in!" Wilkinson called.

Sergeant First Class Segal entered. "Good morning, sir. *Merry Christmas.*" Segal was the ranking sergeant in Wilkinson's Photo Intelligence Section, the enlisted man who was responsible for seeing that Wilkinson's orders were carried out.

"Sergeant, what the hell is going on outside?"

"It's an alert, sir."

"Well, yes. . . . But haven't we had one this month already?"

"Yes, sir," Segal said.

"Then, you think that maybe . . . perhaps . . . this one is possibly not a practice alert?"

"Looks that way."

"Oh, God, and now I've only got sixteen days to go! Segal, I just haven't got time enough to get involved in a war. I've got too little time left in Korea for this to be a real one."

"Me, too, sir."

"Well, round up the section and I'll try to find out what this is all about," Wilkinson said. He checked himself in the mirror, then started out the door.

"Don't forget your steel pot, sir."

"Oh, Lord." Wilkinson went back and pulled his steel helmet and the pressed wood helmet liner off the top of his locker and put them on. He started out the door again and caught Segal smiling at him. "I know . . . I know, Segal. You've told me before. When I'm wearing this helmet I look like the clapper to the Liberty Bell."

"You said it, sir, not me." Segal followed Wilkinson out of the BOQ, then he trotted up the street to collect the other members of the PI Section. Wilkinson watched the lights coming on throughout the compound as he walked up the slight incline to the commanding officer's office. Captain Martin, the executive officer, was there already, looking as crisp and military as usual. Wilkinson noticed that he even had his paratrooper jump wings stenciled on his helmet. Behind the desk slouched Major Sturgess, who was cleaning his fingernails with a half-opened paper clip.

Wilkinson approached the desk, halted, came to attention and saluted.

"Oh, sit down, Wilkinson," Major Sturgess said, halfheartedly returning the salute.

Wilkinson sat down on the cracked and torn sofa opposite the major. "Which diddly-squat down at Headquarters is responsible for this latest bit of idiocy?" Wilkinson asked.

"What?" the major asked.

"We've already had one alert this month," Wilkinson said. "Is this somebody's idea of a Christmas present to the troops? A practice alert on a day like this—they must have something better to do."

"It's Friday morning, Wilkinson," the major said. "A full working day."

"And this alert isn't practice." Captain Martin smiled as he patted his holster with the .45 automatic.

Wilkinson looked at Martin. He could tell the captain was excited. *Oh, you sonuvabitch,* Wilkinson thought, *you really eat this shit up, don't you!*

"How come you're so pale, Wilkinson?" the major asked. "Didn't you get enough sleep last night, or could it be that our Ivy League lieutenant is a little scared?"

Captain Martin laughed.

Wilkinson did not speak. *Lots of laughs, boys, a real shoot-'em-up . . . R.A. all the way!* Wilkinson licked his lips. He could taste the chalky, cottony fear in his mouth, the coldness in his stomach, the damp sourness which filled him. Not practice . . . *I wonder what's going on up north? . . . Who pushed the button?* He looked at Major Sturgess and Captain Martin. *What a pair to go to war with!*

Major Sturgess was the third commanding officer he had served with since he had joined the 258th Military Intelligence Company. Sturgess was the last in the line of paunchy, rumpled majors who had had eighteen years in the service, and were waiting out the time until they completed twenty years and became eligible for a pension. They had been incapable of making a decision, incapable of taking any forceful action which might in any way jeopardize their retirement. They seemed to collect, to gather in the Intelligence branch like fat, lazy flies who did not want to look far for their sugar. And majors soon became anathema to Wilkinson.

Sturgess had wanted to come back to Korea! He loved Korea! The first thing Sturgess had done after he took over the unit was to fire the Korean houseboy whom the former CO had been teaching to play an accordion, then Sturgess moved in some prostitute from the village to take care of his cooking, laundry, and other needs. A new BOQ extension had been built and now each officer had a separate room. In his opening address to the officers, Major Sturgess said, "Now that each of you guys has a separate room any of you who sleeps alone is a damn fool—in fact ought to be ashamed of himself." In other words, they were expected to move in a prostitute from the village—a *moose,* a curious slang word derived from the Japanese musame, meaning "little wife" or "sister." None of the officers complied with the major's suggestion. In fact they did nothing and said nothing, until the major added in a moment of alcoholic confidence, "I didn't realize what a bad lay my wife was until I got over here." Only Wilkinson, in disgust, had said, "Oh, hell, Major, your wife isn't so bad." The major had not been so drunk that he did not hear the remark.

The other lieutenants were present now—Johnson, Korkus, and Pratt. They spoke softly among themselves, lit up cigarettes, rested their steel pots between their feet, and waited for the major to begin.

"All right, gentlemen, at ease," the major said. He waited until there was absolute quiet. "This is not a practice alert. This is a real one." Obviously aware of the dramatic potential of such a line, Major Sturgess paused to let it sink in. Johnson made an exaggerated sound of swallowing. "As far as I know," the major continued, "we have no reason to push the panic button; nevertheless, we must be prepared to move out of here. That means that you in particular, Wilkinson, better get your wise ass on a stick and drive down to your office and stand by. We will remain in phone contact with you."

Lieutenant Pratt asked, "Do you know what caused the alert, sir?"

"Yes, the 313th reports a drop-off in low-level communications indicating that the line units are on radio silence. Also our First Cav reports they could hear a lot of armor moving up toward the Demilitarized Zone during the night. Now there's no reason to get all worked up, they could just be moving into maneuvers instead of preparing an attack."

"Sir," Wilkinson interjected, "for what it's worth, they went on maneuvers this time last year."

"Well, for what it's worth, Wilkinson, we can't take a chance that they're doing the same thing this year."

"If it's all right, sir, I'd like to get going," Wilkinson said. "If we do have to go to Osan we'll have to cross the Han River twice and I'd kind of like to get across it at least once before they blow the bridge up. What condition alert are we on now?"

"Green Three," the major said. "Now get going."

"Yes, sir," Wilkinson said. He stood up and saluted, then started out. On the way he patted Lieutenant Pratt's shoulder and said, "See you in Pusan, old buddy."

The Photo Intelligence Section was waiting outside the major's office. Wilkinson was momentarily startled by the change in their appearance brought about by their wearing battle gear and carrying their carbines and submachine guns. "Is everybody here?" he asked SFC Segal.

"All ready to go. The deuce-and-a-half and three-quarter are both tanked up and in the motor pool. We can move out whenever you say the word."

"Well, I've got to pick up my weapon and the ammunition from the arms room. While I'm doing that—I'll take Ewling with me—get the men loaded in the trucks."

"Sir, what's this alert all about?" Segal asked.

"Well, it isn't practice, that's all I've got time to tell you now," Wilkinson said. "We'd better get down to the PI Center."

At the arms room, Wilkinson turned in his weapons card and was handed his carbine. The truck driver carried the submachine guns—M8 "grease guns" which Wilkinson admired because they were unmistakably designed for killing and nothing else. The carbine was too graceful, too much of a hunter's weapon, but the grease gun—that was for killing men, and it was the type of weapon Wilkinson wanted if he had to go to war.

At the motor pool Segal was calling the roll: "Thorp . . . Ruggio . . . Culcheck . . . Hollander . . . Mendoza . . . Kim . . . Hwang . . ." Wilkinson could never listen to an Army roll call without thinking of the Hollywood version of the platoon in which every racial and ethnic group was represented, and it always amused Wilkinson that Hollywood was never far from wrong.

Segal finished and turned to see if there was anything Wilkinson wanted to say. "Sir?"

"Does everybody have their proper equipment?"

"Yes, sir," Segal said.

"All right then. Let's load up and move out of here."

Wilkinson made himself as comfortable as possible in the jeep while Thorp led their small convoy onto the Main Supply Route toward Seoul. They crossed the Han River bridge and turned off to the Signal Battalion, where Wilkinson's Photo Intelligence Center was located.

When Wilkinson had first arrived in Korea in the middle of December, 1958, he was a second lieutenant and fresh from the Army Intelligence School in Maryland. There were three sergeants in his PI Section at that time—and all three were former captains who, during the Army reduction in force following the Second World War, had been "rif'd" back to sergeants. It was a most uncomfortable situation for a second lieutenant to come into—particularly a second lieutenant who had been ROTC at Yale, who was twenty-two years old, and who had no intention of staying in the Army any longer than the two years required of him. What was even more embarrassing was that Wilkinson was younger by two years than the youngest PFC in the section.

The first afternoon, Wilkinson called the three sergeants into his office. He told them to bring in coffee if they wished, that

they could smoke, and to make themselves comfortable. Once
they were seated, he closed the door and sat down behind his
desk. "I know very little about you gentlemen," he began, "you
know very little about me—but there are a lot of things we can
either guess about or assume. I know you have had more time
serving as officers than I will ever have. You know that I went
to Yale—that I am an ROTC lieutenant, 'Right Off The Campus,'
as I believe we're known. So, I am sure you all are fully aware
of the awkwardness of this situation, and you could make it
very hard for me if you wished. On the other hand, I could learn
to make it hard for you, too. But I would prefer that it all worked
out very well. Let me say right now that I don't know all the
answers. I am not an experienced officer, and I'm going to make
mistakes. But I expect you to help me not make mistakes, I
expect you to tell me when you think I am doing something
wrong, or something's going wrong—in other words, I want you
to look out for me. If you do so, then I'm in a better position to
look out for you. We have one very good thing going for us—we
are three miles away from the rest of the unit. Therefore, any
troubles that we have we can keep among ourselves. But let
me make this absolutely clear: I am as prickly and sensitive
about being a second lieutenant as you are about being ex-
officers. God knows ninety percent of all the jokes ever made
in the Army have as a punchline the answer, 'Second Lieutenant.'
If we work and work hard together, and we look out for each
other, then there's no reason why we should have any trouble. I'm
going to ask a lot of questions, some of them no doubt stupid, during these first weeks—no doubt first months. You men have been
doing this work a lot longer than I have, and you should be pretty
good at it by now. I hope so. I'm not going to change any
system that's been set up, I don't plan to change anything—not
until I know there's a better way. That's about all I have to say.
The ranking NCO runs the section. You are responsible to me.
Let's do it that way at least until I know a little bit more of what
you're doing and how well you're doing it. Are there any questions?" Wilkinson looked across the desk at the three sergeants,
two of whom were old enough to be his father, the other old

enough to be a young uncle. They were looking back and forth at each other, then the oldest one said, "Just one thing, Lieutenant, how do you like your coffee?"

For the next month Wilkinson had watched and listened. He spent as much time as possible in his office studying back photography, checking the reports made on them, familiarizing himself with the North Korean terrain, learning how to distinguish a burial mound from an artillery position on an oblique photograph taken at 16,500 feet. And one afternoon several weeks later, when Wilkinson felt confident enough to make some changes in the routine, the section chief tacked up a sign on P.S.'s office door which read: "The Old Man (Provisional)."

By 3:45 Christmas morning, Wilkinson's small convoy had pulled into the Signal Battalion compound. He waited in front of the PI Center while SFC Segal and Sp/5 Thorp opened the double combination locks on the steel door to the building. As soon as the door was opened Wilkinson went into his office. He picked up the phone and dialed the G2 office at Headquarters.

"Hey, Halihan? This is Lieutenant Wilkinson. Is one of the majors free for a moment? . . . Good, thanks . . . Major Lewis? This is Lieutenant Wilkinson, sir. Good morning . . . Fine, thank you, sir. What I'm calling about is the alert and— . . . Yes, sir, Merry Christmas . . . Look, I was wondering whether the colonel could talk the Air Force into flying a photo mission for us along the trouble area this morning. It might be interesting to find out what this flap's all about . . . You'll suggest it to him? Fine, sir . . . Good enough . . . Thank you. Right, sir . . . Good-by." Wilkinson replaced the telephone and stepped out of his office into the big room. The "classified" room was opened and he went into the locker where the three 1000-pound combination safes were. He opened Safe #1 and lifted out the secret Alert Plan folder. He read down the instructions for a Condition Green Three alert and saw that all he had to do was stand by and wait for it to become Green Two, then at Green One he would start to destroy classified documents, load up the truck, and move out. He looked at the three thermite grenades, one each taped to the tops of the safes.

If the alert got serious he would take what was needed out of the safes, pull the grenades' pins, and lob another grenade into the photo library bins. Then get out fast because once the grenades went off the heat would be so intense that the safes would melt and the whole building would go up like the Fourth of July. SFC Segal had fixed tapes on each grenade so that the pins could not accidentally work loose. Around each taped pin was the slogan "Do Not Flush." Another of Segal's little jokes was a dollar bill taped to the light table for the interpretation of negatives. Wilkinson had discovered it one afternoon and asked Segal what it was for. Segal had answered, "Just something for the draftsmen to practice on."

He could hear the men priming the diesel oil stoves, and there was nothing for Wilkinson to do but make sure that each man in his section knew what the alert was about and what they would have to do if it became more serious. From Green Three the alert progression was Green Two, Green One, Red Three, Red Two, and Red One—Red One was war. Wilkinson waited until PFCs Mendoza and Hollander had started the coffee maker. Then he said, "While we're waiting for the coffee and trying to keep warm I'll tell you what the alert is all about. Then we'll cover the alert plans in case it gets hotter." He walked over to the large wall map and pulled the heavy green curtains which shielded it. He stood to the side of the map and pointed at the area north of the DMZ. "The only thing we have so far is that the spooks have reported a drop in voice and low-level radio communications. This is common prior to an attack." It was so cold in the room that Wilkinson could see the puffs of his breath. "The second thing is that during the night the forward observers at First Cav have reported hearing tracked vehicles moving throughout this area." He indicated the open area just north of the DMZ between the two serpentine hooks of the Imjin River known as "West Dagmar" and "East Dagmar." Wilkinson dropped his arm. "Of course it could be serious. They could be moving armor up for an attack. But as yet there is no reason to push the panic button, or as the flyboys say, have pucker factor on full. They did the same thing at about this time last year, and they scared the hell out of me then, but it turned out they were only going on maneuvers. . . . I hope to God that's all they're doing this time. But, if it does get any more serious we'll have to move out and each one of you will have to know what to do. Therefore, gentlemen, let me have your complete attention and we'll go over the alert plans. Afterwards I'll answer any questions you might have. We've been over this time and time again in practice, so you should know your jobs pretty well. Okay? . . . Okay." Wilkinson began to read through the Alert instructions. When he had finished he looked up and asked for questions.

Ewling held his hand up. "I have a question: Chaplain, is everyone afraid?"

Wilkinson smiled. "If there are no further questions, the red light is on at the coffee machine, so let's all get our coffee and relax until we get some further word."

Wilkinson got his cup of coffee and carried it into his office. He sat down at his desk, opened the middle drawer, and pulled out the Carter Brown mystery and began to read it. It was too early in the morning for his eyes to focus properly, and he put the book back into his desk and sipped his coffee. Then he closed his eyes and rested his head on his arms. But he could not sleep, he felt there must be something he should be doing. He wondered whether he would have time to do everything if the alert progressed into a real war. He began to study the alert folder in front of him, trying to memorize what he would have to do. He looked at his wristwatch. It was almost four o'clock. *What an ungodly hour! And nothing to do but wait it out . . .*

At 0530 hours he left his office and walked out of the PI Center building to look up at the sky. There still was no snow and to the east, behind the mountain upon which Rhee had built his palace, the dark sky was turning red-yellow with dawn. Up at the front line the light reconnaissance spotter aircraft were already flying with the first light to see what was going on. In another couple of hours the sun would be high enough to melt the thin ice on the paddies and the first awful smells would begin to rise. But for the time being it was a cold, quiet dawn and the convoy headlights were still bright in the west. Wilkinson took a deep breath and exhaled. *Great God, with the amount of smoking I've been doing lately, the North Koreans sure as hell better not make me run somewhere unless I can take the jeep with me!* He turned around and looked at his PI Center. The corrugated metal roof, the flimsy sides. *Probably the only thing holding this place up is the metal door! A small kid could trip and fall right through the walls and into the building.* The sign on the metal door read: CLASSIFIED AREA: DO NOT ENTER.

Wilkinson went back inside the building and closed the metal door behind him. On the reverse side of the door was another sign:

WHAT YOU SEE HERE
WHAT YOU SAY HERE
WHAT YOU DO HERE
WHAT YOU HEAR HERE
WHEN YOU LEAVE HERE
LET IT STAY HERE

On the bottom of the sign someone had scrawled, "Velly nice place you have here, (signed) Mao Tse-tung." Wilkinson fixed himself a fresh cup of coffee. He carried it back into his office and sat down at his desk again. He turned on the transistor radio and tuned to the Armed Forces Radio Station. But there were nothing but Christmas carols, so he turned it off again. He again got out the Carter Brown mystery, but he still didn't feel like reading it. He leaned back in his chair, sipped his coffee, and looked at the charts around the office wall. There were the usual "Tasks Assigned—In Progress—Completed" charts, on the other wall a large one listing their photography, and a code key indicating what, if anything, had been of particular interest. One of the most closely watched Communist efforts which had occurred during Wilkinson's tour of duty was the construction of a jet fighter strip in North Korea. It had been started seven months earlier in the beginning of June and was now completed. Wilkinson's section had put out a very snazzy report showing the progress in construction shown by successive photo missions flown over that area. It had been completed on Thursday and was now at the major's office.

The telephone rang, startling Wilkinson, and as he reached for it he heard SFC Segal answer it in the main room. He picked up the phone and waited until Segal had finished the rigmarole of "PI Center, SFC Segal speaking, sir . . ." Then Wilkinson cut in and said that he had it.

"Lieutenant Wilkinson? This is the first sergeant. . . . The alert's over."

"Well, good," Wilkinson said. "Does the major want us to return?"

"He says it's to be a regular working day."

"On Christmas? Well, okay. Listen, Top, since today's a slow day, I'm going to let my section take the trucks to the PX and I'll stay here for a while. I'll keep the jeep."

"Right, sir, I'll let the major know."

"Thanks, Top," Wilkinson said. He hung up and went back to the big room. "The alert's over, gentlemen."

"What was it all about?" Thorp asked.

"Beats the hell out of me," Wilkinson answered. He was a little shocked by the others' lack of reaction. And then shock was replaced by confusion when he realized that he himself had not felt any particular relief that the alert had been called off. "The major says it's to be a regular working day."

"Do you want me to call the battalion mess to see if we can get some hot breakfast here?" Segal asked.

"Sure. I hope we can," Wilkinson said.

He went back into his office and sat down. *I must go in and out of this goddam office a hundred and fifty times a day!* He looked out his window at the brightening sky. It looked like it was going to be a beautiful day. *Or as beautiful as anyone could expect in a godforsaken place such as this* . . . The telephone rang and Wilkinson answered it, "This is Lieutenant Wilkinson, sir."

"P.S., old boy, this is Major Lewis again."

"Yes, sir. I understand the flap is over."

"Yes, it is. I thought I might still catch you there. How have you been?"

"Fine, sir," Wilkinson answered. Major Lewis had graduated from Yale in 1941 and had gone almost immediately from officers' training into the war. When the war ended he discovered that he didn't have anything better to do than to stay in the Army, so he remained in. Major Lewis was one of those men who looked good in a uniform—studiously more English than American—he wore a gold tie pin, and a grenadier guard's bushy mustache. Because Wilkinson, too, had gone to Yale, Major Lewis considered him of similar background and to be trusted with delicate missions. There was no doubt in Wilkinson's mind as to why the major had called. Major Lewis' singular ambition when he had first arrived in Korea was to sleep with each girl in a particular whorehouse at least once. The house had sixteen girls. Major Lewis never made it. The turnover among the girls was so great that by the time he had slept with twelve girls in the space of two months, four of the twelve had left and he still had eight to go . . . four remaining and four new ones. And now he wanted Wilkinson to arrange a meeting with some special girl. Because the Ranch House was closer to the 258th MI Company than to the G2 offices in Seoul, and because P.S. knew some of the girls up there and knew the Mama-san, the major's request was not so surprising. But still, to P. S. Wilkinson, no matter how the pieces were cut they spelled pimp.

"Uhhhmmm, P.S., how come I haven't seen you down at the Officers' Club lately?"

"Well, sir, it's kind of far away for me when I have to go back to the unit to change into the greens, then drive back to Seoul again. I'd like to get there more often, but lately I just don't seem to have had the energy."

"Well, what you need is one of those Martinis we used to have together . . . a little bit of the Good Life we left behind."

"Yes, sir."

"And speaking of the Good Life . . ."

Wilkinson decided to make it easier for Major Lewis. "Yes, sir, which one would you like for tonight?"

"Ah, good thinking, old boy. Due to unfortunate circumstances . . ."

"In other words, the colonel just walked in. Do you want me to call you back?"

"Uh, that won't be necessary. Perhaps you have some questions I can answer?"

"You'd like me to run through the roster so that you can give yes or no answers?"

"Yes, that'll be fine," Major Lewis said.

"How about Susie Serenity?"

"No, I don't think that's what we had in mind. I was thinking that more work on the area closer to the front might be advisible."

"You want one who doesn't wear PXies?" Wilkinson asked, using the GI-Korean slang for falsies purchased at the Post Exchange. The padded brassieres were very popular with the Korean women.

"Correct. Ahh-affirmative."

"How about Gypsy?"

"Good. Excellent."

"The golden girl with the silken behind. And, uh, what time would you like me to arrange this tête-à-tête for?"

"That's for tonight. Jumping off time should be approximately 2100 hours."

"I'll ignore the pun. Fine . . . Tonight at nine o'clock it is. I'll call the Mama-san when we return to the unit."

"Jolly good. Why don't you come along? I can call for you."

"Good, sir. I'd like to. Then I'll see you tonight. Oh, did you ask the colonel about having a mission flown?"

"Yes, well, I went to the colonel with your suggestion for a photo run this morning and he thought it would be a very good idea but feels that by the time the mission was flown there wouldn't be any point to it. The holiday spirit and all."

"My God, sir, if he called now he could have a plane up there in an hour! Isn't he interested in knowing what caused the flap?"

"I'm sure he would be, P.S., but he doesn't think it's important enough to work on."

"*Work*? All he does is call the Air Force. They do the work."

"I'm afraid he considers that too much effort."

"Oh, for God's sake. I guess that's all then, sir."

"Relax, P.S., you'll be out soon."

"Yes, sir."

"Right. Well, then, I'll see you tonight at 2100."

"Yes, sir," Wilkinson said. He hung up the telephone and sat back staring at the phone and the bright red-lettered message on it: DO NOT DISCUSS CLASSIFIED INFORMATION OVER THIS PHONE. Then he pushed himself away from the desk and went into the other room for some more coffee.

Wilkinson had returned to his office when the section sergeant entered. "Oh, yes, Segal, what can I do for you?"

"Cookie says we can go over now."

"What's he serving this morning?"

"Eggs, any style."

"Good enough," Wilkinson said. "Let's lock up the place and get some chow—no, wait. You go on over. Somebody'd better stay by the phone. I'll wait till you get back."

"I've already eaten, sir. I'll stay here and you go over."

"Well, bless my soul. And here I was thinking how good scrambled eggs sounded and nevertheless knowing that according to chapter such-and-so, section so-and-so of the Officers' Guide, I knew that it was my obligation to see that the men got fed first—all part of my looking out for their welfare. 'Know Your Men and Look Out for Their Welfare' . . . that's what I always say. How's your welfare, Sergeant Segal?"

"Not too good. I've been meaning to ask you that, since you're the Club Officer, maybe you could fix those slot machines so that they pay a little better."

"Ah, now wait, you're wrong. I'm the Library Officer, the Claims Officer, the Legal Officer, the Top Secret Control Officer, and the Theater Officer—but I'm not the Club Officer. That's Lieutenant Korkus. But I'll tell you what I've done for you gentlemen, and I did this way before your time here and Lieutenant Korkus' too. Back in the old days when I was Morale and Re-enlistment Officer I hit upon an idea for boosting low morale —high morale was never a problem. The NCO Club sergeant and I decided that drinking, eating, and smoking should be permitted during the movies instead of before and after the way it had been before—"

"You mean we haven't always been allowed to do that?"

"Ahh, no, old soldier. Ah, no, indeed. The only thing you can't do during the show is play the slot machines—they make too much noise. Now, you wouldn't want Lieutenant Korkus to rig the machines to pay more dough, would you? The club would lose money. They'd have to charge more for a drink, and the bartender would water the whisky. And that would be bad, now, wouldn't it?"

"Bad, sir. Very bad."

"I knew you'd understand." Wilkinson got up from his desk. "How were the eggs?"

"You remember eating library paste as a kid?"

At breakfast in the Signal Battalion's mess hall, Wilkinson shared a table with a lieutenant from one of the Signal companies.

"How'd you like the alert this morning?" Wilkinson asked him.

"What alert?"

" 'What alert?'! You mean you weren't alerted?"

"Hell, no, nobody called us. We probably couldn't have gotten up even if they had, after that party last night."

Wilkinson sat looking at the lieutenant. He remembered now that when they had pulled through the gates of the Signal Battalion there was no abnormal activity, no extra guards, no men in helmets and carrying weapons. He shook his head. "Jesus H. Christ."

"Were you guys alerted?" the Signal Corps lieutenant asked him.

"Since three this morning," P.S. said. "And it wasn't practice."

"Three this morning?" the Signal lieutenant asked incredulously. "You mean that this could have been the real thing and nobody called us? That's funny . . . I mean, you would have thought they'd call us. That's really funny."

"You could have died laughing."

3 THE SIGNAL CORPS LIEUTENANT left the breakfast table and P. S. Wilkinson remained over a second cup of coffee. The fizzled-out alert was typical of Korea. There was always some sort of crisis, some sort of build-up, and each one would eventually resolve itself in some sort of anticlimax. The truce in Korea was marked by a constant stream of agents, saboteurs, defectors, and line crossers who traveled between North and South Korea, crossing seemingly at will the 2000-meter-wide no man's land, that barren strip which wiggled irregularly from the west coast to the east coast of the two Koreas: the Demilitarized Zone. The uneasy truce was marked by sporadic machine-gun and rifle fire which tattooed old trench lines. Occasionally as many as two hundred North Korean soldiers would become involved in weird, almost existential attacks across the DMZ, as though lost battalions were emerging aboveground unaware that for six years a truce had been in effect. A South Korean lieutenant would steal an L-19 light reconnaissance plane and fly his wife and child to North Korea for asylum. A month later an American Army Aviation lieutenant would be flying an L-19 on a reconnaissance mission paralleling the DMZ when he would see the stolen L-19, now with North Korean markings, fly the other way. An overly zealous young South Korean artilleryman would unload his 105-mm howitzer "through the bore" and the high explosive shell would land on some North Korean hill. And every two weeks a U.S. Air Force C-47 would take off from Osan Air Base and begin a photo reconnaissance run starting at the southwest coast of North Korea. The plane, nicknamed "One-Eyed Waldo," would fly just behind the DMZ over the South Korean lines and would photograph, using an oblique mounted camera, the entire front lines of the North Korean Army. It was the responsibility of Wilkinson's Photo Intelligence Section to interpret these photographs and report their findings. It was an accurate and safe means of keeping check on what the North Koreans were doing. Each photo mission consisted of approximately 450 photographs which overlapped enough to provide stereo, three-dimensional coverage. During the Korean War most of the usable intelligence was gained from photo intelligence, and now after six years of truce it was still considered the most accurate and definitive means of gathering intelligence. Since the war had not officially ended, it was important that photo interpreters watch for signs of build-ups, of preparation for movement forward, any signs which might indicate that the war was going to commence again. Wilkinson had at twenty-three more responsibility than many men achieve in the Army in a lifetime. He was responsible for selecting what priority should be given what targets. Twice he had represented Eighth Army at targeting conferences with Fifth Air Force in Japan. During his tour he had tried to see that units as small as company size should know what they faced and had initiated two major programs to ensure that this was possible. Wilkinson's section worked out the most impressive intelligence study of North Korean artillery compiled since the end of the war. The study listed every known position, every cave, every artillery storage park, every artillery unit, and in 85 percent of the cases the exact location of each artillery position to the nearest foot of where it actually was sitting in North Korea. In addition to the artillery study the section also developed detailed and annotated maps representing the exact position, size, and composition of every North Korean Army troop concentration north of the DMZ. Wilkinson, through default, knew more about what faced the United Nations Forces in Korea than any other man. Wilkinson's job was important, and he was often made uneasy by the realization of just how important his job actually was. He approached his work with the utmost seriousness. Because it *was* serious.

P. S. Wilkinson finished his coffee, pushed himself away from the table in the Signal Battalion mess hall, and stood up. For a moment he wondered what he would be feeling if the alert had not been called off; if, instead, it had been real, and they were at war. He was a little surprised to realize that, in spite of being scared, his primary worry would have been to get back across the Han River bridge before it was destroyed. He thought about the ammunition back at the PI Center, the submachine guns and carbines now hanging from pegs in the lockers. And he felt the first twinge of disappointment at not being able to use his weapon against an enemy. Then he remembered Captain Martin patting his holster.

As he re-entered the PI building he noticed SFC Segal talking excitedly to Sp/5 Thorp. "What's up?" Wilkinson asked them.

"The major called, sir," Segal said. "He wants to see you back at the compound on the double."

"Did he say why?"

"Yes, sir. It's about that special report we did on the jet fighter airstrip, the one with all the photographs showing its construction during the past months?"

"What about it?"

"Well, the major's sore as hell."

"Why?" Wilkinson asked. "For God's sake, we let him sign it and take credit for it. What's he sore about?"

"You know the heading part, where we gave the coordinates for the location of the airstrip?"

"Pretty well. I don't remember them exactly."

"Well, we reversed the number. On two of the numbers in the coordinates we reversed them and placed the airstrip behind our lines, about a hundred yards or so from First Cav's headquarters. But what makes it so bad is that this is the report the major's been bragging about and—"

"That's why he signed it himself."

"Yeah, sir," Segal said. "He thinks we reversed the coordinates on purpose just to make a fool of him."

"Oh, for God's sake."

"Hollander's out front with the jeep."

"Good. Listen, pull a copy of that report and go over it and prepare a change sheet for distribution. Make absolutely certain that there aren't any other errors in it. Have the changes mimeo'd and see if there is some way to put out that change without having to classify it. Something like 'Change to Report such-and-such.' 'For coordinates given in Paragraph One change such-and-such to read so-and-so' . . . okay?"

"Yes, sir. Good luck. If there are any calls I'll tell them you can be reached back at the unit."

"Okay." Wilkinson smiled. "If I'm not back in an hour, use all those machine guns to get me out of there."

Hollander drove out of the Signal Battalion's compound and onto the Seoul-Inchon MSR which would take them back to the 258th Military Intelligence Company. There was the usual crowd of hopsans—Korean taxies made out of green jeep station wagons—and one of those brightly painted Korean buses built upon old 2½-ton truck chassis with a body made out of hammered-steel oil drums, canting off center like an airplane bucking a strong crosswind. Sometimes, driving to work along this road to Seoul, Wilkinson would hear sirens behind him coming closer and closer. He would pull to the side of the road along with the other vehicles. He would see the old Koreans in their white billowy pants and dark vests hobble to the roadside to rest their A-frames with their incredible loads against the side of a tree—if a tree could be found. He would see the young men with the six-foot-high stacks of crates balanced on the rear fenders of their bicycles drop their bare feet to the road and skid to a stop, the chunky women, babies strapped to their backs, squat down on their calves to watch. Everyone would halfheartedly turn to watch, turning over their shoulders to see without expression, without hope, without feeling, the six rows of black motorcycles blast past, followed by the black, headlights lit, jeeps filled with National Police, then the two 1959 Chryslers with fat, sleek

Koreans, and then, following close behind the Chryslers, the black 1950 air-conditioned Cadillac, its windows tightly rolled up to seal out the stench of the country, the people, their misery, and in the back seat sat the thin, parchment-faced, eggshell man. A few Koreans, not many (there might not have been time to organize a crowd of frenzied flag wavers), would wave their handkerchiefs at him, but Old Nobodaddy would sit, and he would fart, and he would belch and cough, and when he would be gone, and the last wildly careening jeep with siren and horn would have blasted past, the Koreans would hitch up their A-frames, swear at their oxen, soothe their crying babies, and the MSR would once more be clogged with the result of the benevolence of Rhee Syng Man.

Hollander and Wilkinson hunched up to avoid the freezing wind as they crossed the Han River bridge. At the end of the bridge they swerved to pass a horse. It was one of the few horses Wilkinson had seen in Korea. It was all bones, and its left rear leg had been broken and improperly healed. There were practically no cats in Korea. The Koreans ate cats. The only cat he had ever seen had been chained to a tree inside a walled compound. There were occasional dogs, but even dogs were rare. *The Koreans eat dogs too. Hell, they'll eat anything. Dogs, cats, jeep reflectors. Paper towels. Soap. Each other . . .*

Thorp swung off the MSR and after a hundred yards turned right and stopped at the Main Gate of the 258th MI Company. The guard raised the gate, saluted, and Wilkinson's jeep passed on through and up the slight incline to the corner of Yankee and Rebel and parked. The major's office was straight ahead. Wilkinson got out of the jeep, and went around to the orderly room entrance to the quonset and walked up to the first sergeant's desk.

The top sergeant looked up from his desk and smiled. "Wa'al, good morning, Lieutenant."

"Morning, Top, is the major in?"

"Yes, indeedy. I'll tell him you're here."

The first sergeant came back and said that the major would see him now. *The major will see me? I'll bet he can't wait to see me. He's probably been practicing all morning on what he's going to say.* . . . Wilkinson marched into the major's office, positioned himself directly in front of and three feet away from the desk and saluted smartly. "Lieutenant Wilkinson reporting as ordered, sir."

Major Sturgess returned the salute. "At ease, Lieutenant."

"At ease, Lieutenant" . . . *so it's going to be one of those big deals, eh? Not "Sit down, Wilkinson."* . . . *Well, here we go.* Wilkinson assumed the position of "At Ease," his hands clasped at the small of his back, his feet eighteen inches apart.

"Ahh, Lieutenant Wilkinson," the major began. Sturgess was holding a pencil lightly between his thumb and forefinger, eraser down, as though it were a drumstick. He tapped it on his desktop next to Wilkinson's photo intelligence report of the new North Korean airfield. "Ahhh . . . I presume you know why I asked you up here?"

Asked? "Yes, sir."

"Now, I'm going to read you some map coordinates, and I want you to go over to the wall map and tell me exactly where those coordinates are listed. Right?"

"Sir, I don't think that will be necessary. I know—"

"Do as I tell you, Wilkinson. The coordinates are as follows: C,T,1,5,1 . . . 147. I'll say that again. C, T, 1, 5, 1 . . . 1, 4, 7."

"CT 151 147, yes, sir," Wilkinson said. He went over to the wall map showing North Korea, the DMZ, and approximately twenty miles of upper South Korea.

"It's right about here, sir," Wilkinson said, his finger resting on the map not far from the U.S. Army's First Cavalry Division Headquarters.

"Now what country is that?"

"South Korea," Wilkinson answered. *You really want to play this game, don't you!*

"And what does your report say is located there?"

"A North Korean Air Force jet fighter strip."

"And why would the North Koreans put a jet strip in South Korea?"

"Sir, the typist reversed the digits. The coordinates were supposed to be CT 151 *417*, not 151 *147*. I should have caught it when I checked the report, but I didn't."

"And you brought the report to me in person, didn't you? You carried it up yourself for my signature."

"Yes, sir. The report was classified 'Secret.' Since it was classified that high I thought I'd better bring it up myself instead of giving it to the driver. I was responsible for it."

"Ahhh . . . Ahhh, I think you put your finger on it there, Wilkinson."

Jesus, isn't this something out of The Caine Mutiny? *. . . "And how many helpings of strawberries did you have?"* "Sir, I have already instructed Sergeant First Class Segal to prepare a report indicating that the coordinates as listed in Paragraph One were erroneous. As you know, all along in the report where we list the hangars, the abutments, the control tower, the anti-aircraft emplacements and so on—in all those places the coordinates are listed correctly. I am certain that anyone who is reading the report will know that there was an error in the initial listing alone."

"But, ahh, an error does exist. A finished report originating in your section and disseminated by the 258th MI Company contains an error. . . . Isn't that right?"

"Yes, sir . . ."

"And you didn't catch it?"

"No, sir."

"Then would you say that a report containing an error would indicate that your other reports are reliable?"

"Yes, sir," Wilkinson said. "They can tell the difference between a typing error and an intelligence error."

"But you said the report was all right and that I could sign it."

Ahh, here we go . . . "At the time I thought the report was fine."

"Now. Now, would you say this indicates that I should trust your word?"

"Oh, for God's sake, Major Sturgess! I made an error. Our section made an error. It is being changed. A new report will come out on Monday."

The major was drumming the pencil harder. "Ahh, Wilkinson, I am not used—I am not accustomed to being spoken to in that manner by a lieutenant. I am sure that at times I must try your patience . . ."

"No, sir."

"And that the whole Army must seem terribly foolish to you . . ."

"No, sir."

"I realize that a man of your background and education must find the military mind somewhat moronic . . ."

"Sir . . ."

"You went to Yale, didn't you, Wilkinson?"

Oh, God, this old bit again. . . . "Yes, sir."

"And, furthermore, I am sure that you do not intend to make a career of the Army."

"No, sir." *That's for goddam sure!*

"The taxpayers at great expense have made it possible for you to become an officer in the United States Army. Now that may not be very impressive to you. But it has meant a lot to a lot of people."

"Sir, it means a great deal to me, too." *Why in God's name do you think I went through four years of bullshit in the ROTC?*

"Now I shouldn't think that it would be asking too much of you, while you are on active duty in the service of your country, that you should pay a little bit more attention to your duties. You are now a first lieutenant. I can expect mistakes from a second lieutenant—but you, Wilkinson, you who have been with this unit longer than anyone else, you shouldn't make these stupid and careless mistakes. I don't want you to be setting this kind of example."

Wilkinson said nothing.

"It is my personal belief that you should have an opportunity to practice your ability to take responsibility. An officer hungers for responsibility. Isn't that right, Lieutenant?"

"Yes, sir."

"Well then, well then, I want you to make certain that the changes to the report are finished today and as a further method

of ensuring that you learn to accept responsibility, you will be
officer of the day, duty officer, for the next three days. Is that
understood?"

"Yes, sir. What time do you want me to assume the duty?"

"Because of the delayed holiday schedule, we will hold the
Retreat Ceremony this evening. You will assume the duty following the ceremony."

"Yes, sir," Wilkinson said. "Will that be all, sir?"

"That's all, Lieutenant," Major Sturgess said. "Ask the first
sergeant to come in when you leave."

Following the Retreat Ceremony, Wilkinson went to the
orderly room, picked up his officer of the day armband, and
told the charge-of-quarters that he would be at the major's hooch
if he was needed.

"Well, Wilkinson," Major Sturgess said as Wilkinson came into
his rooms. "It's nice of you to join us. Would you tell Miss Lee
what you wish to drink?" Major Sturgess' moose acted as un-
official hostess, to the anger and mortification of the Korean
officers, who felt, quite justifiably, that they were insulted and
degraded by the American major's tactlessness. But Major Sturgess either was not aware of the insult or didn't care. When his
moose entered the room all the officers had to stand up for the
"lady."

"I'm on duty now, sir. Thank you, anyway."

"Ahhh, that's right, I had forgotten our little talk," the major
said. He turned to the other officers. "Perhaps the rest of you
will be delighted to know that Lieutenant Wilkinson will be the
officer of the day through the Christmas holidays. That means
you, Johnson, will not resume duty as officer of the day until
December twenty-eighth. Clear?"

"Yes, sir," Johnson said.

Wilkinson sat down between Pratt and Johnson. Pratt leaned
over and said, "What's going on?"

"Yeah, Jesus," Johnson said, "the major sounds like he's really
out for your ass. What happened? Get caught sleeping with his
moose?"

"I reversed two coordinates on that airfield study," P.S. said.

"Oh, sure, we caught that in the report and just pencilled in the change—you mean he's made you OD for the next three days because of *that*?" Johnson asked. "My God, I can't wait until Herman Wouk hears of this!"

"Who's Herman Wouk?" Pratt asked.

After dinner Wilkinson went back to the BOQ and cranked the field phone. "CQ? This is Lieutenant Wilkinson. I'll be checking the prison compound if you need me."

P.S. then walked up the drive to the barbed-wire enclosure surrounding the few buildings that housed the civilian and military prisoners from North Korea, and paused at the gate.

"Good evening, sir," the guard said.

"Good evening, Temple, how's it going?"

"All quiet, sir."

Temple was an eighteen-year-old newly arrived in Korea.

"How's the old woman?" Wilkinson asked him.

"She's okay, sir. I checked in on her not more than an hour ago. She seemed to have a chill, so I brought her a blanket."

"A chill? With that stove. It must be seventy-five, eighty in that hut."

"Yes, sir, but she was shivering."

"Well, okay," Wilkinson said. "Let's go take another look at her."

The old woman was kept in a separate small fenced-in enclosure within the cage where the other North Korean prisoners were huddled together. This building was used for VIP prisoners or female prisoners, and was strictly segregated from the other buildings and prisoners. Temple opened the gate leading to the building and he and Wilkinson walked up the narrow path. At the door Temple knocked softly. When he saw the surprise on Wilkinson's face he explained, "Well, gosh, sir, after all she's a woman."

"You're absolutely right, Temple. I'd just forgotten such courtesy existed."

Temple opened the door and stood aside to let Wilkinson in.

Wilkinson went into the small room and screwed up his face at the heavy stench of waste inside. "Jesus, Temple, can't something be done about the smell in here?"

"We've tried, sir. We had one of the Koreans show her how to use the toilet, but she won't learn. He said she's too old to learn."

"But can't we open a window or something?"

"We've tried that too. They've been painted over so many times that we can't raise them. We even tried keeping the door open, but she'd always wait until we were out and kick it shut."

Wilkinson looked down at the old Korean woman who lay on the cot with the rough Army blankets tucked tightly around her. She lay with her heavy-lidded eyes half-shut. If she had heard them enter she made no sign. Wilkinson knelt beside her and placed his hand on her brown and wrinkled forehead. "It doesn't feel like she has any fever now. She's dry as a bone." He leaned over her and said, "Hi, Mama-san, Merry Christmas. . . . Anyunghashimnika . . . Chosumnida?" There was no response to his asking her how she felt. He reached down and patted her hand. He squeezed it lightly, then replaced it on the sharp mound of her hip. He watched as her hand moved away from her hip, began to slip down the slope of the Army blanket. As though in slow motion, it fell to the bed, then stopped, curled like a dead spider. Wilkinson pressed his fingertips to her pulse. He moved his fingers around her wrist, searching for a pulse. "Jesus, Temple, I can't feel a thing." He pressed and searched for a moment longer. Then he waved his hands in front of her half-opened eyes. She did not blink. "Get a medic, Temple. On the double! I think the old lady's dead!"

"Dead? *Jesus!*" Temple hurried out of the small building and across the yard. Wilkinson could hear him rattle the chain at the other end, and he stood up. He looked down at the old woman and wondered whether he should try to feel for a heartbeat, but he knew he couldn't bring himself to touch her dry and bony chest. He looked down at her face again. He knew that in movies they always lifted the person's eyelids and looked. But he never knew what they looked at. He didn't know whether a dead person's eyes were supposed to roll upward—or was that an unconscious person's? *Maybe I ought to close her eyes or something!* He reached down to touch her eyelids, then jerked his hand away. *Wait for the medics. They know what to do. . . .* He looked down at her hand with the thin, bony fingers stained with nicotine. He timidly touched her hand, then knelt beside her cot and prayed, "Dear God: Please have mercy on this old lady's soul. Please be kind to her. It doesn't look like anyone else has. . . . Take her into heaven. God bless her. Amen." He got up from his knees. *What a lousy goddam place to die. . . . A prisoner of war camp in Korea! . . . It's too bad she couldn't have lived at least until New Year's . . . but of course it wouldn't have been New Year's Day for her. . . .* He heard the gate open again and stepped aside for the medics to enter.

"Is she really dead, sir?" Temple asked.

Wilkinson was watching the medics. "I think so," he said.

The medics pulled away the blankets and bared the old woman's chest. There was a broad white scar across her chest, and Wilkinson could see the dirt on her body, and the dark-brown nipple over the fold of skin that had once been a breast. One of the medics was listening for a heartbeat with a stethoscope. Then the medic pulled the instrument away from his ears and stood up.

"Dead?" Wilkinson asked him.

"Yes, sir," the medic said. "She was pretty sick just before chow, but she's sure dead now."

"What'd she die of?" Wilkinson asked.

"Probably pneumonia, sir. Pneumonia and dysentery and worms and God knows what else. She was a mess when she was brought in here. She had just about everything."

"Well, what do we do now?" Wilkinson asked the medic.

"We have to report it, sir. I guess we call the dispensary down in Seoul and they'll send an ambulance up for her body."

Wilkinson watched the other medic cover her with a blanket.

"Sir," Temple asked, "do you want to inspect the other prisoners?"

"No, I'll come back and do it later. I'd better report this and see what needs to be done."

"Whatever you say, sir," Temple said.

Wilkinson left the prison compound and went directly to the charge-of-quarters. "Is the major in his hooch?"

"No, sir, he left the compound for Seoul."

"What about Captain Martin?"

"I think he's here, sir."

"See if you can get him on the phone for me, would you?"

The CQ went to the switchboard and rang the BOQ. There was no answer, so he tried the IPW Section. The phone buzzed and then Captain Martin answered.

"Sir, this is Lieutenant Wilkinson. I just finished an inspection of the cage and the old woman's dead."

"Dead? Is the major in?"

"No, sir," Wilkinson said. "He's in Seoul."

"She died? Are you sure she's dead?"

"Sir, the medics checked her. She's dead all right. She must have died about an hour ago. They think she died of pneumonia or something."

"Well, we'd better do something," Captain Martin said.

"Yes, sir. That's why I called you."

"Well, let me think about this for a minute."

Take your time . . . take your time . . . "Sir?" Wilkinson said. "Yes?"

"Sir, I think we should call the G2 duty officer down at Seoul and tell him. Then call the dispensary. They ought to know what to do."

"Good, Wilkinson. That's fine. You do that and let me know what the answer is."

"Fine, sir," Wilkinson said. He heard Captain Martin replace the telephone and Wilkinson rang off. Then he told the charge-of-quarters to get in touch with the duty officer at Seoul and looked at his wristwatch. It was a quarter to seven.

An hour later an olive-drab ambulance with bright red crosses on a white background took away the old woman's body. Wilkinson watched the gate bar lower behind the jeep and bob slightly the sign attached to it swinging gently:

WHAT YOU SEE HERE

WHAT YOU SAY HERE

WHAT YOU DO HERE

WHAT YOU HEAR HERE

WHEN YOU LEAVE HERE

LET IT STAY HERE

Wilkinson watched the jeep turn right onto the MSR toward Seoul, then he looked down at the receipt he held in his hand. *They gave me a receipt for her body. A receipt! Just like she was a piece of equipment or something. My God, what are we coming to?* Wilkinson stuffed the paper into his pocket and walked over to the Main Gate guard post. The guard on duty was PFC Galero from the MP Detachment. When Galero saw Wilkinson approaching he turned down his transistor radio, stepped out of the guard shack, and saluted. "Good evening, Lieutenant!"

"Evening, Galero. Listen, when the major comes back would you give me a call? I'll either be in the BOQ or the NCO Club."

"Well, all right, sir, but I don't think he'll be back for some time. He may not be back before morning. He signed out for Seoul but instead of heading down to Seoul, he went right up toward the Ranch House. Oh, and Major Lewis was here looking for you, but he went up to the Ranch House with the major."

When Wilkinson opened the door to his BOQ room, he saw a piece of paper on the floor. Someone had evidently slid it inside and he picked it up and unfolded it.

HEADQUARTERS SPECIAL TROOPS
EIGHTH UNITED STATES ARMY
APO   301

22 Dec 1959

EUSA STP 201-Wilkinson, Philip S.
05 001 345
SUBJECT: Readjustment of EDDPAC

He felt the blood drain from his face, and he sat down on the edge of his bed. He held the letter under the desk lamp and read on: "Under the provisions of Para 7, EUSA Cir 614-30, the Estimated Date Departure on 1st Lt. Philip Sadler Wilkinson, 05 001 345, AI(QMC) has been readjusted to 10 February 1960." *They've extended me! Those goddam dirty fucking sonsuvbitches have extended me! I won't leave for another month and a half! A month and a half! Ohh, God damn those sonsuvbitches! Oh, Jesus H. Christ. Merry fucking Christmas!*

4   PHILIP SADLER WILKINSON was drunk. He was fully aware that being drunk while officer of the day was a serious offense; but, as he sat there on the footlocker in Pratt's room, he knew that if anything came up either Johnson or Pratt would take over the duty and handle it. P.S. leaned back against the wall. Johnson was making Pratt replay the latest tape which Pratt's wife sent every week, and P.S. shut his eyes and listened to Pratt's wife talking to the baby: "Say 'Daddy,' dear . . . Please say 'Daddy' . . . You were saying 'Daddy' all day . . . Please say 'Daddy' . . ." There was a long silence.

"There!" Johnson said. "You hear it? Right back there. Play it back. You heard it, didn't you, P.S.?"

"Her what?" He opened his eyes.

"It was unmistakable. An unmistakable sound," Johnson said. "It was Pratt's baby vomiting on the tape recorder."

P.S. smiled.

Pratt and Johnson began arguing about the sound. Lying open on the floor was P.S.'s letter notifying him of his extension. He knew that everything Pratt and Johnson had said had made sense. He had known even before they had said anything that his extension was legal. There was nothing he could do about it. He knew that he had been extended because his photo intelligence training was rare, and therefore critical. He knew perfectly well that he would not be permitted to leave Korea until a replacement arrived for him. But none of it made it any easier to accept.

Johnson began telling about Christmas in New Hampshire, and after Johnson had finished, Pratt told about Christmas in Ossining, New York. And Johnson wanted to know whether they crucified convicts for the pageants.

P.S. finished his glass of whisky, and stood up unsteadily for a moment, and then he said that he was tired and thought it would be smart if he went back to his room. "Merry Christmas," he said.

He walked back into the cold night and weaved down to his room in the new section of the BOQ. He picked up the photograph of the stripper he had known in Baltimore before he had been sent to Korea. The caption was "When you're halfway around the world, think of me," and was signed "Polly." Beneath her signature was the imitation signature in a handwriting common to all publicity photographs saying, "Ever Yours, Hippolyte (Queen of the Amazons)." The only other photograph P.S. had in his room was one taken senior year at a dance. It showed him standing with his arm around Hilary Farnum, whom he had proposed to three weeks before. She had married someone else six weeks after P.S. had arrived in Korea. He put down the photograph and fell back onto his bed and shut his eyes. The room was spinning faster and faster, and he lowered one leg to the floor to steady himself. The room slowed and began to spin in the opposite direction. He took a deep breath and swallowed hard. He tried not to smell the diesel oil. It was too cold outside to be sick. He plumped up the pillow, tried to make himself more comfortable. He lay there remembering the run-in of the previous afternoon with Captain Lim, the head of the Korean Photo Intelligence Detachment. Every Monday morning for over a year Wilkinson visited Lim's Korean PI Detachment and every Thursday Captain Lim visited Wilkinson's PI Center. They would always talk and joke with each other. Several times Wilkinson had had dinner at Captain Lim's parents' home, and several times Wilkinson had taken Captain Lim and Lim's wife to dinner at the Officers' Club in Seoul. Early yesterday afternoon, Captain Lim had come over as usual to see if he could beg, borrow, or steal some supplies, and Wilkinson had had to tell him that he couldn't have any more because his own supplies were very low, and they were having trouble getting more. Wilkinson assured Captain Lim that as soon as more came in he would let him know, and suddenly Lim had become furious and said, "Okay, Lutena Wilkinson, if that's the way you gonna be, maybe the next time the North Koreans attack we won't be around to help you!" *Sonuvabitch! Known each other over a year and all of a sudden he goes and pulls that! These Koreans are insane! . . . Forget the Koreans, forget Korea . . . Go to sleep . . . Today's Christmas . . . Only six—only a month and a half to go . . . Don't think about it. . . .* He tried to concentrate on what Johnson and Pratt had been talking about that evening. He tried to picture the Christmases Pratt had spent in Ossining, and Johnson in . . . *Where was it? Plymouth? . . . No, it was Concord. Christmas in Concord . . . That's got a nice ring to it . . . Mine were in Baltimore . . . On Charles Street . . .* With *Charles Street,* he corrected himself.

It was the first Christmas following the divorce; P.S. was in his first year at Yale. He had taken the train to Philadelphia and a cab over to his father's house, and arrived in the late afternoon on the 23rd of December. P.S. paid the cab, pushed the doorbell, and then stood outside in the cold, next to his suitcase, waiting for his father to answer. In a minute his father opened the door, saying, "Come in. Come in, Son. Have a nice trip? . . . Fine . . . Good. Well, come in, come in."

P.S. walked inside the house and his father clapped him on the back a couple of times and said, "You know where your room is. I've got about a thousand things to do. All day I've been bothered by the most extraordinary people. I've got at least a dozen letters to write. Only take me about fifteen more minutes, twenty at the most, and then I'll knock off. We can sit down together then, okay? I'm terribly sorry to run off, but you go on up to your room, and I'll be with you in about fifteen or twenty minutes." Then his father rushed back upstairs in a muck of embarrassment, anxiety, terror—all the emotions P.S. had felt as he stood at the front door with his suitcase. P.S. followed him up and turned into the room his father had so hopefully called "his" room. There was nothing of P.S.'s in it. It was like coming into a guest room at someone's house and having them say "This is your room"—meaning while you were there. The lamp on the bureau P.S. had given his father several Christmases ago and as he stood there looking at it he felt that his father had, in a sense, given it back to him. Because his father often had people staying with him, whatever articles P.S. did have at his father's house were stored in the basement in boxes and trunks. In an attempt to make himself feel it was his own room, P.S. unpacked his suitcase, even though he knew he would have to pack it again the next morning when they drove to Baltimore to Charles Street. On the bureau his father had placed the one or two invitations that he had regretted for his son, there were a few advertisements—fifteen ballpoint pens for a dollar, or a shop where he could have suits altered, or a humorous statuette— that he felt his son would be interested in. There were several copies of *Punch,* with notes telling P.S. which stories he should read. P.S. was trying out for the Yale *Record,* and he was certain that his father was trying to teach him humor. By the time P.S. had unpacked and finished reading what had been set out for him, he heard his father come out of his office. From the hallway—he avoided coming into the room—his father asked, "Is there anything you need?"

"No, sir."

"You saw all the stuff I put on the bureau?"

"Yes, sir."

"Why don't you run on downstairs, and I'll join you in a minute."

"All right, sir."

"And get some ice out. We need ice. Got to have a Martini, don't we." It wasn't a question.

"Fine, sir," P.S. said, a little pleased that even though he wasn't even nineteen, his father thought him old enough to have a Martini with him. P.S. waited until he heard his father go into his room, and then he crossed the hall, walked downstairs, and got out the ice tray.

In a few minutes his father joined him in the living room. Stewart Wilkinson was a very good-looking man, and—P.S. felt —he was aware of it. He was wearing a pair of neatly tailored light-gray flannels, highly polished Peal shoes, a soft tweed sports coat he told P.S. he had had made in Scotland, a tailored oxford blue shirt, a tight-knit Italian tie held in place by a gold pin. He dressed in a style which P.S. referred to as "Fred Astaire East," meaning the type of clothes Fred Astaire would wear if he had never gotten into movies, but he had made a fortune in, say, designing distinguished racing automobiles. He gave P.S. a couple of pats as he passed him, but then continued over to the bar. He made a big business out of mixing the Martinis. He poured a small amount into his glass, which P.S. had brought frosted from the refrigerator, tasted it thoughtfully, then filled both glasses, handed P.S. the drink, and said, "Health, chum."

P.S. said, "Same to you, sir," and they crossed back to the fireplace. Stewart Wilkinson sat in one of the comfortable chairs and P.S. sat across from him on the couch. There was a little sparring while P.S.'s father kicked the footstool over to him and P.S. kicked it back to his father, and his father said, "Well, you look fine, sport."

"Thank you," P.S. said. "You look pretty good yourself."

P.S. lit a cigarette and looked around, in panic, for an ashtray. There were none, as his father had given up smoking and used the no-ashtray business to show how much better he felt. P.S. got up and brought one in from the kitchen, and as he was about to sit down again his father said, "Let me look at you."

P.S. stood there awkwardly and turned around when his father said turn around, and finally he was released and sat down. He put his cigarette in the ashtray and noticed how the smoke was drifting toward his father. His father asked him if he felt all right and added that he thought P.S. looked a little tired and had lost some weight.

"I might have lost a couple of pounds," P.S. said, "but I feel fine."

And his father said, "Well, you look fine."

They sat across from each other, the father looking worriedly at a crack in the wall above the portrait of Great-Great-Grandmother Wilkinson, the son, awkward, noticing his cigarette had gone out and not daring to light it again.

P.S. took another sip of the Martini and tried not to wince at its strength. P.S. had not eaten lunch on the train and already felt a little high at the surge of alcohol. He raced through his activities of the past months, trying to find an incident that might amuse his father. Just as he felt he had one, his father said, "I saw a great friend of yours the other day," and he named a man whom P.S. knew slightly but who was a great friend of his father's. "His son is a junior at New Haven, you know."

"I didn't know."

"Well, I told him you were at Yale and he is going to have his son look you up, take you to dinner at his club or something."

"Good, that would be nice," P.S. said, knowing, as he was certain his father must, that a Yale junior does not invite the freshman son of his father's friend to lunch or dinner or anything at his club. Then P.S. told his father his anecdote, which his father found only mildly amusing, but which reminded him of one of his own, which he told P.S. And then it was time to get dressed for dinner.

"I hope you don't have any plans for dinner," his father said.

"Of course not," P.S. answered, wishing to God that he had.

Then there were twenty minutes of bathing and dressing, before they met back downstairs for a pre-leaving-for-dinner Martini. This one was stronger than the first, and P.S. got a little more tight. They climbed into his father's car, a Lancia, and P.S. hoped that the cold winter air would sober him up, at least enough to have the traditional third Martini when they arrived at the restaurant.

Dinner, too, was dedicated to steering conversation away from any topic that might be revealing or personal. There was anecdote matched by anecdote, discussion of this restaurant compared to another, one foreign beer to another, this year's Yale-Harvard game with games in the past. Finally, there was coffee and the check. Then they got back into the Lancia. His father wanted to stop off at a friend's house for brandy, more coffee, and more anecdotes.

When they came home from his father's friend's house, they went upstairs, and shook hands briskly on the landing. His father said, "It's nice having you home, Son. We had a good time tonight, didn't we."

"Yes, sir," P.S. said.

Stewart Wilkinson was fifty when he and P.S.'s mother were divorced. P.S.'s older brother, Carter, was twenty-three and repeating his senior year in college. Page was twenty-one and beginning her senior year at Sarah Lawrence. P.S. was eighteen and starting Yale. Because he was the youngest, he was supposed to be the one most affected by the divorce. P.S. had already spent most of his life away from his parents; at nine he was sent off to Napier Boarding School. Therefore, he didn't think he was hurt the most by the divorce, but he had no way of telling. What was true was that he had more restrictions placed on his actions when his parents separated. He was the one who was expected to be with the "family" for holidays and special occasions. His father's family was from Maryland, and it was a big family, the type of Southern family that takes enormous pride in turning out for family—family parties, family holidays, family weddings, family deaths. His mother's side were New York, and good New York—the old New York. They had family occasions, too, but these were limited to the immediate family and did not depend so much on tradition to make them successful. To P.S., Christmas with his mother would have been relaxed and warm and good. But Christmas with his father meant going first to Philadelphia, where his father lived, and then driving with him down to Baltimore, in order to spend Christmas with his father's family. There was always a Christmas Eve lunch at his uncle and aunt's house, Christmas Eve dinner at the huge house of his father's first cousin and his family, and Christmas morning would be spent at the house of whomever they were staying with. Then off to Carter Hall for lunch with fifty cousins, aunts, great-uncles, great-aunts, and family friends. Carter Hall was the family house. It had been in the family for two hundred years, and it was traditional for the family to congregate there for Christmas lunch. Although P.S. admitted these big lunches were fun, he could not say they were warm and relaxed. Tradition got in the way of intimacy. And there was one further difficulty: P.S. had been brought up in the North. There were too many anecdotes he didn't understand, too many great-aunts whose names he couldn't remember, too many cousins who made fun of his Northern accent, his Yankee clothes, his inability to tell a Southern victory from a Southern defeat. And he would never forget the embarrassment he brought upon himself that first Christmas as a child when he had gone with his father to the Christmas Day luncheon at Carter Hall and had effusively greeted and kissed one of the maids, whom he had mistakenly assumed to be a great-aunt.

Yet it was P.S. who accompanied his father to the Christmas dinner. Stewart Wilkinson and P.S.'s older brother, Carter, had long since given up trying to understand each other. There never had been much affection between them, P.S. felt, and he thought that this was largely his father's fault. To P.S., his father seemed a man incapable of expressing emotion. During that first year at Yale following his father's divorce, P.S. compared his feelings about his father with other boys' feelings about their fathers. And with the background of a basic psychology course behind him he was more than prepared to make a statement as to what precisely was the matter with his father. P.S. had come to the conclusion that his father was so self-conscious, so self-wary, so self-centered that he wouldn't attempt to understand someone else because it might result in the other person's presuming to understand him. P.S. had watched his brother try to reach their father and had hoped to learn from him. Carter, through the early years, had made every effort to please their father. He had taken a job on an Oklahoma oil rig because his father wanted him to gain "experience." He would play football even though he was too small, just because he wanted his father to be proud of him. Even though Carter was accepted at Yale, he chose to go to the college where his grandfather, after whom he had been named, had gone, and where Stewart Wilkinson had gone, and where nine out of ten of the male members of his father's family had gone. Carter did not join the family fraternity simply because none of his friends were joining (P.S. joined the chapter at Yale), and though Carter was aware that this might be a disappointment to his father, he did not know that Stewart Wilkinson would take it so seriously. Stewart Wilkinson had been on the staff of the college humor magazine, so P.S.'s brother tried out for a place on the staff, too. And when Carter was later elected editor in chief he was sure his father would be proud of him. Carter sent home copies of several issues, which his father sent back with the stories marked "Not Funny" or "Too Long" or "Pointless," and the jokes at the back marked "My God, we had this one when I was there!" or "Bad Taste" or "Dirty!" P.S. remembered once visiting his brother at the university. On Carter's bureau was a framed photograph of Gargantua the Ape, snarling. It was signed, "Love, Dad."

Stewart Wilkinson did not pretend to understand his daughter. He was perfectly willing to love Page, to protect her, but his daughter's world was totally foreign to him. And so Stewart Wilkinson limited his conversations with Page to comments upon the way she dressed, wore her hair, and whom she was seen with.

That left P.S.

Perhaps experience with his older brother and sister had tempered P.S.'s father's touch so that he did not make the same mistakes with P.S., or perhaps Stewart Wilkinson saw enough of himself in his youngest son so that he could guess the effect his words would have on the boy by trying them out first on himself. At any rate, P.S. was left with his father, since even before the divorce his brother and sister would do anything in their power to avoid having to spend any length of time with him.

In those months immediately following the divorce, usually it was possible to work out the times P.S. and his brother and sister would spend with their parents, but Christmas was impossible. It was only one day, and it was possible to spend it with only one of them. P.S.'s mother was living in New York City, his father in Philadelphia. Carter and Page had already decided to spend

Christmas with their mother. P.S. would have liked to have done this, too, but someone had to spend Christmas with their father. And P.S. could not understand why his brother and sister, who were older, did not have the compassion to put themselves in their father's position—the position of a man who knows his children don't want to be with him for Christmas.

The next morning, no matter how hard he tried not to, P.S. slept later than his father. His father had banged on the door and yelled, "C'mon, c'mon! Get outta bed!" P.S. told him that he *was* up, and lay there hating his father for not knowing how to wake up a person. P.S. wished that he had been the first to wake up, so that he could have gone down to *his* room and crashed and pounded insanely against *his* door and shouted at *him* to get up.

His father made another big business of fixing P.S.'s breakfast. There was a slice of cold toast with chips of butter on it, some orange juice, and hot water for instant coffee. He asked P.S. if he was all packed up, and P.S. had to say no, and his father looked at his watch and shook his head. P.S. finished the piece of toast, took the half-cup of bitter coffee upstairs and opened his suitcase again. As he put the shirts in, he saw the brightly wrapped Christmas presents he had brought down with him, and remembered that today was Christmas Eve and felt, for the briefest moment, the tenderness and excitement that the day should hold.

"What's happening up there!"

P.S. finished packing and joined his father downstairs. P.S. was told to run back up to check the lights, and when he came back down his father was waiting in the car. P.S. put in the suitcase, climbed in the car, and locked his door. His father started the car, and P.S. was trapped.

His father fought his way into the traffic, fought his way through Chester to Wilmington, fought the other cars for right of way with an angry determination not to let another car pass him or go slower than he wanted to go; and then they were on U.S. 40, with seventy miles to Baltimore.

P.S. lit a cigarette, bravely ignoring his father's look of pain at having to share the car with someone who smoked. His father opened the air vent, adjusted the vertical side windows, and then said, "I haven't heard a word from your brother or sister."

"Ummm," P.S. answered.

"I'm not sure I have their addresses correctly." He recited their addresses, knowing full well they were correct.

"Well," P.S. said, "senior year is very busy, you know. I mean, I'm sure they have an enormous amount of work to do."

"I suppose so. But somehow, when I was a senior I always found time to write my father. I wrote your brother and sister twice during the past week, asking them whether they would be coming to Baltimore. I haven't heard from them. I can only suppose they haven't received my letters. I suppose the Christmas mail rush is responsible. I'm sure they would let me know. But I haven't heard from them. Maybe they'll be in Baltimore when we arrive."

"No, they're both with Mom," P.S. said coldly. "I have their Christmas presents to you and the family in my suitcase."

"Well, of course, I couldn't get them anything very grand," his father said. P.S. sat there thinking of his father's outrageously expensive foreign after-shave, the shirts which were made to order, the attaché case which would come from a good leather shop in London. It was the little things that offended P.S. the most: these little unnecessary expenses of his father's. His father never used paper napkins, only linen. His father's writing paper came from Tiffany's. And now his father was trying to pass himself off as a pauper! P.S. heard himself say, "Well, I'm sure they aren't expecting much," and was suddenly plunged into the wildly exuberant hope that his father might take what he had said the wrong way and think P.S. meant that because the father had been so cheap with the children in the past they had no reason to expect anything else now.

"So they're spending Christmas with your mother."

"Yeah."

"They won't be coming down to Baltimore then at all?"

"Nope!"

P.S. saw the road sign giving fifty-five miles as the distance to

Baltimore, and he told himself that it was only an hour more, an hour and fifteen minutes to his uncle's house.

"How is your mother?"

"Oh, fine, Dad. Just fine. She looks very well. She sends her best."

"I just don't understand your mother. I just don't understand why she did this to me. She never could understand why I went into the Navy during the war. She always felt I was running away from her. She couldn't understand that I was doing it *for* her, for us . . . so that . . . so that you could be proud, or not ashamed, of me. I didn't have to go. I could have stayed out of it because of my age, and because of you children. But I couldn't bring myself to do that. And your mother never could forgive me for what I *had* to do. She always believed that I volunteered, enlisted just to get away from her and you children."

"Ummm."

Then there was a long pause. P.S. reached for his second cigarette and his father opened the ashtray and double-checked the vent and window. P.S. lit his cigarette, blowing the smoke toward the slightly open window, loving the taste, and his father said, "You really smoke too much." And the cigarette became dry and chalky in P.S.'s mouth. His father told P.S. how he had stopped smoking. How it was a stupid, dirty, expensive habit. And P.S. sat there listening to him, the cigarette burning down between his fingers, not daring to take another puff, until finally, the end glowing hot next to his fingers, he pushed the cigarette out the side vent, scattering ashes onto his father's suit, spreading gray specks up his father's sleeve, and P.S. was horrified. He tried to brush the ashes away and instead rubbed them in; he mumbled apologies. After a period of time, enough time for P.S. to realize how stupid it was to smoke, how obviously dangerous it was inside a car, his father spoke again.

"Do you suppose your brother is all right?"

"How do you mean all right?"

"Is there anything the matter with him?"

"Not that I know of," P.S. said. "Why?"

"Oh, nothing."

P.S. began to think that his father knew something about his brother that he didn't know, and he asked again, "Why did you ask? *Is* something wrong?"

"I don't know. Is there?"

"No, no, there isn't. Not that I know of, anyway."

"Does he write you?"

"Well, no, Dad, but we have sort of an arrangement—an agreement. I don't write him and he doesn't have to write me."

Another long pause. "Tucker Whipple's son is in Carter's class at the university. He says Carter has some girl he's spending a lot of time with."

Judy Perkins! "Who?"

"I don't know her name. But do you suppose he's serious about her?"

"Oh, I doubt it."

"Good," his father said. "I hope not. Your brother certainly isn't in any position to be getting serious about any girl. Or ready for the responsibility of being a husband or father. God knows what kind of job he could get."

"Well, I guess there are plenty of good job openings for seniors."

"For graduates. He has to graduate first. And besides, he doesn't seem to be interested in anything. There isn't a thing that interests him."

"Aw, Dad, he just needs time."

"Time! My God, he already has had— This is his fifth year at the university! How much more time does he need?"

"Well, I think he's interested in writing. I think he wants to write."

"He never tells *me* anything," his father said.

"Umm." *Somewhere along the line,* P.S. thought, *somewhere after Carter was editor of the school yearbook and after he was editor of the college magazine and after he wrote that play for the dramat— Somewhere along the line, Dad, you might have noticed he was interested in writing.*

"He never writes me. As far as I know, he never writes his grandmother either. I honestly don't know what's the matter

with your brother and sister . . . God knows, I've done everything
I could to teach them common good manners . . ."

"Well, it's a little hard to write when you don't have anything
to say."

"You don't need to have anything to say when you write your
grandmother. All you have to do is write her—tell her that you're
fine and you want to see her soon and things like that."

"Ummm."

"That's all it takes."

"Ummm."

"Your grandmother likes to get letters."

"Yes, sir." *Here it comes.*

"When was the last time you wrote your grandmother?"

"I don't know. I don't remember exactly . . . I don't think it
was too long ago—maybe a couple of months."

"I'm sure it pleased her a great deal."

"Yes, well, I hope so."

"I'm sure it did. We'll stop off to see her before we go on to
the house."

"Yes, sir."

They arrived at P.S.'s uncle's house in time for lunch. P.S. got
out of the car and lifted the suitcases out. Free at last. Now there
would be cousins to see, and dogs to pat, and an uncle and aunt
whom he was honestly and deeply fond of. But most of all there
was the relief of knowing it was over—that his father and he
could carefully avoid talking to each other and yet keep up ap-
pearances.

P.S.'s father was Home. It was Christmas Eve. He was with
the Family. He didn't have to think about the divorce. He didn't
have to impress anyone. He was, P.S. thought, the returning
prodigal, the one who led the glamorous life in the outside world.
P.S. heard him tell the others what a good time he and P.S. had
been having together, and how sorry P.S.'s brother and sister
were that they couldn't be there. And P.S. knew that his father
was not fooling anyone; P.S. knew the family understood that
when parents become separated or divorced, their children cannot avoid taking sides. P.S. also knew that the family understood

that in respect to his father and mother, it was an extremely difficult and heartbreaking decision that he and his brother and sister had to make. Neither parent was an ogre, or a lout, or a lush, or a sadist, which, at least, would have made the decision easier. The decision was so terrible because one parent was marvelous and the other was only average. The easy decision, the automatic decision would have been for the child to have gone to the parent who was marvelous, leaving alone the one who was only average. *But what happens,* P.S. thought, *when the child loves them both? What happens when two of the three children have already decided that the divorce was the average one's fault —that it could not have been the fault of the marvelous one?* P.S. wondered whether the family also understood that the third child, the youngest, could choose only to go with the parent who was not marvelous, because, unlike the other two children, he resembled that one, thought like that one, and worse, felt sorry for that one.

Stewart Wilkinson was wearing what P.S. referred to as the Family Occasion Suit—a dark suit, almost a tail coat, the type of suit P.S.'s grandfather had worn at Christmas Eve dinners like this. P.S.'s father was wearing a detachable collar and a silvery tie, the sort seen nowadays only at weddings, and he had a sprig of mistletoe in his lapel. P.S. stood watching his father for a minute, loving his father, who looked so comfortable with the family and with old friends who by this time were almost, if not in reality, family. P.S.'s father beckoned to him, and P.S. went over to listen to a story one of the older-generation cousins was telling about a servant of P.S.'s grandfather. And then P.S. was held there by his father to hear one he wanted to tell. A lot of the pretty young female cousins were listening to P.S.'s father, and P.S. knew how much his father liked having the girls around him.

"Philip is very much like me," his father said, patting P.S. on the shoulder. "We are both tall and skinny—well, I'm not so skinny now—but every time I look at him I cannot help but remember what his grandfather, my father, once advised me to wear when I went trout fishing. My father said to me, 'Stewart?

Instead of going out and spending all that money on rubber wading boots why don't I lend you a couple of my umbrella covers!' "

The cousins were laughing and looking over at P.S., and P.S. walked away from his father, feeling the girls measuring his legs for umbrella covers, and the more he thought about the way his father embarrassed him in front of the girls the angrier he got. The pretty new wife of one of P.S.'s cousins entered the room, carrying her new baby, and the family all circled around her. P.S. watched his father being deserted by the girl cousins, who rushed to coo and sigh with the matrons of the family. P.S.'s cousin was explaining how worried he had been during the delivery, how he had been nervous and sick and twice as scared as his wife, and then how excited he had been when the doctor told him his wife had had a son.

P.S.'s father made his way over to the group and said, "Excited? That's absurd! I never got the least bit excited when any of my children were born, particularly my sons! Never had any reason to."

It was the typical remark P.S.'s father would make, which P.S. had heard his father make before. And he knew he shouldn't have let it bother him, but it did, and P.S. said across the room to his father, "I know you never got excited about us, Dad. Don't you think you've made that clear by this time?"

And when P.S. saw the awful look on his father's face, the pain that lanced through his father's eyes—when P.S. saw him become slightly smaller, trying to smile, trying to turn it into a joke—P.S. could only share the humiliation his father was now feeling, and he hated himself. He hated his brother and his sister, who had put him in the position of being alone with his father in Baltimore for Christmas. But most of all, but most of all he hated his father, who was standing there across the room, showing his hurt, his embarrassment, his bewilderment that his son could have said such a thing to him.

The next morning First Lieutenant Philip Sadler Wilkinson awoke, still fully dressed in his uniform. He sat up on the edge of his bunk, then leaned over and massaged his feet through the boot leather. It was so terribly cold in his room that he could see his breath, and he got up from the bed and lit the diesel stove. Somebody had brought the mail to the BOQ and on his footlocker rested a letter from his friend Charlie Merritt, telling Wilkinson of his intention to get married and hoping Wilkinson could be best man. There was also a thick brown manila envelope from New York City. It was marked "Book" and was the only package that had arrived for him. P.S. knew that his father often Christmas shopped in New York, and he opened the package almost tenderly. He slid away the brown manila envelope and pretended that it was brightly colored Christmas wrappings. The envelope dropped to the floor, and it wasn't a present from his father. It wasn't from anyone, it was merely the gift catalogue from a book company that he had now been receiving for years.

5 AFTER HE HAD READ "Dear Abby" in the Saturday *Pacific Stars and Stripes* and had finished his last cup of breakfast coffee, P.S. stepped out of the mess hall into the crisp morning sunlight. From the top of the steps at the mess hall he could see over the roof of the BOQ and beyond the BOQ the low red dirt hill, its flanks still pitted by artillery shells fired during the war. In the years that had passed since the truce had been declared at Panmunjom, no grass or shrubs or trees had grown along the hill to hide its scars. From the middle of the hill frosted gray rice paddies reached down like old men's fingers, each finger wrinkled by dikes and paths. Wilkinson sucked on a piece of bacon that had trapped itself between his teeth and watched a Korean farmer tightrope along a narrow dike between two paddies. He was balancing his A-frame on the small of his back. At the edge of one of the paddies, the old Papa-san stopped and squatted down to rest.

"*Lieu*tenant?"

Wilkinson turned and saw the first sergeant hurrying toward him.

"What is it, Top?"

"Lieutenant, the major wants to see you in his office right away."

Oh, for God's sake, what is it this time? "Okay, Top, tell him I'll be right there." Wilkinson made certain that his woolen

55

trousers were properly rolled over his boot tops, that the buttons on his olive-drab woolen shirt lined up with the polished belt buckle and fly. He walked down the steps of the mess hall, then up Yankee Avenue to the major's office. He knocked on the door, then walked inside and saluted. "Good morning, sir . . . you sent for me?"

Major Sturgess was, as usual, cleaning his fingernails with a half-opened paper clip. He did not look up or return the salute.

"Wilkinson?"

"Sir."

"You were duty officer last night, is that right?"

"My report was on your desk before breakfast, sir."

"I've read your report. It seems like a perfectly good report, Wilkinson, except for one thing. Nowhere in your report do I find any mention that our compound was broken into last night."

"I didn't know it was, sir," Wilkinson said.

The major tossed the paper clip into the wastepaper basket where it hit with a slight *ping!*, then for the first time the major looked up. "Wilkinson, last night, while *you* were supposed to be on duty, the compound was broken into for the third time in two months."

"Is anything missing, sir?"

"That's what I want you to find out. You're the Top Secret Control Officer, and I want you to take the logbooks and make a complete inventory of every classified document in the possession of this unit in accordance with AR 380-5. If anything is missing I will want to hear about it. Is that clear?"

"Well, sure, sir, but—"

"Don't 'but' me, Lieutenant!" the major ordered. "You *were* the duty officer. You *are* the duty officer—whether you like it or not —for the next two days, and are therefore responsible for what occurs in this compound while I am not present."

"Yes, sir."

"Well, what do you plan to do about the break-in?"

"Notify Lieutenant Pratt and then have the C.I.C. check up here right away."

"I've already done that," the major said.

"Then I'd better have some men repair the fence. Where was it cut?"

"Behind the motor pool. Between Posts Three and Four. I've already sent some men to fix it."

"I can't think of anything else other than check the classified material. What more do you want me to do?"

"God damn it, Wilkinson, I want you to stop these break-ins!"

"But, sir—Major Sturgess, I can't do anything about it. Lieutenant Pratt has all the guards on duty that he can. He's already taken one of the cooks and made him a guard. And he's got two men rotating home this month and they don't have any replacements. He's going to be more shorthanded than he had been before. And those Koreans he had—you know as well as I do that they're worthless."

"In the Army you have to do your best with the best you've got."

"They sure aren't the best—they're the only thing we've got. My God, they drive Lieutenant Pratt out of his mind!"

The major's field telephone buzzed and he lifted it out of the canvas boot. "Yeah, Major Sturgess here . . . Right, Top . . . Okay. Good. No, that'll be all . . . Fine, Top, g'by." The major slid the phone back into the boot and turned to Wilkinson. "Just as I thought. That was the first sergeant. It was a moose. A whore. Just like the last time. Do you see what this means?"

"Sir?"

"God damn it, Wilkinson, it means those mooses are cutting through the barbed-wire fences to shack up with the men. Some goddam moose doesn't get herself a customer for the night, so she cuts through the fence to see who she can pile into the sack with on the inside!" The major slammed his hand down hard on the desk. "This is the goddamdest country I've ever seen! I don't know what the—in the eighteen years—I've been in the Army for eighteen years! Eighteen! I retire in '62—if 1962 ever gets here. This is the foulest, goddamdest country I've ever seen! I've never seen anything like it. Where else—where else in the world do whores cut through barbed-wire fences to climb into the sack with the GIs?"

Wilkinson stood watching him. *You wanted to hurry back*

here. You're the one who loves this country so much. . . . You couldn't wait to climb into the sack with one of those mooses yourself. And here—and here you are, for God's sake, acting surprised that such a thing could happen! "Will that be all, sir? I'd like to get started checking that classified material if you don't want me around any longer."

"Stick around," the major said. "Sit down. Sit down." The major leaned back in his chair and reached behind him for the field phone. He lifted it out of its boot and cranked the buzzer. "Top? Get me Major Kim, see if he can be located at his detachment headquarters. If Major Kim isn't there get one of his captains and have him call that police captain—what's-his-name—from the National Police . . . Chang, that's right. Captain Chang. See if Major Kim and Captain Chang can get here for a meeting at zero eight-thirty . . . Right, Top, that'll be fine." Major Sturgess replaced the phone and swiveled his chair around and smiled at Wilkinson. "Make yourself comfortable, Wilkinson. We'll be here for some time. You might as well wait until Major Kim and Captain Chang get here."

Wilkinson leaned back in the chair opposite the major's desk and lit a cigarette. *The major certainly is happy about something. What's this all about?*

"How's everything going at the PI Center?" the major asked.

"Fine, sir." *Are we going to have a polite little chat?*

"Good," Major Sturgess said. He lifted his feet onto the desktop and looked down at his fingernails. "How long have you been in the Army now, Wilkinson?"

"Nineteen months, sir."

"Do you like it?"

"The Army? . . . Well, there are parts of it that aren't bad."

"But you don't intend to stay in."

"No, sir."

"What do you intend to do for a living?"

"I'm not sure, sir." *What is going on?*

"But you are sure that you don't want to stay in the Army?"

"Yes, sir," Wilkinson answered.

"Why not?"

"Well—well, for a lot of reasons, sir. I'm just not the Army type. I mean I don't like the idea of armies much."

"Oh, shit, Wilkinson," the major said, "if you're going to talk like that, then it's time we got back to business—" The major was smiling again—a fat, feather-mouthed cat smile. "Now, the reason why I've told you to stick around is because I want you here for the meeting when Captain Chang and Major Kim get here. They know you. You've been here longer than anybody else and they seem to like you. So when they see you're here they'll know I mean business—and I do mean business. I'm going to tell them that the next time a moose gets caught on this compound— the next moose who enters this compound, unauthorized, will have her head shaved . . . Clean . . . Bald! Just like they did the collaborators in France at the end of the war. That's the only way to treat those whores. Show them up. Humiliate them. Let the world know they're whores. Once the word gets around that any moose caught here gets her hair shaved, I'm willing to bet that we won't have much more of this fence cutting."

So that's it! . . . "Sir, these girls don't need to be humiliated. They're humiliated enough knowing they're whores. They don't need someone like us to tell them that. In most cases it's the only way they can support their families. I mean there must be some way we can stop this without shaving their heads. Think, think what it would be like if some Koreans shaved the heads of some American girls."

"Girls! . . . *Girls!* . . . Wilkinson, you keep calling them girls! These aren't girls, these are whores who are cutting through the barbed-wire fences of an intelligence unit, a maximum security area, and God knows what they steal or who follows them in. Then they climb into the sack with some GI in the barracks. Now what the hell kind of unit would we have if all the GIs had bedmates in the barracks?"

What about the moose in your own building? "I still think, sir, that there must be a better way."

"Look, I don't like the idea of shaving heads any more than you do, but I have the responsibility for this unit."

"Because I am responsible any means I choose to achieve the

end is permissible." . . . *Jesus, isn't that the way things go?* "Yes, sir," Wilkinson said.

"I can't have this sort of thing going on in my unit. If it makes you feel any better, the last time I was here, not long after the war, the Turks caught a slicky-boy making off with some equipment he had stolen from their compound. The Turks caught him, held a trial, and condemned the kid to death right there on the spot. They carried the kid, who was fighting and kicking, over to the fence line and strung him up across the barbed wire. Then they cut him right down the middle and left him there to die. Everyone in the village could hear the kid screaming, but they didn't dare do anything about it. And you know what? Of all the United Nations forces still in this country, the Turks have the lowest record of goods stolen."

"Well, that doesn't make them right," Wilkinson said. "Why couldn't we, if we catch a moose, turn her over to the National Police? It seems to me, sir, that they're the proper ones to punish her."

"Jesus Christ, Wilkinson, for someone who's always harping about how long he's been in this country you sure are the most naïve— Look, this is not the U.S. of A.! You don't get the same police protection here. *We*'re the foreigners, not the Koreans. Do you remember that man in your section, what was his name, the one who had the moose with the big knockers . . . Culcheck! Culcheck's moose, well, you remember how she was caught stealing a case of Cokes?"

"Sure, and we turned her over to the National Police."

"That's right. We turned her over to Captain Chang. You remember what her punishment was?"

"I don't think so, sir."

"She had to turn half the case of Cokes over to the police."

"But what makes you think shaving the heads of the mooses is going to make any difference?"

"How many GIs are going to lay out five dollars to shack with a moose who looks like Yul Brynner?"

"Maybe none of the mooses will show," Wilkinson said hopefully. "Maybe warning them will be enough."

"Maybe. Maybe. *Maybe!* MAYBE!" Sturgess said, slamming his palm down on his desktop. "But I'll be goddamed if I'm going to be commanding officer of this unit when the inspector general comes around and discovers that we are missing ten secret documents, four hundred gallons of gasoline, several carbines, and thirty percent of the men are on the disabled list with gonorrhea. . . . Which is exactly what will happen if we don't make goddam sure that no Korean whore is going to come on this compound without permission."

The field telephone buzzed and the major picked it out of the boot. "Yeah? . . . That's right, Top, okay . . ."

Wilkinson looked at his watch. It was eight-thirty.

"Okay, fine," the major was saying. "Lieutenant Wilkinson is here with me, and he'll escort him up to the office. Tell the guard to hold him there until Wilkinson arrives. Make sure the guard signs him in as a visitor on official business, and that he wears a tag . . . Right, Top." The major replaced the phone and swiveled back to face Wilkinson. "Okay, boy, Captain Chang's down at the Main Gate."

P. S. Wilkinson stepped out of the major's office and headed down Yankee Avenue toward the Main Gate. The morning sun was warming the rice paddies and he could already notice the fetid smell. In the distance Wilkinson could hear the *pffwhUMP! pfffwhhhhUMP!* of an artillery unit firing on the practice range. Overhead, two F-86Ds banked high and climbed, their silver wings swept back and shining brilliantly for a moment, and then they were gone and behind them raced the throaty whistle of their engines. The jets had to turn back because only fifteen miles farther north were the North Koreans who worked all day on their concrete artillery caves not knowing whether they were to defend or attack. The light Army reconnaissance planes flew along the DMZ, were occasionally shot at when they strayed too close to North Korea, and at Panmunjom the truce negotiators were off for the holiday, but the empty building echoed their voices, their charges that "Your side violated my side's land." Just as they had been charging each other for the past seven years. For P. S. Wilkinson, the Korean War had become the worst sick joke of all time.

The guard stepped out of his shack at the Main Gate and saluted. "Sir, Captain Chang is here."

"Good, did you give him his pass?"

"Yes, sir."

Wilkinson walked over to the National Police captain and saluted. "Merry Christmas. Anyunghashimnika," Wilkinson said.

"Chosumnida," Captain Chang answered, bowing slightly, then he shook hands with the lieutenant.

Wilkinson walked back up Yankee Avenue with the police captain on his right in deference to the Korean's rank. "Nari chosumnida," Wilkinson said.

"Yes," the captain laughed, "but it'll get much colder. You are learning Korean very well, Lutena Wilkinson."

"No, I'm not, sir. You've just heard all the Korean I know. But you speak English without any accent."

"Yes, but I studied it for a long time," the Korean said.

"U.C.L.A.?" Wilkinson asked, but Chang did not answer.

Wilkinson and Captain Chang entered the major's office. Major Kim, the commanding officer of the Korean Intelligence Detachment, was there also. The two Koreans shook hands, spoke to each other briefly, then sat down. Wilkinson remained standing behind their chairs. The major's door opened again and Lieutenant Pratt stepped inside and took a place next to Lieutenant Wilkinson.

"Captain Chang, I believe you know Lieutenant Pratt," Major Sturgess said. "He's our security officer and the CO of the Military Police Detachment, and of course you all know Wilkinson, so we don't need to bother with introductions. Let's get right to the point." He paused to make certain he had everyone's attention. Then he began, speaking almost as though he were giving a prepared briefing, a previously memorized spiel. "Gentlemen, I have asked you to meet me here this Saturday morning so that I might obtain your advice, your assistance, and your cooperation in dealing with certain—with a particularly unfortunate problem which has arisen recently in this unit. As you know, the 258th

Military Intelligence Company is engaged in highly sensitive work, of a nature which directly involves the national security of your country and the security of the United Nations Forces quartered on your soil. Our work is highly classified, of a highly responsible nature and of a highly ahh-ahh highly important nature. For this reason I have been particularly alarmed by the high rate of increase of unauthorized entrance of certain Korean ahh-ahh women." The major paused and pulled out his pack of cigarettes. He passed them first to Major Kim, who declined, and next to Captain Chang, who took two out of the pack and pocketed them. The major continued: "The method of entrance has been to cut through the outer perimeter fence—only the bottom strand. Three times within the past two months this has been done. The most recent was last night. In both of these past two incidents the fence cutting was done by prostitutes. The former time was a slicky-boy. However, it could just as easily have been done by agents or—to use a word I think is somewhat over-glamorized—by spies. But, the main problem so far has been with the prostitutes. Do either of you have any suggestions as to the means by which we might stop these incidents?"

Major Kim was the first to speak. "Of course I shall have a long talk with the Korean guards on duty last night . . . but the main problem still is that, of course, we don't have enough men. Lieutenant Pratt, I am sure, will agree with me there."

"Yes, sir," Lieutenant Pratt said.

"Therefore the only practical suggestion I can make is to lay concertina wire along the base of the fence line and perhaps some mines."

"Well, of course, Major Kim, we would like to use concertina wire," Major Sturgess said, "but we can't get it. It's all up with the divisions along the DMZ. As for mines, we couldn't use them either. The mines would have to be placed near the fence line, and the fence line generally passes within two or three feet of some of our buildings. Anyone detonating a mine would knock out a building. Hardly worth it."

"Perhaps, perhaps . . ." Captain Chang began. He was tapping his fingertips together. "Perhaps you could discourage your men from sleeping with Korean women."

"God damn it, yes, of course we have tried that—it hasn't been particularly successful. There isn't much else the troops can do for entertainment."

"But, ahh, Major Sturgess," Captain Chang continued, "you have your movies, your libraries, your USO clubs . . . you have so many jeeps in which you might travel. You could see our theaters or shrines or treasures, there are so many things you could see here instead of staying on your compounds. We have so many beautiful lakes, mount—" Chang was interrupted by Major Kim, who chewed his ass out in rapid Korean. Kim's tone was harsh, his sentences chopped, his tongue hissing between his teeth. Throughout the harangue the police officer's face remained polite and unchanged except for a slight flush. At the end of it Major Kim leaned back in his chair. And Captain Chang leaned forward again to say, "But, as Major Kim has pointed out, boys will be boys . . ."

Lieutenants Wilkinson and Pratt exchanged quick questioning glances, both wondering what Major Kim had said.

"Right! Right!" Major Sturgess agreed enthusiastically. "Of course! Now, I feel that these unauthorized entrances must be stopped. An example must be made of anyone who is caught. For this reason we have decided that the next prostitute found on this compound without a satisfactory reason for being here— without, as it were, *permission*—will have her head shaved. She will then be turned over to you, Captain Chang, for further punishment if it is deemed necessary. . . . Are there any questions?"

Lieutenant Wilkinson looked from Captain Chang to Major Kim. Their faces showed no reaction at all.

"Good. Fine," Major Sturgess said. "Now, Captain Chang, I would appreciate it if you would sort of pass the word in the village, okay? . . . For the time being that's all, gentlemen. If there are no questions, or there are no comments you would like to make, then I think we can close this meeting. I want to thank you for coming. I know that I have no doubt interfered with plans you might have made for the morning, and I greatly appreciate your coming here." Major Sturgess stood up and waited for the two Koreans to rise also, then he said, "Ahhh, Lieutenant Wilkinson? Would you be good enough to escort Captain Chang to the Main Gate?"

"That's perfectly all right, Major," Captain Chang said. "I can find my way myself."

"No trouble, Captain. Lieutenant Wilkinson would be happy to accompany you."

"Yes, sir," Wilkinson said.

Captain Chang turned in his visitor's card to the guard at the Main Gate, then bowed slightly to Wilkinson. "Your major is a most curious man."

"Yes, sir." Wilkinson smiled.

"Very interesting."

"Well, sir, we all hope that none of this punishment becomes necessary."

"I, too, Lutena. I too." The police captain paused, then smiled. "I almost forgot. Merry Christmas. Have a nice weekend."

"Thank you, sir," Wilkinson answered. "Same to you."

Wilkinson finished the last of the classified documents just before dinnertime. He quickly typed up a report, in triplicate, stating that as ordered by Major Sturgess he had completed a check of classified documents filed at the 258th Military Intelligence Company, and that to the best of his knowledge no safe had been tampered with, no documents were missing, no building had been entered without authorization. In the second paragraph he suggested that the officer in charge of each section should check the documents himself, and pay particular attention to the "Confidential" documents for which no log was kept. He walked over to the orderly room, dropped his report and the first carbon on the major's desk, and kept the third copy for himself. Then he walked back down Yankee Avenue toward the mess hall and saw for the first time the new sign that had been placed on the guard shack by the Main Gate: UNAUTHORIZED PERSONS WILL BE SEVERELY PENALIZED IF DISCOVERED ON THIS COMPOUND AFTER VISITING HOURS. Underneath the lettering was the same message in Korean, then at the bottom, "By Order of the Commanding Officer." *Someone has been busy!* Wilkinson went on into the BOQ. There was a new notice also on the bulletin board: "All personnel of this command are reminded that female personnel are not permitted within the billeting area at any time. Failure to comply with this regulation will result in reduction in grade, fine, and restriction to the compound for a period of not less than two months."

Underneath, in Johnson's unmistakable handwriting, was, "Does this mean no more visits from Eleanor Roosevelt?"

Wilkinson washed up, then walked up the steps to the mess hall. All the officers were talking about the head shaving and because Major Sturgess had not come to chow, they were discussing whether or not it was legal. Johnson strongly opposed the order, Pratt felt there was no other way of handling the problem, and Captain Martin said he would go along with the major. Wilkinson sat down at the table and the Korean waitress came in and asked what he would like to eat. While waiting for his order he stared out the window at the low red dirt hill. *It's unbelievable! This whole goddam head-shaving thing is unreal . . . all of us . . . we're all unreal . . . grown men getting excited about shaving a woman's head!* . . . He rubbed his fingertips across his temples, then dropped his hands into his lap and leaned back in his chair. Major Sturgess entered and went to the head of the table.

"Did you find anything missing, Wilkinson?" the major asked.

"No, sir. I left a report on your desk and made the recommendation I discussed with you earlier, that is, that each section chief check his documents himself."

"Fine," Sturgess said. "It's a good way to start the New Year, anyway."

Captain Martin pushed away from the table and announced that he was going over to his section, the IPW, and do some work. But everyone knew that he went over there to write letters on the typewriter.

Before the captain was able to get up Major Sturgess said, "There is a Christmas party being given tonight by the G2. I have to go to it. And all the other officers of the 258th have been invited." Major Sturgess paused, then continued, "It is important that we make a good showing at affairs such as this, particularly official holidays, so any of you who wish to join me are cordially invited."

"Well, I have a date tonight," Johnson said. "I'd really *like* to go, sir, but I met this American girl in the PX yesterday who had invited me over to her parents' house for dinner."

"An American girl!" Pratt said. "My God, where'd you—how?"

"An authentic round-eye," Johnson said. "Her father is with the Department of Agriculture or something and he's over here to show the Koreans how to plant rice."

Wilkinson looked at Johnson and tried to think how long it had been since he himself had been out with an American girl. The last time had been in Japan two months ago when he saw a girl he had known from New York in the Imperial Hotel. The girl had left the next day with her family on the next leg of a round-the-world tour which certainly did not include Korea.

Lieutenant Pratt said that he thought he would go to the movie and get to bed early.

"How about you, Captain Martin?" Major Sturgess asked. "Are you sure you wouldn't be able to come?"

Wilkinson watched the captain. *Look at that poor bastard. . . . He's trying to decide whether this is going to affect his career. He knows that the party is going to be boring, and he's going to have to pay for drinks. . . . He's wondering if the major knows he isn't going to be doing any work back at the IPW Section. . . . On the other hand, he knows that if he won't go he'll offend the major . . .*

"I'll be happy to join you, sir," Captain Martin said. "I'm sure the work will wait."

"Fine, Martin," Sturgess said. "And you, Wilkinson?"

"I'm the officer of the day still, sir."

"That leaves Korkus. Where the hell *is* Korkus, I haven't seen him since yesterday at the Retreat."

"He's been up to Uijongbu seeing a friend, sir," Lieutenant Johnson said.

"I hope he remembered to take his lighter to impress his friends." Pratt laughed.

"What lighter?" Major Sturgess asked.

"Well, sir, P.S. and I took his lighter, the one he had engraved with his initials, and took it down to the PX and had 'From the Officers and Men of the 258th MI Co, With Esteem,' engraved on it also."

"What the hell did you do that for?" Sturgess asked.

"Well, sir, it was a joke," Wilkinson explained. "We accuse him of having had it engraved himself. That's all."

"I see," the major said, plainly not amused. "Well, Captain Martin? I'm leaving in about fifteen or twenty minutes. Can you be ready by then?"

"Yes, sir," Captain Martin said.

Wilkinson finished his dinner, then walked down the steps and crossed over to the BOQ. He walked into his room, tossed his fatigue cap onto his bed, sat down at his desk, and inserted fresh writing paper and four carbons in his typewriter. He sat there not knowing what to do with his time. He looked down at the typewriter, cracked his knuckles, then wrote, "Now is the time for all good men to come to the aid of yours truly." He pulled out the papers and saw that it had printed well on all four carbons. He crumpled up the papers, threw them into the wastepaper basket, and got up and went over to his bed and lay down on his back staring up at the ceiling. The worst part of loneliness was not having someone to share it with.

Wilkinson had been lying on his bed for about twenty minutes when he suddenly heard a Korean girl shout, "Hey, you, SONNA-BITCH, HEY, HENNERSON, YOU SONNABITCH YOU COMA HERE ME." The next thing Wilkinson heard was the sound of breaking glass. He got up and went outside. As he walked over to the Main Gate he recognized the girl who was standing with her hands on her hips angrily chewing gum. "Hello, Choe," he said.

The girl did not answer. Instead she tucked in her jersey and took a deep breath.

Wilkinson looked at the jeep with the broken windshield and asked what had happened.

"I no mean to hit jeepu," she explained. "I mean to hit Sa'gy Hennerson."

Wilkinson could tell that she was embarrassed to be seen by him.

"Why'd you want to hit Henderson?"

"Hennerson no wanna see me. Lat night he alla time stay club. He no come outta Main Gate to talk when I wanna see him. Tonight when I call him he say he not here. He say he at Uijongbu. But I know he here alla time. So when I see him come outta mess hall I call to him. But he pretend he no hear me. He no speaky me, ne? He no pretend to see me. So I throw rock to catch his eye."

"Well, maybe you'd better wait until Sergeant Henderson does want to see you."

"Lutena, Hennerson no wanna see me. He owe me money."

"Well, I can't do anything about that. In the first place, you're not supposed to have military payment certificates."

"Whatsamattah you? When you used to come to Ranch House when I work there you pay me in MPC."

"Well, I can't—it's different. Look, Choe, I'll do what I can for you. But I don't know if I can help. You go back to your hooch and don't throw any rocks around here. When Henderson wants to see you he'll see you. But you're not allowed on this compound without permission."

"You bring me in? You bring me and I'll go see Hennerson."

"I can't do that, Choe. I'm the duty officer."

"Okay, Lutena," she said. She looked at him, smiling slightly. Then she turned and walked away from the Main Gate. As she rounded the corner she spat out her gum. Wilkinson kept looking at her, thinking about the times he had stayed with her, wondering why she had left the Ranch House.

"Quite a pair, huh, Lieutenant?" Galero said.

"Yes, they are."

"They're real, too," Galero said happily.

Lieutenant Wilkinson walked up to the orderly room and saw that the charge-of-quarters was a PFC from his own section, Hollander.

"Good evening," Wilkinson said.

Hollander rose from his chair. "Good evening, sir. It looks like the fate of the 258th MI is resting squarely in the hands of the PI Section."

"Looks that way," Wilkinson said.

"There's been a change in the officer of the day instruction book, sir. You might want to take a look at it." Hollander passed the book over to Wilkinson. "It's right there at the top, sir."

Wilkinson read the change aloud: " 'Unauthorized indigenous personnel caught on this compound after hours will have their heads shaved. Signed, Baylor Sturgess, Major, AI(Ord), Commanding' . . . Well, let's just hope to God that this sort of thing never has to be done."

"Oh, I don't know, sir," Hollander said. "It might be fun."

Wilkinson went out into the Korean night and walked back to his room. He threw his cap onto his chair and stretched out on the bed. *None of this is real. None of this is happening.*

6

P. S. WILKINSON was awakened by a loud knocking at the door of his BOQ room.

"It's me, sir. Hollander. . . . You'd better come up to the orderly room right away."

"What's the matter?" *Not another goddam alert!*

"The KATUSA at Post Seven caught a moose just after she'd cut through the fence down at the motor pool. We're holding her in the orderly room now."

Wilkinson sat up. "You caught a moose?"

"She's being held in the orderly room," PFC Hollander repeated.

"Oh, my God!" Wilkinson said quietly. Then he stood up and walked to his door. "I'll be there in a few minutes, Hollander . . . see if you can get ahold of the major . . . I'll be there in a minute." He listened to Hollander walk down the hallway and out of the BOQ, then Wilkinson put on his fatigue uniform again and sat down on the bed. *It'll be Choe, God damn it . . . I know it's Choe!* . . . He looked down at his combat boots and considered saving time and energy by putting on his regular black low quarter shoes instead. But he decided that since this was a duty assignment he might as well play it by the book. He began lacing up his boots. When he had finished dressing and had slid the OD armband up his left sleeve, he picked up his fatigue cap and stepped out of the BOQ. It was freezing cold and he looked down at his watch.

It was 3:20. . . . He picked out the Big Dipper and the North Star, then he walked up to the orderly room and saw the Military Police sergeant holding a Korean girl in a chair. It wasn't Choe and P.S. felt relieved.

"Hollander, did you get ahold of the major yet?"

"No, sir," the CQ answered. "I checked with the Main Gate and the major hasn't returned yet. He left at eighteen-thirty and hasn't come back yet."

"Then try Captain Martin," Wilkinson said. He sat down in the chair opposite the Korean girl and looked at her. He could see that she was not wearing a brassiere. When she saw where he was looking she took a deep breath and crossed her legs to let her skirt ride up her thighs.

"Lutena, how 'bout you giva me cigarette, ne?"

God damn you, God damn you! . . . Wilkinson looked away instead to the Military Police sergeant who had brought her in. "Sergeant Raebruck, maybe you'd better tell me what happened."

Sergeant Raebruck cleared his throat. "Well, sir, Private Hwang, the KATUSA on Post Seven, saw her just after she had cut through the motor pool fence. He caught her as she was running and brought her to me. Then I came up here to the orderly room with her and had the charge-of-quarters call you."

"How did she get through the fence?"

"Sir? Lieutenant Wilkinson?" Hollander interrupted. "The Main Gate says that Captain Martin left with Lieutenant Pratt and the major. There aren't any officers back yet. You're the only one here."

Pratt went too? What a helluva way to run an army! "Okay, Hollander. Call the first sergeant. I want him up here."

"Yes, sir," Hollander said.

Sergeant Raebruck handed a pair of GI wire cutters across to Wilkinson. "She cut through the fence with these, sir."

Wilkinson held the wire cutters in his hand, squeezing the handles together. On a piece of adhesive tape on the inside of one of the handles was written 258MIC Supply. "Where did you get these?"

"Me I dunno," she answered. "Old Papa-san in village catchee me cutters. Whatcha gonna do me?"

"Could you identify the old man if you saw him again?" Wilkinson asked her. "Do you know the man? His name?"

"I nevah see him before."

"Just tell me one thing," Wilkinson said. "Why—why in God's name did you cut through the fence?"

"I wanna speaky my boyfriend. I think maybe if I speaky him tonight, I catchee me some money. He no coma my hooch so I hafta come in see him."

"Did you see him?"

"I no catchee chance to see him, Lutena. No good sonnabitch catchee me before I see him."

"Sir?" PFC Hollander said. "I've got the first sergeant. He wants to know if it's important."

"You tell him that I want him up here on the double and that I'm the one who decides whether or not it's important, not him. You tell him the only thing that's important to him is that he gets here no later than five minutes from now!"

"It's important, Top," Hollander said into the phone.

" '*Is it important?*' " Wilkinson repeated. "Jesus H. Christ, does he think I'm getting him out of his sack at three-thirty on Sunday morning to have a drink with me?" He looked back at the girl, who was nervously massaging her hands.

"Hey, Lutena, you gonna giva me a cigarette?"

Wilkinson stood up. "Raebruck, keep an eye on her. I'm going to talk to the first sergeant outside when he arrives."

"All right, sir," Raebruck said.

"Hey, Lutena? Watcha gonna do me?"

Wilkinson walked out of the orderly room and sat down on the curb. *I knew this was going to happen . . . I knew it! . . . Oh, God, why? Why did this thing have to happen to me? . . . Why isn't the major here? Why is he always off screwing around somewhere! . . .* Wilkinson could hear the first sergeant walking up Yankee Avenue toward him and he stood up.

"Good morning, sir," the first sergeant said. "I'm sorry, I didn't know it was you who wanted me. I thought it was the CQ who had some sort of bug up his—"

"That's okay, Top," Wilkinson said. "Sit down here for a moment out of the wind. Something's come up that I want to talk to you about." Wilkinson waited until the senior enlisted man in the unit was seated next to him on the curb, then he offered him a cigarette and lit one for himself.

"What's the problem, sir?"

"Top, we have a moose inside the orderly room who was caught cutting through the fence behind the motor pool. You are aware of the major's new order."

"Yes, sir . . . to shave her head."

"That's right. What do you think of it?"

"What do you mean, what do I think of it?"

"Look, Top, I know I'm putting you in a difficult position. But I wanted to talk to you out here, away from the others. I'd like to talk to you about this, hear you out, and see what you think. You've—you've been in the Army for twenty-some years and I haven't even been in for two yet. You've been in the Army a long time. Maybe you've seen something like this before. But, but I don't think we have any—any jurisdiction over this girl. I don't think we have any right to shave her head. What do you think?"

"The major says to shave her head."

"But I think his order is wrong. I think he's making a terrible mistake. I don't think I should give that order. Tell them to shave the girl's head."

"Look, Lieutenant, you're a nice young guy. But you are the officer. It's your decision, not mine. That's why you wear the silver bar and me all these stripes. It's your decision."

"I *know* that, Top. I'm not asking you to decide for me. That isn't what I want. All I want is your advice. I *need* your advice."

"Well, if I were you, I'd follow the major's orders."

"Even if you thought they were wrong?"

"I didn't say I thought they were wrong. That's what you said. It isn't my job to question the major's orders. He gives orders and I follow them, or see that they're carried out."

"My God, Top . . . my God, that isn't enough . . . you can't just *follow* orders . . ."

"Look, Lieutenant. You want me to tell you that it's all right for you not to obey the major's order. Isn't that it?"

Wilkinson stepped on his cigarette and when he spoke the anguish was clear in his voice. "Top, I don't want anything from you other than your advice . . . You've been in the Army for a long, long time. What's going to happen to me if I don't obey the major's order?"

"I'd obey the order if I were you, sir. . . . Look, you could wait until the major gets back. You could hold her. She could stay in the empty cage since the old woman died."

"The major would know why I kept her here. He'd know it was because I didn't believe his order was right. If I held her, he'd only shave her head himself. And it would be the same thing. Even though I hadn't been the one to shave her, she'd still get her head shaved. What's the point?"

"You're going to let her go, aren't you, Lieutenant."

"Yes."

"All you'd have to hold her for is another five hours at the most. The major would be here. It would be his responsibility."

Wilkinson stood up. "Well, I guess that's all, Top. Thanks for coming up here. I appreciate your getting out of a warm sack for me."

"Not at all, Lieutenant. Not at all . . . but since you asked me for my advice I tell you again. If I were you I'd shave her head and forget about it."

"Good night, Top," Wilkinson said.

Because of the holiday, the Sunday breakfast began at 0830 and ran to 1030. Heavy doughy pancakes were served, and burned bacon; but, as on any Sunday, if you got there early, when the mess hall was relatively empty, it was possible to get eggs cooked to your own taste, bacon that wasn't burned, hot toast, good coffee. The officers started to straggle in at about 0930 with their editions of the *Pacific Stars and Stripes,* they gave their orders to the Korean waitress, nodded at each other. On normal Sunday mornings, they would sit down to read *Orphan Annie* and *Terry and the Pirates.* There would be the usual groans of dismay at *Mary Worth's* latest platitudes, Chester Gould's sadomasochistic meanderings, and the horror of that small dewy-eyed brat

Dondi. But this holiday Sunday morning, the 27th of December, 1959, the officers did not read their newspapers as intently. They spoke little among themselves, and not at all to P. S. Wilkinson. Lieutenant Pratt patted P.S.'s shoulder on his way to get more coffee. Lieutenant Johnson looked up from his plate to glance curiously at him. Captain Martin read predicted bowl game football scores aloud to himself, and Major Sturgess concentrated on his soft-boiled eggs. There was an uneasy truce, the same silent breakfast truce that might arise between quarreling married couples. Wilkinson took a final sip of coffee. He had not slept well the previous night, and he felt the fatigue in the sourness of his stomach, the irritation of his eyes. He considered getting another cup of coffee, then decided he might as well get the action started. He stood up and walked over to the wall rack and picked off his fatigue cap. He took his time getting into his field jacket and liner because he knew the major would speak to him before he got to the door. He straightened his cap on his head and waited.

"Ahh, Lieutenant Wilkinson . . ." the major said.

"Yes, sir?" Wilkinson turned and faced him.

"Would ten-thirty suit you?"

"That would be fine, sir."

"Ten-thirty, then. My office."

"Yes, sir," Wilkinson said. He stepped out and looked across the rooftop of the BOQ at that red dirt hill. He had twenty minutes before he would see the major. Beyond the barbed wire, the muddy road, the frozen rice paddies, there was a Korean leading an ox along the top of the ridge. Both man and beast moved slowly, as though they had all the time in the world. Wilkinson walked down the steps and crossed to the BOQ and went inside his room. He sat down on the edge of his bed and rubbed his tired eyes. In a few moments Johnson entered and stood in the doorway looking at him.

"Look, I know this is none of my business, but what the hell happened last night?"

"Nothing much."

"Oh, come on, P.S., everyone knows something is up. What

happened? Was it something while you were on duty? Did you get caught off the compound?"

"No, it wasn't anything like that, Johnny," P.S. said. "We caught a moose last night who cut through the wire back at the motor pool. And instead of shaving her head like I was supposed to, I let her go."

"*You let her go!*" Johnson said in astonishment. "My God, do you know what that means?"

"I guess so," Wilkinson said. He felt so tired of the whole thing. All night he had thought about his decision, and why he had made it, and what was going to happen to him. And now, even though he hadn't spoken to the major, he just wished it were all over with.

"My God, it means you disobeyed orders."

Wilkinson got up from his bed and walked over to his Japanese phonograph. "That much I know, Johnny," he said. "That much I know." He sifted through his record albums and chose Chris Conner singing Gershwin. He put on the side that had the medley from *Porgy and Bess*. He waited for the record player to warm up, then let the record drop. "Not only does it mean that I disobeyed orders, but I no doubt was disrespectful, I humiliated him in front of the men, and I acted—my conduct was unbecoming to an officer."

"But why?"

"Because, Johnny, I don't think the major's order is correct."

"Jesus, P.S., I think you've been reading too much Herman Wouk. . . . No lie, P.S., *The Caine Mutiny* was fun to read but I wouldn't want to have been there."

"Oh, for Chrissake, I didn't commit mutiny! I merely disobeyed his order."

" 'Merely disobeyed his order!' . . . '*Merely!*' . . . Do you have any idea what can happen to you?"

"Nothing's going to happen to me," Wilkinson said.

"You hope so. . . . You may hope nothing's going to happen to you, but I'd sure as hell hate to be in your shoes. Listen, P.S., I hope you don't expect me to admire you for standing up for your principles. Jesus, you were a fool! This is just plain idiotic!

What the hell does shaving a moose's head mean compared with what's going to happen to you?"

"Nothing's going to happen to me," Wilkinson repeated.

"I wouldn't bet on that," Johnson said.

"Okay, okay, don't bet on it. All the same I did it, it's over with. And I was right. Now go on and talk to somebody else about it. I want to do some things before I go up and see the major." P.S. walked over to his door, opened it, and waited for Johnson to leave.

Johnson shrugged, then said, "Well, good luck, old buddy, you'll need it."

Wilkinson closed the door behind him. He walked over to his wall locker and pulled out a fresh uniform. He put it down on his bed and got out of the old uniform he was wearing. He got out a rag, his can of Brasso, and began polishing his belt buckle. When that was finished, his boots spit-shined, his insignia properly set, he put on his clean winter fatigues. *If I'm going down in flames, I'll do it right . . . I'll look, for once, like an officer . . . like Walter Mitty, but an officer. . . .* Wilkinson checked himself in the mirror, then walked out of the BOQ. At the door he met Lieutenant Pratt, who smiled sadly and said, "Well, hell, P.S., well, hell."

"Yep," Wilkinson said. He continued on up Yankee Avenue toward the major's office. Sp/5 Ewling and SFC Segal were coming down the street toward him. They both threw exaggeratedly proper salutes at Wilkinson. *Good God, now they're getting corny. They make me feel like John Wayne or somebody.* He returned their salutes and walked to the major's office and knocked on his door.

"Come in," Major Sturgess said.

Wilkinson stepped inside, shut the door behind him, then approached the major's desk and saluted. "First Lieutenant Wilkinson reporting as ordered, sir." He held his salute until the major returned it, then dropped his arm sharply to his side and remained standing at attention.

"Oh, shit, sit down," Major Sturgess said.

"Thank you, sir," Wilkinson said. He sat down in the stuffed chair across from the major's desk and watched as the major read through the officer of the day report and the charge-of-quarters report. While the major was reading he was absent-mindedly drumming his fingernails across the desktop. The major finished the reports and looked up at Wilkinson. "This just doesn't seem to be your week," the major said. He paused for a long moment waiting for Wilkinson to answer. But when there was no reply, he continued: "I must assume that you were familiar with my order concerning the shaving of any moose caught on this compound after hours. You were here when I discussed it with Major Kim and Captain Chang. Therefore we must acknowledge that ignorance was not your excuse. Can I further assume that your actions in disobeying my orders were deliberate and premeditated? Is that right?"

"Yes, sir."

"Right. I can further assume that you did so—that you did, in fact, disobey my order knowing that court-martial charges could be brought against you."

"Yes, sir."

"And that you are not going to sit across the desk from me like some Hollywood toy soldier and say, 'No excuse, sir.' Am I still right?"

"Yes, sir."

"Then—ahh—then you'd better explain why you chose to disobey my orders . . . off the record, of course."

"Well, sir, it's a little hard to know where to begin. But I want to try to make something clear at the beginning. I did not do this—I did not disobey your order to spite you, or humiliate you, to show you up, to embarrass you . . . I did it because, sir, I think your order is wrong. I think it was wrong. I could not obey an order which I knew was wrong and which I felt was a serious mistake on your part. Look, sir, I'm not a military man. I suppose I've made that abundantly clear. I'm not a career officer. I don't even like the Army. But I recognize why an army must exist, and I know I owe an obligation to it. Just as I owe an obligation to you. I don't know what a lieutenant is supposed to do. I don't know the channels for something like this . . . I don't know how I was supposed to talk to you, to make you understand how wrong this order is or was. What I'm trying to say is that I couldn't do it. I couldn't shave her head. We can't go around shaving Korean women's heads. I know I'm young, that I'm only twenty-three years old and you're—you're how old? Forty-five? Almost twice my age?"

"Forty-three," the major said.

"But I didn't disobey your order to show you up. I wish to God that girl hadn't cut through last night. I wish I'd had time to talk to you, maybe make you change your mind on this. All I know is—I know that I'm glad that I was the OD when it happened. One of the other officers would have shaved her head . . ."

"You're goddam right they would have."

"Sir, we don't have any *right* to punish a Korean. We just cannot shave a Korean prostitute's head. That's a job for the Koreans and the Koreans alone. It isn't our right. We don't have that right!"

"You know as well as I do that the Koreans haven't done anything, they wouldn't have done anything if you'd turned that whore over to them."

"That's not the point."

"It *is* the point! Who's going to punish them if we don't!"

"Maybe no one, sir. But still, still we can't be the ones. No matter what, it isn't right. It's not up to us. No matter what their laws. My God, if Rhee thinks someone here is an enemy of the people he has him lined up against the wall and bang! That is why, why we don't want—will do anything to avoid having a status of forces agreement with Korea. If we punish Koreans, why shouldn't Koreans punish our men? And don't think our men are such golden boys. How many times do you think some of our GIs get drunk and beat hell out of some Korean? If the Koreans could take our GIs to Korean police, what kind of trial would they get? Look, sir, if we had taken that girl with her shaved head down to Captain Chang and the National Police, what do you think would have happened?"

"You tell me, Wilkinson," the major said. "You're the one who has all the answers."

"Ahh, Major Sturgess. Don't, sir, please. I'm trying to make you understand that I did what I did to help you. Look, if we'd taken that girl down to the police, Captain Chang wouldn't have done a thing to her. He'd do just what you said, nothing. But he would certainly do something to us—the first thing he'd do is call the newspapers, and the government, and the intelligence, and Jesus, before the week would be over we'd be sitting inside an international incident. The—"

"Oh, come off it, Wilkinson!" the major said scornfully.

"I'm serious, sir—you remember the Girard case? The Army guy in Japan who either shot at or didn't see the Japanese woman who was in an unauthorized area picking up brass? Well, it never was shown whether or not he meant to shoot her. The fact is he did kill her and the papers were full of it. The same thing would happen here. You've read the translations of Radio Pyongyang's news broadcasts, you know what a field day they'd have with something like this. My God, the Communists would go wild! They'd step up the broadcasts, they'd beef up the 'Now is the time for our Southern brothers to rid themselves of the imperialistic warmongers who torture and commit atrocities upon the flower of Korean school children.' And they'd—"

"Schoolgirls? Come off it, Wilkinson, come off—"

"Well, all right, *we* know she's a whore. So what if we know it? What's her story? She gave an American sergeant twenty dollars to buy her a PX radio so that she could listen to the Korean National Broadcasts of classical music. She was a poor girl, working as a housekeeper for an American sergeant so that she could earn enough money to take music lessons, and prepare herself for a career in the musical field. And who'd believe us! The Pyongyang broadcasts are powerful enough to reach all of South Korea, and no one outside this area knows the girl has been working as a prostitute. . . . And look at the stink that's being raised about our commanding general's meddling in politics here. The South Koreans themselves have accused us of meddling in their affairs."

"We have a goddam good right to meddle since we support their stinking country."

"But we don't have the right!" Wilkinson insisted. "This is what you don't understand."

"The one thing I understand is that you disobeyed my orders, Wilkinson. And for that you will be punished. And another thing, I don't give a good goddam what you think of that order or any of my orders. Your job is to obey them. I'm the one who is responsible."

"But you're not the only one," Wilkinson said. He sat looking at the major. "Sir, what can I say to you to make you understand what this might have turned into if I'd gone ahead and shaved her head?"

"You didn't shave her head, Wilkinson," the major said. "That's why you're here this morning. You do not deny that you disobeyed my orders?"

"I'd have to disobey that kind of order every time."

"Ahhh, insubordination? No, let's not have that. I'm going to hang you up, Wilkinson. I've got you by the short hairs and I'll make an example of you that the officers and men of this unit will never forget."

Wilkinson leaned forward. He could feel his eyes begin to smart with anger. "If—if you want to press charges against me for disobeying your orders, do you understand what will happen to you? You'll be finished. FINISHED! Don't you see? You'll never even get a cent of your precious ass-grabbing pension!"

"And just how do *you* propose to finish me, Wilkinson?"

"How do I? *Me?* I'm not going to be the one who does it. It'll be you! Your own stupidity, your own blind goddam stupidity that finishes you for good. Good-by, pension, good-by, *Major* Sturgess. What I can't make you understand is that this morning I saved your ass, but ah, no. You're not going to let some twenty-three-year-old snot-nosed lieutenant run things, that isn't the way the Army goes. I honestly saved your ass, Major, and for that you want to court-martial me. And I'd *have* to fight that. I'd appeal first thing to make sure this case gets a lot of attention, and I'll see that as many people as can be rounded up will sit in on it. The head-shaving thing happened at about three-thirty this morning. You were nowhere around. I tried to reach you. As it turned out there wasn't one officer on this compound other than myself. How's that going to look when it's brought up in the trial? They'll ask questions, in particular they'll ask where were the commanding officer and the executive officer of this unit. How would you like to answer that one?"

"I was at the G2 party. So was Martin."

"Until three-thirty? What time did you get in this morning?"

"God damn it, I'm not on trial, Wilkinson."

"But you would be, sir."

"Are you threatening me? Is that what I am to understand?"

"Christ, no, sir, I am only trying to make you see—understand just what position you'd be in if you brought any more attention to your order than you already have. . . . Let me try some other point. Your order states that any unauthorized person found on this compound after hours is to have her head shaved, right?"

"Right, God damn it."

"What about that woman you have in your quarters?"

"What about her?"

"What sort of authorization does she have?"

"She doesn't need any author— She has *my* authorization. She takes care of my hooch, she does my laundry, cooks a meal occasionally. She keeps my place in order. What the hell does that matter?"

"Oh, come on, Major . . . you know as well as I do if it were brought out in the trial that the commanding officer of the unit who ordered the head shaving kept in his own quarters a young and attractive Korean woman, that the other officers of his unit had heard him say that any man who had a single room and slept alone should be ashamed of himself, and further that they had heard him say—in reference to the woman he was keeping in his quarters—'I didn't realize what a bad lay my wife was until I got over here'—how do you think a court-martial board would feel about that?"

"You really *are* a sonuvabitch."

"No, sir, I'm not. I'm only trying to prove to you that your order was a serious mistake and might have precipitated some very serious consequences had your order been carried out. And that the disobeying of your order was not intended as a sign of disrespect, but rather a gesture of respect—an indication that this recent order of yours was not in keeping with the high standards of military competency and responsibility which you have so far displayed."

"Oh, horseshit!" the major said.

"Yes, sir," Wilkinson said. He began to relax. "Would it be all right if I smoked?"

"Why not . . . why not . . ." The major took one of the cigarettes Wilkinson passed across to him, lit it, and leaned back in the chair. "You're not getting out of this unscratched, Wilkinson, I'll see to that."

"Yes, sir," Wilkinson said.

"Wilkinson, I just want you to know that you're not so hot. I don't want you going out of here thinking you're the answer to the world's problems."

"Major Sturgess, no matter what you think, what I did I did because I had to and I did it as much for your sake as I did for mine."

"Don't feed me that line, Wilkinson. You went all the way through that line of crap about international incidents and status of forces agreements—you went through all that crap before you ever got to your real reason for disobeying orders. It wasn't because you believe any of that crap, it was because you wanted to see if you could get away with putting one over on the Army, on me, on the system. That's why. Just so you could sit there with your goddam ego, call me names, and get away with it. You just think you got away with it, Wilkinson."

Wilkinson stood up. "I hope you don't really believe I did it just to get away with something, Major. I hope you don't really think that's why I did it."

"I know why you did it," the major said. "And now, Wilkinson, get out of here."

"Yes, sir," Wilkinson said.

7

THAT SPRING, P. S. Wilkinson was still in Korea; he sent the following letter to his friends:

> 24 April 1960*
> Yongdongp'o, Korea
> *4293, Year of the Rat

Lt. (jg) Wallace: (Somewhere in the Pacific on a DE)
Ens. Gurdey: (Somewhere in the Atlantic on a carrier)
Lt. (jg) Nelson: (Somewhere in the jungle with the Viet-MAAG)
PFC French: (Somewhere in Berlin, hopefully West Berlin)
Mr. Charles Merritt: (Somewhere in his apartment in Washington,
D.C., the lucky bastard, and one whom
I am pledged to defend, and find it trying.)

Top copy goes to Wally this time; the fuzzy bottom carbon as usual is for Merritt. Let me lead with an apology for that insane letter I wrote you at the beginning of last month. But if you had just been extended for the third time and were told that you would not get out of Korea until June 10th, you too would have flipped. That will make eighteen months—547 days in this godforsaken place. I think the straw that really broke the camel's back was that I got that extension on February 29th—that extra little goddam day that doesn't even BELONG in the calendar.

The reason why I haven't written sooner is that it's been a little hectic here. I don't know what you've read or haven't read, so I'll put down as much as I know or can guess at. The riots began in Masan, in southern South Korea. These first riots were against police brutality. What I think happened is that the students were rioting over the sham Rhee made of the March 15th election. Rhee's Liberal

85

Party instituted a sort of "buddy-buddy" system whereby one man in each village was responsible for seeing that the village voted for Rhee. The village poppa-san was bought (for so many hwan his village would vote for Rhee). In other places Rhee's boys would have one man take two others to vote with him, if the man could not get the two men to vote for Rhee then all their crops and huts were burned. But what the Liberal Party did down in the tip of Korea was even wilder! A week before the election the Liberty Party went down there to teach the poor peasants how to vote. They were given practice ballots—obviously no different from the real ones—and the "instructor" would say, "Now, just suppose you wanted to vote for our beloved leader Rhee Syng Man. You would have to check your ballots in that space there . . . Now let's see you do it, just to make sure you know how . . . Good! Now you would have to sign your name, too . . . No, further down in the space provided . . . Let's see you sign your names . . . Good! Now we'll collect all the ballots and—" and, of course, they were the ballots used during the election. But to be safe, they even had their own goons at the ballot boxes to count. If the Democratic Party (Rhee's opposition) seemed to be doing well, they would throw out the opposition votes on grounds of technicalities. There is no doubt in anyone's mind here that Rhee is the crookedest sonofabitch to swim up the Harlem River to Seoul. His opponents have a curious way of dying just before the election. Rumor is that one died of a heart attack brought on by a 38-caliber slug. However, there really does not seem to be any alternative to Rhee. All the ones who would like to get rid of him don't seem to be any better—they don't want to reform the government, they just want their cut of the green that Uncle Sugar's passing around. Still, to me, the big tragedy is that 33,000 Americans died here. And for what?

Anyway, after the first demonstrations against the elections down in Masan, the police moved in on the students. (The colleges teach democracy, unfortunately, which gives the students a chance to see that Korea doesn't have any.) The riots could have ended in Masan had the National Police not caught one student, broken his arms and legs, then forced a grenade through his broken jaws. They pulled the pin and tossed the kid into the ocean. Unfortunately for the police, the body did not stay underwater. The students found it, and they touched off the riots in Pusan, Inchon, Kwangu, and Seoul. Here in Seoul several thousand students charged the Assembly Building and Rhee's home. The police fired their carbines into the air—and, ironically, killed the first man—an American standing on top of the Bando Hotel (owned by Madam Rhee). He was watching the riots. When the rifle fire did not slow the rioters, they brought in the fire trucks, who sprayed the students with their high-power hoses. The rioters threw rocks back at the fire trucks and killed the second American, who had, idiotically, climbed onto the back of one of the trucks to take pictures. Then a ROK Army infantry division with one medium tank company pulled into Seoul. The police and soldiers fell back behind concrete bunkers not used since the war. From the bunkers and from behind barbed wire the police threw tear gas grenades—but, they neglected to check the wind and so, gassed themselves. During the confusion the students got through the barbed wire. They no longer had any control and were acting like a mob. The soldiers cut loose on them, as much to stop the riots as to save themselves. Carbine and machine gun fire wounded several hundred in the first minutes, and gas and clubs dispersed the rest. But not for long. The riots lasted for seven hours that first day, and by the end of the day both newspapers, the National Assembly Building, and a police station had been burned. The riots here started about five days ago, and even now we're not sure of how much has gone on. I never realized how effective censorship could be. The Korean Broadcasting Company plays classical music 24 hours a day. The idiot Armed Forces Radio feeds its same old pap to the sub-teen (mentally) audience which listens to it. And that symbol of enlightened reporting, the Pacific Issue of the *Stars and Stripes,* tells us nothing. On the worst day of the riots the headline was "ATLAS MISSILE SCORES IN TEST." We have all been restricted to our posts by the UN Commander, so we can't see for ourselves. The Korean papers have been cut to pieces by what looks like a palette knife, great hunks of white space where articles were or photographs were which did not please the censors. There is no doubt more news can get out from Korea than we can get here inside it. I know at least 100 have been killed in Seoul and at least a thousand injured. But the riots seem to be over, and it looks like old Siggy will be here forever—like me.

The only other news here is that the CO, Major Sturgess, was promoted to lt. colonel and is now with the Headquarters in Seoul. The exec, Captain Martin, is the new CO . . . I couldn't care less.

It's raining outside again. It's been raining two out of three days for the past month. Jesus, I'm sick of Korea. Everything is mud now and when the rain stops and the sun comes out those goddam rice paddies smell so awful you never get used to it. I don't know which is worse, the mud or the smell. Well, only 47 more days to go . . . My God, I just realized! This is my 500th day in Korea. Highest personal regards to all of you from America's First Line of Defense here in Riot-torn Korea, Freedom's Frontier and all that crap.

P.S.

On the bottom of the copy to Charlie Merritt he added: "Wonderful news about your forthcoming nuptials. Am honored to have been officially asked to be Best Man. I should be home in time. God, I'd better be!"

Book Two

8

FIRST LIEUTENANT PHILIP SADLER WILKINSON
changed planes at Tachikawa Air Force Base, Japan, then took
off again in a military charter flight which refueled at Wake
Island and again at Honolulu, finally landing at Travis Air Force
Base in California. Wilkinson took the bus to the Oakland Army
Terminal and arrived in time to have the sergeant say, "I'm sorry,
Lieutenant, but we're closing up now. You'll have to process out
tomorrow."

He knew there was no use in trying to explain to the sergeant
that he had waited for two years to get out of the Army, that
the past eighteen months he had spent in Korea might possibly
justify the sergeant's staying on the job a little longer. But
Wilkinson knew the system well enough to know that there was
nothing he could do, and he went to the BOQ and signed for a
room. That night in San Francisco he looked at the young girls
with their straight dark hair, their dark glasses, their full-
breasted blouses, their black stockings, their tight, dark skirts,
and the only thing that Wilkinson could think or feel was "What
a waste!" Not because it was wasted youth or intelligence—or
even time—but it was a waste because he was not getting any
of that good-bodied stuff. He walked into a small paperback
book store and bought copies of Ginsburg's *Howl*, Corso's *The
Happy Birthday of Death*, and Ferlinghetti's *A Coney Island of
the Mind*. While he was standing there, waiting to pay the dark-

91

eyed, suck-cheeked salesgirl who was so pretty in spite of her makeup, Wilkinson looked at the young man who was leaning on the counter in front of him. Wilkinson looked at young Mister-First-Time-Away-From-Home, seeing the kid's Oh-Aren't-We-Devils pose, and heard him say, "Well, back to the old typewriter!" And Wilkinson watched him mince out of the shop and felt the anger sear him, the draft-the-sonuvabitch-so-he-can-find-out-what-it's-all-about burn him, but most of all Wilkinson felt the disappointment that on his first night home, there had been no one he had felt he would like to talk with, to be with, and that there was no one who wasn't desperately trying to make some sort of valueless impression, and that all these little men with beards were never really with it at all. He paid the girl for the books, did not answer when she said, "I think you'll like these, generally speaking. Although, I, for one, find Corso a bit precious," and he walked back up Grant Street to find a bus which would take him to Oakland and his BOQ.

The next morning was June 16, 1960 (Bloomsday, Wilkinson recalled), and he processed out of the Army and received a small cheaply engraved card upon which was printed and typed:

This is to Certify That
PHILIP SADLER WILKINSON 05 001 345
1ST LT   AI
Honorably Served On Active Duty
in the
ARMY OF THE UNITED STATES

It wouldn't say "United States Army"—that was reserved for the Regular Army, the professionals. No, his status was as a Reservist, an amateur, who had somehow managed to bumble through.

Wilkinson made a reservation on the first available flight to New York. It wouldn't leave until after midnight, and he had the rest of the afternoon and the evening to kill. He stepped into the phone booth outside the processing auditorium and placed a long-distance phone call (collect) to his mother and told her he would be arriving at Idlewild six the next morning. His mother said she couldn't possibly meet him that early, but that she would make a reservation for him at the Gladstone and that he should go into New York, go to the hotel, eat breakfast, sleep, do whatever he wished, and that she would meet him for lunch and bring him back to Long Island. Wilkinson packed and took a bus into San Francisco, checked his baggage at a hotel, and rode the cable cars again. He had a cocktail at the Top of the Mark, strolled around Fisherman's Wharf, went to a movie, had a lonely dinner, and finally, when he could stand it no longer, took a cab to the airport even though he had several hours before his plane left.

He was not able to sleep on the plane, and he pushed aside the curtain of the small window and looked out at the cities passing beneath them. He saw the little spider necklaces of the lighted streets and highways, followed the highways between the cities, playing connect the dotted lines with the faint headlights of the automobiles below. And then, when the sun began to rise as they flew toward Chicago, the land below was so dazzlingly beautiful that he would not have let himself sleep even if he wanted to.

"Would you care for some coffee, sir?"

"Yes, please," Wilkinson said. He took the coffee from the stewardess and watched her move on ahead toward the other passengers. He wished she would come back and sit with him so that he would have someone to talk to. He remembered how it had been when he had flown from Washington to San Francisco prior to leaving for Korea. The man at the TWA desk had learned he was going to Korea and had felt sorry for Wilkinson and had given him a seat next to a very pretty girl for the trip. Wilkinson and the girl had ten hours on the plane together, and it had been fine. He had asked her for a date that night in San Francisco, and had visions of himself falling prey to some movie-script sort of life in which a young lieutenant, going overseas to certain death, meets a beautiful and amply endowed stranger on the plane. His last night in the States, and they make it together and the next day as his troopship sails for the Far East the girl stands on a cliff overlooking the Golden Gate Bridge. As the ship passes beneath the bridge the girl unwinds a tattered silk stocking from around her neck and waves. The young man, all alone on the turret, unwraps the other stocking from around his neck where he had been wearing it like a scarf and waves back at her. Fade out. Of course it had not worked out that way at all. When the plane landed in San Francisco the girl was met by her married sister who lived two hours out of San Francisco and Wilkinson had had to process all that day and most of the night before leaving for Korea.

The plane was late when it landed at Idlewild and P.S. walked down the ramp and wished for a moment that someone there had a sign saying WELCOME HOME, that someone had been there to meet his plane—he imagined sort of a family picture of everyone standing at the bottom of the ramp with their arms around each other's shoulders, and he would join them—limping slightly. But there was nobody there to meet him and he waited for his baggage, then took a taxi to his hotel. As they approached the city, P.S. told the cab driver that this was the first time he had been in New York in about two years and that he had just gotten out of Korea. And the cab driver said, "Oh yeah? Korea? What's it like now?" And Wilkinson answered, "About the same."

The cab stopped at the hotel and Wilkinson overtipped the driver, had the doorman check his baggage, signed the register, then walked up to the corner of Fifth Avenue. He stood watching the pretty girls getting on the buses to go to work. There was nothing for him to do, so he got on one of the buses to ride it downtown, just to be with the people. As he moved to the rear, remembering what New York was like, a girl hanging from a strap said, "Why, P.S.! P. S. Wilkinson! How are *youuuuu*? I haven't seen you in *ages*!"

P.S. smiled at her, trying to remember her name or where he had seen her before. He knew she was from Darien or Fairfield or some place like that. "It's been a long time, hasn't it."

"How's graduate school?"

"Graduate school?"

"Yes," she said. "I heard from Minnie that you were in graduate school."

Minnie? "I'm afraid not. I've been in the Army."

"You're out now? When did you get out?"

"Yesterday."

"Yesterday! Well, you must feel simply *marv*elous! My cousin Toby's in the Army now," she said. "He's stationed right here in New York. Where were you stationed?"

"Korea."

"*Korea!* That must have been terrific fun seeing the other places and things like that."

"Umm," P.S. said. "Well, this is my stop. It's been nice talking to you." He pushed his way past her to the doors, and when the bus stopped he got out and began walking back up Fifth toward his hotel. He found he could not walk slowly, he could not look through the windows, because everyone else was in such a hurry, with their heads down, coattails flapping, and he was caught up in the rush in spite of himself. He went into his hotel, and rode up with the bellboy on the elevator. At the door to the room he waited for the boy to unlock the door, then followed him in. When the bellboy was gone Wilkinson ran himself a hot bath. He undressed, climbed into the tub and lay back to soak. He closed his eyes and slid down into the tub so that the water lapped his chin. He lay there thinking about the baths he had taken in Korea, then he thought about calling Charlie Merritt to tell him he would be able to make it to the wedding, but he had only Charlie's home address and he didn't know where Charlie worked. He soaked for fifteen more minutes, planning his breakfast: a pot of coffee, a large glass of *real* orange juice, two eggs fried in *butter,* some protein toast, and copies of the *New York Times* and the *Daily News.*

Then he got up, dried himself, opened his suitcase and took out a clean shirt and a pair of flannels. He put them on, phoned room service, and then sat down to wait for breakfast. As he sat there, staring blankly at the curtained windows of his hotel room, he tried to get used to the fact that he was out of the Army, that he had nothing in the world to do except wait until his mother came to New York and took him to lunch. There was nothing for him to do in the future except be in Charlie Merritt's wedding. He had no job. No place to live. He had a little more than a thousand dollars cash—accrued leave pay, severance pay, travel allowance—to do with as he wished. It was his money. He had earned it. He owed no one. For the first time in his life he was on his own. He realized that he had finally finished with every harboring institution. He was free. Independent. He was no longer Philip Sadler Wilkinson—Student: Class of '49, Napier Boarding School; Class of '52 Non-Grad, Virginia Preparatory School; Class of '54, Hotchkiss; Class of '58, *Universitatis Yalensis*. Nor was he any longer an Obligated Volunteer (that curious phrase) in the Army of the United States; he was a Reservist. He was no longer "And this is our youngest" or "We have such trouble making him wear his retainer" or "For heaven's sake, make sure you dance with Mrs. Henderson's daughter." He was neither an "old boy" nor a "freshman" nor a "recruit" nor "cadet" nor "shavetail" nor "lieutenant" nor anything else in the world other than Philip Sadler Wilkinson, son of Stewart Wilkinson and the former Elizabeth Denison Sanford, now Mrs. Warren T. MacDonnell. He was simply Philip Sadler Wilkinson, unemployed nonresident member of the Yale Club of New York City. He finished dressing, repacked his suitcase, and began reading the newspapers.

Wilkinson drove out to Long Island with his mother. He could tell that she was being very careful not to push him, not to ask what he was going to do now. She asked him a few questions about the Army and he told her what he thought might interest her. She did not look any older than she had when he had left; in fact, she looked better than she ever had. She told him about his sister's child, who was named after him, and how the child looked like his sister. And P.S. asked his mother about Carter, his brother. And she said that Carter was in Hawaii working on a magazine. And P.S. told her how his plane had been quarantined at the end of the runway in Honolulu. Throughout the entire conversation, throughout the ride from New York out to his stepfather's house on the South Shore, he had the eerie feeling that he had never really been away, that time had, in fact, stood still, and that the eighteen months in Korea had been nothing more than a brief Rip Van Winkle cat nap. When they arrived at the house and he got out of the car with his suitcase, the dog rushed up to him, grabbed him by the back of his jacket, whimpering with pleasure at seeing him again. He was touched. P.S. walked inside the house. It hadn't changed. His stepfather was still sitting in the comfortable chair by the fireplace, his glasses down on the end of his nose as he read the New York papers. When P.S. entered, his stepfather slowly stood up and said, "Well, welcome home, Lieutenant," and P.S. said, "Thank you, Commander. It's nice to be aboard again. You still running a taut ship?" and his stepfather said, "I've made your mother walk the plank occasionally." Nothing had changed.

Wilkinson spent a week out on the beach with his mother and stepfather. During the mornings he would take long walks up and down the beach to work off the nervous energy and emptiness which the sudden lack of responsibility and inactivity after the Army had brought him. During the evenings he watched television, or read, or had long rambling talks with his step-father about everything under the sun—except what he was going to do now that he was finished with the Army. He knew that they would have been happy to have him stay for as long as he wanted. But he had this compulsion to keep moving—not in any particular direction; he merely felt he could not sit still.

One morning at the end of that first week while P.S.'s mother was in the village shopping for groceries, P.S. and his stepfather were sitting in the small living room looking at the newspapers. P.S.'s stepfather said, "Your mother and I have been invited to a cocktail party this evening at the Bateses. They have a daughter about your age who just graduated from Smith, and they've asked if you'd like to come. I hear she's pretty, so you might enjoy it."

The Bates daughter, Linda, was pretty—but not beautiful. Like so many other Smith girls P.S. had met, she was too broad in the hips. He had grown up with girls like Linda, had gone to dancing class with them, to their debutante parties, he had received his first french kiss from one of them and had, some-what in return, given them gold circle pins or idiotic charms for bracelets already crowded with little symbols of their trip to Europe. He had received innumerable letters from them, the

margins punctuated with grinning faces and extra-large ques-
ion marks, the bottom dot a circle. He had received valentines
signed "Guess Who?" and, since all those girls wrote identically,
it was never possible to guess. Linda Bates was a nice girl, easy
for P.S. to sit with and talk to at the cocktail party. And since
to a certain extent he could depend on her predictability, he did
not have to listen to her all that hard. Besides, Linda Bates was
a blonde, and P.S. had to admit, sitting with her on the Bates
porch overlooking the ocean, that worse things had happened
to him.

"What did you write on at Yale?"

Somewhere along the line she had asked him what he had
majored in, and she had added that she had majored in English,
too.

"You mean, what did I write on for English?"

"What did you do your thesis on?"

"I didn't have to do a thesis, that's only for the people in the
Honors program. I guess the longest paper I did was on Wordsworth, something about child and nature . . ." He smiled at her
and said, "It seems like a very long time ago."

"I love Wordsworth, don't you?"

"In many strange and wondrous ways."

"Is that a quote?"

P.S. laughed and shook his head.

"You know something?"

P.S. looked at her and thought that somebody must have said
that she looked cute when she cocked her head to one side like
that. "What?" he asked.

"Well, I'm almost certain I've seen you somewhere before."

"I thought only men were allowed to use that line."

"No, seriously. I mean it. I'm positive I saw you at Yale . . . I
used to date a boy named Walker Ross. . . . Now I know where
I saw you!" she said excitedly. "You used to date a girl—that girl
who married Bruce Mallory. What's-her-name . . ."

"Hilary Farnum," P.S. said. He looked at the girl sitting next
to him. He found it difficult to believe that she could have known
him while he was at Yale. *She saw me when I dated Hilary. . . .*

"Dated!" God, that's an awful word . . . It seems so very long ago. My God, I feel as though I've aged a hundred and fifty years since then.

"It was about two years ago," Linda said.

"Two years."

"Do you ever see her now?"

"Hilary?" he asked, somewhat startled.

Linda laughed a little embarrassedly. "No, of course you don't. You just got back from Korea. I forgot."

"I wish I could forget it that easily," he said, and then he groaned. "I beg your pardon. That was the most awful line I think I've ever heard myself say. I feel as though I should have just gotten back from Dunkirk. I've sailed a piece of board back across the Channel and I'm dragging my leg—the one attacked by sharks—behind me, and you're my fiancée, sitting on some wind-swept rosebush, and, umm, let's see, of course you've got a lovely complexion, all that rain and fog, and I drag myself up to you and say, 'Hello, Emily,' and then you say, 'Did you hear about Toby Smythe? He came in second at Wimbledon,' and I look up from tying a tourniquet on my leg and say, 'Oh, really? I didn't know that,' and then you say, 'Oh, yes, you just got back from Dunkirk, I forgot.' "

Linda smiled uncertainly. "When did you get back?"

"From Korea?"

She nodded, her smile a bit strained.

"Well, I left Korea on the fourteenth. Not quite two weeks ago."

"It must be a funny feeling to be back," she said. "I mean, just think, less than two weeks ago you were in Korea. . . . What's Korea like?"

He didn't know why he felt that answering her was such an effort. He knew that she meant well, which was an awful thing to say about anyone, but he just felt so much older than she, older than Smith College and cocktail parties. He knew he was just being melodramatic as usual, but still he didn't know how to answer her.

"I guess that's a pretty silly question," Linda said. "I suppose it would be pretty hard for me to tell someone what Northampton was like if they asked me—unless they asked me a specific question, you know, such as what is Rahar's like."

"What *is* Rahar's like?"

"Pretty crumby."

"Well, that about covers Korea, too," he said.

"What about the riots? I've read a lot about them in the papers and everything. Now that Rhee is gone, is it going to get any better?"

"I guess so," he said. "I don't know, really. . . . I guess, I guess I really don't care. . . . No, that isn't true, really. . . . I guess I do care. But I don't know. The whole country is in such terrible shape now that I don't see how it can help but get better." He looked at her helplessly.

"What are you going to do now? What sort of work do you plan to do?"

"Funny you should ask me that." P.S. smiled. "My entire family is interested in the same question. I've been trying to figure out what I do want to do. And I pretty well decided that I'm going to go into the government. . . . At least that's where I thought I'd start first looking for a job."

"I should think you'd have had enough of that after Korea."

"Well, no, not really. . . . I think Korea made me aware of just how bad working for the government could be—but, I don't know. A lot of it—the government—is the people, and there were some pretty terrible people in Korea. I don't mean the Koreans, I mean the Americans there."

"Like whom?"

"Oh, well, Linda, you know . . . you read *The Ugly American* . . ." P.S. looked down at his shoes. He was wearing brown shoes and he tried to think of how long it had been since he had worn brown shoes. He looked up and suddenly realized that she had mistaken his silence for deep concern about her question, and he tried to think of an example of an "Ugly American" in Korea. "You want an example?"

She nodded.

"Well, there was my commanding officer," he said. And then he paused and started again. "In Korea, there was sort of a problem with—ahhh—prostitutes. Ahhh, they were cutting through the barbed-wire fence around our compound . . ."

"Why? Were they trying to steal things?"

"Well, yes and no." P.S. smiled. "Isn't there some song about a stolen kiss, a stolen embrace, a stolen moment with you-u-u-u? Well, it was something along that line . . ." He paused, and then he suddenly assumed a mock paternal pose and placed his hand on hers. "You see, my child, these women would sneak into the barracks with the men, and this was against Army Regulations. . . . Not only because the men needed their sleep, but also because since we were, after all, an intelligence-type unit, we had a lot of stray secrets lying around loose and if those secrets were taken, well, they wouldn't be secrets any more." He had the feeling that he was wrong. He knew, he was certain that Linda thought he was making fun of her. And he wasn't, and he didn't know how to make her understand that. The problem was merely that he was not yet mentally out of Korea. Even though he was physically sitting on the porch with Linda, he found it hard to take her questions seriously.

"But why would the girls cut through the fences? Why didn't they just meet the soldiers outside?"

"Well, usually, the girls knew the GIs and maybe the GIs owed them money, or had promised them a radio, or maybe the GI had gotten tired of some particular girl and had jilted her. . . . Anyway, the commanding officer decided that the only way to stop them from cutting through the fences was to shave the head of the first one caught."

"But that's terrible!" she said. "Why couldn't he just arrest them or something? The girl probably couldn't help herself."

"Well—I keep saying 'well.'" P.S. laughed. "What I mean is that these girls, as you call them—" He thought suddenly of how the major had jumped on him for referring to the prostitutes as girls . . . *Am I so much like this girl, here? Was I that naïve?* "Anyway, they weren't like Dreiser's Sister Carrie . . . And it wouldn't have done any good to arrest them because we would have had to turn them over to the Korean Police, and they wouldn't have done anything."

"Why not? Those girls—prostitutes, broke the law, didn't they?"

"Yes, but cutting a barbed-wire fence is breaking a very minor law compared to their obeying the law of survival."

"But what happened? Did you shave the girl's head?"

"We caught one one night, and I was supposed to shave her head, but I didn't, I couldn't," he said.

"I couldn't have either," Linda said.

I couldn't have either? . . . P.S. didn't know what he could tell Linda to make her understand that it wasn't as simple a decision as she implied. He wanted to make her understand that it would have been far easier for him to have shaved the prostitute's head . . . *Would it have been easier?* . . . He was a little angry at Linda for not realizing how difficult a decision it had been . . . *Had it been difficult? Hadn't I always known that I wasn't going to shave the prostitute's head?* And P.S. knew that no matter how ugly Korea was, no matter how sordid the circumstances, no matter how far he might grow apart from the P. S. Wilkinson Linda Bates had seen with Hilary, there still remained some common bond of behavior. . . . And he began to wonder as he sat there on the porch with the pretty blonde-haired girl beside him, and the sounds of the ocean and the cocktail party all around them, he began to wonder whether or not his act of defiance in Korea had taken any courage whatsoever. *There was never any other choice . . . was there?* He knew that to Linda Bates his decision not to shave the prostitute's head was obvious. One didn't need to spend eighteen months in Korea to understand that. He wanted somehow to make the girl feel that his decision had taken courage.

P.S. knew that now he wasn't sure. He was no longer sure whether he had acted out of instinct or because he had decided for himself that it was wrong. He wished for a moment that Linda could see Korea; if she saw Korea, then she might understand the complexities of the decision. But Korea would never mean anything more to Linda Bates than a place where the United States had fought a war ten years ago—when she was twelve. "Well, anyway," P.S. said, "the head-shaving incident was just an example of how wrong some Americans can be."

"And now you're thinking of going into the government?"

"Yes," P.S. said. He felt a hand on his shoulder and looked up. "Hi, Mom."

"I think we're going, Phil. Mr. and Mrs. Bates said you could stay as long as you like."

"I'd better go with you and Mac," P.S. said. "I've got to pack up and get ready to go." He turned back to Linda, who was now standing and smoothing her dress. "I hope I didn't talk your ear off," P.S. said. "I wish we had more time. I think it would take more time before I could make you understand about this thing in Korea. You said you thought you'd be living in New York. Well, maybe I'll see you there. I'm sorry to run off like this, but I think I'd better start getting organized."

"Well, I hope you didn't think I was too stupid," Linda said.

"Not at all. You weren't stupid at all. It was just hard for me to be objective, that's all. Maybe by the time I see you in New York things will be in a little better perspective."

"Good," she said. "I hope you'll call me."

"I will indeed," he said. He shook hands with her, then followed his mother through the other people standing around the porch and in the living room.

"Linda's a pretty girl," P.S.'s mother said.

"I liked her," he said. "She was very nice."

"She looks very much like her mother."

Back at his stepfather's house, P.S. brought some wood up from the cellar and lit the fire. His mother said, "I heard you tell Linda that you were thinking of going into the government."

"As I remember, you were thinking about the Foreign Service," his stepfather said.

"What about your father?" P.S.'s mother asked. "What does he think you should do?"

"I don't know," P.S. said. "He's still in Europe. I haven't seen him."

"But you do think you want to work for the government?" his mother asked.

P.S.'s stepfather crossed to the fire and stood with his back to it and clasped his hands behind his back. "I know your mother is concerned about you," he said, "and she doesn't want to seem to push you."

P.S. smiled at the two of them. "I understand and appreciate your concern. Mac, you and Mom have been very good about not asking me a lot of embarrassing questions like what I want to be when I grow up." He looked at the two of them again and then laughed. "Oh, come on, you both look like some sort of old engraving where the parents are asking their son whether he might not be wise to go into the family firm. . . . I know this is a serious problem, and I have given it some serious thought, and I've decided I want to be a dress designer."

"A *what?*" his stepfather asked, and then gave a deep, throaty chuckle. "That would make your father very proud."

"Be serious, Philip," his mother said.

"Oh, all right, I will be serious. You're right, you did overhear me tell Linda that I wanted to go into the government. But the only reason I haven't said anything to the two of you is that I'm not sure of the best way to go about it."

"You might get a pretty good job because of your training," his stepfather said.

"You mean the Photo Intelligence?"

"That and Yale."

"Well, I was thinking of something like that."

"Like what?" his mother said.

"I have some friends in most parts of the government, and you might talk to them," his stepfather said. "Or, I could write them a letter. It doesn't do anybody any harm to ask someone for help. It can save you a lot of wasted effort and sitting on your hands."

"Well, I appreciate the offer," P.S. said, "but you haven't let me tell you what I want to do. I mean, I've changed a lot since I listed 'future occupation: government' in the Yale Class Book."

"How have you changed?" his mother asked.

"The two of you have been so nice about pretending not to notice about my missing leg. . . . Oh, all right, we'll be absolutely serious. When I was at Yale I guess I was pretty typical. In the late-night bull sessions I could sling words like 'create,' 'neces-

sity,' 'responsibility' with the best of them. . . . And I think at
Yale I really did want to go into the government. I had a feeling
that I could be of some use." P.S. saw his stepfather's skepticism
and added, "Mac, I knew I wasn't going to shape the world, or
make This World a Better Place to Live In. . . . I may have been
idealistic, but I wasn't entirely out of my mind."

"Fair enough," his stepfather said.

"Anyway, after eighteen months in Korea, I saw just how little
difference I could make, and I learned other things—"

"Like what?" his mother asked.

"Oh, I don't know, Mom. . . . They aren't things you can de-
scribe, it's more just a realization or an awareness of limitations.
It isn't anything you can really measure, like being able to
hold your breath for a minute and a half; it's more a realization
of what, of how far you'd go to keep that breath going in and
out. I know this sounds sort of melodramatic, and I can't really
help it. Korea is unbelievable . . . life in Korea is unbelievable
. . . the values change. This is what I was trying to explain to
Linda at the cocktail party. . . . You learn that your being in
Korea is no different from being an occupying force. The Koreans
hate us, and why shouldn't they? We get drunk all the time, we
spend too much money—a lieutenant like myself makes more
money than a Korean general—and, and I guess after a while
we even start despising the Koreans; but even worse, we degrade
them, we humiliate them and in so doing debase ourselves even
more."

"In what way?" his mother asked.

"Oh, well, Mom, you know . . . it wasn't very pretty." He was
thinking about the "Yongdongp'o Circus" where the officers
from Seoul would go to watch three naked Korean women perform. It meant nothing to the women, it was all rehearsed and
skillfully executed, and the men spent five dollars to watch them
do it. P.S. had gone and was so ashamed that he had contributed
to this, and was so ashamed by the excitement on the other
officers' faces, that he had never been able to go back, or tell
anyone about it, or see those other officers without loathing
them for their knowing he, too, had once gone. "I guess it's just

not what Eisenhower had in mind with his People-to-People program."

"But, Phil," his stepfather said, "you must realize that happens wherever armies go . . ."

"I know, sir, but to degrade people, to turn them into animals is such a terrible, terrible thing. Do you know what the United States and Korea have developed in the ten years of their association? A new form of gonorrhea which is not only resistent to penicillin but which actually thrives on it. And now it's spread to Japan, Okinawa, Southeast Asia . . . and there's no hope that any of this will change. I mean, it's the only thing—this availability of the women—that makes Korea bearable. . . . And the thing you have to understand is that all of this—pardon the expression—all of this screwing around probably is good for Korea and the United States. After all, it helps support Korea's economy, and it keeps the men quiet enough so that they don't get trigger happy. The thing, the one thing that really shocked me in Korea was that we supported Syngman Rhee . . . and after a while I even got used to that. And Rhee would still be there now if it hadn't been for the Korean students' rioting. They're the ones who got rid of him, and last month, when Rhee was granted asylum in Hawaii, he took twenty-eight million dollars with him. But, what this is all about is that I think government is terribly important, someone somehow must make sure that the United States finds better men to support than Syngman Rhee."

"Then you'd want to go into the Foreign Service?" his mother asked.

"Well, no, not right away."

"What do you want to do?" his stepfather asked.

"In Korea I saw that even though I didn't like the Koreans I could work with them, and you can take my word for the fact that their Photo Intelligence was every bit as good and in some areas a helluva lot better than ours. What I'm trying to say is that there has to be a new generation who see that the United States isn't the red, white, and blue answer to everybody's prayer, other countries can do a lot of things better than we can and do it without us. . . . I can't seem to explain this well," he said. "My point simply is that I think our government needs young people who are both idealistic and politically aware of our own country's limitations. . . . I think there has to be a realism which currently our country doesn't have. . . . I am also realistic enough to think that there isn't much time. And because there isn't much time, I've been giving serious thought to going into the CIA."

"The CIA!" his stepfather exploded. "Good God, I preferred it when you said you were going to be a dress designer. At least those fairies are out in the open."

"Why the CIA, Philip?" his mother asked.

"Well, first off, I have no intentions of staying in the CIA—"

"Thank God for that!"

"Let him finish, dear," his mother said.

"As I said, I have no intentions of staying in the CIA," P.S. continued, "but, as we said earlier, I do have this training. In Madison Avenue-ese, it is a marketable commodity, there is a demand for it, and the supply is low. Therefore, I should be able to get very good money while I'm doing it."

"But, Philip, you're not going to do it just for the money?" his mother asked.

"No, not entirely. I like the money, but I'm doing it because of something I think is called a 'lateral transfer.' . . . I already have two years of government service behind me, the Army counts as that, and with my intelligence training I could go into the CIA as a GS-8, GS-9, and maybe even get a GS-10 rating in a year—and that's one helluva lot higher than I would be if I started as a Foreign Service officer trainee."

"But what is this transfer?"

"I'm getting to that, Mom. After a couple of years with the CIA I can cross-transfer into the Foreign Service—"

"As an Intelligence officer?" his stepfather asked.

"Not necessarily. . . . What I'm saying is why not take advantage of whatever head start I can get? Why not let my training and my Army experience work for me instead of starting at the bottom all over again?"

"But if the Foreign Service is what you really want to do, wouldn't you be wiser to start right in?"

"I don't think so, Mom. I think I can avoid an awful lot of crap by going in later." He turned to his stepfather. "What do you think?"

"Well, if you're right about what you're saying, then I guess it makes sense."

"I'm sure I'm right, Mac," P.S. said. "And anyway, it seems to me I would be better off to start doing something I know about, and while I'm doing it I can be looking around."

"Well, I think that makes sense. . . . Look around, see what there is."

"That's what I mean, Mom; if it doesn't work out then what the hell—I've blown a couple of years. I'll be only twenty-seven, twenty-eight at the most."

"God, I wish I were twenty-eight again," his stepfather said. P.S.'s mother smiled. "What would you do, dear?"

"Call you up and ask you to dinner," he said. "That was how many? Twenty-three years ago. I'd like to have known you twenty-three years ago. That would have made it 1937."

P.S.'s mother was figuring dates in her head. "Philip was one year old, Page was four, and Carter was six. . . . Would you have still asked me for dinner?"

"Nineteen thirty-seven . . ." P.S.'s stepfather was thinking. "You know, I had a Packard convertible then. Dark green, almost black . . ."

P.S. Wilkinson called Charlie Merritt that night and said that he would be in Baltimore in time for the Groom's Dinner and wedding, that he would be honored, proud, and delighted to be the best man, and that he would provide his own cutaway, and would he need to bring a dinner jacket? The next morning he said good-by to his stepfather, thanked him for his advice, and said he would be sure to let him know how everything turned out. Then he got into the car with his mother, and they did not speak until they reached the station.

"The train won't be due for another five minutes," his mother said.

"I was trying to think on the way over how I could thank you and Mac, but you in particular."

"For what?"

"For so many things, Mom. . . . I think most of all for not pushing those first days I was back, for understanding . . ."

"I've never worried about you, Philip. I feel you've done everything any of us ever wanted you to do and now it's your turn to do what you want for yourself. You've worked hard and you've earned a rest. Remember, you have that three hundred dollars a month from your grandfather's estate, and I'll give you some to tide you over—"

"You don't have to do that, Mom."

"I know I don't need to. I want to. I'm very proud of you. We're all very proud of you."

"Well, I appreciate it, but I think you'd better save your pride until you see me really do something."

"You'll do all right, whatever you do . . . Mac's very fond of you, you know."

"He's a wonderful man."

"He meant what he said about helping you."

"I know he did. He said something to me about it again this morning." P.S. smiled and added, "He also mentioned that he thinks I'd be a lot better off in something other than the CIA— State, for instance."

"It's your decision, but Mac generally knows what he's talking about. And one thing, Philip, when he says he can help you, don't think he's peddling influence. He'd never do that. And don't be too proud to accept."

"I know, Mom. Don't worry, if I need help I'll ask him. But it's as I told him, I just don't want to waste any of his friends' time until I'm sure I need them."

"Whatever you say."

"Mom . . ." P.S. said. He looked at her and wished he could say all the things he wanted to say to her. He wished he could explain to her why, after the divorce, he had had to go with his father. But he knew that she understood. "It's nice to see you again."

The train blew for the crossing and P.S. got out of the car, removed his bag from the back seat, and walked around to his mother's window. "Thanks again, Mom. For everything. I'll let you know what happens and where I am . . . And thank Mac, too."

"Take care of yourself, Philip."

P.S. leaned through the window and kissed her cheek. "I wish I'd known you twenty-three years ago."

His mother looked a little surprised, and for the first time that P.S. could remember, a little embarrassed. And then she smiled and said, "But you did."

9

P.S. TOOK THE TRAIN to Penn Station, then caught a cab out to La Guardia and flew directly to Washington. He got himself a room in a pleasant and inexpensive small hotel not far from DuPont Circle and went to the Central Intelligence Agency for his first interview. The personnel officer told him that he was in luck, that he could fill out the preliminary forms and take the first tests that afternoon. Wilkinson filled out the personal history form and when he came to the section asking why he wanted to work for the government he knew that he could not put down that he wanted to work there because he had nothing better to do, so he put down instead that he had been trained by the military, that his training was valuable, that he had had actual experience in combat situations, that he thought his knowledge of North Korea could be of use, and that he thought it was the responsibility of every citizen who could afford to to work for the government. He handed in the forms and was told to report at 2:30 to begin the tests. He thanked the personnel officer and left the building, certain that a Soviet agent in the apartment building across the street was taking his photograph, so he shielded his face and went into a restaurant around the corner and had lunch.

At 2:30 he was sent up to the third floor to a small classroom to take the tests. He sat down at a small desk and was given a set of forms with eight hundred questions asking such things

111

as how much would he like to be a member of a sheriff's posse and was he (check one):

—Very scared-
—Scared-
—Didn't care- } to get cancer
—Might like-
—Wanted very much-

He handed his answer sheets to the woman who sat at the head of the classroom and she said, "Thank you very much, Mr., uh, Wilkinson. We'll get in touch with you."

"About when?"

"Well, we can't tell you that," she said.

"But, you see, I'm staying at a hotel here in town. If it's going to be tomorrow I can leave word at the hotel. Or would it be the beginning of this coming week? Next week? Two weeks from now? Next month?"

"We'll let you know as soon as we can."

"Miss, all I want is a rough idea so I can give you an idea of where to reach me. Today is Thursday. I'll be in Baltimore over the weekend, then I'll be back here in Washington on Monday. But, if I'm not going to hear from you for two weeks or so, there's no point in my hanging around Washington. I was thinking of maybe going up to New York."

"Well, you should receive word early this coming week. But we can't count on it."

"I see," he said. "How would it be if I called you should I change my address?"

"But you shouldn't call *me*, sir."

"Then whom do I call? If I move I'd like to be sure that your message gets to me."

"I'll give you a number to call."

Wilkinson watched her tear a sheet off a blank memo pad. She wrote nothing more than a telephone number on it and handed it across the desk to Wilkinson. He half-expected her to say, "Memorize this number, then burn this piece of paper and swallow the ashes."

Wilkinson left the building, this time not caring if a Soviet agent photographed him. He tried to think of what he could do with the rest of the time he had that day. He couldn't remember whom he knew who still lived in Washington. In the year and a half he had been away a lot of people had moved in and out of Washington, so he decided to go back to his hotel, wash up, have dinner, and go to a movie.

P. S. Wilkinson slept late Friday morning. Charlie Merritt had said that he wouldn't have to be at the farm until the cocktails before dinner at seven, but that he was more than welcome at any time he wished to come—especially if he arrived in time for lunch. P.S. knew it would be the last time Charlie would have a relatively free lunch with his parents, and he didn't want to interfere. P.S. made up his mind to get to Baltimore around five, and he strolled out into Washington's pre-summer heat wave.

When he had been a freshman at the Virginia Preparatory School, he and Charlie Merritt used to sign out for Washington every chance they got. They would take the bus which would drop them off on Pennsylvania Avenue and they'd go into all the Army surplus stores, the magic stores, the sports equipment stores, and then they'd try to get into the Pix or one of the other movies showing nudist films. They would sit in the dark, sweaty theaters, smelling the drunks, their cigars, their hair grease, their awful breath and odors, and he and Charlie would try to ignore them to concentrate wild-eyed on the flickering screen, the mammoth-breasted girls who would step-stride-turn, step-stride-turn as they tossed off their sequin-encrusted gowns to the off-music sounds of the bands. And after the movie they would go from bar to bar trying to get a drink, but were, as always, told, "Get outta here, kid. You want me to lose my license? Go home to yur mudder." And they'd end up at the Smithsonian Institution—that incredible mishmash of a museum which had the best aviation building in the world where a couple of small boys could walk right up and—if the guard wasn't looking— *touch* Captain Eddie Rickenbacker's SPAD. The Aviation Building was P.S.'s favorite building in Washington. Glass cases contained the most intricate and beautiful scale models of airplanes a small boy could ever covet and hunger to touch. But even though they could not be touched, they could be seen suspended from thin wires in the case, eternally bucking strong headwinds as they raced over painted landscapes into adventure. The first biplane. The first mail plane. The real hull of the NC-4 seaplane which made the first flight around the world. The real Bell jet fighter, the first jet plane America built. Bits of insignia from World War I German planes. Real uniforms used by the Lafayette Escadrille. Hundreds of photographs of pilots who were braver than God and who stood, smiling crookedly, one elbow on the lower wing of their planes, and at their feet the small mongrel mascot, its head and tail a blur of excitement. And the planes themselves: Sopwith Camels, SPADs, Fokker D-IIIs, SE-5s, Fokker Triplanes, like the one Baron Manfred von Richthofen flew—bright red!—Nieuports, Bleriots, the Gotha bomber, the Albatross with the wings which looked as though Leonardo da Vinci might have designed them, and Bristols. And after they left the aviation exhibits they could always cross the Mall to the National Gallery and look at the nudes. "Well, my God, why shouldn't we? They're ART, aren't they?" And then it would be time to get back on the bus for school. P.S. and Charlie had two years of that, and then P.S. was expelled from the Virginia Preparatory School for cheating on his Latin examination. Charlie was the only person P.S. had ever been able to talk to about that. And they continued to be friends, wrote each other letters, saw each other during the summer. They roomed together freshman year on the Old Campus at Yale, and again sophomore year when they lived in Branford College. But junior and senior years they roomed alone so that they would be able to get some work done. They joined different clubs: Charlie went to Fence and P.S. joined the family fraternity—St. Anthony Hall. But that was all over with. The Charlie Merritt who had sat in the dark girly movies with P. S. Wilkinson was getting married tomorrow. And P.S. could get a drink from any bartender, could go to any movie, do anything he wanted. He took a taxi to Georgetown and spent the rest of the morning walking around the quiet streets, wanting to live there, hoping to run into some young woman, some girl he had known before, and when it was too hot to walk any more he entered a small French restaurant on M Street off Wisconsin Avenue which had red-and-white-checked tablecloths, badly painted murals of Paris scenes, and a waiter came over to take his order. Wilkinson said he wanted a dozen snails and a bottle of ale, and the waiter answered, "Doodah, doodah!" He finished lunch, and since it was only a little after one he thought he might catch a nap before he had to arrange for a rented car, check out of the hotel, and drive up to Charlie's place. He went back to his hotel, went up to his room and called the desk, asking the operator to wake him at three.

10

CHARLIE MERRITT'S PARENTS lived on a farm just outside of Baltimore in the Maryland Hunt Cup country of rolling hills and green grass that should only be seen in the setting sun. P.S. drove through the whitewashed brick gates, then along the long curving drive toward the main building. On either side, white post-and-rail fences and shade trees paralleled the road. One side was farmed, the other was grazing land for the horses. He pulled in behind the house and twisted the rear-view mirror to get a look at himself. He looked tired; but the tan he had picked up from the week of nervously pacing the beach had compensated. It was 5:30; and P.S. got his suitcase out of the back of the rented car and walked up to the house. The Merritt house, framed on either side by oak trees, was a three-story old brick. The house was not as large as the impression it gave; but it was old enough to have assumed the patina of antique velvet, as though the bricks if rubbed might be furry to the touch. P.S. stood for a moment before the house just looking at it, admiring it, remembering it from school vacation visits with Charlie. *My God, it's nice to be back,* P.S. thought. He felt as though he should put his suitcase down and sit on it and just look at the house, and he smiled at the rising excitement he felt. In just a few minutes he would see Charlie Merritt, he would see Charlie's family, he would see some old friends he hadn't seen since college. He would meet the bridesmaids and maybe one of them would love him, if only for the course of the wedding.

116

"P.S.!" The front door of the house crashed open and Charlie Merritt stood on the steps whooping with joy. P.S. put his suitcase down and they rushed toward each other, ran into each other, pushed each other away, and slapped each other's shoulders and backs, then they stood, speechless with pleasure at seeing each other again.

Charlie Merritt was pumping P.S.'s hand and saying, "Lord, I'm glad you could make it! When I got your phone call, I just couldn't believe it. I didn't think you were ever going to get out of Korea, at least not in time for the wedding. I'm so happy to see you!"

P.S. could not stop himself smiling long enough to speak. He just stood there looking at his friend, trying to see how he had changed in the year and a half, trying to see in his friend's eyes whether he, himself, had changed.

"There's so much I want to talk to you about," P.S. finally managed to say.

"My God, it's been a long time since we've seen each other. How long has it been?"

"A long time," P.S. said. "Almost two years—over a year and a half anyway."

"Has it been that long?" Charlie asked in wonderment. "Well, you look just great. Just great. The Army must have done you some good."

"I guess so," P.S. said, the first uneasiness having touched him. There was no doubt that Charlie was happy to see him; it wasn't that. It was Charlie's amazed "Has it been that long?" . . . *You're goddam right it was that long!* P.S. thought, and he could not help resenting Charlie's unawareness of it and, worse, Charlie's having avoided the service. P.S. followed Charlie into the house. They walked down the hallway with the hunting prints, the giant brass umbrella stand, the needlepoint-covered bench, P.S. wanting to pause and touch them all. *Charlie's hair is longer and his face . . . Something's changed . . . Is it thinner? Older?* P.S. wanted time to turn his friend around and look at him, but Charlie was hurriedly leading him through the back and into the kitchen.

"Hey, Mom, Dad, look who's here!"

Charlie's parents were leaning over the kitchen table with a seating plan for the evening's dinner. Mrs. Merritt was the first to speak. "Why, hello, *dear* P.S., it's *so* nice to see you again. It's been *such* a long time."

"Hello, Mrs. Merritt," P.S. said, wanting to kiss her, but he had his suitcase and there was no place to put it down.

Charlie's father patted P.S. on the back. "Well, gosh, boy, it's nice to see you again. You look fine, just fine. It's like old times having you here again!"

Charlie and his father were about the same height, 5 feet 5, and they looked like dwarfs next to P.S.'s 6 feet 3. At the Virginia Preparatory School, P.S. and Charlie had been known as Mutt and Jeff.

"Thank you, sir," P.S. said. "It's nice to be back."

"Where's Nancy?" Mr. Merritt asked.

"Upstairs resting," Charlie said. "She was tired, so I told her to lie down. It's going to be a long, long night." He turned to P.S. "You've never met Nancy, have you?"

"I don't think so," P.S. said.

"You were away, I guess."

You "guess"! . . . Charlie, Charlie, it was five hundred and forty-seven days!

"How's your father?" Mr. Merritt asked.

"Oh, he's fine, sir. I haven't seen him yet. He's still in Europe."

"Well, make sure you give him my best when you see him, will you?"

"I certainly will, sir."

"I'm taking P.S. off now, Dad. I want him to get to know some of the others before he has to call on them for toasts."

"What others?" P.S. asked.

"The bridesmaids. You know most of the ushers. They're all outside playing softball."

"Fine. Anything you say."

"As a matter of fact we have a couple of young lovelies who have been waiting to meet you."

"My pleasure." P.S. laughed. *That's more like it. Take it easy!* He followed Charlie again, this time out of the house and over to the field near the barn. He could see young couples playing softball—the males in khakis and sport shirts, the girls in Bermuda shorts and sleeveless blouses. And P.S. felt terribly out of place. Not just because of his suit and cordovan shoes, but because he didn't care if he ever played softball again. P.S. suddenly looked at Charlie in his khakis, his pink button-down shirt, the bright red-and-yellow belt, the tennis shoes. And he looked at Charlie's face, noticing new lines. . . . *Do you get lines at twenty-four?* . . . Charlie and P.S. sat down together on the edge of the softball field. P.S. felt he should say something to Charlie, something important, for hadn't he been looking forward to seeing Charlie again for such a long time? *But what's the matter? Why can't I—why can't we . . . It's so strange! Is it possible that he feels as uneasy with me as I do with him? We're best friends, he's my best friend!* P.S. turned away from Charlie and stared stony-faced at the softball players as though they, and their softball game, and the Merritt house were a way of life which had become obsolete.

"Got a surprise for you," Charlie said. "Take a look at who's playing center field."

Cheer up, Wilkinson. Make the effort! P.S. squinted into the setting sun. "It looks like Elsa Maxwell. . . . No, it's Mamie Eisenhower. . . . No, don't tell me, let me guess . . . Dorothy Kilgallen?"

"*Sonny Tufts!?*" Charlie laughed. "Look closely."

Because the sun was in his eyes P.S. could not make out who it was. All he could see was that it was a girl. She had her back to him and she was flipping a Frisbee back and forth with the boy playing right field. There was the wet *thunk* of the soft ball being hit, and P.S. watched it loft lazily over the second baseman's head. The girl turned from her Frisbee and ran in to pick up the ball. It was Hilary Farnum—the only girl P.S. had ever really known, who had ever loved him as much as he had loved her, the girl who had got married six weeks after his arrival in Korea, the girl who was now Mrs. Bruce Mallory, and who now had Bruce Mallory's child. P.S. stood up. He was shocked, then embarrassed—as though he had been caught peeping—when Hilary saw him, too. She did not pick up the ball, and P.S. looked away from her to Charlie, then back to her. *God damn them, is this some sort of trick? Is this their idea of a joke?* He turned back to Charlie and asked tensely, "What's she doing here?"

"She's a bridesmaid."

"Good God." He watched the second baseman field the ball and Hilary went back to her position in center field, but she still glanced toward P.S.

"I told you you'd be surprised," Charlie said. "Turns out she's a good friend of Nancy's. I didn't even know Nancy knew her until we were making up the list of whom we wanted in the wedding. She said she wanted Hilary Mallory . . ."

"Jesus Christ," P.S. said. He sat back down on the grass next to Charlie."

"Hilary didn't know you were going to be here either."

"You wanted to surprise her, too?" P.S. asked.

"Take it easy, old buddy, take it easy," Charlie said. "If either of you had known the other would be here, probably neither of you would have come. . . . Nancy wanted her, and I wanted you, were we wrong?"

"What's her husband like?"

"Bruce? I only met him once. Seems like a nice guy. He's not here," Charlie said. "He's in some place like Alabama looking for a factory site."

"*A what?*"

"Factory site. At least that's what Hilary told me."

P.S. looked across the field at Hilary. He knew she was pretending that she didn't know he was watching. But he thought her motions were much too careful, too nervous, too deliberately calmed, to be real. He tried to analyze his feelings for her as he sat on the edge of the ball field watching her. And he couldn't. He didn't know how he felt. There was still the shock but he sensed his feelings weren't the same as they had been before. When they were in love with each other. It was as though he were incapable of committing his feelings until she showed how she felt about him.

"She looks pretty good, considering, doesn't she?" Charlie said.

"Considering what?"

"I hear she and Bruce are having some sort of trouble."

"What kind of trouble?" P.S. asked. He felt the hope flash through him, the hope that it was some terrible, irrevocable marriage problem, that they were going to get a divorce.

"Oh, you know, the usual early marriage trouble."

"Well, I hope not," P.S. lied. "I hope there's nothing seriously wrong. . . . They have a child, now."

The inning ended and the players moved off the field.

"Looks like the game's breaking up," Charlie said.

"Umm." *Oh, my God, here she comes. . . . What can I say to her?*

"When was the last time you saw Hilary?"

"Commencement. 1958. But it was all over by then." P.S. stood up. "I think I'd better hang out my dinner jacket. If I'm going to have to wear it tonight, I might as well try to make it look as though it hadn't been slept in."

"Chicken."

"*Chicken?* What's chicken about hanging up a dinner jacket?"

"Hilary's coming this way and you're running."

"Oh, lay off, Charlie, there will be plenty of time for Hilary and me to see each other during the wedding."

Walking up the stairs behind Charlie, P.S. heard the front door open and Hilary talking to some of the others, then he heard her ask where Charlie had gone.

"What do you bet she comes up?" Charlie asked. "And I'm going to be right beside you, old tennis shoe, old horse trader. I wouldn't miss this for all the tea in Lipton's."

They entered the bedroom and Charlie showed P.S. which bed was to be his. He listened to the sound of footsteps climbing the stairs toward them. He opened his suitcase and began rummaging around busily. There was a light knock on their door and P.S. knew without turning that it was Hilary. He was physically aware of her standing behind him. He could feel it in his skin.

"Well, hi, Hilary!" Charlie said. "I bet you remember my best old friend in the whole wide world, P. S. Wilkinson, formerly of Korea and Yale . . ."

Lay off, Charlie . . . just lay off it for a while.

P.S. turned slowly, preparing himself to look at her and not to show anything. "Hello, Hilary."

"Hello," she said. She was not smiling either.

P.S. didn't know what to say to her. He didn't know whether he should shake her hand or kiss her or just nod. He stood there looking at her, seeing how lovely she was, what the differences were since they had seen each other. Her hair was darker than he remembered, and of course it was worn differently. But those green eyes were the same—maybe a little brighter, perhaps a little more mature than they had been. She was still tall, almost 5 feet 10, that wouldn't have changed, her dark hair almost black and so very fine and framing the pale skin, making her look almost the way high-key photographs make models look.

"I don't want to be in the way," Charlie said. "I'm sure the two of you have a lot to talk about."

"No, stay," Hilary said. "I only wanted to say hello. I've got to check on Nancy."

"Well, how have you been?" P.S. asked her, wishing to God he could think of something sensible to say.

"Fine," she said. He watched her leave, then he turned quickly and messed up his suitcase.

"Well, the two of you certainly went at it like a pair of jay birds." Charlie laughed. "I could just barely squeeze a word in edgewise."

"I'm afraid we didn't put on much of a show," P.S. said angrily.

Charlie walked over to the wall mirror and went through the motions of adjusting his belt, checking his shirt, looking at his teeth. "I'm going to go see Nancy for a few minutes." He started out the door, smiled, and said, "You want me to send Hilary back to you?"

"Lay off, please, Charlie."

"You really are serious, aren't you?"

"Yes," P.S. said and he was distressed by Charlie's surprise, Charlie's mouth silently framing "Good God!"

P.S. unpacked his dinner jacket and trousers and hung them up. He took longer than he needed to unpack, half-hoping that Hilary would return. But when it became apparent that she wasn't going to, he set out his dress shirt, studs, cuff links, on the bed along with a pair of black silk socks, the butterfly bow tie, his vest, and the gold watch and chain he had been given as a graduation present from Yale.

P.S. finished dressing, and while he stood in front of the wall mirror adjusting his tie, fussing with his handkerchief, and waiting for Charlie, he thought again about the curious estrangement he felt from this sort of life. The pomp, the ceremony, the pageantry of a family wedding seemed only pomp, ceremony, and pageantry. He felt no warmth over seeing Charlie. . . . The whole wedding had adopted a secondary emphasis in P.S.'s mind. There was only Hilary, and the confusion he felt over seeing her. And he knew he had to get over that. After all, there was Charlie and the problem of a friendship which had almost ceased to have meaning. Could they get along just pretending things hadn't changed, that things wouldn't change if for one moment he were to step out of character and not be the groom's best friend, but instead indicate that he no longer felt any friendship for him? How could so much have happened since they had last seen each other? He wanted to ask Charlie about the years Charlie had had for his own self, the time to fall in love with a girl and to get married while P.S. had been in the Army, the time to find a job and to start working upwards in it, while P.S. had only a small wallet-sized card saying that he had served honorably in the Army of the United States. P.S. felt as though he was standing absolutely alone and was not moving, and that everyone else was on a sort of moving sidewalk which kept them hurtling through time and space and life in a fixed direction. For the time being he felt that he did not belong. And maybe Charlie sensed that, too.

When Charlie was dressed, he and P.S. walked downstairs to the living room. Mr. and Mrs. Merritt were there, and Charlie and P.S. fixed themselves drinks and sat down opposite Charlie's parents.

"Well, Son, how do you feel?" Mr. Merritt asked. "Nervous?"

"Not a bit. I'm having a ball. If all marriages are this much fun, I'll have to get married more often—to Nancy, of course. . . . When do we expect Mr. and Mrs. Hammond?"

"They'll be here soon," Mrs. Merritt said. She turned to P.S. "You don't know Nancy's parents, do you?"

"I don't think so," P.S. said. "I may have met *him* here during some Christmas vacation, but I don't think I've ever met her." P.S. looked at Charlie curiously. . . . *"Having a ball, I'll have to get married more often!" Christ, what kind of crap is that, Charlie? . . . Do you remember me—me, P.S.! Your old friend who snuck into girly films with you, who had water pistol fights with you in the college dining hall. . . . Do you remember the time we put you in a trunk and left you outside Skull and Bones?* P.S. smiled over at Charlie and Charlie smiled back. P.S. wished Charlie would give him the finger or scream "crap" or whip out a water pistol or anything that would make P.S. feel that they still had something in common. Charlie raised his glass and silently toasted P.S.; and P.S. returned the toast feeling miserable. Then he heard the sound of high heels and his stomach tightened at the thought that it might be Hilary. P.S. turned toward the sound. But no one was there.

The doorbell rang and the first guests began to enter. Mr. and Mrs. Hammond were there, and a couple of the bridesmaids. Mrs. Hammond went upstairs to check on Nancy, and P.S. found himself caught in the corner with Mr. Hammond, who had been a Marine during the Second World War and had taken part in the invasion of Okinawa. He wanted to know if Okinawa looked the same, and P.S. tried to explain that he had never been to Okinawa. He had been in Tokyo a couple of times but the rest of the time he had been in Korea.

"Jesus, that place was green," Mr. Hammond was saying. "Everything was green. The brightest green you ever saw."

An usher P.S. hadn't met came over and said that he had been in Okinawa and P.S. took the opportunity to move away. He saw Hilary standing on the other side of the living room with another bridesmaid, Wendy Potter. Mrs. Merritt was saying, "Why doesn't everybody move outside? It's nice and cool on the terrace."

P.S. crossed to Hilary, swallowed, and asked if she'd like a drink. Hilary shook her head, and P.S. asked the same question of Wendy.

"Nothing for me, thanks," Wendy said. "I'll leave the two of you alone since I know you must have a lot to talk about."

P.S. watched her walk away and wanted to give *her* the finger. "My God, what's going on here? What *is* this? Everyone seems to be—I don't know what—setting up a scene between us or something."

"I've been getting it, too," Hilary said. "Maybe I shouldn't have come. I wouldn't have except that I thought you were still in Korea. I guess if I'd known for sure that you'd be here, I wouldn't have come."

"I didn't know I'd be able to come until a couple of weeks ago. Not until last week, really," he said. Then, after a moment, his tongue black and swollen in his mouth, "You really look marvelous. How are you?"

"Fine. I'm fine," she said. "Just fine."

"That's good." He looked at her, trying to look through her dress, trying to remember.

"And you. You're looking well, too," she said.

"I feel well. I spent a week with my mother on Long Island. I just lay around on the beach for about a week, and I feel pretty good." *I feel awful. I feel stupid. I feel—*

"How is your mother?"

"Fine. She's fine, too." And then he shrugged and laughed. "What the hell, everybody's fine. How about if I get you a drink?"

"Not just yet. We can talk a little longer."

"Would you like a sip of mine? As I remember, you used to drink bourbon."

She nodded, and P.S. handed her his glass. She took a sip and returned it. He looked at her lipstick on the rim of his glass. He suddenly had the most idiotic feeling that he should deliberately drink from where she had drunk. It was such a corny idea that he was furious at himself. Instead of drinking, he continued to hold the glass in his hand, conscious that his hand was so hot the ice was melting too fast.

"You're out of the Army for good now, aren't you?"

"So to speak. I'm going to have to go to Reserve meetings once a week, and two weeks during the summer. But that's all."

"What are you going to do now?"

"You mean what kind of job?"

"Something in intelligence? Like your photo reconnaissance?"

"Something like that," he said.

"The CIA?"

"Not so loud!" he said and forced a smile. *Now, you smile, Hilary. Smile at me. Forget what you're to smile about. Just smile once, once just for me, not for anything I said.*

"But is it the CIA?" she asked again.

"That depends on if they'll give me a job. It depends on a lot of things."

"How much does that pay?"

"God, I don't know," P.S. said. "I hadn't even thought of that." He thought for a moment about her question. One of the reasons they had broken up after Yale was because she was so interested in how much money he would make and not in what kind of job he took. And when she found out how little he would make in the Army she had laughed at him, and he had never forgotten it.

"What about the Foreign Service? I thought you wanted to do that."

"Not yet. I just want to sit down in one place for a while. Get some roots. Some place like Georgetown. And lead a sort of *Saturday Evening Post* cover life. You know what I mean? I mean a good dog, a good pipe, a good fire, a good brandy, a good woman . . . things like that." *Something like what you're doing, Hilary. . . . Only you're doing it with somebody else.*

"Fireplaces bring thirty dollars a month extra in Georgetown."

P.S. laughed and felt his lips were so dry that they would shatter. "What about yourself? How are you doing?"

"How am I doing what?"

"I mean is everything okay with you?"

"Yes, of course. Everything's fine."

Was there something in her tone? "And the baby? I never knew what it was. Cissie wrote me that you'd had a baby, but she didn't say what kind. I mean, boy or girl."

"Girl. She's fine. She's growing up fast. She's not a baby any more. She's ten weeks old. She smiles now."

"And she's—you're living in Washington now?"

"Yes, she's with a nurse. I have to leave tomorrow right after the wedding."

"What's the baby's name?"

"Hester."

"*Hester!* My God, wasn't that the name of the woman in *The Scarlet Letter*? Hester Prynne? And her daughter's name was Pearl. I didn't think anybody was called Hester any more."

"Well, it was Bruce's mother's name."

"Has she got a middle name? Hester?"

"Farnum. Hester Farnum Mallory."

"Why don't you call her Farnum? That's not a bad name for a girl."

Hilary said, "Because we call her Hester." She brushed at her dress—a gesture so familiar to P.S. whenever she was feeling stubborn. "And anyway, it doesn't matter. . . . She doesn't answer to anything."

"After Cissie wrote me I meant to congratulate you, but I didn't know your address. I was—well, anyway, I didn't think I ought to write you."

"She was born on your birthday."

"*My* birthday? I'll be damned. I don't know anyone else who was born on my birthday."

"April twelfth."

"And yours is— My God, yours is tomorrow. June twenty-fifth! Will your husband be back tomorrow?"

"Bruce."

"I'm sorry, Bruce. I knew his name. Will Bruce be back tomorrow?"

"No."

"That's too bad. I guess he has to work pretty hard. Someone —Charlie, I think it was—told me he was down in Alabama looking at plant sites."

"South Carolina. He works very hard."

"So, Hester's birthday is the same as mine. That should be easy for me to remember. You two were married, when? It was just after I arrived in Korea."

"December twenty-eighth. I was a Christmas bride. Hester was born fifteen months later, in case you want to count."

"Ahhh, Hilary," he said gently. "I wasn't going to count. I didn't mean anything, honest. I wasn't sure exactly when you were married, that's all. I wanted to get you a wedding present or something."

"There's no need."

"But I'd like to," P.S. insisted. "At least let me get you a drink."

"No, thanks. Maybe I'll just take another sip of yours."

P.S. handed her his glass again and watched as she tilted it to drink. She looked at him over the rim of the glass and P.S. felt the same almost-dizziness he used to feel whenever she looked straight at him. Then her eyes focused away from him.

"Hey, you two lovebirds, break it up!" It was Mr. Merritt, and P.S. felt himself start to burn. Charlie's father put a hand on P.S.'s shoulder. "My gosh, boy, I'm going to have to stand on a chair if I want to pat you on the top of your head."

"Yes, sir," P.S. said. He had always hated jokes about his height.

"Hilary's about the right height though." He turned to her. "All's well with you, my dear?"

"Fine, thank you," she said.

"I'm afraid I'm going to have to take your beau away from you. He's to be the toastmaster and I want him to learn some names and faces. And besides, it's a little unfair not to give the unmarried bridesmaids a chance at him."

P.S. looked quickly at Hilary and saw her anger for the moment. Then she said, "I was just leaving to talk to the others, too."

Mr. Merritt steered P.S. through the guests. "I feel I know you pretty well, my boy, so I'm going to talk to you like an old friend. I wouldn't spend too much time with Hilary if I were you. People have a way of assuming the worst. They always like a chance to do some talking."

"Oh, come on, now, sir. Hilary and I haven't seen each other for almost two or three years now. We're just old friends. My God, it isn't as though we were going to go to bed together."

"Well, make sure you don't ever let that happen either. She's a very attractive woman, but don't ever forget the fact that she's married."

"I know she's married, Mr. Merritt. Believe me, I know that."

"Well, just a friendly word of advice from an older man. That's all. Now . . . those two old people up ahead are Nancy's grandparents. You're going to have to speak loudly to him, he's a bit deaf and won't admit it."

P.S. half-listened through the introductions, but all the time he was thinking about what Charlie's father had said. Was it so wrong for him to talk to Hilary? Hilary had had that strange look about her. He had seen that look at Yale sometimes—the look of someone who is lonely, a little bit lost perhaps—she used to remind him of a bird with a broken wing. He tried to remember their conversation and whether she had sounded bitter when she talked about Bruce. Had she sounded bitter because P.S. wanted her to be bitter? Was it all in his imagination? And what the hell could people have to talk about if they saw Hilary and him just standing together and talking? What could be more natural than two people talking?

Charlie's dinner did not start until 9:30. And after the main course had been cleared away and the Baked Alaska was on the dessert plates, and the glasses were refilled with champagne, P.S. stood up and started the rounds of toasts. They were about what he had expected. The mother of the bride and the mother of the groom recounted how lucky their children were to find such perfect mates, then each told an anecdote which she felt would indicate how very lucky she felt the other child was to be married to hers. Then the fathers stood and told anecdotes all curiously limited to the period in the child's life at which he or she was eight, nine, or ten—that period at which parents choose best to remember their children. And after the parents came the grandparents, and then the ushers in dinner jackets bought during college days, and bridesmaids in demure, dull little dresses alternated stories—the ushers telling how Charlie failed miserably with girls, and how Charlie was sure Nancy was in love with someone else. And the bridesmaids told how Nancy had plotted to trap Charlie, ever since she had met him at the Maryland Hunt Cup in 1958. And when it came to Hilary, she stood up and looked very scared. And perhaps a little high, and she tilted her champagne glass toward Charlie and Nancy, spilling it a little, and she said, "I hope you two—I just want to say, that I hope you and Charlie—that you, Nancy, and Charlie will both be awfully happy and that married life and everything can be such fun and. . . . And I want to say that I love you both dearly, and I just hope . . . I *wish* you can be happy together and love each other and for ever and ever just be so terribly happy. . . ." She sat down quickly, her face crimson. P.S. stood up at once and called on Nancy's aunt to make a toast. Nancy's aunt was very amusing, and soon made everybody forget Hilary's toast, and the dinner settled back to normal. P.S. felt Hilary's toast was so unlike her, so wrong for her, and he looked at her hoping to reassure her, but Hilary was staring down at her plate. It wasn't until the last of the toasts that she looked up and began again to take part in the dinner. After the toasts everyone pushed back from the table and stood up and moved into the living room where the furniture had been lined against the wall and the rug taken up for dancing.

P.S., too, had made the move into the living room. There was a rush for the bar and P.S. hung back. "Dear P.S.," Charlie's mother said, placing her hand on his arm, "you did such a nice job on the toasts. These stories about Charlie at V.P.S. were *so* delightful! Of course I never knew you two snuck off into Washington!" Nancy's father thanked P.S. for calling on Nancy's grandmother and said, "But of course the grandmother wasn't Mrs. Hammond, it was Mrs. *Lee*—but other than that, young man, you did a fine job." Mr. Hammond was replaced by a bridesmaid who asked P.S. which of the ushers was the one expelled from the Virginia Preparatory School for cheating. P.S. said that he had been the one and he moved back from her and edged out of the living room and around the corner to the front hall and sat down on the stairway beneath a Paul Brown drawing of a mare and foal. He was so terribly disappointed by the dinner and the toasts. He remembered how much he had looked forward to being here. He remembered sitting in his BOQ room in Korea looking at the invitation, knowing what enormous fun he would be having with Charlie, the other ushers, and how there would be bridesmaids, not mooses, and how nice and good it would be to see Charlie's parents and the other older people. He had imagined a weekend filled with friendships and conversations and humor and toasts and love and the kind of warmth which he had missed so much and which his memory would so thirstily absorb after the despair of the past eighteen months. He had wanted this to be a wedding that Charlie, especially, would never forget—a great flood of happiness which would provide such a solid base of shared joy for Nancy and Charlie that the two of them would never be able to think back on their wedding without knowing that everyone there remembered it, too. P.S. had wanted the dinner and the toasts and the interplay of friendships and love to be an evening which would warm even Mrs. Lee's cooling memories. But instead the evening was beginning to become another Christmas with Charles Street for P.S. and not the rich, incredible cornucopia of warm thoughts, visions, asides, memories, which formed the insights, the vignettes of a family's love.

The trio was warming up, and P.S. could hear the rattle of ice cubes dropping into drinks at the bar. He could hear the busyness of conversations, the bright, Christmas-tree-ornament fragility of some girl's laughter. He could hear all the closer conversations just on the other side of the wall—little puffy phrases popping into the gaps left between the fuller murmurings of the room. P.S. leaned forward on the step and peered around the doorframe and into the living room. Some heavy woman whose gray dress with the gold threads pressed so tightly around her rear that he could make out the seams of her girdle stood partially blocking his view. But beneath one dewy arm he could see all the way to the corner and the foot of the trio's drummer tapping, tapping, tapping. Under the woman's other arm he could see the fireplace and over her shoulder to where a great-great-great-grandfather scowled through layers of dust down at the guests spilling ashes, putting wet-bottomed drinks on good wood tables, laughing too loudly. In the other corner of the living room, opposite the band, was the bar and the bartenders who were just now beginning to relax after beating back the first assault from the dining room. P.S. scanned the room quickly for Hilary. He wished she would come and sit with him, or at least come by and see him sitting alone; but he could not see her anywhere. Couples were dancing now and there was Wally Wallace laughing with one of the bridesmaids in the middle of the floor: Wally Wallace, who had been on the *Sherwood*, a brand-new destroyer-escort, which was being used all over the world to impress other nations. He had been in the Atlantic and the Pacific, sailed down the Suez and the St. Lawrence, been off Lebanon and Quemoy. The *Sherwood* had an exec who ran pre-dawn battle drills with all the lights on so that he could watch the men. Once, when another destroyer had blinkered, "What's going on over there?," Wally had sent back, "Shuffleboard on the promenade deck." Wally had come in while P.S. was dressing for dinner, and after the first enthusiastic back pounding and hand pumping, P.S. had felt the same uneasiness, the same shyness he had felt with Charlie. Wally had changed. He was thinner, his face had hardened, there was no sign now that he had once been the College Weekend Beer Chug-a-Lugging Champion. P.S. had looked at him, had seen the lines around the eyes, the wind-burned cheekbones, and asked him what he had been doing on the *Sherwood*. And Wally hadn't been allowed to tell him. There hadn't been time to explore and explain. It had been the same with Wally as it had with Charlie. Nobody seemed to have time, or wanted to make the time. And sitting on the stairs while the party went on around him, P.S. began to feel the familiar, insistent tug of loneliness.

"Hey, you never called on me!" a small boy protested.

P.S. looked up from the stairway. The boy had the fine features of Nancy. He was wearing a clip-on bow tie with one of the clips undone so that it seemed he had a small propeller at his throat. P.S. smiled at him and said, "I never saw you. Where were you sitting?"

"I had something all prepared," the boy said. "I'm Timmy, Nancy's brother."

"Younger or older brother?" P.S. asked.

"Younger," he answered, obviously pleased.

"Would you like me to ask the band to stop so you can give your toast now? It would be easy to arrange. Unless you'd rather wait. . . . Which would you prefer, Timmy?"

The boy thought for a moment. "No, I don't think you'd better do that. . . . Hey, listen, there're going to be toasts tomorrow, aren't there? At the reception and things?"

"Sure."

"Are you going to be the m.c. again?"

"You mean toastmaster? I don't know."

"Well, listen. I'd probably have to make one then, too. So why don't I just save mine for tomorrow. Would that be all right?"

"I think it would be fine. I'll call on you first."

"No, don't do that. Give me a chance to get some champagne from the other toasts."

"What's that you've got there?" P.S. asked.

"It's my camera."

"Are you going to be taking pictures tonight? You any good at taking pictures?"

"Some of them turn out. Anyway, it's fun to shoot the flash off."

"Umm."

"Hey, were you in Korea? When you were there, did you kill anybody?"

"I don't think so," P.S. said. "The war was over."

"Oh. Yeah, well . . ."

P.S. waved good-by to the boy and then got up from the stairs and went into the living room to the edge of the dancers and cut in on Nancy. She squeezed his hand and said that she was just having the most *mar*velous time, that she just *adored* Charlie's friends, that she was just too excited for *words* thinking about getting married tomorrow. P.S. didn't have to say anything to her at all until she asked him if he would please make absolutely certain that he called them when he came to New York and would stay with them. And he said that he didn't know they were moving to New York but that she could count on his mooching a free bed every time he came in, and then he was cut in on and he walked over to the bar to join Wally.

"Well, whaddya say, P.S.?"

"Nothing much."

"What do you think of Nancy?"

"Very pretty little thing, isn't she?"

"Cute as a bug's ear. . . . Absolutely lovely. . . . I told Charlie that if he should decide to chicken out I'll smuggle that little bundle right on the *Sherwood* and whisk her away to enchanted isles. . . . How are you and Hilary doing?"

"Doing what?"

"Where is she?"

"I don't know," P.S. said. "Dancing, probably."

"I don't see her."

"Well, I'm sure she's around," P.S. said. He turned around and looked into all the groups gathered at the sides of the dance floor. He didn't see her among them either, and he realized he had never seen her after the toasts. He picked up a drink for himself and a drink for her and walked out on the terrace to find her. He saw a girl standing alone out on the lawn. Her pale dress was the only thing which showed on the edge of the floodlit terrace. P.S. crossed the terrace to the lawn which was a little damp from sprinklers. He saw that it was Hilary and she had her back to him, apparently unaware of him as he approached. She continued to stand, her arms crossed, looking down at the lawn.

"Hi," P.S. said. "I brought you a drink."

"Hi," she said. "Thanks."

He stood beside her, not speaking. Then he put his drink down on the grass and reached into his dinner jacket for his cigarettes. "You still smoke these things?"

She nodded and took one and waited for him to light it. He lit hers and then his own.

"Is there some place we can sit out of the range of these floodlights?"

"There's a wall," Hilary said. "A stone wall over there."

"Good. Would you like to—mind sitting there?" He picked up his drink and walked with her over to the wall and sat down.

"God, I feel so mortified," she said.

"Why?"

"Oh . . . because of my toast . . . my stupid toast . . . I wanted —I wanted to say that I hoped they would be very happy and no matter how I tried it just didn't sound right. I mean it sounded as though Bruce and I weren't happy . . ."

"Are you?" *Please God, be honest.*

"Happy? Yes, I suppose so."

"Well, then you've got nothing to worry about. I mean your toast wasn't all that bad. My God, it was nowhere near in the same league as Nancy's father's toast about how Nancy wanted to know why she wasn't made the same as her brothers."

"I think she and Charlie will be terribly happy. They're absolutely perfect for each other."

"Whatever that means."

They sat together on the stone wall in the darkness. He felt her warmth next to him, he was overwhelmingly aware of her closeness, her thigh no more than a few inches away from his, as though the air itself between them was thick with presence. He wanted to be able to talk to her, to tell her how much he had thought of her in Korea, how badly he had missed her, how much he wished she hadn't married Bruce Mallory. But he didn't. He sipped his drink. Smoked his cigarette. Then he became aware that the music had stopped and he saw some people start out onto the terrace.

"I guess we'd better go in, Hilary. People are coming out and there's no point in making them talk more than they are already."

He knew that no one could see them, that they were still in the darkness, and he stood up and reached for her hand to pull her to her feet. She took his hand and started to get up, then her high heel sank into the soft grass, throwing her off balance, against him, and P.S. caught her and held her a little longer than absolutely necessary for her to regain balance, but she didn't pull away until after Nancy's brother had taken a flash picture of them and said, "This oughta be a neat one."

"Welcome home," Hilary said.

11

MISS NANCY LEE HAMMOND, daughter of Mr. and Mr. R. Taylor Hammond of Easton, Maryland, and Squam Lake, New Hampshire, was married this afternoon to Charles Merritt, son of Mr. and Mrs. Paul W. Merritt of Baltimore, Maryland. The Reverend Winthrop G. Owen, Jr., performed the ceremony in the Trinity Episcopal Church assisted by the Reverend Matthew Parker III. The bride wore her mother's wedding dress of white satin and a tulle veil fastened to an heirloom lace cap. She carried lilies of the valley, gardenias, and stephanotis. Mrs. Frazer Hempstead, the bride's sister, was matron of honor. Other attendants were Mrs. Bruce Mallory and the Misses Alexandra Stoddard, Margaret Travers, Wendy Potter, Linda MacKenzie, and Peggy Bishop. Mr. Philip S. Wilkinson was the best man.

Mrs. Merritt is a graduate of St. Timothy's School and the Parsons School of Design in New York. Her husband, a graduate of the Virginia Preparatory School, received a bachelor of arts degree in 1958 from Yale University, where he was a member of Fence Club and the Pundits. He has recently been transferred to the New York offices of Brandt & Klein, where he is a junior account executive.

The reception was held back at the Merritts' farm, and after the rush from the church to the farm immediately following the ceremony, P. S. Wilkinson had a chance to relax. The lawn was dotted with the friends of the bride and groom's parents. And near the stone wall upon which Hilary and P.S. had sat the night

136

before, a buffet table covered with a large white linen cloth
had now been set up. Two silver candelabra, at either end of the
table, framed the silver serving platters of sugar-cured smoked
Virginia ham, cold roast beef, slices of turkey, and salad. Flowers
were set in a large silver bowl in the center of the table. The
bowl had been given long ago as a wedding present to Mr.
Merritt by his fellow members of Scroll and Key, the Yale secret
society. P.S. looked upon it as a forceful reminder of how times
had changed. Had Charlie been a member of Scroll and Key,
his father would have been surprised at how much smaller the
bowls given as wedding presents were now.

P. S. Wilkinson, wearing his cutaway, the carnation already
wilting in his lapel, saw that it would be a long, long time before
Hilary would be released from the receiving line, and he circu-
lated among the guests on the lawn and carried drinks to the
older women with the pale, varicose-veined legs and the floppy
organdy hats, who sat beneath the oak trees on folding chairs,
smiling and nodding repeatedly at nothing in particular. P.S.
avoided walking up to the receiving line. He had already been
kidded enough about being caught-in-the-act with Hilary. Charlie,
and others, when they had come inside from the lawn and later
at the rehearsal for the wedding this morning, had made sly
semiserious references to the incident which indicated that even
though they accepted P.S. and Hilary's account of her heel sinking into the grass, they didn't entirely believe it.

And after the incident, late that night in bed, P.S. had looked
over at Charlie, who was asleep, who had had time for one more
drink with P.S. after the party and after kidding him about
Hilary had said, "Well, P.S., how are you really?" to which P.S.
had answered, "Fine," knowing that to try to explain would have
been idiocy. Charlie had fallen asleep almost immediately and
P.S. had wanted to talk because his earlier thoughts about the
evening had changed, and he had seen that everyone *was* having
fun, that the dinner had been a success, that all the warmth did
really exist, that Charlie and his parents were so good together,
and that if the chill existed, it existed only in P.S.'s mind. But
that did not in any way reduce the loneliness P.S. felt; instead

his despair had been intensified by the bitter truth that Hilary was, after all, married and did, after all, have a child. P.S. had lain awake that night thinking about Hilary, not understanding why she had married, why she couldn't know as P.S. did that all he had needed was time. He was even a little pleased that people thought there might still be something between Hilary and himself. Hadn't she held him after she slipped a little longer than necessary, or had that been just his imagination?

The receiving line was breaking up, and he looked at his watch. It was 3:30. He wondered if he would have time to see his grandmother before he had to return to Washington. He knew that he damn well better make time to see his grandmother or his father would want to know why. He knew he would have to check into a hotel again, and he thought for a moment how nice it would be if he could stay just one night with Hilary. But he would not be able to leave in any case until Charlie and Nancy left the reception to catch the flight to New York and from there to Bermuda. An old lady asked him to bring her a drink, and when he returned to her she had two more friends who would like drinks also. At least it kept his mind off Hilary. When he was finally freed he strolled over to the group listening to Wally Wallace reading telegrams and he saw that he had missed seeing the cake cut. There was a telegram from Chuck Gurdey on an aircraft carrier in the Atlantic, one from Bill French, who was still in Berlin, and there was one from Fred Nelson, who was with the MAAG in Vietnam. "And here's one from the White House . . ." Wally Wallace was saying. "It's from the President." The guests quieted down and looked at one another as if to say how nice it was for Mr. Eisenhower to have taken the time. "It says, 'Greetings. You will report no later than—'" That was as far as he got before he was drowned out by laughter.

P.S. looked over at Hilary. She was talking to one of the ushers. He looked at her standing there so lovely in the pale-green bridesmaid's dress and she caught him looking at her and smiled, and he felt the effect of her smile wash over him, and he smiled back at her. Hilary excused herself from the usher and walked over to him. "Hi," she said.

"Hi," P.S. answered.

They stood smiling at each other for a moment.

"When do you think you'll be going back to Washington?" P.S. asked her.

"I don't know. Wally Wallace offered me a ride back in his car. He's taking a couple of the bridesmaids back, but I'm not sure when he's leaving."

"You could drive back with me. I have a car."

"No . . . no, I don't think I'd better do that."

"Why?"

"Well, you know how people are. . . ."

"Yes. Anyway, I guess I'm beginning to find out. But I would like very much to drive you back . . . I really would."

"What time would you be leaving?"

"Well, I can't leave until after Charlie and Nancy leave, of course. And we've all got to change. They won't be catching the plane for another hour or so."

"Nancy's all packed. Her bags are here. I'm sure Charlie is packed too. All they'll have to do is change."

"God, you look nice," he said, and then suddenly added, "Hey! I just remembered! Happy birthday!"

"Thank you."

"I'd almost forgotten. Happy, happy birthday. I'd give you a kiss on the cheek but that would just about fix us for good."

"I know."

"Listen, what are you doing about your birthday? I mean tonight. Are you having some sort of birthday party or something? Is there any sort of birthday celebration?"

"No."

"Well, then look . . . I know this could be kind of touchy or Not Done or whatever, but I'd like to at least do something for your birthday. Couldn't I just take you out to dinner or something some place? We could do it here. I mean, we could go to a restaurant here in Baltimore. I'd have to stop off and see my grandmother for about fifteen minutes or so, but we could do it after that. I could take you to some place like Miller Brothers or Hausner's. Just dinner. Nothing fancy." He looked at her, then said,

"I—I don't think anyone should ever be alone for the birthday. I just don't think it's right."

"I wouldn't be alone. I'd be with the baby."

"But couldn't you ask the nurse to stay longer? I know next to nothing about babies but I don't think I'd want to spend a birthday with one even if it were mine. I think I'd probably end up feeling terribly sorry for myself."

"No, I don't think that would happen."

"But couldn't you call the nurse? Get her to stay a little longer? Miller Brothers is one of the great restaurants. And I've been planning to get there for a meal ever since Korea. I used to dream about that place in Korea. We could have dinner and then drive straight to Washington. How would that be? We'd be in Washington no later than ten or ten-thirty and—and nobody would need to know."

"It's very sweet of you, and I would like to very much. But I just don't think we'd better."

Sweet of me? . . . Is that what she thinks? "Oh, come on, Hilary . . . I'd just like the chance to sit down and talk to you, just be with you without all these—all these flashbulbs and people pointing at us and thinking things or saying things. Just to be able to—to talk to each other. I haven't been able to talk to anyone since I've been back. I don't know why. But I just haven't been able to. Maybe there hasn't been anyone I've really wanted to talk to, but you. And I could talk to you. I'd like to talk to you. It would be an enormous favor to me, and, and besides, it's your birthday. . . . And you shouldn't be alone on your birthday."

"I don't know, Philip. Let me think about it, okay? . . . Look, Charlie and Nancy have gone inside to change and I think maybe we'd better go in there with them."

"Talk to you later?"

Hilary nodded, and they separated. P.S. went upstairs to Charlie's bedroom. The room was filled with ushers, friends, strays, and Mr. Merritt was pouring champagne. P.S. pushed his way through to Charlie and asked him how he was feeling.

"Jush terrific . . . Marvelush," Charlie said, mock drunk.

"I meant do you feel any different? Do you feel *married*?" P.S. had to raise his voice to make himself heard.

"Not a bit. Not one iota."

"Wait until after the honeymoon," Mr. Merritt said. "I bet you lose twenty pounds."

"Bermuda . . . God, I'd love to go there," P.S. said.

"We'd be delighted to have you come along." Charlie laughed.

"If I didn't have to get back to Washington, I probably would."

"Where are you staying in Washington?" Charlie asked.

"I've got a hotel . . ."

"A *hotel*!" Charlie said. "Why don't you— Listen, I've got a great idea. I still have my apartment in Georgetown for the next two weeks. Why don't you stay there? Nancy and I won't be back for another week and a half, and we've both stored a lot of things in it and we're worried about them being stolen. If you stayed there you could look out for them and have a place to stay. It would be a great relief for us."

"I don't know what to say. . . . If you really mean that you'd like someone to stay there it would be like a blessing from heaven."

"Of course I mean it." Charlie rummaged through his pockets for his key chain. "The address is 2908 Q Street, apartment F, can you remember that?"

P.S. wrote down the address on a scrap of paper. "You've saved my life, old buddy."

Charlie got the key loose and handed it to him. "Well, keep out of my personal letters and underwear drawer."

"Speaking of underwear," Mr. Merritt laughed, "you'd better put a clean pair on."

"Oh, my God!" Charlie said and the others laughed.

Charlie put on a light summer suit and stood there suddenly looking very young and vulnerable, and then he lifted his champagne glass from on top of the bureau and said, "Thank you all very much. I want you all to know that you've helped to make this the happiest day of my life. Thank you for coming." Everyone said, "Awww . . ." Charlie finished his champagne and stood beside his father and shook his father's hand. "And you, Dad . . .

especially you . . . Thanks." Mr. Merritt hugged his son, and P.S. thought for a moment they would both cry, and he wondered whether his father and he would ever be so emotional about each other. Everyone joked and laughed and Wendy Potter came to the door and said that Nancy was ready, and Charlie went, "Gulp!"

"Well, this is it, big fellah," P.S. said. "We've taken you about as far as we can. You're on your own now . . . It's up to the big marriage maker in the sky."

"It's murder sending a kid out in a crate like that," Wally said.

"I talked to the squadron leader," Charlie said. "He said everyone's afraid their first time out."

"There goes a great guy," P.S. said. "And his apartment."

"Get a move on, boy," Mr. Merritt said.

P.S. went downstairs and saw that the car was ready. He made it back into the house in time to see Nancy and Charlie pause at the top of the stairway. Mrs. Merritt was passing out little bags of flower petals and Mrs. Hammond was giving the guests cornflakes. P.S. could hear her saying that she was so embarrassed, she was sure she had remembered everything, but she had forgotten the rice. Nancy's younger brother was eating the handful of cornflakes he had been given. Then Nancy threw her bouquet and Wendy Potter caught it, and Charlie threw Nancy's blue garter, and none of the ushers made any move to catch it. It dropped to the floor and some of the older guests went "Ohhh!" until it was explained to them that none of the ushers was particularly eager to get married—at least not immediately. Then Nancy and Charlie ran down the stairs and raced out of the house under the storm of cornflakes and flower petals. Mrs. Merritt and Mrs. Hammond cried, neither attempting nor wanting to console the other, and P. S. Wilkinson went back through the covering of cornflakes and flowers, feeling sad for a moment looking at the fake petals on the floor, and went upstairs to Charlie's bedroom to change out of his cutaway and into his suit. When he had finished with his good-bys and had assured the ushers that he would keep in touch with them he looked around for Hilary. But she wasn't there and he felt a little sick when he realized how much he had wanted dinner with her tonight. He picked up his suitcase and carried it around the back of the house where he had parked his rented car. He opened the back door to put it in and saw Hilary sitting in the front seat. "Hi," he said. "I thought you'd gone."

"No."

"Thank God. I'm so glad you didn't." He walked around to the front of the car and slid in next to her. "Do you have everything? Your suitcase, things like that?"

"Yes. I didn't bring much."

"Then let's be off." He drove around to the front of the house. As he turned into the driveway past the people still standing around on the lawn, Hilary slumped down in the seat so that she wouldn't be seen. P.S. wondered whether she had been right to do that, whether it didn't make their going off together different from what he wanted. And then they were out of the driveway, onto the road to Baltimore, and Hilary sat up again.

She was silent for a while and then she said, "Look, maybe you'd better drop me off at the railroad station. I don't think I should have done this."

"Oh, relax, Hilary," P.S. said. "There's not a thing wrong with what we're doing. It's two old friends going to dinner together on your birthday and afterwards we'll drive straight home to Washington."

"Do you think anyone saw me?"

"So what? . . . Anyway, unless they saw you get in the car, no one saw you."

"No one saw me get in the car."

P.S. laughed thinly. "You make me feel like some sort of counterspy."

Hilary did not speak again until they came to Charles Street. Then she said, "Your family has a house here, don't they?"

"It's further on. We go right by it. I'll show it to you."

They continued driving in silence until Hilary sort of twisted so that she was sitting sideways in the seat with her knees tucked beneath her and she patted his hand and said, "I'm glad I came."

"So am I. So am I. We'd better start looking for a parking space. My grandmother lives in that apartment building up ahead."

"There's one. . . . No, that's a hydrant. There's one though, I think."

P.S. parked the car and turned off the ignition. "Would you like to come up with me and see my grandmother?"

"I don't think so. She hasn't seen you in a long time and, besides, I'd just get in the way. No, I think you'd be better off if you went alone."

"Well, maybe so. . . . I'll leave the key in the ignition. If you want to listen to the radio or something just turn it on. It's a rented car, so there's no telling what you'll find in the glove compartment. Probably rate cards and things to do in case of accidents."

"I'll be fine."

"I won't be long."

"Good," Hilary said.

P.S. got out of the car and walked along the sidewalk toward the apartment building. On the way he wondered whether or not he should have insisted that Hilary come up. He had the feeling that he was not in control of their relationship, that somehow whatever was happening was predetermined to happen in spite of him. He knew the sensitiveness of this situation. Was she, by staying in the car, by ducking down on the way out of the Merritts to avoid being seen, by placing this emphasis upon the furtiveness of their relationship, accepting the moral judgments others had placed on their seeing each other? And, further, was she then by staying for dinner with him admitting her willingness—indeed, committing herself—to having an affair?

He took the elevator up to his grandmother's floor and rang the doorbell at her apartment. The colored maid answered the door and said, "Why, Mr. Philip, how nice to see you again. Please . . . Come right in . . . My word, how you've grown!"

"Hello, Francine," he said. "How is my grandmother?"

"She's just fine. She'll be so pleased to see you. Is she expecting you?"

"I don't think she even knows I'm back in the country," he said. "I've just gotten back from a wedding and I wanted to see her before I left Baltimore."

"Who is it, Francine?"

"It's your grandson, Mrs. Wilkinson, it's Mr. Philip."

"Philip?"

"Yes'm."

"Send him in here."

"Yes'm. Please go right in, Mr. Philip."

"How is she, Francine? Would it be all right if I stayed about ten minutes?"

"You'll be able to tell when she gets tired. Can I bring you some milk and cookies?"

"No, thanks," he said. "I don't think so." He walked into the living room and saw his grandmother sitting with her back to him in the high stuffed chair she had been sitting in for as long as he could remember. He came around the side of her chair and saw her hands, swollen with arthritis, lying half-hidden under a shawl in her lap. "Hi, Grandma," he said. "How are you?" He leaned forward and kissed her.

"My word, Philip! You smell like a distillery. Where have you *been?*"

"Charlie Merritt's wedding." He pulled up a chair and sat down opposite her.

"Oh, well, that's fine then. How is that nice boy? His parents were kind enough to invite me to the wedding, but I'm getting just too old to go to those things any more."

"It was a nice wedding. You should have been there. You might have enjoyed it." He smiled at her. "You've already noticed how freely the wine flowed."

"That's not wine on your breath. But never mind. I like it."

"So do I. Now, I want you to tell me, really. I haven't seen you in more than a year. How are you?"

"Well, I'm not about to die, if that's what you mean."

"That's exactly what I meant. You promised to leave me that mahogany captain's chest in your will, and now that I'm about ready to have a place of my own, I was wondering when I could collect."

The old lady pursed her wrinkled lips and rustled her hands in her lap and pretended to tremble slightly. "I suppose I could give it to you now," she said, then gave a prolonged sigh. "That is, if you *really* want it."

P.S. watched her. He loved this act of hers. She would suddenly change into a helpless, doddering, unloved, forlorn old woman to trick him into being ashamed of himself. And as soon as she would trap him into abject apologies, she would just as swiftly burst into laughter and harass him for being so gullible. But he had been away for a long time. Could she have changed in a year? He decided to risk her being the same and said, "Look, I've got a car outside. I could pick up the chest now and take it out with me."

"Oh, no, you won't!" She laughed. Then she sat back in her chair, smiling with satisfaction. "Philip . . . Philip, at times you're so much like your dear grandfather that it frightens me."

"That's a very great compliment."

"Not so great. He was a rascal, a terrible rascal. Someone who would take advantage of old ladies just like you."

P.S. waited, giving her time to remember. And then he said, "I'm sorry I never knew him better."

"He was a fine man. He certainly never forgot you! Do you know what you did the first time he held you? You couldn't remember, of course. I doubt that you were more than three months old at the time . . ."

P.S. knew the story, but he listened anyway.

"He picked you up and said, 'My, what a fine-looking boy you are!' and you threw up on him. I wish you could have seen the look on your mother's face, she was horrified. But your grandfather said, 'There's no doubt about his being a Wilkinson. He takes right after his father.'"

"I'm afraid I still do," he said.

"Well, you two look a little alike. Of course you look like your mother, too. Now, tell me. I know that Korea was dreadful, so we won't talk about it. Let's talk instead about what you plan to do."

"I'm not sure, Grandma," he said, "I was thinking of working for the government."

"Yes, that would be nice. Your great-grandfather, as you know, was Ambassador to Italy. And your great-uncle Coulter was a delegate to the treaty of something or other. And, let's see, your cousin Tucker is in the Diplomatic Corps now."

"Well, it's a good place to work."

"It's an honorable place to work."

"Umm."

"Have you heard from your father?"

"No, not yet. But, then again, he doesn't know where to reach me. Can I leave my address with you? I'll be staying at Charles Merritt's apartment. I'll write it down and leave it with Francine. When he gets back I know he'll call you. Anyway, I'm sure we'll get in touch when he returns." P.S. looked at his watch and stood up. "I'm afraid I have to go now. I've got someone waiting for me in the car."

"But why didn't you bring her up?"

"How did you know it was a 'her'?"

"Now, Philip, I may be old, but I'm not foolish." She smiled at him. "Do I know her?"

"I don't think so. I didn't bring her up because I hadn't seen you in such a long time, and I thought it would probably be boring for her to have to sit and listen to us talk family talk."

"But it was wrong for you to leave her in the car, Philip. You shouldn't have done that—unless you're ashamed of her."

"Good heavens, no! She's a girl I knew at college and I said I would drive her back to Washington after the wedding."

"Are you interested in her?"

"You mean am I in love with her? I just got back from Korea a week ago. I haven't had time to see anybody, much less fall in love with someone."

"Well, bring her to meet me next time."

"I will, Grandma. I will," he said. He kissed his grandmother on the cheek again, and said, "Take care of yourself."

"Got nothing better to do," she answered.

He could see she was tired and he left the apartment quickly and rode the elevator down and walked out onto the sidewalk. He saw Hilary still sitting in the car and he waved to her, then looked away from her and at the cars going by, until he was abreast of the car and he climbed in. "I'm sorry I took so long," he said. "The only way I could get out was to tell her that I had a lovely young lady waiting in the car for me. She told me I should have brought you up with me. That would have given Baltimore something to talk about. My grandmother loves to gossip."

"I could have slipped off my wedding ring," Hilary said. "She never would have known the difference."

"I never would have thought of that," P.S. said. And he felt a little stunned that it had occurred to her, and then elated. He started the engine and pulled out into the traffic and continued down Charles Street. "That's Carter Hall up ahead. Behind the hedges. It's the old family house. Sort of vintage Charles Addams, but not bad inside."

"It's enormous, isn't it?"

"I wish I could take you inside there, but it's probably filled with people we'd be better off not seeing for the moment, and anyway, I've got to get you some dinner if we're to get you to Washington at the proper time."

"You don't really have to take me to dinner, you know. I mean we could drive straight down to Washington."

"Let's not start that again. I said I'd take you to dinner and I meant it."

They bypassed the monument to George Washington and turned up Lafayette Street to the top of the hill, then parked in the garage opposite where they would eat. Hilary took his arm as they crossed the street, and they entered Miller Brothers' restaurant.

"I like the dining room to the left the best," he said. "It has all these marvelous signs in it—signs about Baltimore Firsts, like the first statue to George Washington was erected in Baltimore on such-and-such a date. Or the first ice-cream machine was made in Baltimore, or the first balloon ascension by a fourteen-year-old boy was made in Baltimore. But the one I like best is the one that says that the first underwater ship of commerce landed in Baltimore harbor in something like 1916. And the painting shows this German U-boat, and you know damn well that that sub was there to photograph the harbor installations. . . . I haven't been in here since I was stationed here with the Army, I mean outside Baltimore."

The headwaiter came over and showed them to a table and took their orders for drinks.

P.S. sat opposite Hilary and looked at her. "I'm very happy you came," he said, feeling that he had said it already a hundred times.

"I'm glad, too."

They busied themselves folding and unfolding their napkins, moving the silverware, smoothing the white tablecloth, and then their drinks came, and P.S. lifted his glass and said, "To you."

"You, too," she said, and she smiled at him over her glass and he tried to smile but all he could think was *Oh, God, I'm falling in love with her again.*

P. S. Wilkinson sipped his drink, then put it down. "You really look so lovely, Hilary . . . I guess this new life must be suiting you."

"It is."

"That's good . . . Well, that was quite a wedding," he said. "I thought it went very smoothly."

"It was a nice wedding."

There was a long pause and then Hilary asked, "Do you think you'll be living in Washington?"

"I don't know. I'd like to. I like Washington better than any other city. But I don't know. If, if I do this thing with the government, then I'll have to live in Washington. But I don't—if I don't get the job, then I don't know where I'll live. Maybe New York."

"What do you want to do?"

"You mean what kind of job? I can't seem to find anything that I really want to do more than anything else in the world. . . . I guess maybe we'd better order. My sister, Page, when we were little always used to say that I talked too much. She used to say to me, 'Babble on, little brook, babble on.' I never knew what the hell she was talking about. I thought she was saying Babylon, that place in the Bible—also Long Island . . ."

"We *had* better order," Hilary said.

P.S. signaled to the waiter. They ordered a bucket of steamers to be split between them, pompano, a Chablis served in chilled glasses, and for dessert, Cranshaw melons. The clams arrived, a bit gritty but good, and they settled down to the ritual of dipping the clams in the broth, in the butter, biting off the necks, piling the empty shells on the plates. P.S. paused and asked, "Are you a good cook?"

"No. I guess I could be if I wanted to. I like to cook. But Bruce doesn't care what he eats. He's happy to eat hamburgers."

"Not me. God, I love food. I'm grateful I'm so thin. I can eat as much as I want. You know what?"

"What?"

"This meal we're having. I've had this meal planned for over a year. I can't tell you how many times I thought about having this meal while I was in Korea."

"You wanted what we're having now?"

"Exactly." *Even to the point of being with you.*

"Then this sort of makes it a special occasion for you, too."

"I know." He ate another clam. "What are you now, twenty-one?"

"Umm-hmm," she nodded. She was struggling with the neck of a clam.

"You always seemed so much older than me. I know that they say women mature faster than men. But I was three years older than you, and yet I always felt like some sort of little boy with you."

"But I was in love with you."

"I was in love with you, too. I've often wondered why we didn't work out." *Oh, for God's sake, Wilkinson!*

"You mean why am I married to someone else?"

"I guess so," he said. "No, look, that's none of my business. I just want to say—let me lay a little ground rules, here. I really did love you, Hilary . . . I loved you more than anything else in the world—anyone in the world. We spent a lot of time together and I'd like to think that we know each other pretty well, anyway a lot better than most people know each other. And I don't want to have to forget it, pretend that it didn't happen. Oh, God, I keep sounding like a bad movie or something. But all I want to say is that we-are-good-friends, aren't we?"

"Yes."

Oh, God damn it! Why do I sound so much like some awful, pimply-faced teen-ager whose best girl in the whole wide world has just told him that she's terribly, terribly sorry but she's fallen in love with the football captain, some bastard with tiny hips and a big chest, and although she thinks the debating team is terribly important, she is sure he will understand that it just isn't the same any more between them, and would he mind if they were just good friends? . . . "Hilary, all I want—all I want is not to lose you again—even lose you just as a friend."

"Okay."

"I've got a few clams left, do you want some more?"

She shook her head, "No, thanks."

"You know what? I'm finally, really beginning to be able to relax. To be sort of, I don't know, *myself* with you."

"I know what you mean. I feel the same way. I'm glad we can relax with each other, I'm glad that other business is all over with."

It was the way she had said it that disturbed him, and he asked, "Why glad?"

"Because . . . you made me so goddam unhappy!" she blurted. "Do you remember when we announced our engagement? And the next week you called it off? And I was so . . . I felt awful, so . . . so USED. And I hated it. I hated you! I felt as though I were groveling."

"My God, Hilary, but why? I never knew I made you feel that way."

"Oh, well, forget it, Philip, it doesn't matter any more. It's over with."

"Are you sorry?"

"Sorry it's over?"

"No—oh, hell, I guess that is what I meant. Don't answer that one either. I had no right asking it. Forget it."

"Well, then, I'll say this much, Philip. I'm glad that it happened, that we did love each other, and I'm not sorry it's over."

P.S. laughed awkwardly. "This is so awful. All I've wanted to do this weekend is talk to you—and now that we're finally alone I can't say what I want to say. I don't know why—it's maybe because I'm so much like my father in some ways, but I always feel so goddam self-conscious when I'm trying to talk to someone, to be honest about something. It's the words themselves in a way. I can't seem to keep from seeing my self sitting back— as though I were a separate self, one of me watching the other. And when one of me says something like 'I want to be serious,' the other of me always sees it as though it were in print somewhere and there's Bodoni type face saying, 'But seriously,' with a comma. And then, without fail, I always bog down and become inarticulate. But the point is that I do want to be serious with you, and I can't help it if it's such an awful word."

They ate silently for a few more minutes, and P.S. sipped his Chablis and cleared his throat, and then he said, "Okay, I'm starting again. Now. First. To begin with . . . I still love you. Now quick before I go any further let me explain, okay?" He saw that she was looking at him. He took another piece of pompano, swallowed, sipped his Chablis, lined up the glass with his butter plate, straightened his knife alongside the spoon. "Oh, God, not like we were in college, I mean, I can't, I'm not allowed to love you the same any more—no matter how much I would like to. But what I hope is that I can still love you in some way . . . I still sound like some awful teen-ager with sweaty palms."

"No, no," she said. She reached over and touched his hand. "Anyway," she said, "your palm is dry. Please, don't spoil it."

"We can't. It's so nice, just to have someone to talk to. I used to go batty in Korea because there was no one to talk to. I was so damn lonely because of that. In Korea I could never be myself, I always had to be—to pretend to be someone, something different. I had to be a soldier, an officer, a sort of professional killer and things like that, and I was always forced to behave like an officer. And all I really ever wanted to do was talk, was to— ready?—here's that awful word: com-mun-i-cate . . . And then, when I got back, I couldn't at home and I couldn't at the wedding, and I wanted somebody so much to honestly talk to me and there just didn't seem to be time. And now, to have someone I love, sitting across the table from me, eating this delicious meal, makes all the difference in the world, do you see what I mean? I want to catch up with you, and find out what you've been doing. What *everybody's* been doing since I've been away . . ."

"Well, I got married, and I have a child."

"That's quite a lot," he said gently.

"Well, yes. It is. It should be the greatest thing in the world. Fulfillment of the woman's role. But it isn't all that exciting."

"Did you ever—you know I thought a lot about you this past year."

"I thought about you, too."

"You know what happened once? This is going to sound so childish. But once, one night in Korea, in the bathtub—we had these marvelous Japanese tubs in Korea, about three feet deep, with some step to sit on, all tile—anyway, I borrowed this other lieutenant's soap, and I used it, and suddenly I felt sort of sick, because I recognized the smell. It was the soap you used to use. I never knew it was the soap that made you smell this way, I just thought that was the way you smelled. And that one smell was *yours*, and it shouldn't belong to some bar of soap. And there I was, up to my chin in this tub, smelling this bar of soap, holding it under my nose, and it was you. You know how it's impossible to remember how someone you really know looks? You can't remember what they look like, because you can never really look at them without all kinds of associations. But there in Korea, I had an absolutely crystal-clear perfect picture of you. And I missed you so terribly much right then. All I could think of was that you were married and that I had no right to think of you at all. Anyway the next day I went to the PX and bought some of that soap, just so that I could think of you and remember you and I even—once I slept with a bar of that soap under my pillow so that I would dream of you."

Hilary would not look at him. She kept her face turned away and hid her eyes behind her hand. She shook her head slowly back and forth and then, when she finally uncovered her eyes and looked at him, P.S. could see the tears.

"Oh, Hilary, I'm so sorry," he said. "I didn't mean to upset you."

She shook her head again.

"Hey, listen, this is supposed to be your birthday party!" He picked up his glass of Chablis and tipped it toward her. "Happy birthday, Hilary, and I hope you have many, many more and that they'll all be happy."

"Thank you, Philip. Thank you for giving me this dinner, thank you for bringing me here." She leaned across the table toward him and brushed her hand across his and squeezed his lightly. "Thank you for giving me the nicest birthday party I've ever had."

He opened his mouth and wanted to tell her he loved her but then she said, "This is a nice restaurant. I like it. If Bruce and I ever come up to Baltimore I'll make him take me to dinner here."

P.S. felt the jealousy and knew she saw it. The melons came and she and P.S. ate in silence, and then P.S. looked up at her and said, "Forgive me, I'm sorry. I can't seem to get away from acting stupidly."

"Don't—" she said, not finishing her sentence.

He put aside his melon, then drank his coffee. He drank the whole cup without stopping, then put the cup down in its saucer and placed his hands palms down on the tablecloth.

"I'll be finished in a minute," Hilary said.

"Take your time."

"No, I'll finish. I can remember you were always so impatient when I took a long time over my coffee."

"No, that's changed. The Army and its endless coffee breaks has changed that. Please. Take as long as you want. It's nice sitting back and being able to look at you."

"What time is it?"

P.S. looked at his watch, "Around a quarter to nine."

"I guess we had better get going."

"We have plenty of time. It's only about forty-five minutes to Washington, an hour at the most." He poured himself another cup of coffee. "See? There's plenty of time. No hurry."

Hilary sipped her coffee and P.S. drank his. The second cup was cool, and tasted like dirt.

"I've finished," Hilary said.

"Would you like a brandy? I forgot to ask before."

"No, nothing for me."

P.S. paid the check and got up to help Hilary out of her chair. As they left the restaurant and crossed the street Hilary again took his arm and pressed it to her, and said, "Thank you, dear Philip, for a wonderful evening."

"I love—" he started. "I loved having you."

The Baltimore-Washington Expressway was surprisingly uncrowded in spite of its being a Saturday night. P. S. Wilkinson was able to keep the car at a good speed, five miles faster than the limit. It was quiet inside the car, quiet within the night, the night broken only by the sweep of his car's headlights. Hilary sat curled up on the other side of the sea, far away from P.S., resting her arm and her head on the back of the seat. Every now and then P.S. would look over at her, see her in the dim light of the glowing dashboard instruments, see the whiteness of her throat, the shadow of her cheekbone, her lips darkened by the dim light. He liked her sitting away from him. There was no need for them to sit close together like two teen-agers racing home from the double feature horror show at the drive-in. He felt no need to touch her, speak to her. He was happy that she was with him. And he knew that this must be what marriage was like. Ahead was his favorite curve on this road, a long open parenthesis to the right, where the tall dark trees framed the road. He pretended he was a racing driver, his arms taut against the wheel, his body and the automobile fused into one perfectly functioning machine. He had thought about this curve, too, in Korea, thinking what he would be doing, whom he would be with, where he would be going when he came into this curve again. He would be back in the States. He would be on his way to Washington. He would be having a good time. Knowing that this curve was always a happy one, one where the speed limit slowed to show that the driver was approaching Washington. He wondered if he could explain this feeling to Hilary, could make her understand what this curve meant to him, why it was something special. And he wondered if other people had their favorite curves. Whether, when they loved a place, they did not think of the place but of some part of the road leading into it like he did. He looked over at Hilary and thought she might be asleep, and he went into the curve, leaning slightly with the car, wanting to whistle or smile or laugh, and then the curve straightened out and he settled back, still very happy. He wondered what Charlie and Nancy were doing now. Maybe they were just finishing dinner and wanting to go to bed and Charlie would be nervous and saying something like, "You know, we don't have to make love tonight, unless you want to." And then Nancy would be put in the awkward position of having to say that she wanted to, which, from what P.S. had seen of Nancy, he thought she would want to do very much indeed. And P.S. smiled again in the anticipation of their first night's confusion, and tenderness, and love. He slowed the car and Hilary stirred and stretched. Her arm touched the back of P.S.'s neck and he jumped slightly. She moved so that her fingers could massage his neck muscles.

"Scare you?" she asked.

"No, no. I guess I was about a hundred miles away." He felt her fingers on the back of his neck and he liked them there and felt guilty and bothered and hated himself for not feeling that it was a natural gesture on her part—a gesture in friendship, not as a prelude to anything else, that she was massaging his neck muscles because she felt he might be tired of driving.

"You were smiling to yourself a moment ago," she said. "Why?"

"I was just very happy."

"Any particular reason?"

"Oh, a lot of reasons. Charlie and Nancy, I was thinking about the two of them. I'm happy for them. And I'm happy about being out of the Army. And I'm happy because of that curve in the road we just took. And I'm especially happy being with you. I guess it's just that for the first time in I don't know how long I'm very, very happy."

"So am I."

"Any particular reason for you?"

"I'm just very happy."

"Good," he said, disappointedly. They drove again in silence.

And then he thought what a horrible thing it would be if the two of them were killed in a car accident. If he and Hilary were suddenly splashed across the road, and people would find them, and then there would be all sorts of talk. Someone would find out that they had had dinner together at Miller Brothers and one of the waiters would say something like, "Well, they certainly looked very lovey-dovey to me." He slowed the car down and tried to think about something else.

"We're almost there," Hilary said.

They could see the lights of Washington ahead. "Hilary? . . ."

"Hmm?"

"Can we have lunch together in Washington sometime?"

"I don't know. I don't know if we should."

"I was afraid of that."

"I didn't say I didn't *think* we should see each other. I just said I don't *know* if we should see each other. I would like to see you."

"I'd like to see you, too."

"Well, we'll have to wait until Bruce returns. I want you to meet Bruce. You'll like him."

The hell I will. "Well, I'd like to meet him, too," he said, "but do you really think he would mind if we saw each other? My God, I know *I* would."

"Well, he's not a bit like you. You two are entirely different. I think you'll like each other."

"I hope so. I'm told he's a terrific guy." *Oh, shit.*

" 'Terrific guy'? Yes, I suppose he is."

"When does he get back?"

"I don't know. He's down in South Carolina looking at a plant site. He's with Massey-Prewitt and they're thinking of building a new plant in South Carolina, not far from Aiken. He said it might take about a week."

"A week? When did he leave?"

"Yesterday. He flew down to be there for the weekend. That's the way business is these days. He spends a weekend at the country club playing golf with the people, drinking with them, smiling at their daughters, then they get around to business at the start of the week."

"Sounds pretty pleasant. I mean a pleasant way to do business."

"Yes, I suppose it is. Actually I don't know—oh, never mind."

"Never mind what?"

"Nothing," she said. Then, after a moment, "Look, Philip, I'm not fooling you any. Bruce and I aren't as wild about each other as I try to pretend. I don't know why, but it hasn't worked out."

He felt as though his stomach had exploded, as though the car should have swerved off the road, as though Hilary would have been knocked senseless by the impact of her words upon him. "In what way?" he asked cautiously. *I want to know everything! Everything that bastard has done wrong!*

"I'm not going to bore you with it," she said. "Sometimes these things just happen. So what if everything isn't roses; that's what happens sometimes."

"I guess so," he said, wondering how she could sound so tough. "I suppose they've given him a lot of responsibility—maybe once he can relax a little from his work, things will be all right between you. I'm sure he works very hard."

"He does. He's their 'golden boy.' He'll probably be president of Massey-Prewitt by the time he's thirty-five."

"God, I hope not!" P.S. laughed. "I'd hate to see anyone my age be that successful."

"Well, he's very ambitious," she said. "In fact, he kind of frightened me when we first met. I mean he knew exactly what he wanted to do and how long it would take him to do it. You know what he wrote his thesis on? The importance of industrial plant sites in the relationship between labor costs and its influence in the community. It attracted quite a lot of attention. They were even thinking of publishing it."

"Who's 'they'?"

"Massey-Prewitt. That's why he got such a good job with them."

"My God, the only paper I wrote was the one I did on the relationship between child and nature in Wordsworth. I don't know anybody who'd want to publish that. In fact, my English professor wrote on it, 'Your style is frequently barbaric.' Maybe I could get someone to publish his comments."

"Massey-Prewitt might like the 'nature' part of it."

"I doubt it."

P. S. Wilkinson found a parking place not far from Hilary's house. He looked at his watch. Ten-o-seven. That's about the time I promised, isn't it?"

"It's fine," she said. "And thank you, Philip. I had a lovely time."

"I did, too."

She made no move to get out of the car.

"What about the nurse? Does she have a way home?"

"She'll sleep in tonight."

"Oh, okay. I was going to offer to drive her home, but since there's no need . . ."

"No, she'll be fine."

"Okay."

"I wish I could ask you in for a drink, but I'd better not. . . . There's just myself and the nurse and Hester."

"No, don't worry about it. It's fine. I don't think I could drink anything more anyway."

"Well . . ."

"Would you like a cigarette?"

"No, thank you. I guess I'd better be going . . ."

"I can walk you to the door."

"No, that's all right. Don't bother."

"It's no bother."

"Then maybe you'd just better not."

"You mean because someone might see us?"

"No, it's not that."

"Then what is it?"

"Someone would come along and see us," she admitted.

P.S. laughed. "Oh, for God's sake. So what? They'd think here is a friend walking you home. Period. That's all. Some friend of yours and Bruce's is dropping you off, that's all."

"Well, okay. I don't like walking around alone in the night anyway."

"God knows you're safe in Georgetown."

"You used to be, but I just get nervous now. So let's go."

"Okay." P.S. opened his door and stepped out, then he walked around the back of the car and opened Hilary's door and helped her out. He glanced away so that he wouldn't be caught looking at her legs. He walked beside her not speaking for the half block to her door, and stood slightly behind her while she fished through her pocketbook for her keys.

"I hope you haven't lost them," he said. "If I have to go around sneaking through windows, then the neighbors *will* have something to talk about."

"I've got them," she said. She pulled out a small red leather key case and opened it. She held up the keys to the dim light from the street lamp. "Here's the one." She pushed the key into the lock and turned it, partially opening the front door. "Well . . . Good night, Phil."

He stood there, wanting to kiss her good night. Not on the lips, but just a gentle kiss on the cheek. But she was facing the wrong way, and he knew that it would be awkward and that he'd probably mess it up. And yet he certainly didn't want to just shake hands with her. He reached out to touch her arm and when he touched her, she jumped slightly, and laughed nervously. "The electric touch of P. S. Wilkinson . . ."

"I didn't mean to scare you."

"You didn't."

"Umm." He stood there with his hands now pushed deep into his pockets. "Well . . ."

"Good night, Philip, I'm glad you're home."

"Me, too," he said. "I'll call you, okay?"

She paused for a moment, then smiled. "Yes, do that. Please."

He waited for her to close the door behind her, and then he walked back up the block to his car. He sat there for a moment, smoking a cigarette, then he pulled out of the parking place and drove slowly toward her house. He could see a light on upstairs now, and wondered if that was her bedroom. Then he saw her shadow move across the shade, and he drove on past her house and across Georgetown to Charlie Merritt's apartment.

12

SUNDAY MORNING P. S. Wilkinson awoke late and it took him a few moments to realize where he was. And then he got up, walked into the living room and sat down at the desk. He looked up Hilary's number in the telephone book, and dialed. After a few moments he said, "Hilary? Hi. It's P.S. . . . Oh, fine, very nice. Once I got to sleep. And you? . . . Good. Well, what I'm calling about is lunch. How about some lunch? . . . Well, you could bring her along. Put her in a box or something. . . . I see, well, I . . . Oh, no, I couldn't do that. It's a lot of trouble. . . . No, really. . . . Well . . . You're sure now? It's not too much trouble? Well, what about the neighbors? . . ." P.S. laughed. "Okay, I'll walk on over. I think I can find you again. If not, I'll take a cab. I might take a cab anyway, it's so hot . . . Fine, fifteen minutes . . . Sure . . . G'by— no, wait, Hilary? . . . Hilary? Is there anything you need? Something I can bring? . . . You're sure? . . . Okay, 'by."

As he entered the taxi and gave the driver Hilary's address he recognized that he was entering a situation of impressive and melodramatic proportions. He was fully aware of the various interpretations one might place upon his going to Hilary's home while her husband was away. P.S. knew that during the past night's dinner and drive back to Washington he had fallen in love with her again—but in the cold light of the rational morning he knew that the love he felt now was not quite so unrealistic.

161

She was, after all, married, and she did, after all, have a child, and he had been, after all, gone a long, long time, and he was, after all, lonely. And as he sat there in the cab he saw himself simultaneously cast in the roles of good friend of the ex-girl, the bitter ex-fiancé seeking revenge, the ex-girl's husband's cuckold, and the nice young man with whom the good wife cheats. He was, therefore, more than willing to accept the risk of discovery and compromise and reprisal merely for the interest he had in the situation. He also knew, however, that he was not at all sure how he would behave should Hilary wish that he become more than an old friend and, rather, become— *What does she want me to become?* he asked himself. *She was certainly eager or at least willing for me to come to her place. . . .* As the cab turned onto her street, P.S. had a sudden vision of Hilary meeting him at the door clad in a near-transparent negligee. She would quickly close the door behind him saying, "I couldn't wait any longer," and he would answer—

"What was the number of that house again?" the cab driver asked.

"That's the one." P.S. pointed. "The red brick with the ivy on the right."

P.S. paid the driver and crossed to the front door and pushed the doorbell. He looked around to see if anyone else was on the street, and then he looked across the street at the houses on the opposite side to see who was watching through the windows. He heard someone walking toward the door and he checked the pocket flaps on his suit coat to make sure they were out, and the door opened. Hilary was wearing shorts and a blouse.

"Hi, Hilary," he said.

"Come in quick, before the house heats up."

He stepped inside and stopped in the hallway while Hilary shut the door. "Well, how are you?" he asked.

"Fine. Hot."

"How's Hester?"

"She's sleeping. I just fed her." She saw P.S. looking at her breast. "Bottle. Bottle fed her."

P.S. blushed slightly and laughed.

"Well . . . well, where would you like to sit? The living room's the coolest. I'm not fixing us anything special for lunch. Bacon, lettuce and tomato. That's all right, isn't it?"

"Fine," P.S. said, nodding. "Perfect."

"Good. Then you go sit in the living room and I'll fix lunch."

"Let me help you."

"There's nothing to do."

"Well, can't I come into the kitchen and watch?"

"It's a mess. I wouldn't want you to see it. I still have all the things from breakfast."

"Oh, for God's sake, I'm not running an inspection. Why do I have to sit in another room? I'd rather be with you."

"Okay then, come ahead." She led him into the kitchen. "Do you want butter or mayonnaise on your sandwich?"

"Whatever's easier," he said.

Hilary looked at him for a moment. "Do you want butter or mayonnaise? They're both as hard to spread."

"Mayonnaise."

"Do you want your sandwich on toast or bread?"

"Toast, dear." P.S. smiled. "My God, you're pretty tough in the kitchen, aren't you! I'm giving you three seconds to make up your mind, Buster. You want mayonnaise or butter? Toast or plain bread? One, two, three!' "

"I can't stand it when people can't make up their minds."

"I was just being nice."

"Well, don't be nice."

"Don't be nice? What do you want me to do? Grab the sandwich from you and belt you one in the chops?"

"All I want you to do is to tell me what you want."

"Peace and quiet, and happiness ever after."

Hilary laughed then, and P.S. walked over to hug her and chickened out before he got to her. "You seem nervous as a cat," he said.

"I couldn't sleep last night," she said. "And when you told me on the phone you slept well I wondered—"

"I never said that. You asked me how my night was and I said, 'Fine once I got to sleep.' If you want to know the truth, I slept lousy. It took me until around two o'clock before I fell asleep."

"Well, I didn't sleep well at all."

"Why not?"

"Well, it wasn't because of the heat."

"You mean because of us?" P.S. asked.

"Eat your sandwich," she said. They sat at the kitchen table and ate in silence for a moment.

"What's Charlie's apartment like?" Hilary asked.

"Oh," P.S. laughed, "maybe a little sweet. Nancy told me he got it from some fag interior decorator. It's got the wildest curtains. They're bright red corduroy and they kind of swirl and droop and swish to the floor."

"How big is the apartment?"

"Living room-bedroom-kitchenette. It's not very big, but then I don't need anything bigger. It's about the same size as my room was at college. Anyway, since Charlie said I could have it for the next two weeks it'll give me a place to stay while I figure out if I want to live in Washington or not."

"I thought that was settled. I thought you did want to live in Washington."

"Well, I do. But I certainly can't live here without a job. Until I get a job there's no point in getting an apartment."

"Oh," Hilary said.

P.S. looked at Hilary. He tried to imagine himself married to her and having lunch across the table any time. "This is kind of nice," he said.

"Well, we're going to put in some more cupboards."

"Oh, for God's sake, I'm not talking about your kitchen." P.S. laughed. "Here I am trying to inject a little romance into our lunch and what do I get? *Good Housekeeping!*"

"Well, it is nice," Hilary said. "You must come to lunch more often."

"Good God," P.S. said, "is this my fault?"

"Is what your fault?"

"The way you're behaving?"

"You don't have to tell me," Hilary said, "I'm acting like the perfect bitch."

"Why? Because you didn't sleep?"

"No, no, not that."

"Well, then, why?" he asked. "Unless it's none of my business or you'd rather not tell me."

"No, it's Bruce. He called this morning and said that it looks like he's going to have to stay in South Carolina longer than he expected."

"Well, that's good news, isn't it? I mean, you said last night that everything wasn't too great between the two of you. I should think a little time away from each other would be good."

"Not if he's with some little dewy-eyed Southern belle it isn't."

"What makes you think he is?"

"He just sounded funny on the phone, that's all."

"Funny how?"

"I can't explain it to you. You have to live with someone before you know what I mean."

P.S. was quiet. He knew that this was not the time for him to remind Hilary that she had lived with him, too.

"Did you have enough to eat?" she asked. "There's plenty more."

"Fine, thanks," he said, "I might take another glass of iced tea."

"He'p yo'se'f," she said.

"Thang kew veddy much." He poured himself another glass and set it down on the kitchen table.

"Let's go sit in the living room."

"Whatever you say, Fang."

P.S. followed Hilary back through the dining room, across the hallway, and into the living room. He wondered whether Hilary would sit on the couch. If she did, would he sit next to her? Hilary sat on the couch, and P.S. sat on a chair opposite her.

He watched Hilary lift a cigarette from a silver cigarette box with the names of the ushers at their wedding engraved upon it. She tapped the cigarette on top of the box, then picked up the table lighter. She flicked the lighter several times, then put it back down on the table. P.S. reached over and held his lighter for her. She took the light, gently touching his hand as he did so. "Thanks," she said.

He watched Hilary inhale, then quickly blow the smoke out,

and he said, "Look, if this is a bad day for you, I could go and we could forget about today entirely."

"No, don't go, Phil. Not yet."

"Well, I'd like to stay, but if you don't feel well . . ."

"I'm fine."

He wished he knew what to do. He wished there were some way he could get her to relax, to be happy, or at least pleasant. He hated not being able to comfort her. He remembered at college when she got this way, it meant her period was coming and they had made it safely through another month.

Hilary lifted her legs onto the coffee table and leaned back on the couch. From the way she was sitting her shorts were pulled tight around her and he could not help but look.

P.S. forced himself to look away. "What do people in Washington do to keep cool on days like this?"

"Either they leave town or they never move away from the air conditioners."

"Where do they go to, Rehobeth Beach?"

"Unless they've got a summer place somewhere else," Hilary said. "Or you get to know someone with a swimming pool."

"Who do you know who has a swimming pool?"

"Well, a couple of people. But I don't like to go there on the weekend since that's the only time the husband has a chance to use it himself."

"Very thoughtful."

"Yes, it is."

"Yes."

"Well . . ."

"My God, you know what I feel like?" P.S. asked. "I feel like we were blind dates or something. I feel like we just met at a dance. You know? 'Where do you go to school?'"

"Farmington," she answered.

"Oh, really? Do you like it there?"

"Yes, it's very nice. . . . Where do you go to school?"

"Choate. Choate School."

"Oh, I've heard of that."

"Have you?"

"Oh, yes," Hilary said, "I've heard it's very nice."

"Yes, it is."

"Yes," Hilary repeated, "very nice. Do you know Rock Murphy, the good-looking football captain?"

"I don't think he's that all-around good looking."

"Oh, yes. All the girls at school say he's good looking."

"Well, if you like that kind of guy, I suppose he is," P.S. smiled, "and evidently you do like that sort of guy."

"Well, I've always had a weakness for good-looking men."

"Ahh."

"Oh, I like people who look like you, too."

"You do?" P.S. laughed. "But not as much."

"Oh, no, it depends."

"Depends on what?"

"Well, if—it depends on whether or not he has a lot of personality."

"Personality. Per-son-al-i-ty, yes, well, I've been told that even though I'm not good looking, I'm a lot of fun."

"Umm," Hilary said.

"Well, what I meant, I mean after all this, I was wondering if you'd like to dance?"

"To whaat, honey?" Hilary's accent had changed to that of a dance hall hostess.

"Dee-yance. I set ya wancha dee-yance?"

"Shooweh, doll. But there's no mew-sick. Ya keyant dee-yance widoud d'mew-sick . . ."

"Ya wanna waitta minute, huh? Ya wanna wait?" P.S. got out of the chair and turned on the phonograph. An Andre Previn record dropped onto the turntable and the music started. "So now there's mew-sick, aw-reddy." He held out his arms to her, and Hilary got off the sofa. She began to dance holding him away from her and she lapsed into the Farmington girl voice again. "I just lahhve Lester Lanin."

"It's Andre Previn."

"Does he give away hats, too?"

"I don't know." P.S. laughed. "One-two-three, ONE-two-three, one-TWO-three."

"You dance as though you were pumping water."

"It's very fashionable," he said stiffly.

"Well, I just think it's funny, that's all. I just think it's funny." Her accent was getting younger and younger.

"If you don't like the way I dance you don't have to dance with me."

"Yes, I do," she said. "My daddy said that if P. S. Wilkinson cuts in on me or asks me to dance I have to dance with him. So that's why I have to dance with you."

"Well, my father said I had to dance with you, too." He continued to hold her away. "And if you—if you don't want to dance with me you don't have to either."

"True."

They danced for a moment in silence.

"P. S. Wilkinson?"

"Yes?" P.S. said.

"They sure fixed the gym up nice, didn't they, P. S. Wilkinson?"

"Yes, they did. The old gym really looks nice and everything. I particularly like the way they painted all the basketballs different colors."

"Umm."

"You know what?"

"What?"

"No, guess. You gotta guess."

"You don't like to dance with me?" Hilary asked.

"No. Wrong," he said. "I don't mind dancing with you at all."

"You don't?" Hilary asked softly.

"No," P.S. answered in his normal voice, "no, Hilary, I like it just fine."

They danced silently and P.S. felt Hilary moving closer to him, but it was done so gently, so sweetly, that he wasn't even conscious of it until he felt her forehead against his cheek, felt her move her head the way she always used to when they had danced together—the slight tilting and lowering of her forehead to keep her hair away from his eyes, the slight nudging of her nose against the bottom of his jaw. And P.S. moved his arm higher up her back so that it rested between her shoulder blades and he pressed her to him softly, like a father comforting a child, and he felt her first tears against his cheek and said, "Ohhh, God, Hilary."

She pressed herself against him, pushed herself, flattened herself against him and clung to him with her arms tightly wound around his back, her fingers crushing his jacket. He could feel the sobs shake her body, felt her back beneath his hands jump with every gasp for breath (*Dear sweet God, she really is in love with me! Oh, God!*) and he tried to soothe her, saying, "Don't, Hilary . . . Please, Hilary . . ."

But she held him tighter and cried, all reserve lost, and there was nothing for him to do but hold her and try to quiet her. And finally Hilary caught her breath and said, "Dear God, Philip, I'm so scared! So *scared!* What are we going to do?"

We? WE! *What are we going to do? . . . What am I going to do, that's the real question!* "I don't know," he said.

She stepped back and looked at him, her fingers on either side of his face, her eyes darting back and forth, shifting from his right eye to his left eye. "Do you love me, Philip? . . . Say you still love me."

"I still love you, Hilary. You know that." And then he took a deep breath and said, "It would be so much easier if I didn't." He wished they could go back to pretending they were at a high school dance. He didn't want to have to think of what they were going to do. He knew what she was going to want to do. *You're going to want to get a divorce. That's what you're going to want. But what about me? . . . My God, my trunk hasn't even gotten back from Korea yet!* He looked at Hilary. *You think you're scared! Jesus, you're not half as scared as I am!*

He walked back to the chair and sat down, unable to look at her. "Oh, God, I feel so—if only I didn't feel so goddam *young!*"

13 HILARY had suddenly looked at her wristwatch and said that it was silly but she had forgotten she was supposed to take Hester to a friend's house in McLean, Virginia. P.S. hadn't believed her, but he knew she wanted him to leave the house as much as he wanted to go himself. He said that he should do some unpacking, and anyway there were some letters he should write telling his parents where he was living, and as he stood there telling her this, he felt so ashamed of himself, so embarrassed because he knew she knew he was running away, but what else could he do? He hurried back to Charlie's apartment, his head down, ignoring the heat, his mind racing through imaginary conversations he might have had with Hilary. In these conversations she would understand completely that it was impossible to expect him to commit himself this quickly to anything so serious as marriage—*and parenthood, my God! I mean, let's try to be realistic, Hilary. I—love doesn't have anything to do with it, oh, sure, well, it has a lot to do with it, but realistically speaking, wouldn't it be wiser for us to continue along the way we are for a little longer—at least until I get a job and settle down? . . . Settle down! Who wants to settle down? I've been settled down all my life! I was settled down in Korea for a goddam year and a half! Settling down is that last thing I want to do! . . . But Hilary would never understand that. . . . How can I make her understand that I just want to have fun for a while?*

170

I, after all, I just got out of Korea and I think I deserve a little fun. . . . But she'll think it's just the same thing as at Yale, that I ran away, that I'm running away again for the same reason, because I'm not ready for marriage, she'll say. . . . Well, goddam, it I'm not ready for marriage. I'm ready for an—I'm ready to go to bed with her again, God, I'd love to go to bed with her again, going to bed with her again would be fine. If an affair is what she wants—sort of a hopeless sort of affair, if only she wouldn't want more—if only for some reason it would be impossible for her to get a divorce, then everything would be perfect. Perfect! I could say—I could tell her I wanted to marry her and "I can't marry you, Philip," she'd say, "You know I can't, it's impossible." . . . But she—it's not impossible at all, in fact the only thing impossible is her not getting a divorce. . . . Why couldn't we just go to bed with each other? Why the hell can't we just be in love with each other and go to bed with each other like before? . . . Why is it going to have to be so goddam complicated?

P. S. Wilkinson entered the apartment building and walked up to his room, turned the air conditioner to its coolest, undressed down to his shorts and lay back on the bed staring up at the ceiling.

"I don't see why everything has to happen so fast," he said aloud to himself. "Why can't everybody just sort of take it easy?"

He got up again and wrote his father his new address, though he was probably still in Europe; then he wrote his mother and said that he had gone through his first tests and he would be staying at the following address, and thanked her for putting up with him that first week back after Korea. He thought about calling the CIA to tell them his new address but it was Sunday, and he thought he'd better call Monday. *I wonder if the CIA closes down over the weekend? . . . Of course not, they couldn't, someone would have to be there. . . . What the hell, call them Monday, that's plenty of time.* He began to unpack his suitcase, then found his bottle of bourbon. He carried the bottle back to the bed and caught sight of his reflection in the mirror. He looked at himself standing alone in an apartment on a Sunday afternoon with a bottle in his hand and said, "Oh, for God's sake! I've seen better plots in *Mary Worth!*" He put the bottle on top of the bureau, turned the television on, and lay down on the bed to watch the Senators lose the Sunday doubleheader.

Monday morning, the 27th of June, P.S. called the number given him by the CIA secretary and was told that a letter would be sent to him at his new address. He thanked her, hung up, and picked up the telephone and dialed the first two digits of Hilary's number and sat there with the phone in his hand, his finger poised over the dial, then he replaced the telephone and sat looking at it. He had done the exact same thing twice before during the last evening. He had stopped for the same reason. He knew that as soon as Hilary would answer the telephone, he would have nothing to say. He just wanted to see her, but he didn't know what to say to her. He didn't know how he could call her without accepting her terms. He was still disturbed by an overpowering sense of unreality—everything that had happened to him since his return seemed to bear no relation whatsoever with what he had assumed in Korea he would find once the Army was behind him. Everything was so complicated. *You can't do "x" unless you agree to do "y" and "z."* . . . But he didn't know who else he could see if he didn't see Hilary. All of his friends were either still in the service or scattered all over the country. None of the girls he had known were still around, and other than Hilary he really hadn't known any girls for the past five years, and he could imagine what might happen if he called up a girl and said, "You probably don't remember me, but . . ." And he had the nagging feeling that no one did remember him. *No, that isn't it.* . . . *It's not that they wouldn't remember me, it's just that I don't mean anything to them.* . . . *I was the guy they knew when, that sort of thing* . . . And they had all had two years since college to meet new people, make new friends, do new things. And he had been in Korea. And of course they had got along fine without him. Why shouldn't they? . . . And so he sat there looking at the telephone and becoming more and more depressed because he had never counted on being lonely when he returned. All he wanted was to mean something to somebody. And to have somebody mean something to him. He wanted someone to like him and talk with him and be with him and share . . . *That's it!*

That's the big thing, I—all I want is somebody to share things with.

P.S. reached for the telephone again. He rested his hand on the telephone without picking it up. *And, who else do I have to share with but Hilary? . . . But what can I say to her? What can I say to her? . . .* He pushed himself away from the desk and paced around the room, then he went into the kitchenette and opened the ice box and—*That's it! Food! I need food! I can call her and say something like, "Hilary, I don't know where the best places are to buy food in Georgetown, and I was wondering if you could tell me?" . . . and then I can say, "Look, if you'd like, it's a beautiful day and we can take Hester for a walk," and of course she'll have the baby sitter . . .*

It was after five when P.S. and Hilary returned to his apartment. They carried the packages to the couch and went back to her car for another trip. P.S. put the food they had bought on the shelves and in the small refrigerator. "Hey, there's some beer in here. You want a beer?"

"Sure," Hilary said.

"Charlie left it behind. But I'm sure he won't mind if we drink it."

"I'm sorry I couldn't find any wooden spoons," Hilary said.

"So what? I didn't even know they were important."

"Well, you can't cook without wooden spoons."

P.S. carried the beers into the living room. He clinked his glass against hers. "Well, here's to my temporary home. If I do work in Washington, I think I may take over Charlie's lease."

"Cheers," Hilary said.

"What time does your baby sitter take off?"

"Margaret? Not till late. Why?"

"Well, I didn't know how long you could stay. I thought if you could stay for a while then I'd take a quick shower to cool off, then sit back. But if you have to run off I'll wait."

"I'm not going anywhere, go ahead."

"I'll be quick," P.S. said. He went into the bedroom and searched around in his suitcase for his silk bathrobe. He had two bathrobes—one silk hand-me-down from his father and a seersucker he had bought for himself. He undressed in the bedroom, pushing his clothes into a bureau drawer, then wrapped the bathrobe around him and crossed back through into the living room and into the bathroom. He took his time in the shower, starting with hot water and gradually letting it get cooler and cooler. Then with it straight cold, he stood under the shower as long as he could stand it, turned it off, and stepped out to dry himself. He had forgotten to bring a towel. *"Hilary . . ."* He opened the bathroom door a crack. "Hilary? I forgot a towel . . . Can you hand me one?"

"Blue or green?"

"Doesn't matter. . . . Blue. Start with blue."

She passed him a blue towel and he dried himself, hopping from one foot to the other in the tiny bathroom. Then he carefully triple-folded the towel and hung it above the bathtub, and put on his bathrobe. He looked at himself in the mirror—wiped a clear spot with his hand—saw that his hair needed combing and realized his comb was still in his suitcase. So he pushed his hair down as best he could with the palms of his hands, opened the bathroom door, and went back into the living room. Hilary wasn't there, but he could hear her in the bedroom. He walked on through and saw she had made the bed with clean sheets. "Hey," he said, "you didn't have to do that."

"I know. But it gave me something to do."

He stood there in his father's silk bathrobe and looked at Hilary and the bed and he walked over and put his arm around her shoulder and said, "You know what? This may be my first home, I mean, the first place I've had to call mine."

"Be it ever so humble."

"It's kind of nice."

P.S. sat down on the side of the bed and tested the softness of the mattress. "The bed's not bad, either," he said. "It certainly beats the one I had in Korea."

Hilary sat down on the bed next to him, and he felt terribly conscious that he had nothing on underneath the bathrobe and that he was too fat in the belly and too skinny in the chest. She was sitting half-turned toward him with her right arm supporting her weight, her left arm loose, the hand resting on her thigh.

"I wish the air conditioner was in this room," he said.

"It's not bad. If you pull your curtains the sun won't heat up the room."

P.S. got up and went over to the window to find the pull cord. It was on the other side and he went back, past Hilary, around the foot of the bed to the window again and closed the curtains. The curtains were a dark green, and the sunlight filtering through gave the bedroom a curiously watery look, as though the entire window space were made up of tropical-fish tanks.

"What time is it?" Hilary asked.

P.S. crossed to the bureau and picked up his watch. "Almost five-thirty."

"It's still hot."

"Why don't you take a shower? I've got another bathrobe. If it doesn't seem too immoral or dangerous for you, help yourself. It's cooled me off."

"I don't know," she said.

"Go ahead." He handed her the seersucker bathrobe. "I'll sit in the living room." He left the bedroom so as not to give her time to think about whether or not she should do it, and sat down on the sofa. He heard her close the bedroom door and knew she was getting undressed, and he nervously patted his hands together, touched his fingertips to his lips, then crossed over to the desk and lit a cigarette. *Well, here we go again. . . .* He went into the bathroom and checked to see that it looked presentable. He used some toilet paper to mop up the floor next to the bathtub, flushed the paper away, and looked in the medicine cabinet. There was a bottle of witch hazel there. He carried it out with him into the living room and the bedroom door opened. Hilary was standing there framed in the doorway, the gray seersucker bathrobe wrapped around her.

"You look marvelous."

She smiled and started toward him. He reached out to hold her, but she put her hand against his chest and said, "No. Wait. Let me take a shower."

"What about your hair?"

"I won't get it wet," she said. Hilary closed the bathroom door behind her.

No. Wait. Let me take a shower . . . Wait . . . P.S. picked up his cigarette from the ashtray and carried ashtray and cigarette into the bedroom. Then he went back into the living room, picked up the bottle of witch hazel and carried it into the bedroom, too. He stood at the foot of the bed looking around at the room. The curtains were closed, the pale-green light was perfect. He put the witch hazel on the bedside table, then straightened the sheets, tucking them in tightly, and fluffed up the pillows. He could hear the water running in the shower, and he sat down on the side of the bed to wait for her to return. He stubbed out the cigarette and lit another. *What, me nervous? . . . Of course not, don't be silly. I always smoke this much. . . . Why should I be nervous?* The cigarette tasted hot and slightly sour, the way the furtive cigarettes used to taste late at night in the bathroom at prep school. He got up from the bed and looked at himself in the mirror. *Hair. Comb, where's the comb?* He went back to his suitcase and searched through the pocket in the lid for the comb, found it, then went back in front of the mirror to comb his hair.

He looked at himself again in the mirror, then went back to the side of the bed and sat down. The shower had stopped and he knew that in a moment Hilary would be back. *Throat's dry. . . . That's great. I'll say something like "Hi, Hilary" and I'll sound like the first tenor in the Columbus Boy Choir. . . .* He got up from the bed and walked through the living room into the kitchenette. He heard the bathroom door open as he was searching in the refrigerator for a beer, and he found the beer, straightened up, and said, "Hilary? I thought I'd get myself a beer. Would you like one?"

"No, thanks."

She had answered from the bedroom and P.S. pictured her pink and nude on the bed waiting for him. He considered putting the beer back in the icebox, then decided that if it was wasted what the hell. He opened the beer, poured it into a glass, and carried it back into the bedroom. Hilary was standing in front of the mirror combing her hair.

"That bathrobe's never looked so good," he said.

Hilary smiled. "I like it. When did you get it? I don't remember you having one before. Not like this. I remember your red silk one . . ."

"Ah, this one's finally falling apart. I think I'm the third generation to wear it. I got the seersucker in Long Island when I went to see my mother."

"How is your mother?"

"Fine. She's fine. Everybody's fine. . . . I think we went through all this at the wedding."

Hilary had her back to him and was still combing her hair.

"Did you get your hair very wet?"

"No."

P.S. sat down on the side of the bed. "You look so lovely standing there," he said, "I wish you could . . ."

"What?"

"I was being stupid. I was going to say that I wish you could stand there forever, but I suddenly had a picture of you doomed to an eternity of standing in a damp bathrobe in front of a mirror combing your hair."

Hilary put down the comb and turned to face him, smiling. "It wouldn't be much fun."

"No, it wouldn't."

She sat down on the edge of the bed and crossed her arms in front of her breast and massaged her neck muscles.

"Stiff?" he asked.

"A little. I played some tennis yesterday afternoon for the first time in months."

"Would you like a back rub? Do you remember the back rubs we used to give each other at college? I think we spent half our time during the weekends giving each other back rubs."

"I know . . ."

"Well, anyway, if you'd like one I'd be happy to give you one." His throat was dry again and he reached over onto the night table for his beer. "Want a sip?"

"No, no, thanks. Beer just makes me hot."

"I love the stuff." He drank some of his beer and put the glass back on the table. They were both silent.

"Philip."

"Yes?"

"About what you said . . . You know, I mean, Sunday afternoon about our not knowing—not knowing what we were going to do. Do you remember?"

"Yes," he said softly.

"Well, I wasn't just talking about just going to bed."

"I know," he said.

She reached for his hand and held it. "Maybe I should go. It's unfair. I'm being unfair to you. I shouldn't have come here unless I was going to make love to you."

"No, don't say that. We don't have to make love. Don't go."

"But it's not fair to you!"

"What's not fair to me? I didn't bring you up here just to make love. I don't think I really wanted to . . . well, I wanted to, but . . . Maybe I feel a little better—more relaxed now. Look, Hilary, I'll tell you what I'll do. Lie down and I'll give you a back rub. We're both worried and nervous and everything and it'll relax you. So don't worry about making love. We don't have to."

She smiled at him, then leaned forward and kissed him gently on the lips, touching his cheek with her fingertips. She stood up and undid the cord to the bathrobe, then, standing with her back to him, let it slide to the floor. P.S. was disappointed to see that she was wearing her brassiere and panties. With her back still to him, she slid onto the bed and lay down, her head turned away from him. He sat where he was, looking at her for a moment, remembering her body, surprised at how thin she was, the ribs showing faintly on her back. Then he got up and knelt over the backs of her legs. "I've got some witch hazel," he said. "Would you like me to use that?"

"Sure," she said, "it would be nice and cool."

He splashed some witch hazel onto his hands and said, "It's going to be cooler than that at first."

"Okay."

He let a few drops hit her shoulder, then he placed his hands on her neck muscles and began gently to massage the back of her neck. He moved his hands slowly, using his fingers to work the muscles of her neck and shoulders. Her eyes were closed and she was smiling slightly. He remained working on her shoulder muscles.

"Feel good?"

"Very," she said.

"Look, I don't want to seem too forward, as it were, but if I can undo your bra I'll be able to do your back better."

"Go ahead."

He had trouble, of course, with the catches. He always had trouble with them. He thought about his brother, Carter, who had once told him he had mastered brassieres and was able with one deft, incredibly suave snap of the fingers to unhook the most intricate brassieres known to women. He finally got the hooks undone and Hilary lifted herself slightly and reached beneath herself and pulled the cups away from her breasts, then took the bra off entirely. She lowered herself again and he could see how her weight pushed the fullness of her breasts to her sides. P.S. leaned forward to take another sip of beer. He became increasingly aware of her thighs touching his where he was kneeling above her, and he splashed some more witch hazel onto his hands and began to massage her between her shoulder blades. Each time he pressed down on her, her breast flattened beneath her and he could hear the slight push of air out of her. With his hands now on either side of her spine, his thumbs working the spine, his fingers the muscles of her back, he began to work downwards, below the rib cage toward the small of her back. He concentrated on the area just above the swelling of her hips.

"That feels good," she said. She brought her hands from beneath the pillow and, hooking her thumbs in the waistband of her panties, slid them down to just cover her buttocks, then she tucked her hands back beneath the pillow. The gesture was so natural, so automatic in its acceptance of what they were doing together that P.S. was a little shocked. He began to massage the base of her spine.

"The coccyx," he said, "man's prehensile tail. His link to the ape. The last bone of the spinal column—and without doubt the most painful bone to break in the body. I knew a guy once who fell and broke his coccyx. There is no way to be comfortable. You can't sit, certainly. But whenever you move or however you lie, it hurts like hell. He was in terrible pain." He raised her panties slightly and began to massage the bulge of her hip. Then he moved his hands back up to her shoulders.

"You must be getting tired," she said.

"No, not a bit. I enjoy it."

"You sure?" she asked. She turned to look at him, slightly raising herself. He saw her breasts hang free, not touching the bed and he could not stop himself. He moved his hand to cover her breast, he felt it fill his hand, the nipple harden against his palm. "Ahh, God," he said. He held her small breast within his hand, his fingertip lightly touching the nipple. He felt Hilary shiver slightly, and then she lay down again, crushing his hand against her. He withdrew it gently and continued to rub her back. He concentrated on the small of her back. It was safe. Harmless. Nothing erotic about the small of the back—at least not as erotic as the breasts, and then almost as though he was unaware of what was happening, his hands were moving up past the marks of the waistband on her skin, up her ribs, and this time, Hilary, too, moved, raising herself on her elbows, her breasts not touching the sheet, and then her sharp intake of breath as his hands cupped her, touched her, moved over her. Hilary, her head lowered, forehead pressed against the pillow, her eyes squeezed tightly closed, did not move, even her breathing had stopped, as she held her breath. P.S. leaned forward slightly, resting his forearms along her sides, his hands beneath her holding her breasts.

"Hilary . . . Hilary," he said. He lifted himself clear of the backs of her legs and lay down on his side next to her and she moved also so that they were lying together. He undid his bathrobe and threw it aside so that they were touching each other. "Oh, God, Hilary," he said, "I've thought of holding you like this so many times." She pressed herself against him, her head resting against his left arm beneath her, his right arm around her. She lay with her eyes closed, her chin buried into the hollow of his shoulder. Her hand moved across his chest, then down his side to his hip, pulling him more tightly against her. They held each other for a moment, and then he gently placed his hand against her shoulder and pushed her so that she lay flat on the bed. "Let me look at you," he said. "I just want to look at you." P.S. lay so that his left elbow supported him and he looked down at her, her breasts flattened against her. With his right hand he traced the small circle of her breast, his fingertips touching her collar bone, her throat, then down her side again to her hip. Her eyes were still closed and he moved his hand from her hip to her stomach, his fingers just beneath the waist of her panties. He fanned his hand across her and she shivered and opened her eyes and looked at him.

"Philip . . ."

"Yes?" His throat was so dry he had half expected no sound to come out.

"Philip, if we don't stop now, we aren't going to stop."

He did not move his hand.

"Philip," she repeated.

He slid his hand beneath her panties and she suddenly, violently twisted away from him.

"Hilary . . ."

"No," she said. "We can't."

"I wasn't going to," he said, "I only wanted to touch you."

"But we can't," she said. "I don't want you to stop and we can't."

He tried to touch her again, but she held his hand away.

"Please, Philip, help me," she said, "don't."

He sat up on the bed and reached for his beer, which was now warm and flat. "Okay," he said. He sipped his beer and stood up and pulled the bathrobe around him.

Hilary remained on the bed looking at him, her eyes worried. "Are you angry?"

P.S. smiled. "No, I'm not angry."

She smiled tentatively. "I'm sorry . . ."

"Don't be. Really, Hilary."

"But I am. I said it was unfair."

"No, there's nothing unfair about it. I'm glad we stopped."

"Are you really?"

"No." He laughed. "I'm not glad at all right now. But I will be."

She crawled across the bed, then rose kneeling and hugged him. And he held her, his arms around her back. She pressed the side of her face against his chest. "I love you, Philip," she said, "I really do."

"I love you, Hilary."

"Are you sure?"

"What kind of a question is that?"

"I don't know," she said. She let go of him and got off the bed. "Where's my bra?"

"Next to the bed. On the floor," he said.

"I'm sorry. I really am. Go into the living room. Let me get dressed. I didn't mean to get you upset."

"Who's upset?" he asked. *Oh, God . . . this is so awful!* He tried to laugh at himself and she laughed a little and he picked up his beer and walked into the living room with it. He sat down on the couch and picked up a cigarette. He saw that his hand was shaking slightly, and he was so sick of himself.

"Phil?" Hilary called from the bedroom. "What time is it?"

"My watch is on the table next to the bed."

"Thanks."

"What time is it?" he asked.

"Almost seven. I told Margaret I'd be home at six-thirty. I'd better be going . . . Phil?"

"Yes?"

"Are you angry with me?" she asked, still in the bedroom.

"No."

"Will you have dinner with me?"

"I don't think we'd better," he said. "Besides, I've got to unpack and put things away."

"Have dinner and then put things away." He could hear her moving around.

"No. If I spend any more time with you tonight I don't know what will happen."

"But we won't have a chance to be together otherwise," she said. "Have dinner with me. I'd like to cook something for you."

She came out of the bedroom. She was slipping the belt through the loops of her dress. "I must look a sight," she said, then continued on into the bathroom. He saw her reflection as she looked at herself in the mirror.

"God, I don't think I look a bit different," she said.

"Why? Are you supposed to?"

"Well, I thought I might look a little different—sort of more like Lucretia Borgia or maybe Catherine the Great . . ."

"You look just exactly like Hilary Farnum," he said and immediately wished he hadn't, since Hilary Farnum was no more. It was Mrs. Bruce Mallory.

Hilary walked back to him and sat down on the couch next to him and held his hand. "I've got to go," she said.

"I'll walk you down."

"In your bathrobe?" She laughed. "Don't bother getting dressed, I can find my way. I'm sorry you won't have dinner with me."

"I can't, Hilary. Really, I'd better get this stuff done."

"Then call me, will you?"

He nodded.

"Promise?"

"Oh, for God's sake, of course I'll call you."

She stood up and he stood up with her and walked with her to the door. He leaned forward to kiss her and she turned her head slightly and he kissed her on the cheek. "Lipstick," she said.

P.S. just nodded and opened the door for her.

"You *are* mad at me, aren't you?" she said.

"No, of course not," he answered. "If I'm mad at anyone I'm mad at myself for being such a jerk."

She looked at him worriedly and he took her hand and said, "No, really. I'm fine. I'll call you later on."

"Good-by," she said. Then she paused at the door and looked at him and said, "And, Philip? Thank you."

He started to ask "For stopping?" but he couldn't do anything but nod.

14

PHILIP SADLER WILKINSON finished his second shower of the afternoon and stood drying himself in the bathroom. He thought of how close they had come to making love. *If I'd really wanted to we could have. She said herself that she wouldn't have been able to stop. So why did I stop?* ...

He went over to his bureau and began to lay out fresh clothes. He had just started matching socks when the telephone rang, startling him. He walked back into the living room and picked up the telephone. "Hello?"

"Charlie?" a man's voice asked on the other end.

"No, I'm sorry. Charlie left a few days ago for his honeymoon in Bermuda."

"For *where*?" The man laughed.

"Bermuda," P.S. repeated.

"Who is this? Who am I speaking to?"

"P. S. Wilkinson."

"*Who*?"

"P. S. Wilkinson."

"Phil?" the man's voice asked. "From the Virginia Preparatory School?"

"Well, I went there, yes . . ."

"Phil, this is Linus Hendricks, do you remember me? I was on the Honor Committee. Well, how the hell are you?"

184

"Fine. Fine," he said. He tried to remember what Linus Hendricks had looked like.

"Listen, you're not just giving me head about Charlie, are you?"

"No. No, he really got married."

"Well, what are you doing?"

"Nothing much. I just got out of the Army. I've taken Charlie's apartment for a couple of weeks."

"Well, that's fine. That's fine. Listen, P.S., my roommates and I are giving a party tonight and want you to come. Bring a date if you'd like, if not, don't."

"I don't know many girls here," P.S. explained.

"Fine, then this'll give you a chance to meet some. Listen, it starts about eight o'clock and it's going to go on all night long, so come whenever you like: 1414 36th Street . . . it's by the university."

"Fourteen-fourteen 36th Street," P.S. repeated. "Okay, fine, Linus. I'll try to make it and thanks for asking me."

"Well, I'm looking forward to seeing you again."

"Same here," P.S. said. "So long."

P.S. hung up the telephone. *Linus Hendricks . . . Linus Hendricks . . . There was Mabrey, of course, the head monitor . . . Hendricks! The President of the Honor Committee . . . a nice guy . . . Why the hell shouldn't I go to a party!*

He arrived a little after ten. It was one of the small houses on Georgetown University's land, and had a garden at the back, two stories, and thin walls shared with the houses on either side.

He walked up to the door and considered pressing the bell. But he could hear the sounds of the party going on and he tried the door, it wasn't locked, so he walked in. He was standing in a small hallway, on his left was a kitchen and directly in front of him was a screen which closed off the living room slightly. He moved forward to the screen and could see into the living room. The people inside were of mixed ages—the twenty to thirty-five bracket—and P.S. stood there, half-hidden behind the screen, trying to see if there was anyone he knew. From the noise he could tell that most of the people had been at the party for quite some time. There wasn't anyone that he recognized. There were obviously others around, though. He stepped into the living room, trying to avoid kicking over drinks which were standing on the rug. He excused himself as he pushed people aside, but it didn't seem to bother them.

"Excuse, please. Coming through," P.S. said. He squeezed past a young man who was saying, "No, that's not right! So, look God damn it a minute, will ya? John F. Kennedy doesn't—God damn it, will you listen to me a minute?"

There's someone who looks familiar, what's his name? He was in Yale . . . Fence Club, friend of Charlie's, what the hell was his name? . . . If he turns this way . . . No, damn! It isn't. You'd think out of this many there'd be at least one person . . . The garden, on through to the garden . . . "Excuse me, please?" *Move it, will you? That's a good fellah. . . . My God, there's a pretty girl, wonder who she is . . . I wonder if I'm overdressed for this thing . . . Well, a suit's a suit . . . Got to get some clothes now that I'm out . . . There's a girl I know . . .* "Excuse me, please? Coming through." *She used to date Wally Wallace, what was her name? Went to Smith . . . something like Beebe, BeeGee, BeeJay, God the number of girls called "B.J." . . . Didi! Didi! That's what her name is. Didi Williams. Used to sleep with Wally . . .*

He made his way over to the girl. She was talking to a young man whom P.S. didn't know. He hoped she would ask him to join them. The girl smiled at him and P.S. smiled back.

"Hello, Didi," he said, "it's so nice to see you again. I'm P. S. Wilkinson, do you remember? It's been a long time."

"Why, yes, P.S. How nice to see you," she said. "P.S., have you met my fiancé?"

"No, I don't believe I have," P.S. said. "How are you? I'm P. S. Wilkinson." *Zip—scratch Didi!*

"Ron Baker," the young man said, shaking P.S.'s hand. "Nice to meet you."

"Nice to meet you," P.S. said.

"Well, how have you been?" Didi asked.

"Pretty good. And you?"

Didi looped her arm through her fiancé's and smiled up at him. "Just fine," she said.

"It is certainly nice to see you both," P.S. said. "When are the two of you getting married?"

"We're not certain yet," the young man said.

"Probably not until next Christmas," Didi said.

"Well, that's great," P.S. said. He nodded to them both. "I hope we will see each other again before then. Will you excuse me, please?"

What the hell, P.S. thought as he made his way out to the garden. *They're probably just right for each other. Jesus, everybody's getting married!* He couldn't find Linus Hendricks in the garden either. All he saw were more couples. There was an empty chair, though—one of those canvas, collapsible director's chairs, —and he made his way over to it and sat down. From the chair he had a surrealistic view of shoulders and rear ends and he decided that the party might become less unreal if he got himself a drink. So he stood up and pushed his way back into the living room. The young man was still standing near the entrance saying, "Hey, no, so look God damn it a minute, will ya? The whole thing is— Look, will ya listen a minute?"

P.S. fixed himself a mild bourbon and water and edged back so that he could lean against the wall. Opposite him was a couch on which a young man with red hair was seated, his head back against the wall, his eyes closed. Sitting on the floor, her legs tucked under her as though she had been kneeling then slipped to one side, was a pretty young girl with very blonde hair, carelessly worn, who was looking down at the rug. Her left arm was resting on the redhead's thigh. P.S. looked at the girl and tried not to listen to the man blocking the doorway who was saying, "Look, God damn it a minute. The point is not whether or not Mitchell and Martin were fairies"—he pronounced it fay-rees—"but what made them feel they had to leave the country in the first place. Am I right?" P.S. looked at the girl's arm. The hairs on her arm were blonde, very light and sun-bleached like her eyebrows. Her hand was pale, nails polished a silver blue. Her arm lay on the redheaded man's thigh as though it were a napkin. She shifted her position slightly and her dress rode up, exposing the tops of her stockings, and she caught P.S. looking at her. Instead of moving immediately, she inhaled on her cigarette and dropped it into a half-filled whisky glass, then she adjusted her dress. She plucked a shred of tobacco from the tip of her tongue and squeezed it like a small brown worm between her long silver-blue fingernails. She looked at the piece of tobacco, wiggled it, then looked up at P.S., and smiled.

Now, something like that little piece would be nice . . . And her red friend doesn't look as though he'd be of much use. . . . P.S. smiled back at her. *Should I go over? Get her a fresh drink.* He pushed himself away from the wall and walked over to her.

"I'm P. S. Wilkinson."

"Hello, P. S. Wilkinson."

Oh, for Christ's sake. One of those! "Can I get you something to drink?"

"Sure," she said.

"Well, then, what would you like to drink?"

"What are you drinking?"

"A weak bourbon and water."

"That's fine," she said.

P.S. started back to the bar and she said, "P. S. Wilkinson?" and he stopped and said, "Yes?"

"I'll drink from yours."

"I'll get you one of your own," he said. *The one in the room I pick and she's probably a writer for* Teen-Times. . . . *My God, I wonder who writes her material?* "Hello, P. S. Wilkinson," *for Chrissake. . . .* He mixed her drink. Then he remembered dancing with Hilary. Hilary had called him "P. S. Wilkinson." He carried the drink back to her. "Here you are."

"Thank you."

"What happened to your friend?"

"Him?" she asked. "He's passed out. He had too much to drink."

"Really?"

"Yes," she said. She shifted the drink from her left hand to her right hand and wiped her left hand on the redheaded man's trouser leg. She looked back down at the rug and began whistling.

P.S. sat down on the rug near her and put his drink where

it wouldn't be kicked over. "Are you from Washington?" he asked. *What school do you go to?*

"Yes. I work at I.B.M."

"Ah," P.S. said. He offered her a cigarette and took one for himself, then lit them both.

"Did you ever see *Snows of Kilimanjaro?*"

"The movie?" P.S. asked. "Gregory Peck? Yes, I think so."

"Well, do you remember how Gregory Peck and Ava Gardner lit their cigarettes? Kind of leaning together, both lighting their cigarettes from the same match at the same time?"

"I'm not sure I remember that."

"It was very sexy," the girl said.

"Yes," P.S. said. "Then, well, I'm sorry I didn't light ours the same way." He added, "I felt as though I should say that. Actually, if I tried I'd probably set fire to the two of us. I'm not very good at that sort of thing."

"Well, it probably takes practice," the girl said. "Practice makes perfect."

"That reminds me of an old two-line college joke about the girl who says she's perfect. The young man said, 'I'm practice.'"

"What?"

"The girl said that she was pra—the girl said she was perfect and the young man said he was practice . . . Practice makes perfect?"

"Oh," the girl said.

"Well, I never said it would be funny. All I said was that it was an old two-line—forget it."

"Do you think Bill is going to come to?"

"You mean wake up? . . . Eventually. He'll come out of it eventually."

"I'm hungry."

"There's some cheese and crackers by the bar."

"I'm more hungry than that," she said. She took her arm down from the redheaded man's leg and yawned. "God, this party's a bore."

"Do you know many of the people?"

"A few. Not many."

"I don't know anybody," P.S. said.

"Then why don't we get out of here and get some dinner?"

"You mean you want me to take you out to dinner?" P.S. asked. "I don't have much money."

"Neither do I. We'll find some place cheap."

We'll find some place cheap . . . First she decides we'll go out to dinner and now she's deciding how much we'll spend.

P.S. helped her up. He looked around the room once for Linus Hendricks. "I haven't see the host anywhere."

"He's around somewhere," the girl said. "But don't worry. If you really feel you should thank him, call him tomorrow."

"Well, I should try to see him." *God damn it, is everybody making my plans for me these days?*

"No, come on, let's get out of here."

P.S. looked at the girl for a moment. "What's your name?"

"Sandy Frommer."

"Well, listen, Sandy Frommer—to use one of your own gimmicks—if I'm to take you to dinner, allow me at least to show some initiative. Okay?"

"Sure. You're cute when you're mad."

"Oh, for Chrissake!" Wilkinson exploded. "Who *does* write your material?"

"What do you mean?"

"Nothing, let's get out of here."

"That's what I've been saying." She laughed.

P. S. Wilkinson took the girl to a small restaurant on Wisconsin Avenue which served good roast beef and good beer and did it inexpensively. And because it was late, the waiters hurried them through dinner, so they decided not to sit around over coffee.

"You want some coffee at my place?" the girl asked.

"Sure. What time is it?"

"About eleven-something," she said. "I don't live too far from here. Across Wisconsin to 31st Street. We can have coffee there."

"Sure," P.S. said. "I could use some. I promise not to stay long."

"Stay as long as you want," the girl said. "My roommate won't be back until next week. We've got to be quiet, though. The landlady started bitching last week that we were too noisy."

"All right," P.S. said.

The girl slipped her hand between his chest and his arm and curled her fingers over his forearm. He looked down at her hand and pressed her arm against him. *What the hell . . .* he thought to himself. *Why not?*

"Do you like working for the government?" the girl asked him.

"I don't work for the government," he said. "I might work for them, but I don't work for them yet."

"I wouldn't work for the government if they paid me," she said.

"They'd kind of have to, wouldn't they?"

"What?"

"You said, 'I wouldn't work for the government if they paid me.' That's something called 'slip talk' . . . it's a mixed-up sentence. Like, for example, 'everyone in the whole room was there.' Follow?"

She said, "I guess I'm just tired."

"Listen, I'll just walk you to your door . . . I'm kind of tired too. I don't think I'll have any coffee. I'll just walk you home."

"What's the matter?"

"Nothing. I'm just too tired to keep up my end of this conversation."

"Well, don't feel you have to," she said. "We can just walk in silence."

"Okay."

"Shh."

They turned down a quiet street, her hand still resting on his arm. It was cool now in the evening and P.S. walked along the curb. He stopped suddenly and swore. The girl giggled slightly as he rubbed his shoe against the curb. Then he found a patch of grass and ran his shoe back and forth. "I hope I got it off."

"Scuff your foot as we walk. You shouldn't have walked so close to the curb."

"Well, how would I know some dog—"

"You should have known."

"What street are we on?" P.S. asked.

"Thirty-first. There's the post office. Now do you know where you are?"

"Oh, sure."

"And this is where I live."

"The Hamilton Arms? Good God, I didn't know *any*body lived here."

"Why?"

"I don't know. It just seems like sort of a home for apprentice beatniks."

She led him through the courtyard and around some corners, then up the outside stairs to a small balcony. "*Voilà!*" She opened the door to her apartment, flicked the light switch and let him in.

P.S. stood looking at the apartment for a moment. All the lights had red bulbs. "Good God."

"Kind of crazy, isn't it?"

"Well, I suppose it's great if you're a night fighter pilot. I should think it would drive you buggy."

"No." She giggled. "I like it. A lot of my friends think I'm sort of a nut, but I like living this way. I think it expresses my personality, don't you? I mean, don't you think it's important that a person live in a place that expresses their personality?"

P.S. walked across the room to look at her paintings. On one wall was a canvas painted entirely white except for the bottom right-hand corner. Although the red light in the room made it difficult to be sure, the colors in that corner seemed to be mostly violent shades of red, orange, yellow, and green.

"Do you like it?"

"This painting? I'm not sure what it means."

"It's called 'Subconscious' . . . it represents all the tensions beneath the surface."

"Well . . ."

"You don't have to like it," she said. "I'm going to get things going, so why don't you make yourself at home. Is instant coffee okay?"

"Fine," he said. P.S. walked toward a chair—one of those canvas and metal batwing chairs.

"There's a more comfortable chair over th—oops!" She

hurried over to the couch and picked up a brassiere and a slip and stuffed them under a pillow. "I wasn't exactly expecting company," she explained.

P.S. sat down in the chair. On the floor was a beige hooked wool rug. The tables were not-quite Danish moderns, and with the exception of the abstract he had looked at earlier, the paintings were fairly common reproductions. There was the standard Toulouse-Lautrec poster reproduction ("May Belfort"), the Picasso blue picture of the family on the beach. There were a few unframed reproductions tacked to the walls. Beneath the Picasso was a stereophonograph. He got up from the batwing chair and sat down on the couch. He heard the toilet flush, then Sandy walked into the room.

"You want to listen to some music?"

"Sure."

"What do you like?"

"Anything that isn't rock and roll."

"Jazz?"

"Most of it."

"How about some Miles Davis? Or Brubeck?"

"I don't much like Brubeck," he said. "Listen, do you have any Charlie Byrd? Not 'The Bird' Parker, but the guitar player? I used to listen to him in Korea. They had a program from the Showboat Lounge."

"Sure."

P.S. stood up and walked over to the phonograph with her. She leaned over and began to sort through the records, and he stood behind her looking at her. He placed his hands on her hips and she stood up, holding his hands away from her, and looked at him. He bent forward to kiss her and she ducked, saying, "No funny stuff, now."

It was one of those phrases which made him feel physically sick. *"No funny stuff"* . . . *funny stuff!*

"No funny stuff," he said. He stood back from her and she leaned over again and looked through the records. P.S. went back to the couch and sat down. The red lights in the apartment seemed to intensify the insanity of the day. The coolness of the earlier part of the evening was gone now and in its place was the increasing stuffiness of the impending thunderstorm. The girl placed the record on the spindle and waited for the phonograph to warm up. Then she let the record drop into place and sat down next to P.S. She picked up his hand and held it in her own, looking at his palm, then turned it over and traced the veins which covered the back of his hand.

"You've got nice hands," she said.

"Thank you."

"No, I mean it. You ought to be a surgeon or a musician or something."

"It's a little late to get started on it."

"It's *never* too late."

"Really?" he asked. He turned on the couch to face her and his knee touched her thigh and she did not move away.

"It was a silly thing for me to say. The coffee water's going to boil in a minute, in fact I think it's boiling now." She got up and walked around the corner to the kitchenette and P.S. could hear her spooning the instant coffee into two cups. "You want sugar and milk?"

"Yes, please."

A few moments later she returned carrying two cups of coffee. The cups and saucers were the same white Woolworth's china that Charlie had in the apartment. He took a sip and said, "This is good."

"Glad you like it."

They sat together in silence on the couch for a few minutes, then P.S. said, "Whew, it's hot. I hope the storm breaks soon."

"I've got a fan," she said, getting up. "The fan will cool us off." She turned on a fan, one of the swivel kind, and sat back down on the couch.

"This is very nice," P.S. said, as the fan began to blow the cooler air across them.

"Thank you."

"This has been a funny day . . . Well, not *funny* . . . It was probably perfectly normal. But it's been so strange in a way. I guess I've been out of the country too long. It just hasn't seemed

very real. Oh, blah-blah-blah," he said. "I'm just making talk
and I don't have anything to say. You talk, Sandy, I feel like
listening. Tell me about yourself."

"Like what?"

"Personal things. Tell me personal things about yourself. We're
at the best stage right now to tell each other personal things. It's
late at night, the fan's cooling us off . . . coffee . . . music . . ."
He stretched out his legs so that only the base of his spine and
the back of his neck touched the couch. "And if we get too personal then we just won't see each other again. But, I think it's
good to tell people personal things. It sets them in the proper
perspective. . . . You want me to tell you a personal thing?"

"I'm not sure."

"Oh, for God's sake." P.S. laughed. "I'm not going to talk to
you about—don't be— Listen, let me tell you something, Sandy.
How old are you, twenty?"

"Nineteen."

"Nineteen, okay, I'm five years older than you. Which doesn't
necessarily mean anything except that I've been around five more
years— Anyway, listen. With people, a lot of people you know—
I mean really know—you can never talk to them. Or if you do,
the only things you tell them are exactly what you want them to
hear, and you only tell them the good things—the things which
you think will make them appreciate you or think how great you
are. I can't stand all that old blah-blah-blah. The weather. Problems with the boss. What baby said. All that crap. I keep thinking
that my brain, that soggy gray thing inside my skull, it's been all
sort of tamped down like a baseball diamond by a lot of crap.
I mean there's about an inch and a half of air space there now
at the top which used to be good live brain cells, but it's been
all beaten down by crap. People telling me about the weather.
. . . They say the brain never forgets. It stores everything. Jesus,
I bet forty percent of my brain cells, the memory cells, have been
used up storing worthless bits of knowledge like, 'Nine July
1947, Boy it's hot today. Place sure needs rain,' things like that.
. . . Do you pray?"

"Yes."

"So do I. So there. There's something personal. We could have gone months and months without knowing that about each other. Think of all the married couples who don't know if their other half says prayers before going to sleep. See what I mean? We know that much about each other already."

"But everybody prays."

"Maybe so, but not everybody admits it. Listen, Sandy, are you sure you feel like talking?"

"Yes, but what about you? I thought you were very tired."

"I was, but the coffee's picked me up. I feel fine. But you have to go to work so mayb—"

"No, I don't."

"I thought you said you worked for I.B.M."

"I did, but I got fired."

"Fired? How come?"

"Well, I just didn't like the job and I kept coming in later and later. So they gave me a two weeks' notice, this morning."

"Ah, that's a shame. That's too bad—except, you didn't like the job, so you said. What are you going to do now?"

"I don't know. Maybe nothing."

"Well, then we can sit here and talk."

"Fine," she said. "Why don't you take off your coat? I think I'm going to get into something else."

P.S. laughed. "Aren't I supposed to suggest you do something like that? Doesn't the evil old man always say, 'Hey, baby, why don't you slip into something more comfortable?' "

"No, the girl's supposed to say that. And then the man's supposed to worry that the girl meant she was going to slip into a pair of slacks instead of a negligee."

"Well, which one do you mean?"

"Which one do you think I mean?"

"Ahh, you're a very lovely girl. I like blonde hair, particularly long blonde hair like yours. And I like your eyes, they're a good blue. But I'm not wild about silver fingernails, though I prefer that color to orange . . . Probably slacks."

"What do you mean 'probably slacks'?" She laughed. "After a snow job like that what makes you think I won't slip into something black and sexy?"

"Like an underwater rubber swim suit? . . . Do you own anything black and sexy?"

"I've got a set of leotards." She smiled. "And a pair of black slacks."

"But not a negligee?"

"I have a blue negligee. But it's a shorty . . . it only comes up to—I mean *down* to here." She traced a line with her fingertips across the tops of her thighs.

"Well, if the choice were mine, I'd say wear the negligee—but that's because I've had the feeling lately that I must be some sort of a sex fiend."

She looked worried for a moment. "You aren't, are you?"

He saw that she was serious and he laughed and said, "Good God, no!"

"Well," she said, "a girl's got to be careful."

"I'm sure she does," P.S. said, and he finished his coffee.

"Would you like some more?"

"Do you have any beer?"

"In the icebox. Help yourself."

"I'll tell you what I really need is a bathroom."

"Right in front of you as you go out to the kitchen."

"Are you—where are you going to change?"

"In here."

"Okay. I'll get myself a beer and hide in the bathroom until you're ready. Call me when you're ready."

"I will," Sandy said.

P.S. got himself a beer and then he went into the bathroom. He looked at his teeth in the mirror, saw that he had a small piece of roast beef stuck between two teeth and tried to pry it out with his fingernail. That didn't work, so he tried sloshing some beer around in his mouth. He finally worked the scrap loose and finished up in the bathroom. He leaned against the wall waiting for her, but there wasn't much room, so he put the lid down on the toilet and sat. From where he was sitting he could see just the top of his head in the medicine cabinet mirror. His forehead was mirrored in the chrome stripping around the cabinet. And he moved his head up and down watching the distortion in the rounded chrome which caused his forehead to bulge. He took a sip of beer and placed the glass on the sink. He looked down at his feet and his glance caught the keyhole in the bathroom door. He looked at the keyhole for a moment, wondering what he could see if he looked through it, and he was suddenly struck by the thought that he could create a new saying to go along with "The grass is always greener on the other side of the fence." It would have to do with the fact that the view is always better on the other side of the keyhole. *The view is always better on the other side of the keyhole? . . . The other side of the keyhole has the better view? . . . No one likes the view on their side of the keyhole? . . . Looking at life through a rose-colored keyhole . . . How's that for the name of a book?* "Life Through a Rose-Colored Keyhole!" . . . P.S. suddenly remembered reading somewhere about Victorian women who stuck long hatpins through keyholes when they were staying at hotels. He sat there looking at the keyhole. *And then there was the one about the beatnik who had his keyhole fitted with dark glasses . . . Hey, hey, P.S., that's pretty good. Maybe you should write gags for—*

"I'm ready," Sandy called.

"Okay," he answered. As he opened the bathroom door he thought about telling Sandy his ideas about keyholes and then thought if he did she would immediately think he had been watching her through the keyhole and decided against it. He crossed through the kitchenette and into the living room. She was sitting on the couch and was wearing shorts and a sleeveless blouse.

"A bitter disappointment," he said. "For sure I thought you'd be lounging in your scanty panties."

"In my *what?*"

"Scanty panties," P.S. repeated. "Aren't they the things that are always being advertised in the backs of men's magazines? Scanty panties and peekaboo bras."

"Well, to be honest with you, I wasn't *about* to put on a negligee."

P.S. said, "How about some more music?"

"Okay," the girl said. She got up and walked over to the phonograph. She put on some records, started the first one playing, and then walked back to the couch.

"You know," P.S. said, "my brother says that he can tell by the way a girl walks whether or not she's a virgin."

She sat down hurriedly.

"Do you think that's possible?" P.S. asked.

"How's your beer doing?"

P.S. looked at her. *Oh, God, I'm boring the ass off her.* "My beer's fine," he said. *Try once more . . . Just once more . . . And, for God's sake, make it mean something.* "Sandy, I can't seem to be able to—I haven't been able to talk to many people since I got back. Really talk, and—"

"You mean communicate? But we are communicating. Anyway it's such an awful word."

"Yes, yes, it is. Just as awful a word as saying it's an awful word. Look, will you do me a favor? I mean it's not anything you'll have to get up to do, it's just something I have a feeling that you might be the type of girl who does it—these things. First of all, never draw faces on letters. Never draw little smiling faces on letters. I don't know why girls do that. It makes me sick. Next, while on the subject of letters, if you're going to dot your 'i's,' dot them, don't put little circles above them, *dot* them for Chrissake or leave them alone. And don't for God's sake write poetry about lonely children on beaches, or a happy little girl on a calliope . . . Is she happy? I mean, what the hell, we think she's having fun because we're all ready to believe that calliope ride means more to her than anything else in the world. Actually she's probably worried about some kid party she has to go to, and she's eleven years old and her mother's making her wear a training bra and twelve-year-old Morris Edelman is going to try to touch her between her legs—that's what she's worried about, not whether or not she's going to catch a brass ring."

"It's—"

"What?"

"Nothing," she said. "It's not a calliope. It's a merry-go-round." She turned his wrist over and looked at his watch.

"All right," P.S. said. "I'll go."

"I didn't mean for you to leave," she said. "I was just noticing it's almost two o'clock."

"I guess I was just talking to you and trying to make things mean something to me." He stood up and took another sip of his beer, then drained it, and put the glass back down on the table. "Look, you yourself said that you were fired, or quit your job because it didn't mean anything to you. What, what does mean something to you?"

"What do you mean? Do you mean what do I want to do?" she asked, then said, "Well, I want to get married, and I want to have children."

"All right, I suppose that's fair enough. What do you want your husband to do?"

"I don't care. I don't care what he does."

"You wouldn't care no matter what he did?"

"I don't want him to be a crook . . ."

"What if he went into the government? I mean not the Foreign Service or CIA or something, but went into politics. Would you want your husband to be a politician?"

"That would be nice."

"Would you respect him if he were a congressman?"

"Of course I would. I'd respect my husband no matter what he did."

"Well, then, do you think other people would be impressed if he were a congressman?"

"Sure they would."

"Really? Would you be impressed if you met a congressman?"

"Probably."

"You don't think that congressmen aren't sort of—you don't think they have sort of a reputation for being ambitious and conceited and interested in themselves and money more than in the people they represent?"

"Of course they aren't. Not all of them."

"Why should politicians be such awful people? Who makes them become awful people? Or is it that only the awful people want to become politicians. And *Presidents!* When I think of the type of Presidents we've had—well, Roosevelt did do a lot. And Truman turned out a lot better than anybody thought, but still— maybe this is silly—but I know damn well he wouldn't have been invited to dinner at my grandfather's house, President or not.

And Eisenhower? How in God's name did that man ever get to be elected President? Well, maybe Stevenson wasn't much of an alternative. He wasn't a war hero, he didn't have a particularly fetching smile, but at least he had *brains!* But Eisenhower, Jesus! And all his 'I wouldn't know about that' and 'I haven't checked these figures . . .' I once was looking at the transcript of one of Eisenhower's press conferences, and he started out his answers with 'well' something like seventeen out of twenty-four times . . . Well . . ."

"What do you think of Kennedy and Nixon?"

"I haven't been here enough to know that much about them. I guess I hope Kennedy wins. . . . My God, he's got everything going for him. He looks good on television, he's handsome, good rich family, and he can always buy votes if he needs them."

"Why are you so cynical?"

"Cynical, Sandy? Jesus, I'm not cynical. I'm an optimist, I pray to God things get better. There's nothing in the world I'd rather see than a government I can respect for this country. Hell, I love this country. I just don't happen to be wild about the people who run it." He paused, then added, "And speaking of running, I guess it's time for me to run along home. Thank you very much, Sandy, I'm sorry I stayed so long." He stood up.

"Not at all," she said, rising from the couch. "I'm glad you did."

He was a little disappointed she didn't ask him to stay. "You're very lovely, and very nice, and I had a very good time."

"So did I," she said.

"Well, I think you're being kind." He walked to the door and she opened it for him and held it.

"Thank you again, Sandy. For the beer, the coffee. Maybe I can repay you soon."

"No need to. I'm glad you rescued me from the party."

"You rescued me," he said. "Anyway, tomorrow I'll probably have changed my mind about everything I've said, and I'll regret it terribly."

"Well, I won't draw faces on my letters any more."

"Okay," he said. P.S. leaned forward and kissed her lightly on the cheek. "Good night, Sandy."

"Good night."

P.S. found his way out of the Hamilton Arms and began walking up 31st toward Q Street. He pictured Sandy getting undressed and going to bed and he wondered whether or not he'd call her again. He was already beginning to feel a little bit embarrassed by his pretentiousness, his pompousness during the evening, telling her not to draw faces on letters. *She had seemed nice enough. And God knows it was better than sitting around an empty apartment all night. . . . Pretty little girl . . . Nice figure, not very bright, but what the hell? . . . What was her name? Frommer? . . . Probably not in the phone book.* He reached for his cigarettes and suddenly noticed he had forgotten his coat. *Oh, for God's sake! I left it at Sandy's!* There was a slight flicker of lightning and a rumble of thunder and the wind began picking up. He hurried down 31st Street. *Stupid jerk, forgetting your coat—your coat! My God, how can I forget something as big as a coat? . . . Maybe Sandy hung it on the door for me . . . No, she probably heard the thunder. She knows it'll probably rain, so she wouldn't put it outside . . . Maybe she doesn't know I forgot it. But she must have noticed it, it was on the chair by the couch. She would have had to move the chair to open up the couch into a bed. A bed . . . maybe she's in bed. In that negligee . . . Maybe she knew I'd left the coat behind and didn't say anything so I'd come back for it . . . Maybe she thinks I really am a sex fiend and I left it behind deliberately . . . My God, she probably does, the coat's so goddam big. Only a sex fiend could forget a coat that big! . . . She's there waiting for me. In that negligee . . .* "Hi, Sandy, I forgot my coat, pretty stupid of me," *and she would be kind of sitting up on one elbow in that negligee and she'd know I'm not so fiendish and she'd say something like,* "Hi, I'm glad you came back . . ." *and then because it will be raining she'll say,* "You can't go back out in the rain . . ." *and I'll look miserable, but game . . . I'd say something like,* "I don't mind the rain . . ." *and she'll say,* "I can't let you go out on a night like this . . . maybe you'd better stay here," *and then she'll move over in the day bed and . . .* "Gang busters!" he said to himself. He reached the entrance of the Hamilton

Arms just as the first drops of rain began to fall and threaded
his way through the narrow alley until he came to the outside
stairs leading up to her apartment. Just as he reached the stairs
P.S. saw her door open, a quick flash of red light, and a man
entered her apartment, the door swinging shut behind him. *What
the hell?* P.S. thought. He tiptoed up the stairs and heard Sandy's
voice saying, "I thought you'd never get here!" Then there was
silence and the man said, "Why did you wait so long before you
called?"

"I had a visitor," Sandy said and P.S. stood there on the top
stair, frozen, listening.

"Who?"

"A boy named Wilkinson."

A boy?

"Well, so what? Let's—"

"No, wait, listen," Sandy was saying. "You've got to hear this.
He was a real nut. Listen, let me tell you what he said . . ."

"Can't it wait until morning?"

"No, this is too good. The first thing he asked me was if I
prayed."

Oh, God . . .

"Is there any beer left?" the man asked.

"Sure, in the icebox."

P.S. could hear the icebox door open and then the sound of a
can of beer being pierced. It began to rain, large drops splashed
on the wooden steps leading up to the girl's apartment. P.S. sat
down on the top step and hunched up his shoulders and rested
his elbows on his knees.

"And then, Bill, he asked me—he practically came right out
and asked me if I was a virgin."

"What did you tell him?" the man asked.

"Well, he didn't really ask me. He said that he could tell by the
way a woman walked whether or not she was a virgin and then,
and then, now listen to this, this'll kill you. He—" She started
to laugh. "He told me to dot my 'i's'?"

"Your eyes?"

"In letters when I write letters he said I shouldn't put circles over the 'i's' I should dot them . . . and, and he said—" she was laughing harder now—"he said I shouldn't draw faces on letters."

"Draw what?"

"*Faces* . . . you know, pictures."

"Oh, for Chrissake." There was a pause and the man asked, "How old was he?"

"Twenty-four . . . he said he was twenty-four."

"Where'd you find him?"

"At that party. He took me to dinner after you passed out."

"I didn't pass out. I fell asleep. I was tired."

"Oh, come on, Billy . . ."

"I *did*. I fell asleep. You know how little I slept last night . . ."

The girl laughed again and P.S. sat on the top step, the rain soaking his shirt, his hair wet and flattened on his head, his hands covering his face.

"Hey," the man's voice said, "this his coat?"

"He forgot it. He'll come back for it. That means I have to see him again."

"Throw it out."

"I *can't* do that! . . . Oh, and, hey, listen to what else he said. He said that—he had a real *thing* about congressmen . . . He said all congressmen were crooks and only interested in themselves and—"

"Shit," the man said.

"And he asked me about the meaning of life. He wanted to know the meaning of life."

I did not! P.S. thought. *I asked you what meant anything to you . . .*

"Jesus, will you listen to that rain!" the man said.

"I hope it rains all night. I love to sleep in the rain . . . Hey, I got a new record today. You want to hear it?"

"What are you going to do about his coat? It's got his wallet in it and papers."

"Leave it, he can get it when he comes by in the morning."

"In the *morning!*" the man protested. "He'd better not come by too early!"

"Well, he needs his wallet, doesn't he?"

"Did he say how early he's coming by in the morning?"

"No, of course not, he didn't know he'd forgotten his coat, silly. But I'm sure it'll be in the morning. . . . He seemed so lonely."

The music started playing again and, even if he had wanted to, P.S. could no longer have heard what they were saying. He got up from the top step and walked down, then back through the alley and out onto the sidewalk. Because he was soaking wet already he knew there wasn't any point in hurrying back to the apartment—in hurrying back home.

15

THE TUESDAY MORNING MAIL contained a letter from the CIA (with the letterhead folded down so that the print would not be legible through the envelope), telling him to report to Building 4133, Room 117A, at 0930 hrs, Wednesday, 29 June 1960.

There was also a postcard from his father saying, "Welcome home, chum! Must clear up few items then will return Philadelphia July 1. See you then?"

P. S. Wilkinson carried the mail back up to his apartment. He sat down at his desk and could still smell the bacon he had cooked for breakfast two hours earlier. He reread the letter from the CIA, smiling slightly at the elaborate security precaution of a special fold in the letter, and wondered why they bothered to use a letterhead at all if they didn't want anybody to see it.

He telephoned Sandy Frommer and arranged to pick up his coat. She was very cheery on the telephone and so sorry that she would not be able to see him when he came by, but she would leave the door open and his jacket was on one of the batwing chairs next to the couch. P.S. thanked her and hung up, grateful that he would not have to see her again. *Did I spend all that time in Korea to come back to this?* He leaned forward against the desk, the drawer pressing against his diaphragm as he stared down at the blotter. *Why did I even go out to dinner with her?*

206

Because I hoped it might be fun, because she was an alternative, because when she was at the party I could see her thigh above the stocking . . . He remembered coming up behind her at her apartment. He remembered putting his hands on her hips and her turning around and saying, "No funny stuff," and he was embarrassed all over again. *Jesus, what is going to become of me? What did I even bother to come back for if I can't do any better for myself than this? Than a Sandy Frommer with silver-blue fingernails and red bulbs in her apartment.* . . . *Is this all the goddam "fun" I've been looking forward to? Is this the sort of stupid goddam thing I'm going to be doing for the rest of my life? Running after little half-assed Sandy Frommers?* And he knew the rage he felt for Sandy Frommer was no more than a cover-up for the fury he felt for himself. But there wasn't anything he could do. He could continue to see Hilary, but for what? To what end? *My God, I didn't spend all that time in Korea just to come back and get married either!* He decided to window-shop down Wisconsin Avenue, then go to Sandy's apartment, pick up his coat, and come back. He wanted to be certain to miss her.

After P.S. had picked up his jacket he took a bus into the center of Washington and walked around downtown until he got tired and took a taxi to the Smithsonian. He looked at all the old airplanes again, and at the little boys looking at the airplanes, and they depressed him; so he crossed to the National Gallery and looked at the young girls looking at the paintings. He had always heard that a museum was the place to find pretty girls, but all the pretty girls really were looking at the paintings, and were not looking for anything else, and he didn't know how to start up a conversation with any of them, and didn't really want to start up a conversation with any of them, and so he left the museum and returned to his apartment. He lay back in the bathtub, then slid down as far as he could, bracing his legs against the far wall so that he could let the water lap against his chin. It reminded him of the tubs in Korea and Lieutenant Pratt. *At least Pratt had something real to come home to. He had his wife and the daughter. He had a home. . . .* And he remembered being jealous of Pratt and thinking how marriage must be so pleasant. Pratt had asked P.S. why he didn't get married, and P.S. had laughed and said there was plenty of time and that he wanted to have fun. *But what the hell kind of fun am I having? . . . What am I going to do with all that time? Maybe Hilary's right. Maybe she should get a divorce and we would get married. . . . But what about Hester? . . . It's that damn child; if it weren't for that baby then it wouldn't be so bad. . . . What could I possibly do with a child? . . . Yet, if it weren't for Hilary then I'd really be alone. . . .* P.S. wished he could see his brother. He wished he could call up his brother in Hawaii, but he didn't know where to find him. And there was his sister, but she was married and had children and knew what she wanted to do. *And Charlie Merritt's married now,* and P.S. knew that the days of running around with Charlie were over. *At least they're over until I get married, and we can be young-marrieds, or whatever they're called, together. . . . Everybody else is gone. Wally'll be back on his destroyer, Gurdey, Nelson, and French are all out of the country. . . . There really isn't anybody around now . . . No real friend . . . There's only Hilary . . . Maybe the only way to get back to—what is it, reality? Meaning? Maybe the only way for me to get out of this mess is to say, "Okay, Hilary, we'll get married" . . . but that child! There must be some other way! . . . And maybe Hilary's changed her mind. . . . She certainly changed her mind yesterday; there we were all ready to make love and zip! she ran away. . . . Well, I ran away the day before. But maybe, maybe she realizes that we have to take it slowly. . . . Maybe if we just don't rush, everything will be all right.* P.S. got out of the bathtub and walked into the bedroom to catch the 6:30 news. He turned on the television and a commercial told him to guard against Pain! Pain! Pain! Monotonous Pain!

After the news and after he had finished dressing he sat down at the desk and looked at the telephone. He got up again, found himself a cigarette, and carried it back to the desk with him. He lit the cigarette, centered the ashtray on the middle of the desk blotter, then dialed Hilary's number. She answered on the third ring.

"Hi, it's Phil. How are you?"

"Fine," she said. Her voice was very low and soft. "Where are you?"

"At the apartment. Look, what I'm calling about is that I feel so stupid about yesterday. I wanted to apologize and—"

"I tried to call you last night. But you weren't there. Where were you?"

"I went to some silly party where I met some awful girl. . . . Hilary? I want to see you. Can't we just take it easy and go out to a movie or something?"

"I can't. I have the baby."

"What about the sitter?"

"It's her night off."

"Oh, damn. . . . There's a Bogart at the Georgetown and I thought it would be nice . . ."

"I'd love to, Phil, but I can't leave Hester."

"We couldn't sort of take her along?"

"She's much too young. Anyway, I swore I'd never take a baby into a movie."

"I really wanted to see you tonight." He rolled the cigarette ash into the ashtray and pushed it around with the tip of his cigarette. Then he rested both elbows on the desk. He was holding the telephone in his right hand, and with his left hand he supported his forehead. He was trying to think what to do.

"You could come over here," she said. "We could watch television."

"Anything good on?"

"Tuesday night? . . .Tuesday night there isn't much. . . . Have you had dinner?"

"I had hoped we might get something before the movie."

"I've already eaten, I ate early with Hester. . . . Why don't you grab yourself a bite and come on over?"

"I feel I've sort of invited myself. I—"

"No, don't be silly."

"Well, that's awfully ni—"

"Oh, for God's sake, hurry, will you! I've missed you."

"Ah, Hilary, that's so nice to hear," he said. "I've missed you, too, so very much. I'll be over as soon as I can."

P.S. hung up the telephone and ran his hand over its arched back, then he sat back at the desk. He looked at his cigarette burning in the ashtray, the smoke rising unperturbed toward the ceiling, then he stubbed it out and walked into the bedroom. He was happy again, and he chose a bright striped tie, and used a gold tie pin to keep his collar in place. He splashed some Old Spice on his cheeks, checked his pockets, patting them to make sure he had his lighter and keys, then he hurried back through the living room, the kitchenette, and out of the apartment.

Twenty minutes later he pushed Hilary's doorbell.

"It's open!"

P.S. walked inside. "Where are you?"

"Kitchen."

He walked through the dining room and into the kitchen. Hilary was heating some coffee and she turned when he came in. "I thought you might like some," she said. He kissed her lightly on the cheek. "Hi."

"Hi." She looked at him with those sad, dark eyes.

"What's the matter?"

"I'm just glad to see you."

"Then why do you look so sad?"

"Sad? Do I?"

"A little."

"I guess I am, a little."

"Why?" he asked.

"Because I love you."

"I love you, too. . . . That doesn't make me sad. It's the only thing that keeps me from hanging myself," he said and tried to smile.

Hilary suddenly looked frightened and she clung to him, squeezing him, burying her head against his shoulder.

"Hey, hey, hey," P.S. said, "we can't go through this all over again."

"I love you," Hilary said. "I love you and it scares me. . . . I tried to call you last night to tell you."

"Can you tell me now?"

"Not here. Not in the kitchen. Let's sit down in the living room."

P.S. sat down on the couch next to her and took a sip of his coffee, then put the cup and the saucer on the coffee table. "What did you want to tell me?"

Hilary took his hand and began squeezing it nervously. "I used to think—when I discovered, no, that isn't the right word . . ." She let go of his hand and started again. "When I finally admitted to myself that I didn't love Bruce, I used to think that it didn't matter. That Bruce and I could stay married and that maybe in time we could grow to love each other the way, I guess the way couples did in arranged marriages. . . . And for Hester it would be all right, she would grow up with both of her parents and be happy—but I don't know any more. Today I was so miserable, I missed you so much that I knew Bruce and I could never—I couldn't be happy knowing that I still loved you, knew that I was still young and couldn't have you. . . . And I know it isn't going to work out with Bruce now," she said. She picked up his hand, then dropped it again. "It's only a matter of time."

P.S. took her hand and squeezed it. "I don't know what to say . . . I wish there was some easy sort of thing I could say, but there isn't." He held her hand, awkwardly pushing his fingers through hers until he noticed that his fingers were resting on her wedding ring. "The whole thing, the whole thing, Hilary, is this thing about time. There's been so little time—"

"We've known each other for how long? How many years? Two years, two and a half years at college and all the time afterwards?"

"It's not only us, Hilary, I'm not only talking about us. It's everything. Everything that has happened since I came home— I don't seem to have any control. Everything's happening in *spite* of me . . . it's all happened so fast that it's—all I can think of is that my trunk hasn't even got back from Korea yet."

"But your job?" she said. "You'll have that job with the CIA."

"Well, I guess if I get the job then a lot of my problems are solved."

"But what about *us*?"

"But, Hilary, we can't just rush right into everything. I mean, we have to be a little realistic. Please, Hilary, please try to under-stand this . . . I've got to have a little time. All I want to do is take it easy for a little longer . . . And yet everybody seems to be pushing and rushing. I'd like to relax."

"You won't be able to," she said.

That was the kind of smug remark which infuriated him. It was as though she knew him so much better than he knew him-self and that she could look down at him from her Olympian perch and guide him through the stages of life. "What makes you think I won't?"

"You just won't. You aren't the type of person who can just sit around and coast."

"What makes you so sure?" he asked, still irritated.

"Because I *know* you," she said. "In the first place, your family wouldn't let you just coast. They, especially your father, would—"

"Oh, for God's sake!"

"Phil, I'm not being mean when I say that. Look, you've always done what your family wanted you to do. I remember you once telling me that someone in your family had been an officer in our Army for every war this country ever fought. Did it ever occur to *you* not to be an officer?"

"Sure, but what would be the point? What was I supposed to be proving, Hilary, what are you getting at?" P.S. had the uneasy feeling that he was being cross-examined. "What is all this about? It's obvious that you aren't just talking about the Army. What is it you're really after?"

"I remember how toward the end of your final year at Yale there was some problem of whether or not you were going to get commissioned because of your eyes. And you had to get a waiver to stay in, right?"

"I'd already spent four goddam years in the ROTC and to have to chuck it all away at the end seemed kind of stupid."

"But what about your eyes? You were disqualified from the service because of your eyes, weren't you? In fact you never had to go into the Army at all."

"So that's what you're driving at."

"You didn't have to volunteer for Korea."

He got up from the couch and strode across the room, then turned and angrily said, "For Christ's sake, Hilary, you're not going to try to tell me that I volunteered for Korea to please my family!"

"You know why you went there as well as I do."

"I know why I went, but I don't know why you think I went."

"You think you went because you wanted to see whether or not the Korean War was worth it. But what was the real reason!"

"The *real* reason! *You* just gave the real reason!"

"Wasn't it because you wanted to run away from your family and me?"

"From *you*! *From you!*" Suddenly P.S. felt himself become entirely detached from the argument. "Hilary . . . Hilary, please don't try to tell me that I went to Korea—that I spent five hundred and forty-seven days in Korea—to escape from you. The reason I went to Korea was—and maybe this doesn't sound very important to you—but the reason I went was because I felt a certain obligation, I felt the Korean War had been my generation's war. And I wanted to see if the thirty-three thousand Americans killed there had died for something worthwhile."

"In other words, you had a good, a *great*—a decent excuse, an *honorable* excuse to run off."

"RUN OFF!" P.S. shouted. "Just what in the hell was I running off from! My God, two weeks after I arrived in Korea you were married."

"Why do you think I got married!" she cried, rising from the couch.

"I don't know!" he said.

She ran from the room and he was left behind. "Hilary . . ." he said. "Hilary?" *You're the only thing I've got left.* P.S. started up the stairs . . . *What can I say to her? What, what in God's name does she expect me to do?* At the top of the stairway P.S. looked to see which bedroom Hilary was in. He found her at the other end of the hall, the bedroom facing on the street. She was lying on her stomach, her face buried in the pillow. All the lights were on in the room.

"Hilary . . ."

She did not answer.

P.S. entered the bedroom and sat down on the side of the bed near her and touched her shoulder. "Hilary . . ." He began to stroke her shoulder absent-mindedly. "Hilary, I'm sorry. . . . Honest, please believe me."

She still did not answer. He leaned over so that his arm rested on the other side of her, his side touching her back. He continued to move his hand across her shoulders. "Hilary, please don't cry." He looked up and away from her and saw that the curtains had not been drawn across the windows and anyone in the houses across Prospect Street could look right into the bedroom. He got up and pulled the curtains. Hilary had rolled over and was watching him. He smiled at her and said, "Do you want a Kleenex?"

Hilary nodded. "There's some on my dresser. And turn off that top light, will you? It's terribly bright."

P.S. picked up the box of tissues, then walked over to the door and turned off the overhead light, then he sat down on the bed next to Hilary and gave her the Kleenex. Hilary pushed herself up and turned her head away to blow her nose. Then she pushed the box aside and, still sitting up in bed, smiled at P.S. "I'm a mess, aren't I?"

"We're both pretty messy," he said. "But I love you."

"Even with my hair all mussed, the mascara running, lipstick all bitten off?"

P.S. picked up another tissue and wiped away the smudged mascara. "You're lovely no matter what."

"Come here," she said. She held out her arms to him and he moved closer to her and held her. They held each other tightly and Hilary said, "Philip?"

"Umm?"

"I'm sorry I was so awful."

"I'm the one who's awful."

"If I'm a bitch it's only because I love you so much." She sank back in the bed so that she was lying flat. "Stretch out next to me. I want to feel you next to me."

They lay down on the bed together, still holding each other tightly.

"Do you want to turn the lights out?" she asked.

"Not all of them." He got up from the bed. As he walked across to turn off one of the lights Hilary got off the bed also. She stood with her back to him and unbuttoned her dress. He watched as she pulled her arms out of the dress and let it drop to the floor. Then, still with her back to him, she reached behind herself and undid the catches of her brassiere, and P.S. had the uncomfortable feeling that again the initiative had been taken away from him, that he never had a chance to decide for himself. She lay down on the bed again wearing her panties and the unhooked brassiere. P.S. undressed down to his underpants and lay down on the bed next to her. There was an unfamiliar warmth and discomfort in his temples, not a blush, nor anger, but a curious uneasiness which he could not explain. He reached out and pulled Hilary against him and touched her bare back with his hand, ran his hand down her back across her buttocks, her hip to her thigh. He heard her sigh, felt her push herself against him, felt her hand on his side, his hip—felt these things as though they were happening not to himself but to someone else in his body. He again saw himself standing apart watching himself.

"You have a nice chest," she said. She moved away from him slightly and ran her hand across his chest. Then she lowered her head and kissed him in the hollow below his collarbone. "That's nice," she said. "I like you there."

He felt himself smiling, and he moved his hand up to touch her cheek and then he kissed her. He pressed his leg between hers and she opened her legs slightly and pushed herself close against him again. He was aware of the fabric of her brassiere against his chest and he ran his hand up her side and held her breast, his fingers brushing across the brassiere. She pushed her shoulders together and he pulled the brassiere away and she quickly pushed herself against him half in embarrassment, half in eagerness to feel his warmth against her. She raised her leg and pinned his thigh between hers and the warmth in his temple became worse. And when, several minutes later, they lay nude, the whole length of their bodies touching, he could feel his hand behind her clutching the sheet tightly, his fingers gnarled and strained squeezing the wrinkled sheet. He felt her hand move down his side to his stomach and he squeezed his eyes shut. *Oh, God . . . God, what's the matter with me?* He felt her touch him and then, in surprise, touch him again, and knew her question even before she asked, "What's the matter with you? Why aren't you . . . ?"

"I don't know," he said, his voice showing his misery. "I don't know. I can't—it won't—I don't know what's the matter . . ." He thought his temples were going to explode, the heat was so intense.

"Oh, God," Hilary said. Her voice was cold and flat. She rolled over onto her back away from him and their bodies no longer touched. He took his arm away from her and lay on his stomach his hands against his face, his fingers pushing against his temples trying to squeeze out the heat, the shame. And his hands became fists, the knuckles pressing into his cheekbones, his teeth clenched so tightly his jaw ached. He did not dare open his eyes to look at her.

There was nothing he could say. He fully understood her frustration, her anger—worse, her own embarrassment and shame. And he didn't know what to say. There was nothing—no way he could explain to her that if he could, if there was some way that he could, he would make love to her. But the other self, the self which had stood apart and watched, was now inside again and in control and would not let him. All he could do was to repeat again those miserable meaningless words, "I'm so sorry."

"Well, I guess we might as well get dressed," she said. He thought she had tried to inject lightness into her tone and had missed. Instead of joviality, her tone had been harsh and cold. He felt her get up from the bed and go to her side of the room. He heard the rustle of clothing as she kicked the brassiere over to her dress. And he, too, got up, unable to face her. *If only she would understand. If only she could know that it was because we were wrong, that we can't—if only my goddam body wouldn't listen to my mind!*

They dressed not looking at each other, he wanting nothing more in the world than for her to come to him and touch him. Hilary finished first and hurried out of the bedroom saying, "I'll fix some more coffee."

"Fine," he said. P.S. sat down on the bed again and put on his socks and shoes, then got up and walked over to the mirror and brushed his hair. When he came back downstairs to the kitchen, Hilary was just pouring the coffee. "I forgot you wanted to see Hester," she said.

"No, that's all right. It's late. I'll just drink this cup of coffee and go."

"Whatever you say."

"Hilary, please, don't be angry . . . It's not—it wasn't your fault. I'm sorry it—it just didn't work out."

"Forget about it," she said. "Really. It's all right. It doesn't matter."

"Jesus, God, I wish it didn't."

They finished their coffees in silence, and then P.S. stood up and said, "I guess I'd better be going."

Hilary carried the cups and saucers over to the sink and stood there with her back to him. "Good-by," she said. "Sleep well."

"I'll call you tomorrow."

"Okay."

16

WEDNESDAY MORNING, the 29th of June, P. S. Wilkinson dejectedly got out of the taxi and walked across the street to Building 4133. He entered the building and walked past two uniformed policemen and up to the desk. There was a dumpy, gray-haired woman sitting there reading a paperback novel and he stood submissively in front of her, patiently waiting for her to look up. Finally she folded over the corner of a page, closed the book and said, "Yes?"

"I'm Philip Sadler Wilkinson. I was told to report to room 117A."

"What is your name?"

"Philip Sadler Wilkinson," he repeated without inflection.

"May I see your identification?"

He opened his wallet and showed her his driver's license. She carefully copied his name down in the space on the chart in front of her, then said, "Room 117A is down the corridor to the right. Third door. Report to the secretary at the desk as you enter."

"Thank you," he answered mechanically, but she had already opened her book and was reading again.

P. S. Wilkinson walked down the corridor and stopped at the entrance to Room 117A. A few people were sitting on the peeling sofas flipping through copies of *Reader's Digest* and *Saturday Evening Post*. He walked up to the desk. This secretary was younger than the other, and instead of reading a paperback book she was doing a crossword puzzle.

"My name is Wilkinson. Philip Sadler Wilkinson. I was told to report here."

"Yes, Mr. Wilkinson, just a minute, please."

He again waited submissively while the young woman checked through a mimeographed sheet of names and then saw her put a mark beside his. She pulled out a small mimeographed card and handed it to him. "Read this carefully," she said. "Then sign."

"Yes, ma'am." P.S. took the card back to the sofa with him and sat down to read it. It was a standard release form stating that the undersigned was willing to submit to a polygraph test the results of which would be kept in the strictest confidence. *A lie detector! Do they give these things to everybody?* He looked at the others seated around the room and wondered if they, too, were waiting to be given lie detector tests. The card further stated that if the undersigned were unwilling to submit to a lie detector test his application would be considered canceled. *Everyone knows that a polygraph is not infallible, that it's not admissible as evidence* . . . P. S. Wilkinson signed the card obediently and handed it back to the secretary.

"Thank you," she said. "Be seated and you will be called when the examiner is ready."

"Thank you," P.S. said. He went back to the sofa and sat down and dejectedly crossed his legs. He looked around the room at the furniture, which appeared to have come out of old military day rooms, the stacks of old magazines, the bored faces of the others waiting to be pried into. He reached into his breast pocket and pulled out a cigarette and lit it.

"I'm sorry, sir. There's no smoking."

P.S. looked vainly for an ashtray. "Where can I put it out?"

"You'll have to take your cigarette out in the hall."

He stood up and walked out of the room and back down the corridor toward the dumpy secretary he had seen when he first entered. She did not look up until he pushed out his cigarette in her ashtray and when she did look up, he was already turning to go back to the room. He sat down again on the sofa, picked at a copy of the *Reader's Digest,* and closed it because he could not think of anything but the horror of the evening with Hilary.

He felt awful, depressed, totally demolished. He felt so ashamed of himself, so embarrassed. He tried to convince himself that the only reason it had happened was because he was tired. But it had never happened to him before and he wondered what it meant. Whether even his body was deserting him, leaving him alone and trapped with his mind. *Why did my mind permit me to go so far with her—far enough to get into bed with her, to get to the point where I could not make love to her? What's the matter with me? Why did it happen? Hilary's so pretty. She has such a marvelous body . . . Couldn't help but want to . . . Weekends at college . . . All those times . . . But this time I couldn't. Her body wasn't the same, she wasn't the same. . . . Oh, God, why? And she asked what was the matter with me. The way she asked it! As though I were a homosexual. A queer. A fairy!*

"Mr. Wilkinson?"

P.S. looked up at the secretary who was sitting behind the desk. "Yes?"

"You can go in now. It's Room 4. Through the door and second room on your right."

"Thank you," he said. He wondered why he had been put ahead of the others, or whether it might not be possible that a couple of them were "plants" put there to watch his reaction, to see if he was nervous. But none of them were even looking at him. *Why not? Isn't it logical that at least one of them would be looking at me? Somebody moves in a room, others usually look up. . . .* He looked at the secretary. She was doing her crossword puzzle again. *No one will look at me. Why?* He walked down the narrow corridor to the second door on the right. There was a small lettered sign on it beneath a red light bulb: BOOTH # 4. POSITIVELY NO ADMITTANCE WHILE BULB IS LIT. P.S. knocked on the door.

"COME IN!" The loudness of the voice startled him. It seemed to have come from overhead and he looked up and saw the small loudspeaker. P.S. opened the door and stepped inside.

"Close the door behind you, please. Make sure it is tightly shut." P.S. closed the door hard and heard the latch click. When he turned back, the first thing he noticed was the polygraph machine. A long, black rectangular box with dials, scopes, pens attached to thin wires, a long roll of graph paper. As though deference had been paid to its importance, the machine took up most of the long side of the reverse L-shaped desk. The shorter leg of the L was covered with papers and on top of the papers P.S. saw a brown manila folder with his name on it.

"Mr. Wilkinson?"

"That's right," P.S. said.

"Good morning. My name is Williams. Have you ever taken a polygraph test before?"

"No, I haven't."

Williams remained seated behind his desk and P.S. detachedly compared Williams' features with his own stock image of the harsh Nazi interrogator. Williams did not match up at all, except perhaps for the lips. Williams' lips were full and a little wet—but not as full and wet as the drooling stock interrogator's should be. Williams was leafing through P.S.'s personal history form. P.S. looked around the small room. It was certainly no more than twelve feet long and eight feet wide. There were no windows. No pictures. No ornaments. The four walls and the ceiling were covered by soundproofing boards. There were two chairs, one occupied by Williams, enclosed on two sides by the reverse L-shaped desk. The other chair, the one in which Wilkinson was to sit, was situated so that Wilkinson's back would be to the machine and the interrogator, and that by stretching slightly his legs could touch the forward wall. There was nothing in the room to distract his attention—except the machine. High up in the back wall, an air conditioner whispered softly. The light in the room was good, not harsh or glaring. Wilkinson looked down at the chair in which he was to sit. The right arm of the chair was worn slightly, reminding him of the chair in which he had been seated while facing the Honor Committee at the Virginia Preparatory School, and he felt his heart begin to race.

"Please sit down, Mr. Wilkinson."

"Thank you." P.S. sat in the chair in front of the desk. It felt a bit awkward to be facing away from the man, and he started to turn the chair, but discovered it was bolted to the floor.

"There will be no smoking," the man said into the back of P.S.'s head. "The nature and general purpose of this test is to determine whether or not the statements you have made on your personal history form are the truth. We use the polygraph, or lie detector machine, to provide the immediate disclosure of facts which under normal circumstances and methods of investigation might take weeks or possibly months. Therefore, the immediate advantage of the lie detector is that it saves time."

Wilkinson nodded.

"Of course the most important object of this test is to penetrate the outer defenses of lies. Many repressed ideas and emotions which the subject might not even be aware of, which he might have succeeded in deceiving his conscious self about, can be discovered by means of the lie detector test. Many people come away from these tests with a new appreciation of themselves, a new understanding of their personalities, for the machine serves to strip away disguises, mental masquerades, deceptions—*self*-deceptions—and the power to deceive. It acts, therefore, as a purgative to the personality, freeing it from all conflicts, repressions, withdrawals, twisted truths, distortions, and leaves the mind clean and free."

"Sort of washes it out?" P.S. said dully.

"We don't brainwash here," Williams said. There was no lightness in his tone. "This machine serves only to determine whether or not the subject is telling the truth about any given matter."

"But it's not infallible," P.S. protested. "Everyone knows that lie detector evidence doesn't stand up in court."

"This is not a court, Mr. Wilkinson. The machine does not gather evidence. It merely documents responses and provides a means of gauging a subject's reaction to certain questions. It is up to the examiners to determine the meaning and significance of the subject's responses. The polygraph records certain bodily changes such as changes in respiration, pulse, blood pressure. The polygraph will not cause you any pain except, perhaps, for a slight discomfort caused by the tightness of the blood pressure cuff. In addition to the polygraph, we employ the psychogalvanograph, which is designed to measure electrodermal responses."

"Measure what?"

"The response to certain excitements or stimuli. The psychogalvanograph measures the amount of perspiration, constriction of the pores, the electrical resistance of the skin . . . Now don't let the word 'electrical' bother you. The amount of electricity used is so slight the subject never is aware of it."

"Good," Wilkinson said. He knew he was getting nervous, and he tried to calm himself by thinking about something other than the test. But all he could think of was his failure of the evening before.

"If you are telling the truth," Williams continued, "then you don't have a thing in the world to worry about. And this instrument will indicate when you are telling the truth as well as when you aren't. If you do tell the truth, then it will be known. If you aren't telling the truth, as I've said, the machine will show it and I'll tell you so, and I'll ask you to let me hear the truth. . . . That's fair enough, isn't it? . . . And you don't mind taking this test, do you?"

"No, I guess not. Do anything you want. Help yourself."

"Fine," Williams said. "Now I'm going to attach the blood pressure cuff. Don't worry. Everyone's a little nervous at first, and it wears off. If there are any problems, we'll just go over them again until they're solved, okay?"

"Yes."

Williams got up from behind the L-shaped desk and walked around to Wilkinson. "You'll have to remove your jacket. You can hang it on that hook behind my desk, and roll up your left sleeve all the way, please."

Wilkinson hung up his coat. There was just the one hook. He noticed his hand was shaking slightly as he unbuttoned his cuff. Then he rolled up his sleeve as high as he could and sat down in the chair again. Williams wrapped the blood pressure sleeve around his arm and buckled it. Then Williams told him to lean forward slightly, and P.S. looked down at the hose that was being looped across his chest. The hose was ribbed, and looked like a smaller version of one of the hoses found in an automobile. "Just one thing more," Williams said. He slid a spring and soft rubber "bracelet" over Wilkinson's fingers, and then he went back to the desk and pumped up the blood pressure cuff until it was almost painfully tight. The next thing P.S. heard was the click of the machine being turned on, and he involuntarily stiffened. There was the light hum of the motor which unrolled the graph paper. P.S. heard Williams move his chair, then there was the sound of a pencil being picked up. *Was it a pencil?* A faint scratching sound. *The pens moving on the graph paper! It's started!* The cuff was so tight he could feel his own pulse beating in his arm. He took a deep breath and heard the pen move sharply. "I'm sorry," P.S. said.

"No talking," Williams answered.

The room was silent for half a minute.

"Now, Mr. Wilkinson, I am going to begin the test by asking you several questions which should be answered by either a yes or a no answer. If you have any qualifying remarks we can discuss them afterwards."

Wilkinson nodded. He tried to concentrate on the facing wall. But his eyes would not focus on the dotted soundproofing panels.

"Is your name Philip Sadler Wilkinson?"

"Yes."

(Pause.) "Are you twenty-four years old?"

"Yes."

"Are you residing at the Connecticut Avenue Hotel?"

"No, I've moved. I'm living at . . ."

"That's enough. I told you I only want yes or no answers."

Wilkinson heard the man stop the machine. He tore off the portion of graph paper used so far, then threaded the new portion in. Before he started up the machine again he asked, "You've moved where?"

"Q Street. 2908 Q Street."

"All right. But from now on only yes and no answers. If there's anything you feel you want to add, we can cover it afterwards. Now, I'm going to start the instruments and I want you to remain silent until I ask you questions."

P.S. nodded. He heard the machine being turned on again, the sound of the pens moving across the graph paper. There was absolute silence, unbroken but for the mechanical sounds around them, for approximately forty seconds and then P.S. heard Williams shuffle some papers and ask, "Is your name Philip Sadler Wilkinson?"

"Yes."

(Pause.) "Are you twenty-four years old?"

"Yes."

(Pause.) "Are you an American citizen?"

"Yes."

"Are you residing at 2908 Q Street?"

"Yes."

"Is your father Stewart Wilkinson?"

"Yes."

"Are your parents divorced?"

"Yes."

(Pause.) "Your mother is now Mrs. Warren T. MacDonnell."

"Yes."

"Do you know of any reason why you should not be hired by this agency?"

"No."

"Are you now or have you ever been a member of the Communist party?"

"No."

"Do you belong to any organization whose intent is to overthrow the rightful government of the United States by force?"

"No."

"Are you now or have you ever been employed by a foreign government?"

"No."

"Have you ever worked for a member of a foreign government's intelligence offices?"

". . . No."

(Pause.)

"Have you ever been in the possession of classified information?"

"Yes."

"Have you ever disclosed classified information to unauthorized persons?"

". . . No."

"Have you ever served in the military forces of the United States?"

"Yes."

"Did you serve in the intelligence branch of the United States Army?"

"Yes."

"Were you serving overseas?"

"Yes."

"Were you at that time in the possession of classified material?"

"Yes."

"Did you at any time come in contact with material classified as high as 'Top Secret'?"

"Yes."

"Did you at any time disclose Top Secret information to members of a foreign government?"

". . . No."

"Were you born in New York City?"

"Yes."

"Do you have any brothers or sisters?"

"Yes."

"Is your brother Robert Carter Wilkinson?"

"Yes."

"Your sister is Page Wilkinson Shaw?"

"Yes."

"Are any members of your immediate family living outside the continental limits of the United States?"

". . . Yes."

"Your brother is living in Hawaii, isn't he?"

"Yes."

"All right, now I want you to be absolutely quiet for thirty seconds."

P.S. nodded. He listened to the hum of the machine and the

scratching of the pen. He became aware again of the beating of the pulse in his arm and the slight tingling in his fingers beneath the spring and rubber "bracelet." Then the machine was turned off. P.S. leaned back slightly in the chair to stretch his back. Williams let the air out of the blood pressure cuff, then said, "Let's talk about these questions concerning classified information which seemed to have bothered you."

"I was with intelligence in Korea and you asked whether or not I'd ever worked with a foreign government's intelligence offices." He felt so detached from this unreality that his own voice surprised him. "If I am to take you to mean have I ever worked under the *employ* . . . or whether I worked under the direction of a foreign government's intelligence system, the answer is no. We did work very closely with the Koreans. The Korean intelligence was good. In many ways superior to our own."

"Then what about the classified material? The question about disclosing classified material to unauthorized persons also gave you trouble."

"Anyone in intelligence is constantly in contact with people who aren't—who don't *need to know* what is being done. And yet I'm sure you're familiar with the same amount of needless briefings, displays, talks that seem to go on in intelligence offices whenever somebody of some importance passes through. It was common in Korea for intelligence briefings to display more and more knowledge if only to show the people one was briefing that one was important. It may not have been the briefing officer's wish to do so. But one would be told by his superior to tell an individual about something that that person had no reason—no need to know."

"But that is the extent of your disclosure of classified material. You disclosed material when told to do so. And you felt you shouldn't."

"That's right."

"Now what about this Top Secret information?"

"What about it?"

"Did you disclose Top Secret information?"

"No. I released information which up to that time had been classified Top Secret but which for special reasons had been downgraded or which, when separated from other documents, was no longer Top Secret. My reaction to that was simply by association. No matter what the change of classification, the material was of a highly classified nature to me."

"But, again, you were in this instance instructed to do so by the proper military authorities."

"That's right."

"Then, let's see, Mr. Wilkinson. If I were to rephrase those questions to read something like . . ." He paused and P.S. could hear his pencil moving on a piece of paper. ". . . Have you ever disclosed classified material to persons without proper authorization and without prior clearance from superiors? . . . Would that give you any trouble?"

"I don't think so," P.S. said.

"The question remaining is about the family outside the country. The anxiety was caused, I assume, by whether or not Hawaii was considered out of the country?"

"Yes, sir."

"So if I were to ask you, 'Other than your brother living in Hawaii, are there any members of your immediate family who reside outside the continental limits of the United States?' would that give you any problems?"

"No, I don't think so."

"Fine," Williams said.

P.S. felt him pumping up the blood pressure and pulse sleeve on his upper arm, and then he heard Williams turn on the machine again and lower the pens to the graph paper. "Now, Mr. Wilkinson, I am going to ask you the exact same questions with the exception of those previously noted and changed, and they will be in the exact same order as before. I want you to remain silent for the next thirty seconds and then answer my questions only with a yes or no answer."

P.S. tried to make himself comfortable and waited for the questions to begin. The blood pressure cuff seemed even tighter than before, more uncomfortable. He considered asking Williams to loosen it, but decided against it. The room was silent except for the machine, humming, scratching, clicking.

"Is your name Philip Sadler Wilkinson?"

"Yes."

"Are you twenty-four years old?"

"Yes."

Ten minutes later the machine was stopped and Wilkinson was told to relax. "Can you loosen the blood pressure thing a little next time? It was somewhat painful, and tended to distract me from your questions."

"Too tight?"

"That's right."

"Sure."

"May I smoke?" Wilkinson asked.

"No, there's no smoking here. This next series of questions is of a more personal nature designed to find out more about the character of the subject. Don't let them upset you. Everyone who comes in here is asked these questions. I've asked these questions a thousand times and you'd be surprised by the answers I get during the discussion periods afterwards. So don't let them bother you. All right?"

"Yes."

"Good. You ready to go again?"

The interrogation continued and P.S. could not believe the questions he was being asked. With increasing horror he answered them and when, after ten minutes, he was told to relax he did not change his position. He could still hear the sound of the drum moving beneath the pens, he could still feel the tightness of the blood pressure cuff on his arm, and he felt slightly sick to his stomach.

"Well, Mr. Wilkinson, would you like to talk about those questions which seemed to give you so much trouble?"

"I don't know. Which ones do you mean?"

"You know the ones I meant."

"Which in particular?"

"Let's start with the first one, shall we?"

Wilkinson wondered why the machine was still running. He

could hear Williams sorting through some papers and then Williams asked, "Are you a homosexual?"

"*No!*"

"Have you ever had any homosexual contacts?"

"No . . . no, not that I remember."

"What do you mean *not that you remember?* . . . This is the sort of thing that you remember very distinctly. You know whether or not it happened, unless you *repress* it. There is no such thing as 'not that I remember.' . . . Now I'll turn off the instruments and you can just think about this question."

Wilkinson heard a click. but he couldn't be sure that the machine had been turned off. The blood pressure cuff was still very tight on his arm; he thought he could still hear the drum rolling the graph paper beneath the pens.

"I'll tell you why you're saying 'not that I remember.' It's because you're not telling the truth. You find it easier to tell half a lie than a whole one. I know from experience that when a man uses the expression 'not that I remember' he's simply not telling the truth. If he were telling the truth he'd be able to give a simple yes or no answer and he wouldn't have to resort to evasions. He'd have no trouble answering the question and the machine wouldn't show so strong a reaction."

"Well, my God, a strong reaction doesn't mean I'm lying," P.S. protested. "You asked me if I was a homosexual—a *queer!* And you expect me to react to that question the same as if you asked me if I liked cream in my coffee."

"I just want to know the truth. That's all I'm here for. I'm not here to pass judgment on you or humiliate you. As I said, these records are kept in strict confidence. I know this sort of questioning is embarrassing. But if you could only think of me as a doctor—"

"Oh, for Christ's sake!"

"Look, it's my job. Nothing you can say could possibly surprise or shock me. I've listened to thousands of men tell me the same things. All of them thinking that it's never happened to anyone else. Eighty-five percent of the men who apply here have had one sort or another of homosexual contacts. You'd be surprised

how many. The chances are the thing that is bothering you—
whatever it may be—is something that I've heard time and time
again. All I'm trying to do is to determine to what extent you've
had homosexual contacts."

". . . Well, nothing more than the usual."

"What's the usual?"

P.S. gripped the arm of the chair. *Jesus, why does he have to
ask about these things? I've told him I'm not a queer, what more
does he need to know?*

"What's the usual?" Williams repeated.

"Oh, you know . . ." *Is this how he gets his kicks?*

"I don't know, *you* tell *me*."

"A man sitting next to me in a movie, or someone sitting next
to me on a train . . . Things like that."

"How many things like that?"

"Those are the only two that I can remember—and that's the
truth."

"But did they excite you?"

"Jesus, no! Of course not. I got up and moved away from them.
I sat somewhere else."

"How old were you?"

"I don't remember. Sixteen, seventeen . . ."

"What about before?"

"Nothing. I just told you. That's all I remember."

"Is that so? . . . I see," Williams said. "Well, we'll come back to
that later. Now we'll start the instruments and—"

"They've been running all along," P.S. said. *What was that
click before? My God, maybe it was to that microphone outside!
Maybe everyone in the hall could listen. Maybe that stupid sonuvabitch made a mistake. Thought he had turned off the machine
and instead turned on the microphone outside! Would be typical
of this goddam place!*

"I want you to sit perfectly still for about twenty seconds, just
to establish your normal responses. . . . Is your name Philip
Sadler Wilkinson?"

"Yes."

(Pause.)

"You are currently residing at 2908 Q Street, Washington, D.C.?"

"Yes."

"Are you a homosexual?"

"No!"

"Have you ever had any homosexual contacts?"

". . . Yes."

"Have you, yourself, ever initiated an overt homosexual act?"

"No!"

"Do you prefer the company of women to men?"

". . . Well, it depends."

Wilkinson heard Williams swear to himself as he turned off the machine. "Mr. Wilkinson, these are simple yes or no answers!"

"Then, yes and no! I prefer to dance with women but drink with men. There are times when I prefer the company of women over men and men over women."

"All right, we'll eliminate that question entirely."

"Okay with me."

"I'm starting the instruments again . . . Be still . . . Now, answer these questions with a simple yes or no answer . . . all right, Mr. Wilkinson. Is your date of birth 12 April 1936?"

"Yes."

"Were you born in New York City?"

"Yes."

"Do you know any homosexuals?"

"Yes . . . no . . . Jesus, how can I—"

"Look, if you won't cooperate, we're going to have to mark you as unfit, or unwilling to submit to polygraph, in which case your application will be canceled." Williams turned off the machine again.

"Well, how the hell do you expect me to answer these questions with a simple yes or no answer? You don't ask simple yes or no questions! You ask, 'Do you know any homosexuals?' And what the hell, do you mean do I know any by name? Do I *know* them in the biblical sense? Are they my best friends? Do I know them by sight? What do you mean?"

"All right, we'll try again. I'll ask you do you know any homosexuals meaning do you hold any homosexuals among your acquaintances. Will that be all right?"

"Fine. Yes. Yes, I do."

"Wait till the machine is running. . . . All right, I'll ask you that question in about twenty seconds . . . ten . . . Do you know any homosexuals? Do you hold any homosexuals among your acquaintances?"

"Yes."

"Are any of your closest friends homosexuals?"

"No." *But some of my best friends are Negroes.*

"Do you know the names of any homosexuals?"

"Yes."

"Have you ever had—engaged in homosexual activity with them?"

"No."

"Are you in the habit of seeing homosexuals?"

"No."

"Have you had any homosexual contact within the last six months?"

"No."

"Have you had any homosexual contact within the last year?"

"No."

"Five years?"

"No."

"Other than the two times already mentioned—once in a movie theater, another time on a train—have you had any homosexual contact within the last ten years?"

"No."

(Pause.)

"Do you have regular sexual contact with women?"

". . . Yes." *As regular as I can make it.*

"Do you enjoy sexual intercourse with women?"

"Yes." *Oh, for God's sake!*

"Have you ever experienced any difficulty in enjoying sex with women?"

God, last night, Hilary. "No."

(Pause.)

"Do you have any habits, perversions, fetishes, which make the sexual act more attractive to you?"

"No." P.S. had visions of straps, boots, whips, and smiled grimly to himself as he thought of possible answers.

"Can you think of any reason whatsoever as to why you might be open to blackmail?"

"No."

"Prior to the time you were sixteen or seventeen years old, did you ever engage in any homosexual activity?"

P.S. concentrated on controlling his breathing. *Slowly . . . slowly . . . don't let it show. . . .* He could hear the pens scratching back and forth behind him. "No."

"Did you ever—at any time—commit a homosexual act with another boy?"

"No!"

"Did you ever—at any time—commit a homosexual act with an older man?"

"No."

"Do you contemplate any future homosexual acts?"

"No!" *Oh, for God's sake, what an asinine ques—*

"All right . . . just sit still for the next thirty seconds."

P.S. sat quiet, feeling the relief, the temporary respite from the questioning wash over him. He heard Williams turn off the polygraph machine, and the rustle of papers. P.S. looked down at his left hand and noticed that his knuckles were white from the strain of gripping the chair seat.

Williams pushed back his chair and came around to P.S.'s side and undid the blood pressure cuff, then slid the galvanograph off P.S.'s hand. P.S. massaged his arm and hand, then took a deep breath and leaned back against the hard wood chair.

"How do you feel?" Williams asked.

"Fine."

"Not too tired?"

"Not really. It's almost interesting—in an awful way."

Williams seated himself in the chair behind the desk and Wilkinson again. "In what way is it awful?"

"I don't know," P.S. said. "It's just like—it's sort of something out of Kafka. Being plugged into a machine. Being humiliated by a machine."

"Do you feel humiliated?"

"Well, no, maybe that isn't the word I meant. Not exactly. I just don't happen to like being examined on the end of the pin like some sort of insect specimen."

"It shouldn't bother you if you have nothing to hide."

"Well, I don't."

"Look, we can sit here all day if you'd like, or if you'd prefer we can go back over those questions that gave you trouble—"

"What questions?"

"You know the ones I mean."

"Oh, God, it's cat-and-mouse time again. . . . Well, let's go at it again. Turn it on again."

"I don't think that's really necessary, do you?" Williams asked. "I mean, we can both pretty well tell when you're lying without the machine, can't we?"

"Can we?"

"I think so," Williams said smoothly.

P.S. wished he could have a cigarette.

"One of the questions which gave you difficulty was . . . let's see . . . 'Prior to the time you were sixteen or seventeen years old, did you ever engage in any homosexual activity?' "

"I told you no!"

"Not even as a small boy at school? . . . You went to quite a few schools . . . Small boys at school often do things they're ashamed of later."

"Did you?" *I bet you did, you bastard. I bet you were the biggest—*

"Look, Mr. Wilkinson, we're not getting anywhere with you behaving like this. You realize that you must be cleared through this examination to be hired?"

"Yes."

"This whole problem of homosexuality seems to be bothering you. You have shown strong reactions on every question asked of this nature; now I want you to know why. I want the truth."

How do you explain to a man of this type that the whole prep school career of a boy is shaded by the other boys' acceptance of his manhood, his masculinity. If a boy does too well in school, or if he's not very good at sports, or if he sticks to himself, the other boys immediately label him a "fairy." . . . *I spent my prep school days being terrified of being called a fairy because I was never any good at sports.*

"So, let's go back and see what it is that's been bothering you. If you answer this question with the truth, we can end this examination quickly. When you were a boy did you ever have any homosexual contact?"

". . . All right. Yes."

"Go on."

"Go on? There's nothing very much to it."

"Tell me."

"Well, when I was nine. Ten maybe. I don't know how old I was. It was the beginning of my second year at Napier, so it was —I must have been eleven. I was eleven."

"What happened?"

"Nothing much."

There was a long silence and P.S. waited for Williams to ask him more questions, but when it became apparent that Williams was waiting for P.S. to speak, P.S. finally blurted, "I was eleven and it was in the shower and there was a boy who wasn't circumcised and I touched him."

"That's all?"

"Of course that's all!"

"You're sure now? That's all you did?"

"I just told you that's all."

"And that was your only overt homosexual act?"

"Well, I don't think that just because an eleven-year-old boy is curious, he should necessarily be labeled queer."

"But why did the question give you so much trouble?"

"I don't know," P.S. said. "It's not something I generally go around telling people about."

"And if I were to ask you, if I were to phrase a question, 'Other than your touching another boy when you were eleven years old, have you ever committed an overt homosexual act?' That question would no longer bother you. You would be able to answer yes—honestly?"

"Yes."

"All right," Williams said.

It's all over, P.S. thought to himself. He wanted to smile, to laugh, to pump Mr. Williams' hand. *It's finished. I'm through! No more ques—*

"There just seems to be one more region we haven't explored," Williams said. "The polygraph indicated a very strong reaction to the following question: 'Have you ever experienced any difficulty in enjoying sex with women?' Can you think what might have caused that?"

Hilary! God damn that machine. "I don't know why," P.S. said. "I honestly can't think why."

"I don't need the machine to show me that you're lying."

"I'm not lying!"

"All right, let's attach the blood pressure cuff and the galvanograph again and I'll ask you the question, then show you the chart. Will that prove to you that you're lying?"

P.S. sat and looked down at his hands. "I—well, last night, I was in bed with a girl and I couldn't get an erection."

"Was she colored?"

"Colored? Why?" Jesus, what kind of question is that?

"Many young men from good families pick up colored prostitutes and go to bed with them and find they can't get an erection. It's perfectly normal. They may want to make love to the girl but there are too many social or racial or discriminatory or psychological reasons why they aren't able to go through with the act."

"That's very interesting," P.S. said, eager to be off the subject.

"Was the girl you were in bed with last night colored?"

"No, she was married."

"Was that why you couldn't go through with the act?"

"Probably. And I was tired, too, I guess."

"But other than this one time—normally you are able to perform the act satisfactorily?"

"Often to the ecstatic applause of the assembled guests."

"You have done it in front of other people?"

"No," P.S. said. "Excuse me. I was being funny."

"I see," Williams said.

P.S. heard Williams push his chair back, then come around the desk. He thought for a minute that Williams was going to hit him. P.S. had a sudden vision of the Gestapo interrogator smashing the prisoner's teeth in, shouting *"Schweinhund!* Take dot for being fonny!"* but the man was only attaching the blood pressure cuff to P.S.'s upper arm. P.S. slid the galvanograph over his own hand. "Now, I'm going to ask you the questions in the exact same order as they were given you previously. The questions will be the same except for those we have discussed. I want only yes or no answers. If there are any problems, we will discuss them after the test." Williams seated himself behind P.S. again and pumped up the blood pressure cuff. "Is that too tight?"

P.S. shook his head. "No."

"All right, relax." Williams turned on the machine. Once again P.S. could hear the mimeograph roll moving across the drums, then the pens were lowered and P.S. was aware of his chest pressing against the respiration hose. Williams said, "I want you to remain still for the next twenty seconds. Good."

P.S. could hear a light rustle of papers behind him.

"Is your date of birth the 12th of April, 1936?"

"Yes."

"Were you born in New York City?"

"Yes."

Fifteen minutes later Williams said, "Well, that does it."

"We're through?" P.S. could scarcely believe it.

"That's right."

P.S. looked down at his watch. It was only eleven o'clock. He had been inside the small room for just a little over an hour.

Williams undid the respiration hose, the blood pressure cuff, and slid the galvanograph off P.S.'s hand. P.S. was terribly conscious of the man's hand when it had touched his, and he thought of the time that had been spent discussing whether or not he was a homosexual.

"How did I do?" P.S. asked.

"Okay."

"But I mean, did I pass? Everything all right?"

"It's too early to tell. I have to go over the test in detail."

"But you don't think there are any problems?" P.S. wanted desperately to ask the man if he was thought to be a homosexual. He wanted to make sure that both the man and the machine believed him.

"Take this card and go back to the secretary. She will tell you where to go from here."

"There's more?"

"It's common for the subjects to go directly from here to the psychiatrist's office. It's just a short examination. Part of the routine."

"Well, okay," P.S. said with enormous relief. He stood up and rolled his left sleeve down and buttoned the cuff. Then he walked over to the coat hook and took down his coat. He put it on, trying not to look at the sheaf of papers on Williams' desk. He wondered for a moment whether or not he should shake hands with the examiner, then reached out his hand. Williams shook it, looking somewhat surprised, then walked over and held the door open for P.S. P.S. thanked him and walked up the narrow hallway back into the sitting room and handed the card to the secretary. The secretary made a few notes on it and said, "Go up to the second floor to Room 230 and see Dr. James."

"Room 230, Dr. James," P.S. repeated.

"That's right."

P.S. walked up the stairs to the second floor, turned down the corridor labeled 216–230, and stopped outside Room 230 and knocked. A man said, "Come in."

P.S. walked into the office. A soft, pudgy man with no hair and wearing steel-rimmed glasses was seated behind an enormous mahogany desk which took up almost the whole room.

"What's *your* name?"

"Wilkinson, sir."

"Hello, Wilkinson. I'm Dr. James."

"Yes, sir." *His voice* . . .

"You look very young. How old *are* you?"

P.S. felt the hair rising on the back of his neck. There was something horrible about the man's voice. Its tone. "Twenty-four," P.S. said.

"You don't *look* that old."

A shiver ran through him, and P.S. started to sit down.

"No, no!" the doctor protested. "Don't sit down yet. Let me *look* at you."

P.S. remained standing where he was. His skin felt cold and damp.

"My, you're *tall!*" the doctor said. "Are you long all over?"

17

THE LIGHTS CAME ON at the end of the second feature and Philip Sadler Wilkinson blinked owlishly for a few moments, massaged his temples where the first warning pulses of a headache had made themselves felt, then stood and walked up the aisle. He waited for the couple in front of him to step aside, heard the woman between gum chews say that she thought Doris Day was simply the most wonderful and dreamy girl in the wor-uld, and the man said that anyone would look wonderful and dreamy if they were photographed through eight inches of gauze. P.S. passed them and stood outside the movie theater waiting for the readjustment to reality, waiting for the frothy candy-cotton world of Rock Hudson and Doris Day to become the real world of this lonely Baltimore night, waiting for the memories of Washington to rush back in, engulfing him in the stagnant wash of embarrassment, impotency, innuendo, and despair which culminated in standing once again before the giant desk, facing the fat, pasty-faced, puffy-palmed psychiatrist, seeing the fluorescent lights reflecting in the man's steel-rimmed spectacles. And again P.S. felt the horror, the nausea as he saw the pursed lips, the pink tongue licking those lips before the psychiatrist said, "My, you're tall . . ."

P.S. hurried away from the theater to East Baltimore Street. When he had been first in the Army, stationed outside Baltimore at the Army Intelligence School, he had learned to love this street

with its bars and strip joints, its drugstores advertising in red
neon SANITARY RUBBER GOODS just around the corner from the
Salvation Army's neon cross which advertised GOD IS LOVE. P.S.
loved the street with its cheap clothing stores, its tattoo parlors,
its dirty book and magazine stands with rows upon rows of
magazine covers depicting mammoth-breasted girls chewing
plastic flowers or hayseeds or fingertips while lying upon satin
pillows, or bales of hay or rumpled sheets, with all of its books
with the slack-faced women in black leather corsets and black
leather boots that laced all the way up the thighs, with its women
in furs, with its women in silk, with its women in rubber skin-
diving suits with special hoods which hid their faces while they
whipped men who supposedly didn't mind it at all. East Baltimore
Street was the only reality left; it was P.S.'s last remaining link
with his life before Korea. It was where he had known Hippolyte.

Hippolyte . . . Polly Hippolyte. P.S. smiled to himself. He really
wanted to see her now. He remembered how the master of ceremonies at the Club 88 would say, "And now, ladies and gentlemen
. . . our very special attraction . . . The only woman in the world
who was more than a match for Hercules [snicker]. . . . The
one woman whose girdle [snicker] it was Hercules' task to
steal! . . . And it wasn't supposed to be easy [guffaw]! . . . The
Club 88 is proud to present the star of its show, the Queen of the
Amazons herself . . . HIPPOLYTE!"

And when the m.c. and Polly were quarreling, as was usual,
he would introduce her not as Hih-pol-at-tee, but instead he would
pronounce it Hippo-lite, and Polly would come on smiling at him
and the front tables would hear her say something like, "Go find
yourself a poisoned choirboy." Hippolyte was the star stripper of
the Club 88. Before her performance she would circulate around
the nightclub pushing drinks, which was how P.S. had first met
her. She used to wear dresses that appeared to have been put on
backwards. The cleavage dove down to her belt, exposing her
breasts like two parentheses back to back. She clearly wore nothing under her dress. She kept her black hair very short and
streaked with gray to hide her youth. During her act she wore
a long black wig. Her nose had been broken and badly set years
ago, and her makeup did not entirely hide her freckles. And she

was a Lesbian, though not as much or not as complete a Lesbian as her girl friend Faith. *Faith, Jesus, was she a mean one! I'd forgotten all about her.* Faith had left her husband and gone to live with Hippolyte. Faith was a true Lesbian with all the meanness and possessiveness of her kind. She would not go to bed with a man unless she desperately needed the money and only for fifty dollars. *Which was no bargain.* She hated P.S., hated Hippolyte for liking him. Faith constantly had to be told by Hippolyte that Hippolyte loved her. But Hippolyte was not a true Lesbian, she was AC-DC, and Faith despised and distrusted that side of her.

P.S. walked down East Baltimore Street looking at the neon signs of the clubs on either side which advertised girls with names like Toni, Jerri, Betti, and Billi; Torrid, Tawny, Flame, and Blaze; Cuddles, Cupcakes, Ti-Ti, and Lulu; Elvesa, Rita, Kim, and Marilyn. There was Virginia (Ding-Dong) Bell, and fabulous Irma the Body, and then P.S. was in front of the Gayety Burlesque with its architecture as bawdy as its billboards and its gold paint as chipped as the ticket taker's teeth. The colored man in the doorman suit three sizes too large was saying, "*Show*time! *Show*time! Showzahboutah begin!"

P. S. Wilkinson with other second lieutenants going to the Army Intelligence School had spent a lot of time at the Club 88 because the acts came faster, there were no awful comedians, and the girl singer was pretty good. No one had ever tried dating any of the girls, since the club had a reputation for Lesbianism. The October evening after P.S. had received his orders for Korea, he and some friends went back to the Club 88 and they dared him to make a date with Hippolyte. When Hippolyte had sat with them and P.S. had bought her a Scotch, he asked her to go out with him after the show and she said, "It will cost you twenty dollars." P.S. said that he thought he could afford it and she said, "Come back to my place. Meet me outside the club after the show. You got a car?" P.S. borrowed the keys to one of the lieutenants' cars, and after the show he waited around the corner from the club. It was cold that October evening and he had his overcoat collar turned up against the wind and he worried that Hippolyte would pull a no-show. He was about to give up when she came around the corner, linked her arm through his and said, "Okay, let's go."

P.S. drove her back to her apartment in the borrowed car and parked behind an apartment house not far from the library. They said very little to each other on the way back other than asking where to turn and being told where to stop. Hippolyte lived in a basement apartment and when she held the door open for him and he stepped inside he was speechless. It looked like the whole apartment was filled with books. Bookcases lined one whole wall to the left and books were piled up on the two deep recessed windowsills to the right. Separating the efficiency kitchen from the living room were two more small bookcases also filled with books. P.S. walked around to look at the books and they weren't all trash. There were good paperbacks on poetry and art and a whole section devoted to Greek mythology and history.

"Have you read all of these?" P.S. asked.

"A few of them."

P.S. sat down and pulled out the Penguin paperback of the *Aeneid*. "Is this where you got the idea for your act?"

She smiled. "Well, no, not really."

P.S. had never seen her really smile before.

"Vergil never had much to say about the way the Amazons danced. Did you like it?"

"The *Aeneid*?"

"My act."

It was P.S.'s turn to smile. "My God, yes. It's very effective. Particularly your cape work. When you're down on the floor. I didn't know Amazons wore capes."

"They didn't. They wore togas mostly. Or things that looked like togas in the early pictures or representations of them. They carried bows and spears and things like that. It wasn't until later on that they wore thin dresses with high hems so that they could run fast."

"How do you know all this?"

"I read all about them in the *Encyclopaedia Britannica*."

P.S. sat down on the couch. "Incredible," he said. "I think you're the first girl I've ever met who's read the *Encyclopaedia*

Britannica. Most people just stick them into bookshelves and forget about them."

"Well," she laughed, "I haven't read all of them."

"Just 'A through Argo' or whatever it is."

"More like just 'Amazons.'"

"You mind if I look around for a few minutes?" P.S. asked. "Unless, of course, it's too late and you're tired. What time is it?"

P.S. saw the hardness take over her face. "Look, you want a quick lay we can go back into the bedroom right now."

"Oh, God, I didn't mean that at all. I'm sorry," P.S. said. "I just thought that since you've been working all night you must be very tired and I thought you might want me out of here."

"Okay," she said. Her expression softened. "Hey, what is your name? I forget."

"Philip. P. S. Wilkinson. People call me P.S. or Philip or Phil, it doesn't matter."

"Which do you prefer?"

"They're all the same."

"Then I'll call you Philip," she said. "You're in the Army, aren't you?"

"That's right."

"I've seen you at the club before. You get to the club pretty often."

"Well, I like the place."

"Did you learn about the Amazons at college?"

P.S. smiled. "I learned something about them there."

"Where'd you go?"

"Yale."

"I had a friend who went there," she said. "In fact I almost went there myself."

"You mean the nursing school?"

"No, the college."

"But they don't take women," P.S. said.

"I mean Harvard."

P.S.'s eye was caught by one of the modern paintings on the far wall. The painting was a bunch of bright orange streaks on a black background and it was signed "Faith."

"My roommate did that," Hippolyte explained. "She went home to her mother's for the weekend."

"She painted all of these?"

"Yeah. They're pretty awful, aren't they?"

"Yeah," P.S. said.

"Well, she wanted to hang them and there wasn't much I could say." She carried the coffee into the living room and put two cups on the coffee table in front of the sofa. "Sit down before it gets cold."

"Those really are the weirdest paintings."

"Well, they're good therapy for her."

"*Therapy!*" P.S. laughed.

"Yeah, she gets a chance to work out all her aggressions."

"*What* aggressions?"

"Penis envy."

P.S. burst out laughing. "Oh, God . . . oh, God . . . that's too good to be true." He tried to stop laughing and looked over at Hippolyte and saw that she was laughing and she said, "Penis envy" again and P.S. just let himself laugh. Finally he said, "Oh, God, I don't think I've laughed so hard in a year." He wiped his eyes and looked over at the paintings and he saw the one with the yellow background and the large green tree and the great flowery branches and he started laughing all over again. "Did you look at the one over there? The one with the tree and the leaves and everything? It's too much!"

"That's her favorite."

P.S. calmed down and leaning back against the sofa cushions said, "This is kind of nice, you know? I mean it's such a different world from the club."

"Well, you have to get away from that place. It gets on your nerves."

"I bet it does."

"It pays well, though. I make a good living."

"I guess that's the only way they can keep the girls."

"I get over a hundred a week," she said. "Depending on how much the customers drink I get even more."

"Listen, I know that you must get asked this question a hundred times, but there's one thing I've been wanting to ask you—"

"You mean, 'How did a nice girl like me end up like this?' "

"No," P.S. smiled. "I meant those times I bought you Scotch, did you really get Scotch or was it something like tea?"

"The water's unsafe. I drink Scotch."

"Real Scotch?"

"Well, it's not very good Scotch, but it's not Coca-Cola either."

"Then I don't mind paying so much for a drink, just so long as I'm not paying a buck and a half for a glass of tea. When you don't make much money every little bit hurts."

"How much do you make a month?"

"In the Army? About two hundred, two-twenty a month, it depends."

"And you're what? A sergeant?"

"No. A second lieutenant. The lowest of them all. Sergeants make much more money than I do."

"You mean you only make a couple hundred dollars a month? A little more than fifty a week?"

"That's right." P.S. smiled.

"I make twice as much money as you do!"

"That's not hard."

"But twenty dollars is a lot of money to you. It's almost a week's work, half a week's work. How come you want to spend twenty dollars just to go to bed with me?"

"Well, it's sort of my going-away present to myself. I just got orders to Korea and I'll be gone for a year and I thought I'd give myself something nice."

"When do you leave for Korea? Soon?"

"No, not for another six weeks. It's still pretty far off. I just got my orders, that's all."

"And I'm your going-away present?"

P.S. nodded.

She leaned over and kissed him on the cheek. "That's the sweetest thing I've ever heard."

"Well, it's not the same as if I were leaving tomorrow."

"All the same," she said. "I think it's very nice."

"Thank you."

"Hey, how about a drink?"

"No, nothing, really. If I drink then I can't—you know. Say,

I keep wanting to call you something. But Hippolyte is sort of unwieldy. I mean it's kind of long. What's your real name?"

"Call me Polly."

"Short for Hippolyte?"

She nodded.

"But that isn't your real name, is it?"

"It doesn't matter what my real name is. Why are you smiling?"

"I don't know. It was just such a corny line in a way. I mean, like something you'd expect to hear in a bad movie . . . 'It doesn't matter what my real name is . . .' "

"I love movies."

"So do I."

"I always wanted to be in movies."

"Who didn't?"

"You, too?" she asked, surprised.

"Well, I never told anybody, but I always hoped that one day somebody would see me and put me in a movie."

"*You?*"

"For God's sake, Polly, don't be so surprised." He laughed. "I— well, I wasn't all that serious about it, but I was serious enough to know that if some big producer would say, 'Kid, you could be the new Cary Grant,' I'd want to believe him and take him up on it."

"You just don't look the type. You look more the scholarly type."

"Because of my glasses?"

"No, not only them, it's the way you dress, too."

"Tweed jackets with patches."

"Uh-huh." She nodded. She reached over and patted his hand. "Don't worry, maybe you'll make the big time yet."

P.S. laughed.

"Say, come on and have a drink, okay? You don't have to leave right away do you, Phil?"

"I don't have to be anywhere until Monday morning at 0800."

"Good, then let's have a drink. I like you."

"Well, by golly, Polly, I like you, too. So let's drink to that."

"Scotch?"

"You have any bourbon?"

"I think so." She got up from the sofa and walked back around to the sink. "I keep all my liquor under the sink. That way the water's nearby. Take off your coat and tie. Relax. Put your feet up. You look too formal."

"Okay." P.S. stood up and took off his coat, then hung it over the back of a chair. He remembered that he kept his wallet in his coat and he considered shifting his wallet to his back pocket. But it would have been uncomfortable to sit on, and besides, Polly might see him do it and think that he didn't trust her.

Polly came back with the drinks. She handed the glass to P.S., clinked hers against his and said, "Past the lips, down the tongue, look out, stomach, here it comes! Cheers."

"Skoal."

"What's that mean?"

"Health, I guess. I got it off a cocktail napkin."

"You know what?"

"What?"

"I've got a feeling this is going to be a good night. I really feel like—you know. Tonight I think is going to be good."

He wondered if she was saying that to get him excited. At any rate it worked. "Well, I'll do my best," he said. "You ever read any Browning?"

"Sure. 'Auld Lang Syne.'"

"That was Robert Burns. I was thinking of 'Grow old along with me, the best is yet to be.'"

"I like that."

"You know," P.S. said, "what we should really have on a cold wintery night like this is a great big crackling fire."

"You'll be plenty warm, don't worry."

P.S. looked over at her and saw that she was smiling. "I'm looking forward to it," he said.

"You want to—now?"

"What do you think?"

"I think it would be nice."

"I do, too."

"All right," she said, standing up.

P.S. stood up also, and reached in his jacket pocket for his wallet. "Let me get the awkward part over with now, okay?" He pulled two ten-dollar bills out of his wallet and handed them to her. "Here. In advance. I don't want your mind on whether or not you'll be paid."

"I wasn't worried," she said. She put the money inside a cardboard box on the windowsill. "I'm sorry I have to take the money. But I need it for something."

"Don't worry, Polly. We agreed on it in advance."

"I know, but all the same . . ." She picked up her drink and clinked her glass against his and said, "*Bon voyage*, Philip."

P.S. followed her back into the living room. Polly, in her bathrobe, walked directly to the cardboard box, opened it, and handed P.S. the twenty dollars. "Here. Take it," she said. "I enjoyed that much too much to take your money."

"What do you mean?"

"You're the best lay I've ever had."

P.S. stood there in his shorts, looking down at the two ten-dollar bills in his hand. The only thing he could think of was that if he ever told anybody about this, no one would believe him. "But, Polly, I can't take this money. You said you needed it."

"I was only going to buy some shoes. I don't need them right away. I'm not going anywhere."

She looked so young standing there without makeup, her hair tousled, in an old, loosely tied bathrobe. In the dim light of the living room she did not look at all like the tough East Baltimore Street stripper he had bought drinks for. She looked more like some girl who had got out of bed and walked into a room surrounded by books in the hope of finding the fragmentary quote in Bartlett's *Familiar Quotations* that had been plaguing her all night.

"You look wonderful," he said.

"I look a mess." She automatically ran her hand through her hair.

"No, you don't." He hugged her and said, "My God, that was nice. So very, very nice."

"Was I good for you?"

"*Good?* Jesus, I thought you were going to make my ears pop!"
She reached up and cupped her hands over his ears. "*Pop!*"
"Pop."
"Our drinks have melted. You want some more ice in yours?"
"Don't you want me to be getting out of here?"
She hooked her arms together around his back and squeezed
him. "You're not leaving until Monday."
P.S. laughed. "I keep thinking I should pinch myself."
"Why?"
"Because this doesn't—this sort of thing doesn't happen. I
can't believe you really want me to stay."

That had been the beginning of it. P.S. was tired of walking
and he looked at his watch. It was not quite eleven and he knew
that there was no point in going to the Club 88 for another hour.
He went into a dimly lit piano bar and ordered a drink. An
enormous woman sat diagonally across from him in the darkness, and he thought it might be Fat Sally, the singer at the Club
88. But when she turned and her face was lit by the glowing
Miller's High Life sign on the wall behind her, P.S. saw that it
wasn't.

Fat Sally was a Lesbian too, of course. She had a scar running
from the corner of her right eye down to her right nostril and to
her lip. It was an old knife fight scar and sometimes when the
spotlight was on her and she was singing, the scar glistened as
though her face had been cut in half. Fat Sally and Hippolyte
were good friends—not lovers—just friends. Fat Sally had a
great barrel laugh and a husky voice that was perfect for the
sort of blues she sang. P.S. sat at the piano bar and thought
about the time he and Polly and Fat Sally and Connie, a pretty
little stripper from the club, and Faith and a professor from
Johns Hopkins had spent all night Saturday through Sunday
morning playing penny ante poker. P.S. had just dealt a hand
when the doctor suddenly dove out of his chair to the floor, kicking over the card table with the poker chips and drinks on it.
P.S. knew the man was having an epileptic seizure and he told
Polly to roll up a wet handkerchief or washrag as tightly as possible and to bring it to him. P.S. forced the man over onto his

back and knelt over him, pinning his arms to his sides, then he took the washrag and rolled it even tighter and pinched the man's jaw until he had opened the man's mouth and he forced the washrag over his tongue and between his teeth so that he wouldn't bite through his tongue or choke on it. P.S. kept pushing the cloth back so that the man would be able to breathe through his opened mouth without swallowing his tongue. Every time the man shook he bled more from his mouth where he had bitten his cheeks and tongue. The seizure lasted only a few minutes. P.S. saw that Polly was holding a towel full of ice cubes against the back of the man's neck and he wasn't sure whether it was the right thing to do. But bit by bit P.S. felt the man relax and finally they got him up onto the sofa where he sat back limp and trembling slightly. P.S. was just getting ready to light a cigarette when the door burst open and in came two firemen followed by several policemen. He looked at Polly and Polly looked at Faith and Faith said, "I'm the one who called." P.S. got out of the way while one of the policemen checked the professor. Polly was telling the other firemen what had happened and P.S. took time to look around the room. Polly was standing with her bathrobe half open, Faith was in a pair of khaki pants and a tee shirt, Fat Sally was wearing a slip, and Connie, the pretty little stripper, was holding onto Sally's hand for dear life. There were ice cubes and poker chips all over the floor and the rug was damp from whisky and beer. The Johns Hopkins professor was sitting dazed on the sofa and P.S., covered with the man's blood, could only think of what his family and all the old aunts on Charles Street would say if a picture of all this were to appear on their breakfast tables with the Baltimore papers. And then of course there would be a similarly awkward situation with the Army. But fortunately the police did their duty and left with the firemen and all was quiet. When the university professor had been loaded into an ambulance for a checkup, and the apartment had returned relatively to normal, P.S. listened to the girls go at each other. Polly was furious at Faith for calling the cops and the Fire Department, Faith was mad at Polly because Polly hadn't called them herself. Fat Sally was mad at Connie for being so scared, Connie felt sick because she had never seen an epileptic before and blamed Sally for making her be there. Nobody felt like playing any more poker and the party began to break up. Faith came out of the bedroom with P.S.'s coat and Polly told her that P.S. wasn't going anywhere. Faith said that if he was going to stay she was going to leave. And Polly said, "Go ahead. Go dive off a bridge." Faith burst into tears, scooped up her overcoat and ran out of the room. When she still hadn't returned within three hours, Polly began to worry. She said that Faith just might do something like jumping off a bridge, just to be dramatic, and that maybe they'd better find her. P.S. drove Polly's car around Baltimore down to the harbor, through the parks, along the side streets, over to the railroad station, but without any luck. Polly was exhausted and nervous and they decided to stop back at the apartment on the chance that Faith might have returned while they were gone. Faith was, of course, in the back bedroom asleep. The whole time in which P.S. and Hippolyte were together during those six weeks before he shipped out to Korea, Faith was a constant irritant. Faith despised P.S., hated the time he spent with Hippolyte, and when P.S. mentioned that Polly enjoyed going to bed with him Faith screamed that it wasn't true, that Polly only did it because she needed the money. He looked at Polly and Polly changed the subject. When they were alone later he asked her what Faith had meant. And Polly told him that she had had to make Faith believe that he was paying her to go to bed with him. "But how do you explain the money?" P.S. asked.

"I tell her I'm sending it to my mother."

"Does your mother need money?"

"Shit," Polly said, "I wouldn't give her the time of day."

What time is it? P.S. looked at his watch. *Twenty past eleven.* He looked at the piano player behind the bar, a thin-faced Negro who played with his eyes closed, his head tilted down toward the keys. P.S. ordered another drink. When it came and he had paid for it, he got up from the bar and walked back to the men's room. He stood in front of the urinal trying not to notice the smell and the mess of the place, and read the messages on the wall.

"I like to————" (scratched out.)

"So do I." (Different handwriting.) "I will be here Thursday night between ten and ten-thirty to meet you."

"I was here." (Third handwriting.) "Where were you?"

"I was ——ing a ———— that was ———— with a ————" (All magnificently obscene.)

And there was more. A message said that Donald Duck was a Jew, and then the best: "Do fairies fuck?" and the answer in a different hand: "If you believe in them they do."

P.S. walked back to the bar and sat down. The fat woman was still in the corner and he wondered what kind of life she had. *Lousy. . . . Anyone that fat must have a lousy life. . . . Except Fat Sally was that fat. And she seemed to have a pretty good time.* P.S. remembered how he used to go into the Club 88 and ask for Hippolyte.

Fat Sally and P.S. would drink together until Hippolyte would come over and hold up her cheek to be kissed. He would bend over to kiss her on the cheek and she would twist her head and plant her lips squarely on his and hold onto him until Sally would say, "Sonuvabitch!" All the tourists at the bar would look on, eyes rolling, and Hippolyte, conscious of the audience, would hook her arm through P.S.'s and announce, "This guy's the best lay I ever had."

P.S. would stand there blushing and smiling and Fat Sally and Polly would laugh at him. He almost wished she wouldn't say that. Almost.

It was eleven-thirty, and he had had three drinks and now would be the best time to see Polly. He left the piano bar and took his time walking the five blocks to the Club 88, marveling at the different types of people who came to this part of Baltimore and at how, as far as the family was concerned, this part of Baltimore simply didn't exist. *Well, not all the family,* P.S. thought to himself. *The topic does arise occasionally over cigars and brandy in the back room. And there was the time that Cousin Leland had that stripper as a patient, the one who tried a do-it-yourself abortion and almost killed herself. Everybody had wanted to know why she had come to him instead of some other doctor. And, of*

*course, the answer was that he was the best doctor, and there
was no other reason.*

The Club 88 is a walk-down club located just off East Baltimore
Street, one block away from the Salvation Army Mission. P.S.
walked down the steps to the front door and stepped inside. For
a Wednesday night the place was pretty crowded. There were a
few men with cards on their lapels—conventioneers from some
place, and they were always good for drinks. P.S. waited in the
gloom until he could see who was standing around the bar. He
saw the manager walking towards him and he steeled himself
for the man's request to see his ID card.

"Can I help you, sir?" the manager asked.

"No, I think I'll drink at the bar."

"You can see the girls much better from the tables."

"Well, all right—"

The manager started to lead him to a table in the rear and
P.S. said he wanted one closer to the stage and the manager
waited for a tip. P.S. gave him a dollar and he got a table in the
second row behind the ring of tables around the stage. P.S. sat
down and in a few moments a waitress came over. P.S. ordered
a bourbon and asked her if Hippolyte still worked there. The
waitress gestured toward a table full of conventioneers at the
back, but it was so dark where they were seated that he couldn't
be certain the girl was Hippolyte. When the waitress returned
with his drink, he asked her to tell Polly that he was there. The
waitress walked away and P.S. looked down at his jacket, brushed
a few specks of dust and ashes off his sleeves and straightened
his tie. He saw the waitress move away from the table
and he waited for Polly to get up and come over to him. But there
was no further movement at that table except for the occasional
sparkle of the light hitting the cellophane cover of one of the
conventioneers' name cards. P.S. picked up his drink and watched
the next girl come on. She danced to "Harlem Nocturne" and
wasn't much to look at. And, as if to emphasize the sexlessness
of her dance, she would occasionally turn and smile tenderly at
the next girl waiting to go on. The girl's costume was a fringed
bra and a fringed skirt, and when she removed the skirt P.S. saw

the long scar on her stomach. . . . The act ended, and the m.c. came back on to lead the scattered applause. P.S. looked over at the conventioneers' table. *It is Polly!* He saw her stand up and P.S. watched her, preparing himself to smile when she came over, but she didn't even look his way. *Come on, Polly, come on, please!* Instead, she walked behind one of the men and leaned over him so that her breasts were on either side of his bald head. The man reached behind him in his chair and ran his hands up her thighs and Polly disentangled herself as the men at the table laughed and laughed. P.S. watched her walk away in the direction of the dressing room and he ordered another drink. He knew that she wouldn't come out again until it was time for her act. And that wouldn't be for another thirty minutes or three quarters of an hour. A girl cruised by and stopped and came back to his table. "Would you like a little company?"

"No, thanks," he said.

"You sure?"

P.S. looked up at the woman. Her makeup, though probably fine under the lights, made her face look orange in the dimness of the tables. P.S. tried to guess how old she was. Thirty-five, maybe forty. At an age where she should be at home with her husband, the children in bed.

"You sure you wouldn't like a little company?"

"Yes," he said. "I'm sorry."

He felt humiliated for her. He sipped his new drink slowly knowing he was getting drunk. He didn't care.

There was a drum roll and flourish, and the master of ceremonies came mincing out and said, "And now, ladies and gentlemen—if there are any of either sex present [*snicker*]—the Club 88 takes great pride in presenting its very special attraction. . . . The only woman in the world who was more than a match for Hercules [*snicker*]. . . . The one woman whose girdle it was Hercules' task to steal—as if she really needed it anyway . . ."

That's a new line.

". . . The Club 88 presents the star of its show, the Queen of the Amazons herself . . . HIPPOLYTE!"

The band and waitresses applauded and the house lights went

black for a few moments, then came up again to reveal Hippolyte
standing, legs apart, in a thin toga-like skirt. In one hand she held
a spear, over the other arm she carried a cape. She began her
dance and P.S. watched her eyes, hoping she would look his way
and show some sign of recognition and warmth. But she directed
her act to the tables up front, and occasionally at the table full
of conventioneers farther back. Polly began the part of the act
where she would play with the spear and P.S. knew the act would
end soon. He finished his drink and waited.

The act ended and Hippolyte hurried to her dressing room and
P.S. sat watching the door, waiting for her to come out. When
she finally did emerge he got up from his table and intercepted
her and said, "Hello, Polly."

"Hi, fella," she said and started by.

"Wait, Polly, don't you recognize me? It's me. Phil Wilkinson?"

"Who? Oh, sure! Hi, how are you?" she asked. "I didn't recognize you. Long time no see."

"I know," he said. "Will you sit down for a few minutes and
have a drink with me?"

"Well, I was supposed to join my friends at the other table."

"Your friends? Can't they wait? Just one drink. Come on." He
half led her back to the table and she sat down with him and
crossed her legs so that her skirt rode up her thigh. The waitress
hurried over and said, "Your order?"

"Champagne," Polly said.

"*Champagne!*" P.S. protested. "Jesus Christ, Polly, not champagne. Don't do that to me, please!"

"But I *like* champagne."

"Can't we just have a simple drink and talk?" *God damn it!
What kind of crap are you trying to pull? Champagne!*

"I'm *working.*"

"I know. But for old time's sake?"

"I'm very busy," she said, turning to look at the table full of
conventioneers.

"You want that champagne?" the waitress asked.

"No," P.S. said. "Give her Scotch. A good Scotch on the rocks."

"Look—uh—Phil, why don't we meet after the show?"

"After the show?" he repeated.

"Sure," she said. She turned back to look at the other table again.

"Around the corner?" he asked uneasily.

"Sure."

"Same place?" *Polly, don't you do this to me, too!*

"Yeah, sure."

"You'll be there?"

Hippolyte stood up. "Sure, I'll be there."

P.S. knew she was lying. He felt slightly sick at his stomach and he stood up with her and put his hand on her arm. "Hippol—"

"Let *go!*"

Out of the corner of his eye P.S. could see people at other tables turning to watch what was going on. "Polly, I'm sorry," he said. "I don't know—I have the feeling you don't *know* me, don't remember me . . . don't you remember?"

"Sure," she said, "I remember. Look, I'll meet you around the corner when the place closes up, okay?"

"Polly . . . look, sit down, I'll buy you the champagne."

"No, I gotta run."

"But after the place closes?"

"Yes."

"And we can go back to your place? You still live in the same place?"

"Huh? No," she said. "I've moved."

"Where do you live now?"

"I've *got* to run," she said.

P.S. sat down dejectedly. "Okay, Polly, sure. Around the corner. I'll see you."

She stood for a moment looking down at him. "I've got to sit with those fellahs," she explained. "I promised them. Look, I'll tell you what. I'll tell them to meet me around the corner after the place closes. And when they leave, I'll come back and sit here with you, okay?"

"Okay," P.S. said.

"Now you have a drink and wait, okay?"

"Sure, I guess so," P.S. said.

Polly signaled the waitress back over.

"Bourbon and water," P.S. said. *What the hell . . . what the hell . . .*

Polly took the receipt from the waitress and stuffed it in her dress. When she saw the look P.S. gave her she smiled. "Every little bit helps."

He watched her walk back to the other table, heard her say something, then heard the men laugh and look over at him. He rested his elbow on the table and looked down at his drink. He sat there trying to keep the table from moving. The ashtray blurred. Everything was becoming blurred. It was all a blur in his mind, except for the uncomfortable certainty that he was being taken. That the Polly he had spent so much time with prior to Korea was not the same Polly who was here. That he, himself, had changed so much that perhaps she didn't recognize him. But he hadn't changed. He couldn't have changed that much. *Not in a year, just over a year . . . My God, she treated me as though I was just another customer. . . .* He was drunk. And he knew that not all of the whisky had taken hold yet. He would get drunker even if he didn't finish his drink. *Why not get drunk? Good a time as any.*

Another hour dragged by until finally P.S. heard chairs scraping back, away from tables, and he saw the conventioneers standing up. One of them was whispering to Polly. He saw Polly smile and nod, and then the men were going out. In a few minutes Polly was at his table again. She sat down and smiled across at him. *"Whew!* I thought I'd never get rid of them." She pulled out her drink chits and counted them. "This has been a good night for me. I like conventions."

"I guess they do spend a lot."

"Well, now." Polly sat back and crossed her legs so that her skirt rode up her thigh again. "Long time no see."

"I know."

"Where'd you go to?"

"Korea," he said.

"Korea? Why?"

"The Army," P.S. said. "You *don't* remember, do you?"

"Of course I do, sweetie."

"Sweetie? Polly . . . Polly, it's *me*. Phil Wilkinson . . . the guy who used to live with you? Don't you remember?"

"Of course I do. Can't I call you sweetie if I want to?"

"Anything but sweetie."

"Well, I'm glad you're back," she said. "It's nice to see you again."

"It's nice to see you."

"You want another drink?"

"No, thanks, I've had enough."

"Come on, one more. I'll have a drink with you, and then we'll go. I'll meet you around the corner and we'll go back to my place."

"Like those conventioneers?"

"What do you mean?"

"Oh, Polly, look, please . . ."

"*What?*"

"Oh, hell, nothing."

"Good, then. Let's have a drink, okay?"

"But no champagne."

"Okay," she said. "I don't really like the stuff anyway." She only had to look up and the waitress came over.

"Bourbon and water," Phil said. "And a—what?"

"Scotch on the rocks," Polly said.

The waitress went back and Polly leaned forward again. "Say, Phil?"

"What?"

"Phil, listen, I'm kind of in a little trouble . . ."

He felt his stomach go sour again. *Oh, God . . . oh, God . . . what she must think of me!* "What kind of trouble?"

"Listen, can you lend me some money?"

"How much do you need?"

"Twenty-five dollars?"

"Twenty-five? Where am I going to get money like that?"

"You're rich, aren't you? I remember you come from a good family. They'll give you the money, won't they?"

"Not any more," he said. "I'm on my own. I can't give you twenty-five . . ."

"Twenty, then? Can you lend me twenty?"

"Lend you?"

"I'll pay you back, you know I will."

"Here. I've got twenty." He took two ten-dollar bills out of his wallet and handed them to her. "I guess I owed you these anyway from the first night."

The waitress brought back the drinks and P.S. said, "You might as well give me the check, too, please."

The waitress remained standing beside the table as she added up his bill, then she tore off the check and slid it face down across the table to him. P.S. looked at it and couldn't believe it. "*Thirty-five dollars? Jesus Christ,* where do you get that!"

The waitress walked away. The manager edged in.

"Thirty-five dollars!" P.S. repeated in a fury. He tried adding up the figures. But he still couldn't come anywhere near the total on the bottom of the check.

"Can I help you, sir?"

P.S. looked up at the manager. "Yes, you can goddam well tell me how I can have a bill of thirty-five dollars for four drinks?"

"The lady had one."

"All right, five drinks."

"Five drinks, that's seventeen-fifty—three-fifty apiece. Then there's the cover charge—ten dollars, that's twenty-seven-fifty."

"Nobody said anything about a ten-dollar cover charge. You never had a cover charge here before."

"Then there's the entertainment tax and liquor tax, sales tax. I believe you'll find your bill's in order."

P.S. looked over at Polly, who was watching him. "Polly," he said. "I can't pay this check. I only have thirty dollars left. I'll have to get ten of that twenty back from you."

"Ten of what twenty? I don't have any of your money."

She pushed away from the table and started to walk away. He got up quickly and reached out to grab her arm. But before he could touch her, the manager threw him back. P.S. fell back against the table, knocking it over. He was ashamed and furious and he started up again. The manager pushed him back into the chair. "Thirty-five dollars."

P.S. in a rage rushed out of the chair toward the manager and felt two arms clamp around his, pinning his arms behind his back. "POLLY!" P.S. shouted. The manager punched him in the stomach. P.S. knew he was going to be sick. P.S. kicked backwards as hard as he could and felt his heel connect with the man's leg. "Sonuvabitch," the man said, clamping P.S.'s arms harder. P.S. saw the manager getting ready to swing again. P.S.'s glasses flew off with the force of the blow. He had a brief flash of gratitude for the man who was hitting him, for being adept enough not to smash his glasses into his eyes. He knew there wasn't any point in struggling. He knew they had him, and yet . . . He kicked forward, trying to jerk free and was hit again in the stomach. As he tried to straighten up he saw Polly watching. P.S.'s lip was bleeding and he thought his lip might be torn. The manager hit him again. P.S. felt himself slipping. He didn't want to let himself be knocked out. He wanted to stay conscious. The manager hit him in the stomach and P.S. vomited, knowing he was vomiting on the manager as well as himself.

"Sonuvabitch," the man holding him said.

P.S. felt his arms being released and he tried to run forward to grab the manager. He had the peculiar feeling that his feet were moving minutes after his brain told them to. He saw the manager backing away from him and then P.S. was sapped from behind.

I'm not unconscious . . . I'm not unconscious . . . I'm just tired. They didn't knock me out. They didn't hurt me badly. They couldn't knock me out. Those two big bastards couldn't knock me out. Took two of them. Maybe more. They couldn't knock me out. Now get up . . . Get up . . . What's the matter with the floor? Why's the floor so cold? So wet? . . . P.S. felt the ground beneath him. He tried to focus on the ground in front of him. It was black and rough. *My glasses . . . My glasses . . . What did I do with my glasses?* P.S. pushed himself up on his knees, conscious of a terrible pain in his stomach. He looked down at the ground. *It's a street . . . I'm in a street.* He saw a slight shine and ran his hands along the ground toward it and felt his fingers close over the familiar shape of his glasses. He slid them over his nose and waited for his eyes to adjust to them. *I'm in an alley!* He wiped his nose with the back of his hand and saw the blood on his sleeve. He looked around to see if there was anyone else.

And above a lighted doorway about a hundred feet away from him down at the end of the alley was the white neon cross of the Salvation Army with the neon-illuminated GOD IS LOVE. P.S. looked at the sign and began laughing. Even though it hurt he couldn't stop laughing. "Oh, God, oh—oh, God! Perfect! What a perfect touch!" P.S. stood up, holding his stomach, and with his shoulder bouncing along the brick walls he made his way toward the lights at the end of the alley. When he reached the street he stopped. He could see some men inside the Salvation Army building. "Maybe I ought to give myself up," he said, and he tried to laugh again, but his side hurt. He turned away from the Salvation Army place and walked along the sidewalk looking for a window he could see himself in. Before he did anything else he wanted to see how he looked. He found a window and cupped his hands over his reflection to cut out the light. "Not bad," he said. "Not good either . . . but not too bad. Except for that lip. That lip ought to be stitched up. . . . Where does a guy get a lip stitched at this hour?" He could feel the beginning of a giggle again. "Lip-stitch . . . You got to go to a drugstore to get lip-stitch. You say, 'Please, sir, may I have some lip-stitch,' and he'll say, 'What shade?' " P.S. leaned back against the wall and held his sides while he laughed. He saw some headlights. He stepped out to the curb and held up his arm. The taxi slowed and P.S. could see the driver looking him over. When the taxi stopped he leaned over toward the driver and said, "I know I look awful, but I promise I've done my fighting for the night. Will you give me a ride?"

The driver thought for a moment and then reached behind and unlocked the back door. P.S. opened the door and climbed in. "Thank you, sir. Thank you. I'm most grateful to you."

The driver continued to look at him.

"Ahh," P.S. said. "It's good to sit down again."

"You okay?"

"Well, I've felt better."

"You wanna go to the hospital?"

"Hospital?" P.S. thought about it for a moment. "What do you think? You think I need to?" Then he added quickly, "I'm serious. I can't tell how bad I look. I don't think I'm hurt bad. If I go to the hospital then I've got to go through all sorts of shit about signing in and maybe police. No . . . no, I don't think I'd better go to a hospital . . . How do I look?"

"You're a mess, buddy."

"Umm."

"Well, where to?"

"Maybe I'd better go to my cousin's place. He's a doctor . . . Take me to Cousin Leland's house."

"Sure, buddy, but where does Cousin Leland live?"

"Charles Street," P.S. said. "All my family lives on Charles Street. I don't know the number, but I'll tell you when we come to it."

The driver flipped down the flag and started off and P.S. sat back against the cushions. He watched the meter ticking away and suddenly patted his pockets. His wallet was still there, but, of course, it was empty. He wondered whether he should tell the driver that he didn't have any money and that he would have to get some when they got there. And then he decided he'd given the driver enough to worry about.

"That's the one," P.S. said after they had driven up and down Charles Street twice. "That's the one. I'm sure."

"Okay." The driver pulled over to the side.

"Uhh, I'll have to get some money inside," P.S. said. "Would you mind waiting?"

The driver looked back at him and then shrugged.

P.S. got out of the car and walked up the long path to Cousin Leland's house. There were lights on downstairs. He rang the doorbell and waited. He heard footsteps and then the door was opened by Matthew, Cousin Leland's colored butler.

"Matthew, it's me, Philip Wilkinson."

"Lord Jesus, Mr. Philip, what's happened to you?"

"Listen, can I borrow a couple of dollars from you to pay a cab?"

"Sure," Matthew said. "I'll pay the cab, you go right on inside."

"Is Cousin Leland there?"

"Yeahs. He's there with youah father."

18

PHILIP SADLER WILKINSON had not counted on his father's being at Cousin Leland's. He leaned against the front doorframe sick at his stomach, drunk, and he ineffectually dabbed at the blood on his lip with his handkerchief. He knew that in a moment Cousin Leland would call to Matthew to find out who was at the front door, and when there wouldn't be any answer Cousin Leland and quite possibly P.S.'s father would come to see for themselves. The last time P.S. had seen his father had been in Philadelphia, the night before he had left, when his father had given him a bottle of bourbon. They had spent the last night together in P.S.'s father's house outside Philadelphia, and his father had made a small speech to the effect that when P.S.'s great-great-grandfather went off to fight the War between the States, *his* father had given him a bottle of whisky. When P.S.'s grandfather had gone off to fight in the First World War, *his* father had given him a bottle of whisky. And when P.S.'s own father had gone off to fight in the Second World war, P.S.'s grandfather had given him a bottle of whisky. "And now, Son," P.S.'s father had concluded, "here is a bottle of whisky for you."

P.S. remembered trying to make a joke, saying that he felt a little ashamed that there wasn't a war on in Korea at the moment, and would he be permitted to drink the whisky anyway or would he have to wait for it to start again.

"Hell, no, drink it," his father had said, "and celebrate your luck that there's peace."

And P.S. had said, "Well, thank you very much, Dad," and felt as though he were in some sort of Old Crow advertisement.

P.S. stood now against the doorway wondering what he would say to his father, whom he hadn't seen for over a year. *How about, "Dad, I finally got around to drinking that whisky"* . . . *No, he wouldn't know what I was referring to.* P.S. smiled to himself. *I know. I'll say, "Trick or Treat?" and then I'll—*

"Matthew, who is it?"

P.S. swallowed hard. That was Cousin Leland. He could hear the sound of chairs being pushed back and then footsteps crossing the living room. P.S. decided the only thing to do was to face it. And he walked out of the doorway to meet them.

"My God!" was the only thing his father said.

P.S. shook hands with his father, then his older cousin, and said, "The only thing I can think of to say is that right now we are in the middle of what will someday become an amusing anecdote."

"What happened to you?" his father asked. "Are you all right?"

"I think the term is, I was 'rolled' . . . except that's an understatement. I think I'm all right . . . I was wondering whether before I go into the whole story there mightn't be something I ought to do about the lip."

"Come into the bathroom where the light's good," Cousin Leland said.

P.S. followed the doctor into the bathroom and stood with his face turned up to the light while his lip was looked at.

"I don't think any stitches will be necessary. Let me wash it off. This will probably sting . . ."

"I'm not in too much pain," P.S. said, and was gratified to see in the mirror the reflection of his father's smile.

"You're going to have a beautiful mouse."

"I hope not. The guy didn't hit me in the eye, he hit me in the cheekbone."

"That's probably the one you remember."

"Oh," he said, and a few minutes later, *"Ow!"*

"Well, you'll be as good as new in a few days. But you'll have that shiner a little longer. You have any dark glasses?"

"Yes, sir," P.S. said.

"Wear them."

"Okay."

P.S.'s cousin released him and he followed his father out of the bathroom and back into the living room. "Dad, I had to have Matthew pay for the taxi. If you'll lend me a couple of dollars, I'll pay him back."

"I already took care of that."

"Good. Thank you, sir." P.S. sat down gingerly on one of the chairs, and looked across at his father. "Well, if you don't mind a pun," he said, "I'd say that you're a sight for sore eyes."

"Phil, do you think you'd like a drink?"

"Thank you very much, Cousin Leland, but I'm not sure I need one."

"I didn't ask you if you needed one, I asked you if you wanted one."

"Well, sir, if you put it that way, then yes. I'd like one very much." He got up from his chair, wincing slightly at having to use his stomach muscles. "Can I help you?"

"Keep your seat. Matthew will bring you one. What is it you're having?"

"Bourbon. Bourbon and water, please." He sat down again and faced his father. He tried to make out his father's expression. He had the same old worried look, but he couldn't be sure that it wasn't amused-worry or anger-worry.

"Son, how in the hell could this happen to you?"

"You mean getting beaten up?"

His father nodded.

"Well, do you know the Club 88 on East Baltimore Street?"

"I am relieved to say that I don't."

"Well, you're lucky."

"I assure you, luck has nothing to do with it." Stewart Wilkinson stood up and regarded his son. "What are we going to do with you?"

"He will stay here."

"No, no, we can't permit that."

P.S. was too tired to argue with them and permitted his fate to be solved by the two older men.

"He certainly can't stay with you at your mother's," Leland said. "So, he'll have to stay here."

"I can't impose upon you in that way."

"Nonsense, Stewart. I'd like to keep an eye on him anyway. Doctor's orders."

"Well, I'm sure Philip is very grateful to you."

"Yes, sir," P.S. said. He stood up carefully and walked over to stand beside his father.

"Son, what are your plans now?"

"I don't really know, except to get my car out of a garage."

"You've bought a car?"

"No, sir, it's rented. But it has all my stuff in it."

"Your pajamas?"

"Yes, sir," P.S. said.

"Well, what were you planning to sleep in tonight?"

"I'll lend the boy a pair of mine," Leland said.

P.S. felt himself getting one of the old looks from his father, the oh-my-God-what-am-I-going-to-do-with-this-boy version.

"And your car, Philip? What do you propose to do about it?"

"I had planned to turn it in in the morning and take a train up to New York to look for a job up there."

"What kind of a job?"

"I don't know, Dad . . . I just don't know."

"I don't know what kind of job you could get looking the way you do," his father said.

"I don't either."

"You could drive with me as far as Philadelphia. I'm going home tomorrow morning. You could come home tomorrow with me while your face heals and go up to New York the next day if you'd like."

"Well, I don't know, Dad . . ." He could not stop thinking about the car trips with his father in the past. "Actually I sort of have a date," he lied. "I told this girl that I'd meet her in New York tomorrow night."

"Oh . . . In that case I suppose you'd be better off to take the train," his father said.

P.S. looked at him. He thought about his father driving back to Philadelphia alone; he thought about all the lonely nights his father had spent in the house since the divorce. He thought about his father saying, "You could come home tomorrow with me," and knew that his father meant it to be home for P.S. "I'll tell you what, Dad," P.S. said. "There was nothing really definite about this date. I can call the girl and tell her I'll see her the next day. Anyway, I'd like very much to come home with you tomorrow. Who knows? We might even decide what to do with me."

"We can talk about it on the way up," his father said.

"All right, sir, fine."

"Would you like to talk about it?" Stewart Wilkinson asked after they had cleared Baltimore and were on U.S. 40 for Wilmington.

"No . . . I don't think so, Dad," P.S. said. "I don't think it would do any good."

"Try."

"I can't, Dad . . . I wouldn't know where to begin."

"You've been hurt, haven't you?"

"Hurt? . . . Yes, yes, I suppose so."

"I don't mean just physically."

"I know."

"Well, Philip, sometimes when a person talks about it, you— it sometimes makes it a little easier. You might feel a little better if you'd talk to me about it."

Talk to you about it! When have you ever talked to me about anything? "Have you ever tried to talk about being hurt, Dad?"

"I used to," he said. "I used to try to talk to you about it."

"When was that?"

"After the divorce. When we used to drive down for Christmas together."

"I don't remember you talking about anything like that."

"You never listened. I used to try to tell you that I could be hurt, too."

"You mean by Mom?"

"Not only your mother, Son," he said sadly. "There was your brother and sister and even you . . . even you. And when you turned against me it hurt especially."

"I never turned against you, Dad."

"Not even that Christmas at Carter Hall?"

"Dad, I didn't turn *against* you."

"It's a terrible thing, Philip, to be alone."

"Yes, it is." P.S. reached inside his jacket pocket for a cigarette. "The lighter doesn't work."

"I've got a light, thanks, Dad."

"Do you feel alone?"

P.S. lit his cigarette and opened the side vent. "Not *alone,* Dad. Maybe a better word would be 'lonely.' "

"Because none of your friends are around?"

"No, not just that, Dad. That and other things. . . . Look, Dad, maybe—"

"I'm trying to help you, Philip."

"I know, and I appreciate it, but—"

"Then why won't you let me? I'd like to help you if I can. I want to help you."

"I don't think you can, Dad. Thanks though."

"You won't let me?"

"It's not a question of not letting you. I just don't think that there's anything you could do."

"You could at least let me try."

P.S. turned slightly and looked at his father. "You really *do* want to help me, don't you?"

"Of course I do! Does it surprise you?"

"I guess it does—a little."

There was a long silence.

"Dad, when you came back from the war, were you disappointed?"

"In what way?"

"While you'd been away had you kind of built up some sort of image or picture of what everything was going to be like when you returned?"

"Yes, I guess so."

"And were you disappointed when nothing worked out the way it was supposed to?"

"I think the disappointment came later. I was more confused, more puzzled than I was disappointed." There was a pause while he switched into the proper lane to get through the Wilmington interchange. "I was confused most of all by you children. You had changed so much that I hardly knew you. Let's see . . . when the war began you were . . . you were five. Page was eight and Carter was ten. And when I returned you were ten, Page thirteen, and your brother fifteen. I missed five of the most wonderful years a parent can have with his children. There's an enormous change that takes place in a child between the ages of eight and thirteen. He becomes—he's no longer a child, *your* child, he becomes a person. And I never saw it. When I returned I didn't know you—you didn't know me. And you had shown that you didn't need me, you hadn't needed me—no one had needed me—except in the war. It's difficult to make yourself needed again. It was difficult for the three of you to love a stranger." He took a deep breath and exhaled slowly. "It was difficult for everybody."

P.S. told his father about Korea, about the head shaving and the return from Korea. He told him about Charlie Merritt's wedding and the unreality that had descended upon him, the feeling that he had never been away, that no one had missed him, and then he told him about Washington and "a girl there I used to know who got married while I was in Korea." And his father said, "Hilary?" and P.S. told him about Hilary and the next day with the CIA and why he had gone to Baltimore and why he had wanted to get into a fight. P.S.'s father had listened to all of this and then he said, "You probably wouldn't remember this . . . Before the war when I was in your grandfather's law firm in Baltimore there were a couple of very bright young men from Harvard Law. They both had spent a considerable amount of time on the Continent and spoke flawless French. When the war came they suddenly were sent for by Washington. They never returned to the firm, and I did not see them again until—oh, well, after the war, 1953, 1955, thereabouts. They were both living in Paris and I saw them when the Red Cross sent me to France to set up that medical assistance program for the French in Indochina. They had just come back from Saigon and it took no great imagination on my part to know what they were doing there. One of them is still in Paris, but the other is back in Washington. If you think the CIA is really what you want to do, then I'll get in touch with my friend in Washington and see if we can't patch up your application. . . . My guess is, however, that you probably won't be wanting to work for the CIA after what you went through."

"Understatement of the year," P.S. said.

"So what are you going to do? You mentioned looking around in New York for a job. What kind of job?"

"I don't know." *Here we go again.*

"You must have something in mind."

"I suppose so," P.S. said.

"Like what?"

P.S. gritted his teeth and shrugged.

"What?" His father asked. "I didn't hear you."

"I didn't say anything."

"You can't just go into New York without some idea of what kind of job you'd be looking for."

"Well, I have some idea," P.S. said. "But it's too early to tell. Look, Dad, why don't we just forget about it for the time being? Ever since I got back everyone's been asking me what I was going to do. And, well, frankly, I'm kind of tired of it. Whatever I'm going to do, I'll do it."

"When? When you feel like getting around to it?"

"Dad, I'll take as long as I need."

"Why don't we set a time? Otherwise you could keep on looking without ever doing anything."

"Why don't we change the subject? Let's talk about you. . . . What's new at the Red Cross? What have you been doing this past year and a half?"

"Son, I'm only trying to help you."

"I'm sure you are, Dad."

"What about Denison & Sanford?"

"What do I know about investments? I don't understand the first thing about them. Every time I get a dividend check I'm surprised. I can't even balance my checkbook."

"You could learn investments."

"I know, Dad. But don't you think it would be a little awkward to have to learn in Grandfather Sanford's old firm? I mean, wouldn't it be better, that is, if I *did* want to get into that business, to learn somewhere else and *then* come into the firm."

"If they'd take you."

"If they'd take me, yes."

"Is that what you'd like to do?"

"I don't know, Dad. *I don't know.*"

There was another long silence, broken when Stewart Wilkinson said, "Well, you've got to do something."

"Yes, sir."

"How long do you think it will take you to decide what it is you will want to do?"

"I have no idea, Dad."

"You must have some idea, Son."

"But how can I? How can I know how long it will take?"

"I think we should set a time."

"*We . . . WE!* Why are 'we' setting a time for me to get a job? My God, I mean, so the time runs out, then what? What's my punishment?"

"It's not a punishment, Son."

"What will I have to do, enlist in the Army again?"

"Son, all I'm trying to do is help you."

"Dad, this is ridiculous! I'm not a child, don't you think I realize how serious all this is? Don't you think I want to get a job? Want to get started in something? What do you think I've been doing? I just got out of the Army. I just got back to this country, and I already tried out for one job and they told me they thought I was a fag. So, maybe I'll just take a few weeks off. My God, I worked my ass off in Korea and I'd like to think that instead of everybody like you pushing me into another job I—one of you might say, 'Well done, Son, you deserve a rest'—in fact, what the hell am I talking about? That's what Mom did say. . . . I think she's got a good point. I've got some money saved up from the Army, which I saved solely so I wouldn't have to rush right in and get a job. All I want to do is to do it my way, to take the time to find out what does interest me, what I *can* do, and when I do find something, then I'll do it. I don't think I'm asking a helluva lot. I'm not asking for any money or anything else. I'm perfectly willing to listen to advice—"

"That's all I've been trying to give you, Son," his father said. "I've been trying to make you understand the importance of starting something instead of just sitting around."

"And that's what I've been trying to tell you. I *am* going to start something."

"When?"

"*As soon as I find the right thing to do!*"

"Don't raise your voice against me, Son."

P.S. braced his hands against the dashboard and pushed back against the seat, his head lowered. In a few moments he relaxed and said, "I'm sorry, sir."

"Fine," his father said. "Now, let's try to discuss this like two gentlemen."

Book Three

19

PHILIP SADLER WILKINSON left the bank at the end of the day and walked slowly up Fifth Avenue. He caught himself watching his reflection in the large department store windows, and he made himself look beyond his reflection at the bright summer displays of mannequins doing fun things in fun places; and he tried to remember when was the last time he had had fun. He tried to remember whom he had been with, where he had been, what he had been doing; and he felt a little bit sick and very, very tired when he realized that he could not remember having had fun at any time since he had been sent to Korea two and a half years ago. He realized that there had been no real honest-to-God, light-up-the-face, race-the-blood, exhilarate-the-mind fun. And who was to blame?

P. S. Wilkinson had been home from Korea for a little more than a year. It had taken him one month, that first month after Washington and Hilary, to realize that it didn't make the slightest bit of difference to him which kind of job he took—that it merely depended upon who would provide him with the most benefits, the most pay, the best hours, and the least supervision. And when the choice came down to working either in the copy writing department of a large advertising firm or entering the training program of a large New York bank, he chose the bank for no better reason than a preference for thinking of himself as "in banking" rather than "in advertising." P.S. knew that others

277

might feel there was something terribly wrong in his way of choosing a career; but he knew that for him his career was what went on outside of the bank, not inside. The job meant nothing more to him than the money it paid, and he was not surprised to find that a large number of young men in his training program felt the same way. He also knew that it wasn't a search for security, for it never occurred to him that he would stay in banking, nor did he ever think of himself as a banker. The bank provided him with an income, and a satisfactory answer to what otherwise would have been the bothersome question: "What do you do?"

If someone were to ask P.S. what had happened during his first year on his own, he would be able to answer only in terms of what had happened around him: that John F. Kennedy had become the 35th President of the United States, that Adolf Eichmann had been captured in Argentina, that a CIA-sponsored invasion of Cuba had failed, and that others like Major General Walker, Yuri Gagarin, Patrice Lumumba, Shepard, Grissom, had had a great deal happen to them; but nothing had really happened to P.S.

And that was destroying him. He knew it. He knew that it had already changed him. While he worked at a job which didn't interest him, in a city he despised, he tried to find something—anything—which would mean something to him, something to which he could devote himself, to give his new life meaning. And his search lent him an intensity which made others shy away from him, bringing him only more loneliness, more boredom, more despair. And his despair alienated the few friends he saw, for his despair made them aware of their own. So he tried to make it as easy for his friends and himself as he could. He remembered their birthdays, their anniversaries, the birth dates of their children, and he sent them all cards and letters—he started a calendar book filled with dates of friends' births, anniversaries, the names of their new children—but it didn't really help, for other than Charlie and Nancy Merritt, few of his friends called him any more. He now made it a point never to invite or call them more than three times. If they regretted three times, he knew he had lost them. But he continued to send them cards and letters as though to urge them to bear with him for just a little longer, that he knew he made them uneasy, but if they would just give him a little more time he would snap out of it. He felt he had suffered some sort of breakdown—not mental, but verbal. He suffered from an inability to communicate. His picture tube had gone black, and all he could do was hope that friends would stand by and understand that service had been temporarily disrupted. P.S. wondered whether it was just himself. Whether it was he alone who had lost sight of the meaning behind getting a job, getting married, having children, believing in God, loving America, hating the Communists. He felt as though he had been betrayed. But by whom? The editors of the *Reader's Digest*? Ed Sullivan? Dwight D. Eisenhower? Walt Disney? Jack Armstrong? Beatrix Potter? How was everyone else able to cope? How were they able to ignore the meaninglessness of what was happening every day, which every day made front-page news? It must be possible to keep going. Couldn't he just continue doing what everyone thought was best? *If I did that I'd have to marry Linda . . . You spend a lot of time with a girl and everybody starts telling you to marry her . . . Marry Linda? . . . Well, she's sweet . . . she's good in bed . . . but, my God, marry her? . . . No, there must be something better to do than that. . . .*

During this past year there had been times when P.S. had enjoyed himself; but those times had almost always been in bed with Linda, or at crowded parties where he would not have to think. There had been times when a classmate or a friend had stopped off in New York and had had lunch with P.S. He could always pretend things were different during those lunches. He could tell the friend wildly amusing stories about life inside one of the nation's largest banks. P.S. could edit and enlarge upon whatever excitements he had had in the past year or years since their meeting; and he was able to eliminate, or at least gloss over, the tedious and the trite which had become so major a part of his life. P.S. caught himself looking at his reflection again. He saw that the windows reflected his height, his stoop, his youth, his long, thin face, his horn-rimmed glasses. He felt that the windows filled with shiny, sunny mannequins were a perverse mockery of his very own lack of life. And P.S. turned his eyes away from the windows to look at the real people, the not-so-much-fun people with whom he shared the sidewalk. P.S. could see his face twenty years from now in their turned-down mouths, their dulled fury, their disappointed eyes, their blotchy hands clutching sagging chins. He could feel their hate, their envy for his youth, washing over him. And he could see in the dumpy, awful women who wore brightly colored bandannas over their plastic curlers or frizzled hairdos, their disgust for his imagined desires, and contempt for whoever submitted to them.

It was late July, 1961, and the city was thick and wet with grime and almost-rain. P. S. Wilkinson turned east on 52nd Street and crossed to Madison Avenue, where he waited for the light. P.S. was pushed aside when the light changed and he watched the others scurrying across like gray, corpulent pigeons, hurrying away from the weight of the city which pressed down upon them. He had brief, abridged memories of walking with his grandfather and the dog to the park. Of the Christmas tree lights and recognizing Charles Boyer. Then visionary memories of a young Scott and Zelda Fitzgerald dripping wet from a frolicsome plunge in the Hotel Plaza fountain. Then a return to actual memories of vacations from Hotchkiss and the excitement of knowing that the pretty girl who had stood next to him at the Joint New England Prep School Concert at Hartford would be at the "Mets," the "Gets," the "Colls" and half a dozen little tea dances which he might be able to go to if his grandparents would let him stay. He crossed Park Avenue and turned uptown past the broad courtyard in front of the Seagram Building. On the steps by one of the shallow pools a male model posed idiotically in a heavy tweed winter overcoat and a furry hat, stood braced with his ecstatic smile which told how happy he was with his wonderful reduced-from-$89.95 overcoat. The model held the pose, ignoring the passers-by who broke stride to stare incredulously at the handsome young man standing in the July heat and grime in a hevy overcoat with an open briefcase at his feet displaying a host of Very Important Papers, who held in his manicured hand a vaseful of bright red plastic roses.

"Now where do you want me?" the model asked.

And Wilkinson, feeling a depressing kinship for the man, hurried on. And as he hurried he kept hearing the male model's perfectly modulated voice asking again that humiliating question, as though to ask the photographers where they wanted him to put it—himself; as though Wilkinson, himself, with his new summer suit, and his own imaginary briefcase full of meaninglessly important credentials showing he had graduated from the right schools and knew the right people, had had to ask someone, too, "Now where do you want me?"

P.S. paused at 54th and 3rd, where two artists had their studio over the Brauhaus. The door was locked, and he would not be able to climb the stairs to share even for a few minutes their creativity, their satisfaction, their success, their pleasures at doing things for themselves. They were not in. And there was nothing left for P.S. to do but to continue down to his own apartment on the fifth floor of a brownstone.

When he arrived he saw that it was six o'clock. He would have to hurry if he was to shower, shave, and get into his uniform in time for his Army Reserve meeting.

Philip Sadler Wilkinson's notebook was open and beneath his name he had written "Weekly Reserve Meeting, Wednesday, 26 July 1961. Lecture Subject: Frostbite." In the left-hand margin he had carefully printed "Notes:" the space was empty except for a large doodle of a labyrinth he had been working on for the major part of the class. He had nearly finished with shading in the false corridors, the phony doors leading into empty rooms, when he heard the class erupt into laughter. P.S. looked up at the speaker, Specialist Fifth Class Fowler, and heard him repeat, "I'm not kidding, that's what it says in the book. It says if your feet are frostbitten you should put them next to something warm or against your buddy's belly."

The class laughed again and Lieutenant Price leaned toward P.S. and whispered, "I'll be goddamed if I'd ever let you put your goddam feet against my belly."

P.S. smiled and continued doodling. The door to the classroom opened and Major Emil Torfus, the commanding officer, entered and stood at the side of the classroom until the speaker had finished. Then he stepped forward to the lectern and said, "Thank you, Fowler, for a most interesting and informative lecture. I'm sure the men benefited a great deal from it." He paused and riffled through some papers he held against the slanted top of the lectern and said, "I have a few administrative announcements and then you can all go home. There will of course be the usual meeting next Wednesday the 2nd of August, then again on the 9th, the 16th, the 23rd. Our next weekend drill is the 26th, that's Saturday, August 26th, make a note of it . . . I thought that the turnout for the Saturday drill last weekend was, quite frankly, disappointing. Now I realize that many of you were on vacation, but let's make a real effort on this next one. That's Saturday, the 26th of August . . . Captain Edgeworth?"

The executive officer stood up. "I have nothing, sir."

"Lieutenant Flanders?"

"Nothing, sir," the adjutant said, and sat down.

"Sir?" someone behind P.S. said.

"Yes, Almquist?"

Private First Class Almquist stood up. "Sir, last night on television President Kennedy said that he had asked Congress for authorization to recall certain Reserve units. Will that affect us?"

"I have no way of telling for certain," Major Torfus said. "I've received no word on that. My own guess—and I am only guessing—is that what the President is referring to are certain specialized units such as transportation units. As you know, on July 8th, I think it was, Khrushchev made a speech to the effect that he was not—he was going to suspend planned troop reductions from—I think Lieutenant Price, our order-of-battle officer, might help me out on this. . . . Price?"

"Sir," Price said, rising, "I have the clipping here. Would you like me to read it?"

"Go ahead," Major Torfus said. He looked at the other members of the Reserve unit twisting in their seats and knew that they all wanted to get out of there. "Make it short, Price," he added.

"All right, sir. Khrushchev made his speech to the graduating class of one of the military schools and he said that the Western military buildup resulting from the continuing Berlin crisis compelled—that's Khrushchev's own word, 'compelled'—the Soviet government to suspend planned troop reductions. The three-year draft cycle of 1,200,000 men would not be released but instead they would be kept on. He also said that he was determined to sign a separate peace treaty with East Germany by the end of this year. The Soviet Army now stands at about four million men, less than that, three point six is closer . . ."

"Thank you, Price," the major said. "So, Almquist, your question was whether or not the President's warning affects us and—"

"Sir?" Price said.

"Yes, Price?"

"Sir, I have the President's comments on that, too, if you'd like."

"Oh, sit down!" someone in the back said, and the rest of the class groaned with frustration at being kept longer. It was, of course, exactly the wrong thing to do, for the major said, "Read it, please."

Price held up the clipping. "The President said, and I quote, 'We cannot and will not permit the Communists to drive us out of Berlin—either gradually or by force. For the fulfillment of our pledge to that city is essential to the morale and security of West Germany, to the unity of Western Europe, and to the faith of the entire world. . . . So long as the Communists insist that they are preparing to end by themselves unilaterally our rights in West Berlin and our commitments to its people, we must be prepared to defend those rights and those commitments. We will at all times be ready to talk, if talk will help. But we must also be ready to resist with force, if force is used against us.' And then he went on to say that he was asking Congress for an additional three and a quarter billion dollars for the armed forces and an increase in the Army's authorized strength from 875,000 to one million. He also said he wanted increases in the Air Force and Navy and ordered draft calls doubled and tripled and also he wanted Congress to authorize his recalling to active service certain Reserve units, extend tours of duty, and activate some Air Transport squadrons and Air National Guard squadrons. That's about it."

"Sir?"

"Yes, Almquist?"

"Sir, all I wanted to know was whether or not this would affect us. I know what he said, I mean I watched the President, and I'm sure the rest of us did, too. Is this going to affect us?"

A few of the enlisted members of the unit smiled at Almquist for "putting down" Price.

"As I said, I've received no word from DA on this. My own guess, and again I repeat this is only a guess, I don't think this will affect us. I'm sure we'll be all right. Is there anything else?"

There was a moment of silence.

"All right, then," the major said. "I'd like to see Lieutenant Wilkinson for a moment. . . . *Dismissed!*"

P.S. got up and walked over to the major. "Yes, sir?"

"Be with you in a moment."

P.S. waited for the major to finish talking to the adjutant. When he had finished the major said, "Come on into my office, would you?"

"Yes, sir," P.S. said. He tried to think if he had done anything wrong. He silently counted up the number of meetings he had cut, and he seemed to be well under the limit. He followed the major into his office and sat down when the major told him to.

"I've got good news for you," the major said.

"Good news, sir?"

"Captain Denton is leaving the unit and that means we have a slot open. You've been pretty good about attending these meetings, being only attached to the unit, and now that there's an opening we can assign you and you can draw pay."

"Well, good, sir," P.S. said. "That's fine, I guess."

"Don't—aren't you sure?"

"Sure? Yes, sir. Sure I'm sure. I'm certain. That's good. I'd like to be assigned."

"Well, all right, then, P.S. I'll have the adjutant, Lieutenant Flanders, put your papers through."

"All right, sir," P.S. said. He stood up. "Will that be all?"

"What's your rush, P.S.?" the major asked. "Sit down, I like to get to know the men in my unit. You have to rush off somewhere?"

"No, sir," P.S. said. "I just thought I'd get back to the apartment."

"You aren't married, are you?"

"No, sir," P.S. said, and sat down again.

Sp/5 Fowler stuck his head into the office and said, "We're ready to close up now, sir."

"Fine, Fowler," the major said. "You gave a good class tonight." The major stood up. "Come on, P.S., let's get a drink and talk —that is, unless you have to rush off."

"No, sir, I can stay as long as you'd like."

"Good, let's get out of here."

P.S. got back to his apartment just before midnight. He was grateful that the stairway was empty and that he had met none of the other occupants. He did not like to be seen in his uniform. It wasn't that he was ashamed of it, he was simply bored by it. He had worn it for two years in the Army, and he had worn it practically every Wednesday night for the past year—except for the meetings he had cut. He had done his two weeks' summer camp. He felt the Army was behind him. It was in his past. It did not belong in his present life, which consisted of the bank training program. He knew others at the bank who belonged to Reserve units, and it wasn't because he worked now for a bank that he would rather forget the Army. He didn't know how to explain it, really. But he felt it was just one more *institution,* just one more big sheltering all-embracing womb that he wanted out of. It was not something he had chosen; he felt that he had never had any real choice about the Army other than serving as an officer and serving in Korea. He had always known that someday he would have to go to school and from there to college. Just as he had always known that he would have to come home from vacations. But now he felt that he was on his own.

He began getting out of his uniform, the starched khaki shirt with the silver bar on the right collar and the Military Intelligence Reserve insignia on the left collar. He carefully placed the shirt on a hanger so that he wouldn't have to get it washed and pressed until after the next meeting, then he stepped out of his khaki trousers and hung them up, too. He stood for a minute in the center of his small one-bedroom apartment trying to decide whether or not he wanted a beer before he went to bed. He knew that if he had a beer he would watch the *Late Show*, and he would stay up until one o'clock instead of going to bed right away. He decided to go to bed. He sat down on the edge of his bed and undid his shoes and slid off his socks. While he was doing this he tried to remember what he had done with his pajamas. He knew they were probably in a pile in the bottom of his closet along with his other shoes and the laundry he had neglected to take out yesterday. He got up and opened the closet door and was down on his knees when the telephone rang. *That could only be Linda!* P.S. crawled backwards out of the closet as the telephone rang again. He walked back into the small living room and sat down on the couch and picked up the phone.

"Hello?" he said.

"Hi, Phil, it's me, Linda."

"Hi, dear, what's up?"

"What are we doing—um—Friday night?"

"Friday? The day after tomorrow?

"Yes, this Friday."

"I don't know. I don't think we're doing anything, why?"

"Well, listen, I've got two tickets to *Irma La Douce*."

"How'd you get them?"

"Someone at the office couldn't use them. She gave them to me. . . . Where have you been all night? Usually you get back from the meetings by eleven."

"I had a few drinks with the major."

"What did he want?"

"What do you mean, 'What did he want?'"

"Well, you never had a drink with him before. I bet you had a date."

"Oh, for Christ's sake." P.S. laughed.

"Come on, tell me the truth. Who'd you have a date with?"

"Well, if you really must know, I snuck out with Zsa Zsa Gabor."

"I don't believe you."

"I didn't think you would."

"In fact," Linda said, "I don't believe you went to your Army meeting at all."

"I did. God's truth. In fact I'll tell you what the lecture was on tonight. It was on frostbite. You know what you're supposed to do if your feet get frostbitten? You're supposed to stick them against your buddy's belly. What do you think of that?"

"Barefoot?"

"No, for God's sake, you're supposed to take your muddy boots and—"

"I was kidding."

"Well, I did go to the meeting and I did have a drink with the major afterwards. He was lonely, that's all. And he didn't want to go home right away, and since I just became a member of the unit he wanted me to have a drink with him. That's all there was to it."

"You just became a member of the unit?"

"I've been attached up to now. But there's an opening now and I can get paid for going to the meetings. About seventy dollars a month, which will keep us in beer and cigarettes."

There was a slight pause and then Linda said, "Are you coming over?"

"You mean now? What time is it? Are you sure it isn't too late?"

"I've been doing all our ironing and I'm wide awake."

"Sure, then. I'll be right over as soon as I put some clothes on."

"About fifteen minutes?"

"It'll take a little longer. But I'm on my way . . . Say, why don't you put on some coffee?"

P.S. hung up the telephone and walked back into the bedroom. He dressed, putting on the suit that he would be wearing to the office in the morning, then he kicked shut his closet door, turned out the lights, and left his apartment.

Linda Bates had come to New York at about the same time P.S. had. They met again at Wendy Potter's cocktail party and P.S. and Linda had asked each other what they had been doing since they had last seen each other on Long Island. P.S. had apologized for his behavior at the party and explained that he was just beginning to get over the jitters he had been going through following Korea. Linda had taken a job as a secretary in one of the advertising firms and P.S. had just started his bank training program. Since neither of them knew many people in New York they drifted together. And he didn't mind. They performed little chores for each other. She would occasionally mend his socks or remind him about appointments and he would escort her to shows she wanted to see. What had started out as a casual and friendly relationship had developed into a more serious one. They began spending the night with each other for no better reason than loneliness, and now, among their acquaintances in the city, they were known as a couple, invited as a couple, and P.S. was not sure that he wanted this. Sometimes he thought how it would be to take out any girl he wanted again, to go anywhere he wanted, to do anything he wanted. No matter how late he finished work, there was always something Linda wanted him to do. A trip to the market. Some cigarettes. Flowers, because a high school classmate of Linda's was dropping by for drinks on her way through New York, and Linda wanted to show her friend what a nice apartment she had. Kitty litter for Linda's cat—that wretched, scraggly, mewling, obese, egotistical, furniture-scratching beast Linda insisted she loved. Napkins. *TV Guide*. And later, when whoever-it-was had finally gone, they would have dinner sitting across the small table from each other, or in the bedroom behind TV trays, with nothing more to say to each other than, "The liver's nice tonight, Linda," and "Thank you, Phil." And after dinner, when he felt that he might like to unwind a little from the day's work by reading a book or an article which interested him in some magazine, she would say, "Philip, you aren't going to bury yourself behind some book, are you? I haven't seen you all *day*!" And he would put the book down and say, "What would you like to talk about?" And she would say, "Why don't we play Scrabble?" And after Scrabble there would be television. P.S. would open his book or magazine again, and he'd hear, "You mustn't be a bit nervous. Try to get some sleep. Dr. Casey is an experienced neuro-*surgeon*." During weekends, when he most wanted a little privacy, a moment to himself in his own apartment, there was always something Linda wanted him to do. Saturday, the stores would be open. She still needed a rug for her dining area and had decided that a dark Spanish rug would be nice since it would hide the stains and footprints. But when they would get to the store and look at the rugs, Linda would be unable to make up her mind, and P.S. would stand beside her in a rage thinking how much reading he might have been able to do.

He thought the time had come for him to break this off before he couldn't. P.S. took the self-service elevator up to Linda's floor and got out. And as he stood at her door he realized he had forgotten his toothbrush.

"Philip?"

He woke up startled. "Yes?"

"Do you love me?"

He rolled over onto his back and stretched, yawned, then turned his head to look at Linda. The pillow blocked his view, and he flattened the pillow and said, "What, dear?"

"I don't think you really love me," Linda said.

"What time is it?"

"Look at your watch!"

"I forget where I put it." P.S. rolled onto his side and reached across to the bedside table and patted through the debris until he felt a strap. He ran his fingertip up the strap, then tapped the crystal to make sure it was a watch. He lifted the watch and held it up to the light coming in through the Venetian blinds from the street lights. "Three-thirty?" He rolled back and looked at her. "Couldn't you sleep?"

"No," she said. "I've just been thinking about us, that's all."

"What have you been thinking?"

"Philip, do you love me?"

"Sure."

"Just 'sure'?"

"Linda, of course I love you," he said. He turned toward her and moved his hand down her neck to her breast and then down to her stomach. And later, while they were making love again, he could not help feeling sorry for her. He remembered how young she had looked when he had first met her at the cocktail party on Long Island, and how she was the first girl he had talked to after Korea. He made love to her tenderly, wishing that he did love her. And when her breathing quickened, he brought her to her climax.

Afterwards, while Linda lay sleepily beside him, he tried to think of how he could leave her without hurting her. He knew he would never marry her and he also knew he liked her too much to be cruel. He tried to think whether there was anyone at the bank she might like to meet.

20

Hopes for a peaceful solution to the Berlin crisis, which had been brewing all summer, diminished during the month of August.

On Monday, August 7, P.S. was promoted to a new job in the Credit Department and Soviet Major Gherman S. Titov, 26, landed back in the Saratov region after he had completed seventeen orbits of the earth and traveled 437,500 miles. Later that same day Khrushchev, in a televised speech, said that Kennedy "had allowed himself to resort to threats" and had confronted the Soviet Union with "something in the nature of an ultimatum." Khrushchev announced, "It may be that we shall have to increase in the future the numerical strength of the Army on the western frontiers by moving divisions from other parts of the Soviet Union." Listening to the news that night back in his apartment, P. S. Wilkinson felt the same, cottony feeling in the mouth that he had felt back in Korea when the major had told him that the alert was very real.

On Wednesday, August 9, Khrushchev warned that the Soviet Union had a 100-megaton bomb and a rocket capable of delivering it. He said that the Soviet Union did not want war, but that if war resulted from an attack by West Germany, "All Germany will be reduced to dust."

That weekend East Germany closed the borders between East and West Germany—the escape route used by more than two million Germans since 1949 to flee to the free world.

On Wednesday, August 16, the Soviet commandant in Berlin rejected Allied protests and said that it was an attempt on their part to interfere in matters that were exclusively the concern of the East German government. Mayor Willy Brandt, addressing a crowd of 250,000 West Berliners at a rally, warned that Berlin must not become another "Munich." He announced that he had sent a personal message to President Kennedy asking for "not merely words but political action."

Just so long as it remains a "political action," P.S. thought.

On Friday, August 18, President Kennedy ordered a 1500-man battle group to West Berlin to reinforce the U.S. Army Garrison already there. East Germany tightened its border curbs and cut down its crossing points to seven. They then started a wall of concrete blocks.

On Wednesday, the 23rd of August, the Soviet Union sent similar notes to the United States, Great Britain, and France, charging that the Western Powers were abusing their rights to the air corridors over East Germany by flying anti-Communist spies from West Germany into Berlin.

And on Thursday Philip Sadler Wilkinson still had not decided what he wanted to do with Linda.

He stopped off at her apartment after work that night to pick her up. They were to go to the Merritts' for dinner. He rang the buzzer and waited, then used his key to open the door, and walked in. He could hear the water running out of her bathtub.

"Philip, is that you?" she called.

"Hi, dear," he answered.

"Make yourself a drink, I'll be right out."

"Can I make one for you?"

"No, thanks. Help yourself. I'll be right out."

P.S. fixed himself a drink and carried it into the living room. He sat down on the couch beneath the travel poster and leafed through a magazine. A few minutes later Linda came out of the bathroom. She was wearing a terrycloth bathrobe, and her wet feet left damp prints on the rug as she came over to him. He looked up and smiled. "Hi."

She kissed his cheek. "Hi," she said. "What time is it?"

He looked at his watch. "Six-thirty about."

"What time are we supposed to be at the Merritts'?"

"Seven, wasn't it?"

"You wrote it down."

"I did?" He thought for a moment. "Then it's seven. I'm sure of it."

"I guess I'd better start getting ready."

"Okay," he said.

"Say, Philip. Do you have any stamps?"

He reached into his jacket pocket for his wallet. He fished out some stamps. "How many do you need?"

"Just one. I have to mail a letter to my mother."

He tore off a stamp and handed it to her. She took the stamp and he thought she was going to say something, then she turned and walked into the bedroom. It suddenly occurred to him that he hadn't kissed her, that he hadn't said anything nice to her. He got up from the couch and walked to her bedroom. He knocked.

"Come in."

He opened the door. She was standing in front of the mirror brushing her hair.

"Would you like me to mail the letter for you? I could do it now if you'd like."

She looked at him, surprised. "There's no rush. I can mail it on the way to the Merritts'."

"Oh, sure. Of course. How stupid of me." He started out of the bedroom.

"Don't go. While you're here, what'll I wear tonight?"

"Anything you like."

"*Think*. What should I wear?"

"Wear the green one. I've always liked that. Charlie's mother and father will be there."

"It's at the cleaner's."

"Well, then, how about the black one? Your new one?"

"Okay," she said. She began to push dresses around in her closet, then she emerged and tucked the black dress, on its hanger, beneath her chin. "Look all right?"

"Belle of the ball."

"Good." She laid the dress on the bed, then undid her bathrobe and slid out of it. And as he stood there looking at her he felt himself beginning to want her, and he stepped toward her.

"We don't have to be exactly on time at the Merritts'," he said, touching her.

She looked at him, and when he kissed her, he felt her still looking at him and he pulled away. "What's the matter?" he asked.

"Ohh, Philip . . ."

"What is it?"

She sat down on the edge of the bed and leaned forward to pick up the bathrobe and then she covered herself with it.

"What's the matter?" he repeated.

She shook her head.

He sat down on the bed next to her and took her hand. "Tell me, Linda, please."

She lifted her hand in his and pressed the back of his hand against her cheek. "I don't know, Philip . . . I don't know what it is. It's just that—I mean, all we ever seem to be able to do together is sleep with each other. We never seem to talk."

"We *do* talk to each other."

"But why, Philip, why do we always end up in bed?"

"Because—because we need each other," he said.

"Why do you need me?"

"You? Because, it's not just my needing you. There are so many reasons, Linda. I think we need each other—I'm not talking about just physically. When you're lonely you just need someone."

"But what happens if I get pregnant?"

Oh, my God . . . ". . . You're—you're not, are you?"

"No, but what if I were?"

"I'd marry you, of course."

" 'Of course.' . . . Philip, what kind of marriage would that make?"

"How can I answer a question like that?"

"I don't know . . . I just sometimes wish, I guess, Philip . . . I mean, do you think you could ever want to marry me? NO! DON'T

SAY ANYTHING! DON'T ANSWER THAT! I had no right to say that. Don't say anything."

P.S. could not look at her. He knew she wanted him to say something, that she desperately wanted him to say that he loved her, that he did want to marry her. But he was silent. Suffering. And finally Linda spoke again. "I guess I'd better get dressed," she said.

He stood up and walked into the living room and stood looking through the Venetian blinds at the street below.

They didn't speak again until she called, "Phil?"

He turned back from the window. "Yes?"

"I'm sorry."

"Don't be."

She walked into the living room. "I'm ready. Do you think we'll be able to get a taxi?"

"I hope so." He kissed her cheek. "You look very nice."

They sat together silently in the taxi to Charlie Merritt's apartment. Linda nervously tugged at the fingertips of her gloves, and P.S. reached over and patted her hand. She took his hand and squeezed it tightly. "What are Charlie's parents like?"

"They're very nice. Don't worry, they'll only be there for about twenty minutes and then they're going to the theater."

"What will I say to them?"

"Anything. You'll think of something. It won't be hard." And to himself he added, *At least I hope so.* The last time they went out to dinner with Charlie and Nancy, the Taylors had been there, and Linda had sat like a lump on the sofa the whole evening without saying anything. P.S. had told the Taylors that Linda was terribly shy with people she didn't know well. And when on the way home he had asked her why she hadn't tried to talk to anyone she said she had been bored. *Bored! . . . Jesus, think how boring she must have been to them!* P.S. turned to look out the side window. *And the Taylors will probably be there tonight, too.*

"I never know what to say to people."

"Well, Mrs. Merritt will do most of the talking."

"What's she like?"

"You'll like her, don't worry."

"But I *do* worry. After all, Charlie's your best friend. You've known the Merritts practically all your life and they're very fond of you. They know all about you. They *like* you. And . . . well, I want them to like me."

"They will."

"I hope so."

He squeezed her hand and was conscious that he should say something positive to her. Something that would encourage her.

The taxi stopped and P.S. paid the driver, then helped Linda out. He held the apartment house door open for her and Linda ducked beneath his arm. He followed her through the lobby and waited while she checked herself in the lobby mirror.

"You look lovely," he said.

"Do you really think I look all right?" she asked as they entered the self-service elevator.

"Beautiful . . . except for one little thing. It probably doesn't matter."

"*Tell* me! What *is* it?"

"Well, it's just that you have your dress on backwards."

"Oh, I do not!" she giggled.

It wasn't until Charlie opened the door and P.S. started to say hello that he realized he had been gritting his teeth. P.S. helped Linda off with her coat and handed it to Charlie. In the living room P.S. could see Charlie's mother and father. He put his arm around Linda's waist, and as they came into the living room, Mr. Merritt said, "Well, gosh, boy, how are you?"

P.S. introduced Linda to Mr. and Mrs. Merritt, and then Nancy came in from the bedroom and said, "Hi." Charlie brought drinks for P.S. and Linda, and the men drifted over to one side of the living room. Mr. Merritt began talking about the last time he had gone duck shooting. P.S. glanced across the living room to see how Linda was doing. She was sitting on one end of the long couch, Nancy on the other, with Mrs. Merritt between them. Nancy and Mrs. Merritt were talking and Linda was looking down at the rug, listening to them. Mrs. Merritt turned and said something to Linda, and Linda looked up from the rug and said, "Well,

Phil and I want very much to have children."

"Oh, my GOD!" P.S. said to her silently.

". . . It was one of the most beautiful jobs of retrieving I have ever seen," Mr. Merritt said, "except, of course, it wasn't my duck."

"At least the dog didn't bring back a decoy," P.S. said, and the three of them laughed together. Then, after a brief pause, Mr. Merritt said, "Well, P.S., how do you like living in New York?"

"Fine, sir."

"I thought you might. She's a damn sight prettier than you deserve, you rascal."

"Yes, sir," P.S. said.

"Well, gosh, boy, it's good to see you," Mr. Merritt said again. "Last time I saw you you were just getting out of the Army."

"Well, it looks like I might be going back in again," P.S. said.

"Why? This Berlin thing? Just because they built this dinky wall last week? Cinder blocks?"

"It's a little more serious than that, sir," P.S. said.

"You really think you'll have to go back in?" Charlie asked.

"I hope not. I don't know."

"Oh, they have these Berlin crises every year," Mr. Merritt said. "Probably won't mean a thing. Hell, boy, it's just politics."

"Yes, sir," P.S. said. He saw that Mrs. Merritt was coming across the room to speak to him.

"We have to rush off soon," she said, "and I do want a few words with you before we go. It's been so long."

"I know, not since Charlie's wedding," he said. "It certainly is nice to see you again."

"It's nice to see you," Mrs. Merritt said. "Now tell me, Phil, where did you find that little girl of yours?"

"I met her on Long Island."

"I think she's just the sweetest thing, and so perfect for you. Are you going to marry her?"

"Nothing planned yet, but I'm very glad you like her," P.S. said.

"But I do! And you really must get Charlie to bring the two of you down to the farm sometime. We'd love to have you stay with us."

Then Mrs. Merritt looked around for her husband and said, "We must be going. Right this minute."

At the door, with her coat on, she shook hands with Linda and P.S. and said, "It's so nice to see you two together. You make a very sweet couple." She gave P.S.'s hand an extra little squeeze.

In the confusion of the good-bys, P.S. asked Linda how she was doing.

"Okay," she said.

"How did you like Charlie's parents?"

"Well, I never really spoke to Mr. Merritt. I didn't have much of a chance to speak to Mrs. Merritt, either. I mean there just wasn't much I could say."

"Did you try?"

"Oh, Phil . . . of *course* I tried! It was just that she and Nancy hadn't seen each other in some time and they were talking about the baby and all. And—and I just felt that they would probably rather talk to each other than to me."

P.S. looked at her, noticing how sad her tone was. "Mrs. Merritt said she liked you a lot," he said.

After the baby sitter arrived, they all went to a German restaurant for dinner, and from there downtown to the Taylors' apartment. A friend of the Taylors' dropped in, and now there were seven of them in the tiny apartment. Paul Taylor worked downtown on the Street, and Alice Taylor worked as an interior designer. P.S. ended up in the kitchen with Paul Taylor and Nancy Merritt. P.S. sat leaning back in his chair against the kitchen table, listening to Nancy say how great it was being married to Charlie, and he was thinking how great it would be to be married to Nancy. He turned and looked out into the living room at Linda. She was sitting next to Alice Taylor, who was talking about cooking. Linda caught his eye and made the "I-want-to-go-home" sign, and P.S. ignored it.

"I think Linda is absolutely the sweetest person," Nancy told him.

"Yes, she is," P.S. said.

"You two are so cute together. I mean you always seem to be worrying about each other."

"We do?" P.S. asked, honestly surprised.

"Of course you do! Even right now. I can tell you weren't really listening to a word I was saying. You were thinking about Linda, now, weren't you?"

"Yes, but—"

"See? I think it's just marvelous," Nancy said. "If you can keep it that way, you'll have a wonderful marriage. Honestly, after just over a year, I don't even think Charlie notices I'm in the room. When we go to a party he just drops me at the front door, and that's the last I see of him until it's time to go."

"It doesn't seem that you and Charlie have been married that long. You were married just after I got out of Korea—that doesn't seem that long ago."

"It was, though. I'll never forget you. You'd been home just about a week, and the whole time you kept saying, 'This is the first champagne I've had in eighteen months.' Or, 'You're the first white woman I've seen in over a year.' You were hilarious."

"That doesn't sound too hilarious to me. It sounds pretty awful."

"Well, you were very funny."

"And probably very drunk."

"But funny," Nancy said. "Especially getting caught in the bushes with Hilary— Oh, by the way! She wrote me that she was back in Washington now with Hester and that she was terribly lonely and upset, but at the same time relieved that it was all over. You know she got her divorce."

"Her *divorce!* My God! I hadn't— Do you have the letter? She got a divorce? When?" P.S. asked. "Do you have the letter with you?"

"It's at the apartment."

"Well, what did she say? Can you remember what she said? Why was she upset? Because of the divorce?"

"Of course. She said that she thought she had failed and—"

"She thought *she* had failed—how? Why did she say that?"

"I don't know why, P.S., it was a very short letter. Just a few lines really. She said that she was back in Washington, that she was lonely and upset and—"

"She just said that? That's all? 'I'm back in Washington and I'm lonely and upset'?"

"Oh, Philip, for heaven's sake! I can't remember exactly what she said."

"Where in Washington?"

"I suppose the house where she and Bruce were living."

"Are you sure?"

"Well, I think I am. That was the address on the stationery, and I'd think if she had moved she would have crossed it out or put in a new address."

"Maybe I should call her," he said. "When did the letter arrive?"

"Oh, a couple of days ago. . . . Can you reach me those cups up there?"

"Hi," Linda said. "Can I do anything?"

P.S. looked at Nancy in desperation.

"Yes." Nancy laughed. "You can calm P.S. down."

"Nothing's the matter with me," P.S. insisted.

"What's the matter with him?" Linda asked.

"Oh, he's all excited about Hilary's divorce."

When P.S. and Linda returned to her apartment, P.S. changed into his pajamas without speaking to Linda. Then he glanced at the newspaper he had bought on the way back. He read that the White House had warned the Soviet Union not to interfere with free access to Berlin, but all he could think about was Hilary. *She's free! She's got her divorce. This is the answer to everyth—*

"Phil?" Linda called.

"Yes, dear?" P.S. picked up a book he had been reading.

"Are you coming to bed?"

"In a few minutes. I want to finish this chapter, and then I'll be right there. You go on to sleep. I'll be in soon."

"Okay. . . ."

He watched her leave and could hear her climbing into bed, but he could not hear if she had turned out the light. P.S. sat with his thumb marking his place in the book, thinking about her, how sad and forlorn she appeared at times. He tried not to feel sorry for her. If he felt sorry for her, the next step would be pity, and after pity would come hate. He wished he knew how he could make them both happy, how he could end this relationship neatly and quickly, how he could make everything become all right. He tucked the book jacket into the book to mark his place, and stood up, and walked through the apartment turning out lights. Linda was lying on her back, her eyes open and staring blankly at the bedroom ceiling. He got into bed next to her, reached up, and turned out the light. Then he leaned over her, kissed her, and said good night. She did not say anything, so he rolled over onto his side and lay with his back to her. In a few moments he felt her move and rest her cold foot against his calf, and he jerked his leg away. In a spasm, he crushed his face into the pillow, pressing his hands against his temples. *Oh, my God, my God, what can I do? Am I stuck? Stuck with her?* He rolled over onto his back. In the light coming through the Venetian blinds from the street, he could see that Linda was sitting up in bed, her arms clasped around her knees. He looked at her for a moment, wondering whether he should risk asking her what was the matter, knowing that he would have to pry the words out of her, squeeze her into talking. But she looked so sad, so lonely sitting up in bed next to him. He reached over onto the night table for a cigarette, lit it, leaned back against the pillow, and asked, "What's the matter?"

She did not speak.

"Linda, it's after midnight. Tell me, what's the matter?"

There was another long silence. P.S. considered going to sleep, but he had started it and he knew he would have to continue. He took a puff on his cigarette and watched the red tip glow in the darkness. Then he looked over at her again and patted her hand. "Linda, you can't just be sitting up in bed and staring off into the darkness unless something's bothering you. Now tell me, what is it?"

"Nothing."

"What?"

"Nothing's the matter, Philip."

"Well, then, what were you thinking about?"

"Nothing."

"Look, you can't just be sitting in bed and not thinking. The mind doesn't work that way. You must have been thinking about something. Now tell me, what was it?"

"It wasn't anything."

"What *was* it?"

She slid down into the bed so that she was lying flat on her back. He could see that her eyes were still open. She took a deep breath. "I was thinking about us."

"What about us?"

"Nothing."

"Oh, for God's sake!" P.S. said. "Please, let's not go through this whole thing again. I mean, if you've got something bothering you, let's talk about it. If we can't even talk about it, then we've really got trouble. We've got a great big zero as far as any sort of life together goes. Now, come on. It isn't hard. Just tell me, tell me what it is that's bothering you. What—what were you thinking about us?"

"I was thinking that—I was thinking that—" she took another deep breath—"I was thinking that I don't—I can't seem to make you happy. Everything I do is wrong."

"That isn't true!" P.S. said.

There was another long period of silence. He was still sitting up on the bed looking down at Linda, she lying there with her eyes open not looking at anything. "Linda, would you like a cigarette?"

She nodded.

"Where are yours?"

"They're in my pocketbook."

"Where's your pocketbook?"

"I think it's on the chair next to my bureau."

P.S. got out of bed and felt his way over to the bureau, then down to the chair. "Could you turn on a light?"

"Sure."

P.S. lifted a pair of her slacks and a blouse off the chair, then hunted around inside her pocketbook until he found the cigarettes. He lit a cigarette for her, and then carried the ashtray from the night table to the bed. He placed the ashtray by her side and gave her the cigarette. He slid into bed again. They lay in bed together, not touching, not speaking, and he tapped his cigarette ash into the ashtray.

"Phil?" Linda asked quietly.

"Yes?"

"Phil, what's the matter with us?"

"What do you mean, 'what's the matter with us?'"

"I mean—oh, I don't know. I mean, there's just something the matter with us, that's all."

"I don't know," he said. "I'm not sure I know what you mean."

"We don't seem to have any fun together."

"We have fun," he said.

"Not as much as Charlie and Nancy."

"Well, they're different."

"Why?"

"Why are they different?" P.S. asked. *Because they're in love with each other.* "I don't know, maybe I'm wrong. Maybe they're not so different."

"But they *are* different," Linda insisted. "You said so yourself. Why—what makes them different?"

He was silent for a moment, and then he said, "Well, maybe because they just know each other better than we do. Maybe they share things. They're enthusiastic about each other and what they're doing. They can talk to each other. They grew up together. I mean, there are a lot of things. They *are* different." He put out his cigarette. "I mean, look, Linda, what are you interested in? You never ask me about my job, for example."

"You never tell me anything about it."

"Well, all right then, but what interests you?"

"I don't know."

Oh, God! "But you must be interested in something. Music? The apartment? New York? The theater? I mean, you have to be interested in things or there isn't any point in being alive."

"I'm interested in you," she said.

"That isn't fair!" P.S. protested. "Other than me, what are you interested in?"

"Nothing."

"Oh, come on now, Linda . . . you know that isn't true."

"Phil, are you happy we're together?"

"What? What kind of question is that?"

"A simple question. Are you happy with me?"

". . . At times."

"Not all the time?"

"No, not all the time. I wouldn't be that unrealistic. For God's sake, are you glad twenty-four hours a day you're with me?"

"Yes."

"Be honest."

"I *am* being honest," she said.

"Well, I don't believe you."

"But I *mean* it. I am happy with you."

"Let's go back to the first part. Are you—what are you really interested in? What do you really want of life?"

"I want to have a baby."

Oh, God, that would really slam the trap shut! "Linda . . . Linda, we've got plenty of time. We can wait. Let's at least make sure we can be happy with each other, be sure of each other before we get married and certainly before we have a baby."

"*I'm* sure of us."

"Well, then, for my sake, let's wait. Please?"

"But what if I can't have a baby?"

"Oh, for God's sake!" He reached for a cigarette, lit it, and sat back. *If she won't go to sleep, I'll never get a chance to call Hilary.*

"What are you thinking about?"

"Nothing," he said. Then, remembering what he had said when Linda had answered "Nothing," he added, "I was thinking about being a father."

"What were you thinking?"

"I was thinking how many changes it would bring."

"Ummm."

Again silence.

"Would you like another cigarette, Linda?"

"No, thanks."

He got out of bed. "I think I'll get a beer. Would you like one?"

"I'll take some of yours," she said. "If you wouldn't mind."

"Sure," P.S. said. He walked into the kitchen and got a beer out of the refrigerator. He filled a glass, drank what was left in the can, and walked back into the bedroom. Sitting on the edge of the bed, he passed the glass of beer across to Linda. "Here, take some."

She pushed herself back up into a sitting position and sipped the beer. She passed the glass back to P.S. as he got into bed. He slid his feet beneath the covers and leaned back holding the cold glass between his palms. He looked down at the monogrammed top sheet. The monogram was backwards; the sheet had been put on wrong side up.

"God, I think the Taylors are bores," Linda said.

"They aren't all that bad." He put the beer glass on the night table. "And, besides, I watched you at their apartment. You never said a word to Alice."

"I did too!" Linda protested. "We talked for a long time about the apartments and decorating them, and then she wanted to know how to cook something Nancy had told her I could make. And I told her. That's all there was to it. It was boring. And they're bores."

"But they mightn't be. If you just made the effort to talk to them and find out about them. I mean, they could just as easily think that we're bores."

"You mean maybe they think *I'm* a bore."

"I didn't say that, and I don't mean that."

"Does it bother you when I don't talk to people?"

"Of course it does. Sure it does. I like to see you have a good time."

"Well, I wasn't."

"And it looked it."

"Were you ashamed of me?"

"Why should I be ashamed of you?"

"Because I don't talk to people."

"No, I—it doesn't make me *ashamed* of you. I just worry about you. I mean if you aren't having a good time you show it. Other people see it, and it makes them feel uncomfortable, that's all."

"But what could I do? I didn't have anything to say to them. I mean Mr. Merritt was talking to you about duck shooting. Mrs. Merritt was talking about Nancy's baby. Alice Taylor was talking about a soufflé, and Charlie was reading a magazine. You and Nancy and Paul were in the kitchen most of the time. What could I do?"

"You could do anything. I don't care. But, Jesus, Linda, you've got to make the effort. So what if talking about cooking and interior decorating and duck shooting isn't the most exciting thing in the world? At least, it's something that *they* are interested in. I mean, you've got to make the effort like I said. When we go out together it isn't always going to be fun. You've got to carry your share of the load. When you don't it makes it pretty hard for me."

"Maybe you'd be better off at those parties if you didn't have to bring me along."

"Now what the hell does that mean?"

"I mean . . . I mean, maybe you'd be a lot better off if we weren't together so much."

"Why do you say that? Do you think you'd be better off if we didn't see each other?"

"No, Philip, of course that isn't what I was thinking."

He took a sip of beer and handed the glass across to Linda. She finished the beer and passed him back the empty glass. He looked at the empty glass, then put it on the bedside table. He turned back to her. "How come you're thinking about breaking up all of a sudden?"

"I didn't say anything about breaking up."

"What were you talking about then?" he asked. "You said maybe I'd be happier if we didn't see each other. If that doesn't mean breaking up, I'd like to know what it does mean."

"Would not seeing each other make you happy?"

"You haven't answered my question."

"You answer mine," she said.

"Which one?"

"Do you want to break up?"

"Do you?" P.S. asked.

"Do *you?* Of course, I don't want to."

He paused.

"You're thinking about it, aren't you?" Linda said.

"Well, yes and no."

"You mean, yes, you would like to break up, but no, you wouldn't?"

"I mean, yes, I was thinking about it, but no, I don't want to. All it means is that I'm tired."

"But the idea did seem attractive."

"No, it means I'm very tired." He lay flat in the bed, thinking about the life he would lead if he were free again.

"Have you reached your decision yet?" Linda asked him.

"Linda, at this point I'm so tired that I can't even decide whether I'll be more comfortable sleeping on my back or on my side. Can't we just talk about this at a more sensible hour, please? Why do women always want to talk to men at one o'clock in the morning?"

"In other words, this doesn't seem very important to you."

"Of course it does. Of course it is. But can't we talk about it later?" *Do I want to break up? I don't know whether I want to or not, I know I don't not want to break up. It's just that I—*

"You mean, you're going to drop it right here. Leave it the way it stands?"

Linda, I can't tell you the way I feel because you love me. I can't be that cruel . . . I can't hurt you . . . I can only hurt myself. . . . He looked over at her. She was sitting up in bed again, hugging her knees. He pushed himself up on one arm and leaned over and kissed her. *Oh, God, she's crying. She's crying!* He lay back in the bed, and pushed the pillow around until he was comfortable. He lay on his side, took a deep breath, and exhaled slowly.

"Phil?"

"Hmm?"

"Do you love me?"

"Yes, dear."

"Are you sure?"

"Yes, dear."

"I love you."

"Yes, dear."

"Are you being patient with me?"

He reached behind his back for her hand and squeezed it. "Yes, dear."

"Good night, Phil."

He let go of her hand. "Good night, Linda." He felt her roll over toward him and he squeezed the pillow between his fingers, despising his cowardice.

After a while she fell asleep, and he got up very quietly and walked into the living room. He looked at his wristwatch. *It's a little after two. I can get back to my apartment by two-thirty . . . call Hilary . . .*

"Are you just going to stand there?" Linda asked from the bedroom door.

P.S. jumped at her voice. "I'm sorry," he said. "I couldn't sleep. I was thinking."

"About Hilary?"

"No, actually, I was thinking I was pretty tired and Friday's always a big day at the bank."

"You're still in love with her, aren't you?"

"Who, Hilary?"

"Oh, Philip . . ."

"What?"

"Nothing, Philip. Good night," Linda said. "I had a lovely time. Thank you very much." She turned and walked into her bedroom.

"Linda, please, don't be that way," he said, following her.

"What way do you want me to be? How do you expect me to feel? What do you want from me, Philip? What do I have to do for you?"

"Linda, I'm sorry—"

" 'Sorry' . . . Sorry! I just bet you're sorry!" She began to cry.

"Linda . . ."

"Go away, Philip, please."

"I—" He turned, picked up his clothes and walked out of the bedroom. After he was dressed he went back inside. She was sitting on the edge of the bed looking down at the floor. "I'll call you," he said.

She did not look up at him, and P.S. left her apartment. While he was waiting for the self-service elevator to come up he wondered what he could have said to Linda. And then he had the sudden panic that she might dart out of her apartment after him, and there would be more despair, more tears, more silences. But the elevator door opened, he stepped in, and rode down to the street. It was two-twenty, and he hurried back to his apartment.

P. S. Wilkinson got out enough ice to make himself a bourbon on the rocks, then he carried the drink and a clean ashtray and cigarettes over to the coffee table and sat down. He looked at the telephone and clenched and unclenched both fists as though in preparation for a piano exercise. Not until he had lit the cigarette and taken a sip of his drink was he able to call the operator and ask her to place a long-distance, person-to-person phone call for him to Mrs. Bruce Mallory, "and if there's no number listed there, you might find it under 'Hilary Farnum.'" He held the telephone tightly against his ear and he listened to the operator asking routing and then the electronic clicks and stutters as the call went through. *One ring . . . two rings . . . Don't be asleep . . . three rings, ah!* And the operator: "I have a person-to-person telephone call for Mrs. Bruce Mallory, is this she?"

"Yes, it is."

"Go ahead, New York," the operator said.

"Hilary?"

"Yes. Who is this?"

"It's P.S.," he said.

" . . ."

"It's Phil . . . how are you?" *Inane goddam question.* "Did I wake you up?"

"Where are you?"

"New York. I was—"

"How are you?"

"Fine. Fine . . . Everybody's fine," he said, remembering their first meeting after his return from Korea. "Hilary, I had dinner with Charlie and Nancy Merritt and—"

"How are they?"

"They're fine, too. . . . Hilary, what I'm trying to say is that Nancy told me about your getting a divorce, and I'd like to see you."

". . ."

"Would that be all right?" He hated having to raise his voice because of the bad connection. "May I come down to Washington to see you?"

"Fine."

"You don't sound very enthusiastic," he said, trying to make his voice sound light.

". . . I haven't heard from you in over a year. It's three in the morning. You never wrote me or called—"

"How could I? I—"

"Why couldn't you? Why did you decide to call me now?"

"Well, that's—that's what—that's why I want to see you. I want to talk to you. . . . If I catch a shuttle flight after work, I can get into Washington by seven. Would that be all right? Can I take you to dinner?"

"Philip, why have you waited this long to call me?"

"I couldn't call you. Your husband— Why didn't you write me? I never knew you were getting a divorce, that you'd gotten a divorce. Why didn't you tell me?"

". . ."

"At least you could have told me."

"I didn't want you to think you were responsible."

To think I was responsible, but—

". . . Well, come down if you'd like, Philip."

"I'd like to very much. I'll call you when I get into town."

"Call me from the airport."

"You're still at—in the house?"

"Yes."

"Good. Then, I'll call you there from the airport."

". . ."

"Good night, Hilary."

"Good night, Philip."

"And—and, Hilary?"

"Yes."

"I'm looking forward to seeing you again."

He hung up and looked at the telephone for a moment, then he reached for his cigarette. It had gone out. He didn't bother to light it again, and he picked up his drink and emptied it in the sink.

21

ON THE FLIGHT to Washington he thought about how good it would be to see Hilary again. He knew that as soon as they were together he could make her understand why he had been unable to write her. *What if Bruce had seen the letter? What could I say? The year away from you hasn't changed my feelings for you . . . Everywhere I went I saw you . . . I would think I saw you and chase after you, but it was always someone else . . .* He imagined himself holding Hilary's hand. *Every time I saw something new I'd want you to see it with me. I'd wish you were there. I thought of you every day. I couldn't write you; not while you were married—and I never knew, you never told me about your divorce. I don't even know where you went. I kept thinking I'd meet you on the street. That you'd have come up to New York to shop, buy clothes. I'd go to Saks, and expect to find you there. I'd always look for you in Saks. A hundred times I thought of writing you, even a postcard. I'd think of how I could write you on bank stationery, so that your husband would think it was a business letter—but still he might open it and what then?* And because all of it was true he knew Hilary would believe him. She would want to believe him. And everything would be all right between them; the year apart would not matter. It would be as though it had never existed.

He was excited about seeing Hilary. And at the same time he was aware that this was the first excitement of any kind he had felt in a long time. He was determined to help Hilary, to love the baby, to mix the proper amount of respect for Bruce with support of Hilary's decisions about the child. Hilary would need him. Nancy Merritt had said she was lonely and upset. P.S. knew he could fix that. He had sudden and warm kaleidoscopic images of himself with Hilary and Hester: during the winter, laughing . . . a snowball fight . . . Christmas. . . . Walks during the spring . . . bedtime stories . . . Sunday papers. . . . He knew how good they would be together. *Maybe we'll take trips. I'd like Hilary to see where I worked out west* . . . and he knew that he and Hilary would have a son. They'd all be living in the country by then.

The stewardess announced that they would be landing in Washington in a few minutes. P.S. looked at his watch. It was a quarter to seven. He leaned forward to look out the window. Washington's marble monuments and buildings were pink in the sunset. The final approach was made along the Potomac River, and as the plane's flaps and gear were lowered they passed over Arlington Cemetery, and through his window P.S. could look down the Memorial Bridge to the Lincoln Monument, the Reflecting Pool, and beyond that the Washington Monument and the Capitol.

P.S. called Hilary from the airport, then he picked up his small suitcase and caught a taxi. By the time they reached the Memorial Bridge the lights were on, and they crossed the bridge, P.S. twisting to look at the Lincoln Memorial, and they turned down to the Rock Creek Parkway, passed under the bridge by the floating amphitheater.

Maybe there'll be a show, I could take Hilary to a show there tomorrow night. We could even rent a canoe or something and listen to the music from the water.

"Driver? Do you know if there's a show at the amphitheater. that floating thing, tomorrow night?"

"At the Watergate? On the barge? I think so, you'd have to check the papers."

"Okay, fine."

They turned off the parkway and up to P Street and then through Georgetown. The taxi stopped and P.S. paid the driver and crossed the street to Hilary's house. He put down his small suitcase, checked the flaps on his jacket pockets, brushed off the ashes, and rang the doorbell.

Hilary opened the door and said, "Is your taxi still here?"

P.S. turned. "It's gone."

"That's too bad. I should have told you to hold the taxi. They're hard to get at this hour."

She stood blocking the door, and P.S. stood looking at her. "May I come in?"

"We've got to hurry," she said. "Put your suitcase in the hallway, you can pick it up later."

"All right," he said. She stepped aside and he put the suitcase down. When he came back to her she suddenly shoved her hand out and shook hands with him. "How are you?" she asked.

"Okay, fine. . . . What's all the rush?"

"Friday night. It's hard to get a reservation. I made a reservation for us for seven-thirty at Martin's, so we'd better start if we're to get there on time."

P.S. shrugged. "Let's go then."

Hilary started walking and P.S. had to hurry to catch up with her. He came up beside her and said, "Our troops will be in no condition to fight those Apaches if we keep up this pace."

Hilary gave him a fragile smile.

What the hell's going on here? P.S. thought. *A handshake and that smile?*

"You've eaten at Martin's before, haven't you?" she asked.

"Which one? The tavern or the carriage house?"

"The tavern. I think you'll like it. It's very much like Mory's in a way."

"Everybody's singing 'To the Tables down at Martin's'?"

Another fragile smile. "Their roast beef is excellent."

"Excellent, eh? Well, that's nice."

After they had walked a couple of blocks, neither of them speaking, P.S. said, "How's Hester?"

"She's fine," Hilary said. "She's grown up so much in the past year that you won't even recognize her."

"I wouldn't recognize her in any case. I've never seen her."

"You never saw her? I thought you saw her when—the last time you were here."

"She was asleep. We didn't—I didn't want to disturb her."

"Well, she's changed a lot."

"I guess we all have," he said.

"Have you?"

"Haven't you?"

"Well, of course I have," she said.

They walked again in silence, and they did not speak until they had entered the tavern. P.S. stood looking at the crowd waiting for tables. The room was noisy, smoky, and bright; and although there were wooden booths and a long wooden bar, it did not remind him so much of Mory's as it did of the dozens of places like it in New York.

"Hilary, for God's sake, let's go some place else."

"But we have a reservation. Where will we go?"

"Any place that's quiet. Some place where we can talk, please? I'll tell the man to cancel the reservation."

"We won't find any place that isn't crowded."

"I'd like to try," he said.

They had to wait only ten minutes at the Town House, farther up Wisconsin Avenue, and they were shown to a small corner table with a crisp white cloth.

"Now, isn't this better?" he asked.

"Yes," she said. She began fiddling with her pocketbook and P.S. could see how nervous she was. The waiter came over and asked if they would like a cocktail, and P.S. said that he would, and asked Hilary what she would like.

"I'd like a Martini," she said.

"Two," he said. And to Hilary, "I haven't had a Martini in I don't know how long. Over a year certainly."

"Why? Don't you like them?"

"I think they're too strong."

"Then why did you order one?"

"I figured I'd probably need it," he said and smiled.

She did not return the smile.

"Was it very rough?" P.S. asked.

"The divorce? I guess so. But it—these things happen. That's all. Now it's over. That's all there is to it."

"But it couldn't have been—" He was going to say "much fun," instead he said, "easy."

"Well, it was as easy as these things can ever be," she said.

"You seem to be pretty casual about it."

"Bruce and I agreed to be sensible," she said. "We didn't want to give each other any more trouble. He pays child support. I didn't want—I didn't think it was fair to ask for any alimony. I have enough money. He could have the house and half the furniture . . ."

"But you're living in the house now."

"I'm moving as soon as I can find an apartment."

"Where's Bruce now?"

"He's looking at some factory somewhere."

The drinks came and P.S. fingered the thin stem of his Martini glass. He raised the glass, then paused and tried to think of a suitable toast. Idiotically, all he could think of was Major Lewis' "Cheers!" and his father's "Health, chum." He sat there with the upraised glass in his hand for a moment, and then he said, "It's nice to see you again."

"Thank you," she said.

The waiter asked if they would like to order and P.S. asked Hilary what she would like. She said it was up to him.

"I think we'd like to wait," P.S. said. And to Hilary he explained that he would like to talk for a while. "After all, we have a lot of catching up to do."

"More than a year. Why did it take you a year to want to catch up?"

"How could I do anything else?" P.S. protested. "Your husband—"

"We were supposed to be friends, Philip. Friends don't spend a year without trying to get in touch with each other."

"*Friends!* . . . Were we just friends?" he asked. "Did Bruce think we were just friends?"

"He didn't know anything about us."

"Well, why wouldn't you write me?" He thought briefly of all the things he was going to say to her on the plane. "You could have told me about the divorce without my having to find out about it from Nancy Merritt."

"I told you on the telephone. I didn't want you to—to think you were responsible. I didn't want you to do anything foolish."

"Foolish?" He looked down, shaking his head. "Why? Hilary, why?"

"Why what? Why did I get a divorce? Because I couldn't stand living with my husband. I didn't love him. I couldn't love him. And I knew that if I was willing to go to bed with you, then I would be willing to go to bed with others . . ."

With others?

"We were just being polite with each other," she said. "And toward the end we didn't even bother being polite."

"My God, Hilary, I'm sorry."

"Why? Why are you sorry? It's over with. We're divorced. These things happen in the best of families. That's all there is to it."

"I guess so."

Hilary pulled out a cigarette, and P.S. lit it for her. She took a deep breath, then exhaled, and said, "Now, tell me. What brings you to Washington?"

"Oh, for God's sake! What—just why do you think I came to Washington? I came to see *you!*"

"Well, yes, but I thought maybe you had decided to work for the government."

"No."

"You're doing what in New York? Nancy told me you were doing something like—"

"Banking. I am a banker. I work in a bank."

"I used to do that—before Bruce and I were married. I worked at the Riggs Bank down the street." She took another quick puff on her cigarette.

"I didn't know that," P.S. said. "I never knew you worked in a bank."

"That's where I met Bruce." She put her cigarette out.

"At the cashier's window?" he said. "No, of course not. You

were probably in the Accounting Department." ,

"How do you like working in a bank?"

P.S. said that it wasn't too bad, that he'd been taken out of the Custody Department and moved to the Credit Department, which he felt was the most interesting part of banking. He told Hilary about the electronics company that had applied for a loan six years ago. "The company made transistors or microelectronics or something," he explained. "They wanted to expand and they needed the money and they talked to Mr. Murdoch, who's my boss. He recommended that the bank grant them a long term, low interest loan and, my God, that company's worth a fortune today. All they do now is build one tiny electronic panel—about the size of a matchbook—and it goes into just about every missile we make. . . . I'd like to get in on the bottom of something like that—help some company and watch them skyrocket, if you'll pardon the expression."

"I suppose it could be very exciting."

"Oh, it is."

The waiter came and asked if they would like to order now, and with relief, P.S. said that he thought they would. The waiter handed them a menu and P.S. looked at his, trying to concentrate on the food, but all the time he was having to readjust himself to Hilary. He could only suppose that the divorce had been hard on her and that she was covering up. But he couldn't be sure. He had expected her to change during the year, but she was nearly unrecognizable. And now he didn't know what they could talk about. He certainly didn't want to ask her anything more about the past year—it had been taken up by the divorce. *My last year? . . . I don't even want to think of it! I've already tried to pass off the banking as something interesting.* He wondered what he would say if she asked him what he was going to do now. *And what if I ask her what she's going to do? She certainly doesn't seem to want to include me in any part of the future. . . . My God, I thought it was all going to be so nice.*

"You just can't imagine what going through a divorce is like," Hilary said after the waiter had taken their order and moved away.

"I hope the crab is good," P.S. said.

"You just can't imagine," Hilary repeated.

"I guess not. It must be quite an experience."

"An 'experience'!" She laughed. "One must certainly say going through a divorce is an experience!" She pulled out a cigarette.

"I'm sorry," P.S. said. "I didn't mean to sound facetious." He lit her cigarette.

She took two puffs, then exhaled. "Oh, I didn't think you meant to be at all. I wasn't—oh, no, I know you weren't being facetious. I was just going to say that in spite of our divorce—Bruce's and mine—being as easy as these things go, it still was a terrible thing to go through. It was a case of constantly having to meet and talk when that was absolutely—" she paused and laughed lightly—"but absolutely the last thing in the world either of us wanted to do. And I honestly think I saw even more of Bruce during divorce proceedings than I did before."

"Is that so?" P.S. asked.

"Oh, yes, I saw him all the time." She blew a thin gray stream of smoke toward her plate. "And when I wasn't seeing him, we were on the telephone together. He was calling from his office most of the time—and then I'd get his secretary, and she'd say, 'Mr. Mallory is calling you.' . . . She had always said 'Hi, Hilary, Bruce wants you.' "

P.S. listened to her long, involved story of the procedure of getting a divorce and he felt that he didn't want to hear it. It had an anesthetizing effect upon him, numbing him into a lack of feeling toward her. He only half listened to her telling about friends who felt forced to take sides and thereby complicated matters, the difficulty of packing, which she had already started. Which books were his, which were hers. Records, too, were a problem. Personal property—a small toad which was worth, perhaps, twenty cents, but which had great sentimental value for them both—who got it? And always the lawyers and telephone calls. And P.S. was distressed because even though she was talking about herself, she wouldn't mention what he knew would be the real hurt: the loneliness, the guilt, the necessity of calling someone up to ask them if they would like to go out with her, the embarrassment of meeting people in the street who would say, "Hi, Hilary . . . how's Bruce?" But most of all, P.S. wished she would just once mention Hester. And when she didn't he tried to break through this wall.

"Who will Hester stay with?"

"Me, of course," Hilary said and went right on telling about the mixed feelings she had about a table which she and Bruce had bought together. Although it was a lovely piece, she would never be able to look at it without thinking of him. "On the other hand," she added with a certain malice, "if he keeps it, it will always remind him of me."

"Don't you feel sorry at all for Bruce?" he asked.

"Oh, Bruce will do fine. He can always go back to those plant sites and see his *old friends*."

"You must be glad that it's over," he said, hoping to close the subject. "It sounds as though it is a terrible thing to go through."

"Do you think it's changed me?"

"I don't know. That depends," he said.

"Depends on what?"

"It doesn't seem to me that you're the same on the surface . . ."

"Of course I'm not. You just don't know what it's like living with a man like Bruce."

P.S. smiled. "No, I guess I don't."

"Well, it was awful. I never felt so—so much like something—so, I don't know, he had a way of making me feel ashamed of myself. He used to—he was so different before we were married, and then after we were married he changed. It was almost as though by marrying me he had proved himself better than me. And from then on he always treated me as though I were some sort of inferior. He—"

"Hilary," P.S. interrupted, "are you sure you want to be telling me this?"

"Why shouldn't I?"

"Well, it just seems that this sort of thing is better off kept in the family."

"Oh, don't be so pompous. Why shouldn't I tell you? After all . . ."

"After all, what?"

"Well, we're good friends," she said.

"Oh, crap."

"But we are!" she insisted.

P.S. looked at her. He had the feeling that Hilary had arbitrarily assigned him the role of "good old friend." "All right, chum," he said. "If that's what you want."

Hilary then proceeded to tell P.S. about Bruce. She told him how he always stayed later at the office than he had to, how he flirted outrageously at parties, how he would wear the same shirt for three days, how he often used her toothbrush, and finally, when he could stand it no more he said, "Hilary, please . . . I don't want to hear about it. Not because you shouldn't be telling me, but because I think less of you for hearing it. These aren't the reasons why someone—these complaints aren't why someone gets a divorce. And I don't know even if I want to hear the real reasons. And I don't want to hear any more about the divorce unless you tell me the truth."

"What do you mean, the *truth*?"

"It's just that you seem so callous about it, so flippant . . . and that's not like you, Hilary. That's not like you at all. So, all right, a divorce happens in the best of families, so these things happen every day—but, God damn it, Hilary, they don't happen every day to you. And I think I know you well enough to know you're covering up. That you're hiding. If you insist on thinking of me as good old P. S. Wilkinson, then use me that way. Cry on my shoulder. But cry for the real reasons, don't give me a lot of crap about the trouble you have choosing books, or telephone calls. From the way you've been talking you make it sound as though it had all been just some inconvenience you had to go through."

The waiter served their dinner and Hilary made no further reference to her divorce. She said that she thought her dinner was very good and that the Town House was quite a pretty restaurant and that she had never been there before. So P.S. went right along with her and told her a few more stories about banking and friends who had passed through New York.

"Do you see the Merritts often?" Hilary asked.

"Quite a lot. I see Charlie at least once a week. He works not far from me and we have lunch together about once a week."

"What is he doing?"

"Oh, the same sort of thing," P.S. said, and he wondered whether Hilary and Bruce had been polite in this manner.

They continued eating in silence and P.S. considered going back to New York on the late plane. He could understand why Hilary would be upset that he hadn't called in over a year, but there hadn't really been anything he could do. Especially after the debacle of their last night together in Washington.

"Philip?" Hilary said after the main course had been cleared away. "Has it been a good year for you?"

"On the whole it has. It's been interesting."

"In what way?"

"Oh, well, you know," he said, "being on my own in a place like New York, it can't help but be exciting. There's so much going on . . ."

"Have you been to many plays?"

"A few . . . I finally got to see *My Fair Lady*. Do you remember when it opened in New Haven senior year? You wanted to go to it and I said, 'Why bother, it's just another Shaw's *Pygmalion*' . . ."

Hilary smiled. It was her first warm smile of the evening.

"Well, I saw that and I saw *Irma La Douce*."

"Yes, I saw that in Washington."

"I liked it."

"So did I," she said.

"Well, I don't really go to the theater very much. I usually go to a movie."

"Do you go alone?"

"Sometimes," P.S. said. "Or I go with friends."

"Well, have you had any fun?" Hilary asked. "I know you said when you got back from Korea that you wanted to have fun."

P.S. thought for a moment. He couldn't stand this game any longer and he said, "No, Hilary, I haven't had much fun at all. I guess I haven't had fun for as long as I can remember. Not since you and I were together at college. Oh, I had fun a couple of times when I was in Baltimore with the Army, but aside from that I don't remember having much fun. Not any real fun."

"I haven't either," she said.

"That's what I want you to tell me about, Hilary."

"There's nothing to tell."

"Then just stop trying to be so brave about this—all this that's happened to you."

"Let's just have coffee," she said. "I don't want to talk here."

P. S. Wilkinson sat back in the overstuffed chair in Hilary's living room remembering the last time he had sat there. Hilary had been wearing shorts and she had lifted her legs onto the coffee table. He was a little embarrassed remembering how they had danced together pretending to be high school dates. And then when they had no longer been high school dates she had clung to him and said she was scared and he had been unable to help her. Now the coffee table had a small red mover's sticker on it, as did the couch. The bookcases were depleted. The paintings over the hi-fi had been taken down, and only the lighter shade of wall and the nail holes indicated where they had been. Sitting there listening to Hilary talk to the baby sitter in the hallway, P.S. became depressed, and he could imagine how depressing it must be for Hilary. Hilary came back into the living room carrying Hester. P.S. stood up and looked at the child who clung sleepily to her.

"Hester, this is Mr. Wilkinson," Hilary said.

"Good evening, Hester," he said. The child opened her eyes and looked at him.

"Say hello, Hester," Hilary urged. "She says 'hello' and 'good-by' and a few other things," she explained. "She has about the same vocabulary as a good parrot."

"How old is she now?" P.S. asked.

"Sixteen months."

"I had no idea a baby was that big at sixteen months. She's huge!"

"Well, she's about right for her age."

P.S. looked at the child wondering whether she would look like Hilary. She had Hilary's dark hair and incredible eyes. *Or does Bruce look like that, too?* He had a sudden uncomfortable picture of Hester saying "da-da" to him.

"I guess she isn't going to speak," Hilary said. "She's very tired, poor little mouse."

"Good night, Hester," P.S. said. "It's been very pleasant talking to you."

"Good," Hester suddenly said and she smiled at him, reaching one fat hand toward P.S.'s tie. P.S. bent down and gravely kissed her hand. Then Hilary carried the child upstairs and P.S. heard her wind up some toy. He walked over to the fireplace and looked at the photograph in the silver frame. He could hear the light tinkle of a music box playing "Over the Rainbow" and he looked at the suntanned dark-haired young man with the broad shoulders who was smiling handsomely as he pushed a piece of wedding cake between Hilary's smiling lips. Looking at the photograph P.S. suddenly realized how little he knew about her. He had somehow thought that her husband would be more like P.S., himself. He had pictured Hilary married to some tall young man, who didn't necessarily have light hair but who certainly didn't have black hair. *Of course a cutaway does make a man look stronger, more broad shouldered . . . but Bruce obviously does have a good build.* P.S. was painfully conscious of his own thin chest. He could imagine Hilary comparing his build to Bruce's, and then he heard her coming down the stairs and he turned away from the mantel. "Everything all right?" he asked.

"Yes, she's asleep."

"Would you like me to make you a drink?"

"Oh, Phil, I'm terribly sorry! I should have offered you one. Of course, help yourself to whatever you'd like. I'm not sure what we—what there is . . . It's so hard not saying 'we' any more."

"Can I make you something?"

"Whatever you're having."

"A brandy?"

She rubbed the back of her neck. "I think it's a little too warm for a brandy."

"Brandy and soda? . . . If there's tonic, I could make you a gin and tonic."

"Sure. Fine."

"Which one?"

"What are you going to have?"

"I think I'll have a brandy and soda."

"All right. That's what I'll have then." She sat down on the couch.

P.S. went into the kitchen and filled the ice bucket, then he walked back into the living room and over to the bar beneath one of the bookcases. He fixed the two drinks and carried them over to the couch and sat down next to Hilary.

"Philip," she said after a while. "I wish you'd written me."

"I wish I knew how I could have."

"When you left me last time, I felt so dirty—so cheap."

"Hilary, I—"

"You don't have to say anything. I think I know why it happened. I was pushing you too hard . . . but, but what I can't understand is why you didn't call me afterwards. You never called me. You didn't take the job with the CIA and you suddenly ran off to New York. Why didn't you tell me anything?"

"Something happened at the CIA."

"What?"

"Oh, Hilary, it seems so silly now. So—sort of unreal. But it upset me and—upset is too weak a word. It was, I don't know, it was sort of the last straw. I don't know what happened. I just suddenly felt either I was insane or everyone else was."

"What happened?"

"They thought I was a queer."

"A *what*?"

"They had this lie detector machine. And, well, they plugged me into it and asked me all sorts of questions about homosexuality."

"But why? Why did they think you were—were homosexual?"

"Well, it's part of the test. They do the same thing to everybody."

"I know it's part of the test, but why did they think *you* were?"

"Because every time they asked me a question about it, the machine went berserk."

"Maybe the machine was homosexual," Hilary said.

P.S. looked at her, and then he laughed, and he couldn't stop laughing. He imagined a homosexual machine in a very tight-fitted case, with lots of dainty little dials, and all the needles had long lashes, and he couldn't help himself. It was as though the laughter that he hadn't used in the past years had been stored up, saved for this moment, and Hilary, too, began to laugh. Each time they looked at each other they would laugh. One of them would say, "the machine . . ." and it would set them off again, ". . . lots of little buckles . . .", ". . . a suède carrying case . . .", ". . . it would make little sounds, little simpering noises," and they laughed until they were weak, until P.S. had to get away from her. He stood in front of the bookcases, his back to her, and each time he would start to get himself under control he would hear her burst out laughing again and he would laugh, too. He told her about the bracelet that measured his pulse. "When the man put it on I distinctly felt it squeeze my hand." He tried keeping his back to her, but she would see his shoulders shaking, and laugh again.

"Oh, God," she said.

He finally stopped laughing and turned around. There were tears running down her cheeks, and she sat on the couch and would suddenly bounce with the last little laugh, and he walked back to her and said, "God, I don't think I've laughed that hard in I don't know how many years."

"What—what happened next?"

"Well, the next thing was they sent me to a psychiatrist . . . and when I got there he said, 'My, you're tall, are you long all over?' "

Hilary burst out laughing again, and she said, "I know that isn't funny. It's terrible!" And she laughed all over again. "Maybe he wasn't a psychiatrist," she said. "He was probably the machine's mechanic."

And as they sat there together P.S. thought that at least the worst might be over.

"It must have been awful," Hilary said. "Dear, dear Philip . . . especially after the night before. I'm so sorry for you. And, well, I'm just sorry, that's all. You went up to New York then?"

"I spent one night in Baltimore."

"But you like your job now, don't you?"

"It's a living."

"It should mean more than that. You shouldn't be doing something you don't like."

"Well, I don't think I'll be doing it for much longer," he said, not having any idea what he would do instead. "But, as the second thief on the cross said, 'That's enough about my troubles, now you tell me about yours.' "

"I don't know what to tell you, except that it's been an awful year for me, too."

"Go on," he urged.

"Oh, Philip, there were just so many things that were wrong— that are still wrong. The loneliness . . . Once you live with someone, no matter what you think of that person, it's hard to get used to being alone again. I—I hate loneliness. It's something I can't get used to. I hate sitting alone night after night watching television—I can't seem to read any books. I can't concentrate."

"Couldn't you go stay with your parents? Are they still living in Tuxedo Park?"

"I probably will do that for a while, but I don't want to go back there. It's just admitting such complete defeat. I can't—I don't want to do that. And the Park's such a small little island, everybody knows everything about everybody else. I grew up there, spent my summers there. And I just don't want to have to go back to that. Anyway, Mummy's in Southampton, which is even worse. I spent two weeks with her last summer while Bruce was away, and the place was filled with divorced girls my age. It's just too depressing."

"Then you think you'll stay in Washington?"

"I guess so. At least I have friends here. And I can get a job."

"Doing what?"

"Anything. It doesn't matter. I could probably get a job in a dress shop. Something like Dorcas Hardin's . . . or even the Saville Book Shop . . . Little Caledonia."

"Have you tried any of them?"

"Not yet, but I'm sure I can get something. At least during the fall and then through Christmas."

"Is that what you really want to do?"

"I don't know any more what I *really* want to do."

"Yes, well, if you'll pardon a glittering generality, that seems pretty much to be the malady of our age . . . the malady lingers on."

"It's awful to feel this way, though."

He stood up and walked to the bar. He dropped some ice into his glass and poured in the brandy. "You wrote Nancy that you thought you had failed." He added the soda. "How? In what sense do you think you failed?"

"In every sense. The marriage. Bruce. Hester. When you swear—you promise to love, honor, until death do you part and then, two years later, you get a divorce. I just feel so guilty about it. As though I didn't try hard enough. But I *did* try. And I thought of Hester and what would happen to her, and so I wanted to make it work. But I couldn't. And I couldn't stand it any longer. I even went to a marriage counselor. I just looked one up who seemed to have a good address . . . you can't just ask someone to recommend a marriage counselor. I went to her and I told her what was wrong, and I asked her what to do. And do you know what she said? She said, 'Go out and buy yourself some long black silk stockings and wear them to bed. And if that doesn't work,' she said, 'if that doesn't work, lipstick your nipples' . . .

"And you know what, Philip? I did. I was so desperate to try anything, that I did everything she said and that night he, Bruce, laughed at me . . . *laughed* at me as—God, as though I weren't feeling humiliated enough already."

"Was there anything, I mean, was something wrong with him?"

"*Nothing* was the matter with him! It was just that he didn't *want* me. He didn't want me in any way. He didn't *need* me. Because he had this thing, this feeling that once he had married me he had me. He owned me. I was like the television set. Something he would turn on when he got bored. And then when you—you didn't want me either . . ."

"When did all this happen?"

"About the stockings? That was just before Charlie Merritt's wedding. Just before I saw you again. That's why I was so glad to see you. And when you told me at dinner about the cake of soap—that's why I cried, because it meant you liked me, or loved me, or needed me enough to take a cake of soap to bed with you. It was so silly and so sweet—innocent in a way, and just a couple of nights before I had had to put on black stockings and lipstick . . ."

"How little I know you," he said.

"Why do you say that?"

"I don't know. I guess it's because I've just spent all night learning how little I know you. Listen, tomorrow, why don't we —do you have a car?"

She nodded.

"Let's go somewhere. Let's take Hester for a drive. We can just get away from here and have a picnic or something like that. Take a walk. But just get away and talk."

"I'm supposed to go to a friend's house in Virginia. Swimming. There's sort of an informal luncheon . . ."

"Oh."

"But *we* could go. *You* could go with me. I know they won't mind. I can call them tomorrow morning and ask them. I think they'd be happy to see me with someone. . . . That's another thing about a divorce. Everybody's always worried about whether or not you're seeing someone. And—well, I know it's meant well, but I just wish they wouldn't worry about me."

"I worry about you."

"Well, you're different. You're more than just a friend."

"That, dear lady, is what the man's been trying to tell you all night."

"All right." She smiled. And then she stood up and said, "It's pretty late. I guess I'd better go to bed."

He walked with her to the foot of the stairs and kissed her lightly on the cheek. "Good night, Hilary, I'll call you in the morning."

"Good night, Philip. I'm glad you're here."

He picked up his suitcase and walked out of her house and down the street to look for a taxi.

22

HILARY was bouncing Hester in her lap, the next morning, while P.S. drove across the bridge toward Mc-Clean.

"Mrs. Harris says that she thinks she knows your father," Hilary said.

"She's the hostess?"

Hilary nodded. "She says she used to date a Wilkinson in Charlottesville."

"*At* Charlottesville," he corrected her. "There were a great many Wilkinsons there. She may have known one of the others."

"You turn off up ahead at that traffic light." Hilary said.

"Isn't the new CIA building out here somewhere?"

"We turn off before it."

P.S. slowed the car. "Which way do we turn?"

"Right."

P.S. moved into the proper lane and turned off onto a narrow blacktop road. A white board fence separated the fields on either side of the road, and at the far end of the field on their left they could see the big red rooster tail of dust from a pickup truck hurrying along a dirt road. The fields were dry and barren in the hot August sun. "What do you suppose they grow here?" P.S. asked.

"Farm subsidies," Hilary answered.

"In August?" P.S. laughed. "That's only a cash crop in the spring."

"See the gatepost on the right, about—oh—two tennis courts ahead?"

"White brick?"

"Turn in there," she said.

"How's Hester doing?" P.S. glanced down at the child, who lay flat on Hilary's knees, with her legs braced against the dashboard.

"This is the way she likes to ride," Hilary said. "She doesn't like to look out the windows. I don't know why, I think she thinks the windshield is a television screen and when nothing happens she gets bored."

P.S. looked at the signpost as he turned in. "A. T. Harris. . . . You don't suppose these are the same people who rent cutaways in New York, do you?"

"He's a lawyer."

"Well, they charge enough."

They climbed a slight rise and then they had a view straight down the driveway to the house.

"My God!" P.S. said. "This is quite a place!"

Directly ahead lay the house—a large white stone and pillared house with wings on either side. The white columns were the height of two floors, and as P.S. rounded the circular entranceway he said, "Two Mercedes, a Cadillac, a Rolls, and that's not counting the Ford."

He stopped the car and went around to Hilary's door and picked up Hester, holding the child gingerly. "I've never held one of these things before."

"Don't drop her," Hilary said. She was rummaging around the back seat looking for towels and bathing suits and bottles.

"Good morning, Miss Mallory," P.S. said. "You're fat enough to bounce, aren't you?"

"Goob," the child said and pulled the glasses off P.S.'s nose and smeared the lenses in her hand.

"Can't you say anything better than 'goob'? I knew a parrot who got shipped back to Hong Kong because he only said 'goob.'"

"B.S.," the child said.

"B.S.!" P.S. laughed. "I hope she was trying to say my name.

If she wasn't you were right last night when you said she had the vocabulary of a parrot."

Hilary got out of the car. "I thought I'd surprise you," she said. "I was trying to teach her your name this morning, but she can't tell the difference between 'b' and 'p' yet."

"Should have taught her 'Philip.' "

"B.S.," Hester said and smiled. She bit down on his glasses.

"Well, let's go," Hilary said.

"Not until I can see where I'm going."

Hilary wiped his glasses on her shirt front, then slid them back onto his nose.

The swimming pool was behind the house, down a slight embankment. At either end of the pool were dressing rooms, and at one side there was a canopied area with cushioned garden furniture, glass-top tables, and a white lacquered bar. P.S. counted five young men seated beneath the faded blue canopy, and there were two young women sunning themselves by the sides of the pool. One of the young men was wearing a bathing suit. The other four wore linen trousers, one pair white, one red, and two yellow. The one wearing white trousers also wore a blazer with a silk ascot at his throat.

In the center of the pool, in what appeared to be an amphibious beach chair, floated a deeply tanned and silver-haired woman. One arm of the chair held her drink, the other her ashtray.

"Hello, children," the woman called gaily, waving an empty cigarette holder.

"Mrs. Harris, I presume," P.S. whispered, then ducked as Hester made another pass for his glasses. He held her arms down as they walked to the edge of the pool.

"Hello, Mrs. Harris," Hilary said, "this is Philip Wilkinson."

"Hello, Mrs. Harris," P.S. said. "It was very nice of you to let me come."

"Nice to have you," Mrs. Harris said.

Hester was squirming in P.S.'s arms and he leaned toward her ear and said, "Knock it off, kid, or you'll be fitted for a pair of concrete step-ins."

Hilary was saying something to Mrs. Harris, and then Mrs.

Harris said, "I think I knew your father, Carter Wilkinson."

"That's my uncle," P.S. said, "although it's also my grand-father and brother."

"I'm sure it must have been your uncle," Mrs. Harris said.

P.S. wondered if she said that because she felt he had meant to suggest it could have been his grandfather. He considered appeasing her by saying that it might have been his brother, but discarded that as too obvious, saying instead, "My father is Stewart Wilkinson."

"Yes, of course, and your name is Philip," Mrs. Harris said. She paddled herself around to face the sun, and said, over her shoulder, "Well, children, make yourselves at home."

"Thank you," Hilary said. P.S. lowered Hester gently to the grass and they walked toward the canopied area.

"Do you want to change now?" Hilary asked.

"If I'm going to have to meet these people, I'd rather do it behind my protective coloring—that is, dressed."

Two of the young men were with the State Department, one was in the Peace Corps and on his way to Nigeria, one was an assistant to a senator, and the last said he worked for the govern-ment, meaning, of course, the CIA.

They all seemed to know Hilary, and as P.S. was introduced to them and told what they did, he tried to keep their names straight. None of them asked what he did, and he and Hilary stood to one side as they continued their excited discussion of the Berlin crisis.

"Well, all right," the man in the bathing suit was saying, "take a look at what we're faced with. What we're faced with ultimately in Berlin is a showdown."

"And it's going to be a showdown," the one in red linen trousers said. "Khrushchev is going to try to push us, and push us as hard as he can."

"Wouldn't you, after the way we blew the Bay of Pigs?" the man in the bathing suit asked.

"Well, okay, we blew it," the red linen trousers man said. "But this time we can push back a little harder. This time we won't have to use Cubans."

"The one thing we've got to make certain of this time," said one of the men wearing yellow trousers, "the one thing we've got to impress upon not only Khrushchev but also the Allies is that we mean business. And putting SAC on fifteen-minute alert won't be enough, either."

"Close the embassies," the man in the blazer and ascot said.

"Jesus Christ, Harry!" red linen trousers laughed. "That sort of thing hasn't had any effect since the Spanish-American War." The others joined in the laughter. "No, Harry," he continued, "sending those troops to Berlin was a step in the right direction. The Berliners know we wouldn't send fifteen hundred men to Berlin just to lose them. The thing they have to know, too, though, is that we've got something to back them up."

"How many divisions do we have in NATO?" the man in the blazer and ascot asked.

"None, unless NATO understands that the U.S. is willing to go into Europe and fight alongside them."

"But of course we will," the second man wearing yellow linen trousers said.

"We know it, but they don't."

"Then call up the Reserves. What the hell, we did it for Korea, and a lot less was at stake there. If we call up a million troops, it should certainly convince everybody that we're not fooling around."

"Where are we going to get a million?" the red linen man asked.

"Oh, hell, it doesn't matter how many we call up. We can just tell them we're calling up a million. Just so long as we call up enough to show them we mean business."

"Take *that*, you nasty Russians!" P.S. said. "And I hope all our diplomats will leap over the Berlin wall to embrace the Russians, saying, 'Good show!', 'Well hit!', 'Lovely match, what?' "

The young men looked at him curiously, and one said, "I take it you're not with the government."

"I work in a bank," P.S. said. "In New York. I'm one of those Reservists."

During the lunch of smoked salmon, sliced turkey, and salad,

P.S. talked to the young man who was being sent to Nigeria as a Peace Corps volunteer.

"I don't deny that the Peace Corps's a catchy idea," P.S. said, "it's just that I don't think it's going to do much."

"You can't expect to accomplish much. All we're going to try to do is to help these people. Maybe raise their living standards, show them how to make better use of their land, teach them sanitation, build roads, help them set up schools."

"You're going to do all this yourself?"

"I'm going to teach in a school."

"What will you teach?"

"English," the young man said.

"How does that raise their standard of living?"

"Teaching's only a small part of my job."

"Well . . . I admire your going there," P.S. said. "I just don't see how you're going to do much good. I know that when I went to Korea I—well, you can't compare Korea to Nigeria—but I found it very discouraging. I guess I used to have all the ideals, too."

"I hope I don't lose my ideals so easily. But I guess I won't find out until I get to Nigeria."

"I guess not," P.S. said, as he watched the young man join his friends. P.S. sat alone looking down at his empty plate, and then he felt a tugging on his arm and looked down at Hester. "Hi, what's up?"

The child took his hand and said, "Wok."

"Walk? You want to take a walk?"

"Wok," she repeated.

P.S. looked for Hilary. She was lying at the side of the pool talking to the girls. P.S. stood up and Hester took his hand and together they walked away from the pool and down the grassy embankment until they came to the edge of a field. P.S. sat down, resting his elbows on his knees, and watched Hester bounce away to pick flowers. He thought about the young men and the excitement with which they had discussed their jobs, politics, the Presidency, and P.S. admitted that their excitement was somewhat contagious, especially when they spoke about Kennedy with that strange mixture of awe and cynicism in referring to the pure professionalism of the man. He thought of the many times he had watched the President on television, and how he had been proud of the way the President answered questions, proud of the way he looked, intrigued by the man as well as the office he represented.

Hester puffed along the side of the field and back up to P.S. Both of her fists clenched grass and daisies complete with roots, and she dropped all of these at P.S.'s feet and wiped her hands on her thighs.

"Thank you very much," P.S. said, as Hester weaved and bobbed in front of him. He picked out one of the daisies and twirled the stem between his fingers and propellered it against her nose. Hester snuffled and giggled, rubbing her nose where it had tickled.

"Do you have a boyfriend?" P.S. asked. "If not, I'd like to volunteer—but first we'll have to find out how you feel about me." He began to pluck the daisy's petals. "You love me . . . you love me not . . . love me . . . love me not." The child crowded against him, fascinated, as he plucked the last petals. "Love me not . . . there! You love me," he said and showed her the one remaining petal. He bent over and kissed her forehead. "I'm very flattered that you love me," he said.

Hester clamped her arms around his neck and pressed her lips against his cheek.

"*Luff!*" Hester said and smiled ecstatically at him, and P.S. looked at the child's happiness, her excitement, and he lowered his head onto his arms so that she wouldn't see him cry. He sat there with his head between his knees, knowing exactly why he was crying and feeling so completely stupid about it, until he felt a hand on his shoulder.

"Hi," Hilary said.

He hid his face from her so that she would not see him.

"What's the matter?"

He wiped his face on his arms and looked away from her.

"What *is* it, Philip?" She walked around to his front, "You've been crying!"

"Something in my eye," he said. And then he laughed at the foolishness of his excuse and said, "I was being silly."

"Why? What's the matter?" She knelt on the grass beside him. "Are you upset about something?"

"No, really, I'm being stupid."

"Please tell me, Philip."

"Luff!" Hester squealed.

P.S. stood up and patted the child's head. "Hilary, can we leave soon?"

"That's why I was coming to get you. It's time for Hester's nap. I was wondering where the two of you had gone."

"We went for a walk," P.S. said. He held out his hands and Hester took one and Hilary took the other, and they walked together back up the embankment to the pool.

They returned to the house in Georgetown and P.S. followed Hilary inside. He lowered Hester to the floor and looked around. "You really weren't kidding when you said the movers were here."

"I know," Hilary said. "It's kind of sad, isn't it?"

"I guess so."

"Come on, Hester . . . time for bed."

"Can I help?"

"Well, you could carry her upstairs for me."

"Okay," P.S. said. "Allez-oop, Hester, up we go again." He lifted the child and followed Hilary up the stairs. "I can see why fathers get bad backs. All this lifting."

"Fathers are generally at the office all day," Hilary answered.

After Hester had been changed and put into her crib, they closed her bedroom door and stood in the hallway. "The only cool place to sit is the bedroom," Hilary said.

"Fine," P.S. said. He closed Hilary's bedroom door behind them.

"Sit down," she said.

"No, thanks, let me stand for a while. I've been sitting, it seems, all day." He went to the window overlooking Prospect Street and looked out.

"Philip . . ."

"Yes?" He turned back from the window.

"Why did you cry? I've never seen you cry before. It made me very sad."

"I don't know why."

"Was it something I did or said?"

"No, it was just one of those typically stupid things I do. I was thinking about us, that's all. About you and me and Hester."

"What about us?"

He walked over to the bed and sat down. He lit a cigarette. "Well, I suppose in a way it's almost amusing."

"Not if it made you cry."

"On the plane coming down here I had all sorts of pretty pictures in my head. Pictures of the three of us together in some sort of Norman Rockwell *Post* cover, we'd all be having fun. I had all these pretty pictures, oh, you know what I mean, in front of a fireplace on Christmas morning . . . together at home . . . and, well, I guess sitting out there in the field I realized how impossible it was . . . well, no, not impossible, I guess just improbable. But I thought it would all work out so neatly. You were lonely, upset, and you needed someone to help you get over this divorce."

Hilary sat on the bed next to him and covered his hand with her own.

"So then, I sat there thinking about those guys by the pool, so full of their own self-importance, so eager to get me back in the Army, so full of their own self-righteousness. . . . they were all working for the government, serving their country, all dressed up in their red, white, and blue blazers and sneering at me for working in a bank. . . . And I thought, Screw them. Who needs them? Screw them all! Because you know? They didn't even have the faintest idea of what working for the government was all about—except for that one guy who was going to Nigeria, and I don't even know for sure if he's going for any of the right reasons. But there I was mentally knocking all those people for their beliefs, and then I was thinking of you in your black stockings and lipstick, and I knew that it excited me, that I wanted to see you like that, and that made me even worse than Bruce because I would have liked you that way and he just laughed. . . . All these things were kind of whirling around in my head, and all of a sudden your daughter said 'luff' . . . as though in spite of all I was thinking she loved me, and I cried. I guess I cried for all the same reasons that old men do in mediocre poems. I guess I was even thinking of us back at college. I think we might even have really been in love with each other then. But this last time in Washington, last year . . . You weren't in love with me and I guess I really wasn't in love with you. I think we both just happened to need each other at the time and I think we both tried to pretend that it was the same between us as it had always been, or as we thought it had always been, back in college. And it was easy because we didn't want to admit, or accept, whatever it was that we'd been through during the years in between. I couldn't accept my eighteen months in Korea as ever happening because to do so would be to admit that I had lost time, that everybody else had been able to live perfectly normal lives while I was gone. And you, on your part, didn't want to admit your marriage was a failure. You had your own Korea. Your own despair. Your own feeling of wasted time. And so, when we got together again at the wedding it was too easy. So easy that both of us, perhaps, should have been a little more suspicious."

"Were you crying for me or was it for you?"

"I think it was for both of us. For us."

"Then I think you're assuming too much."

"What, for instance?"

"I think you're maybe taking too much for granted, but go on."

"If I'm taking too much for granted, then now's the time to tell me. Unless, of course, you want to pay out more rope. But I think the time for us has come to start trying to get back together. To stop running."

"Do you really think you're through?"

"I'm trying to be," he said, a little irritated.

"Well, maybe . . ."

" 'Maybe' *what*?"

"I just don't think you're through running yet—I think you may be *getting* there, but I just don't think you're through yet."

"Now what, just what the hell does that mean, 'but I'm getting there'? Honest to God, Hilary, you have one—there's one thing about you that just irks hell out of me." He walked to the window overlooking Prospect Street again. "I don't know why you think you know so much about me. After all, if I admit that I don't know everything about you, you might at least not presume . . . might admit to the same lack of knowledge about me." He turned back and looked at her. "What's so funny?"

"You are."

"You think I'm funny?"

"I think you're being a little bit ridiculous."

"How? You tell me how? If you think I'm so goddam funny, you tell me how. Jesus H. Christ, when you get into this sort of omniscient Mother of Men mood, it really burns me off."

"Philip, I'm not trying to make fun of you. It's just that you get so pompous at times. What was it you said? Something about if you admitted you didn't know everything about me then I should not be so presumptuous as to think I knew everything about you." She smiled at him again, worriedly. "Philip, *if*, as you said, you've stopped running, what are you going to do with yourself? What are you going to do now? You couldn't be happy working in a bank for the rest of your life."

"I have no intention of working in a bank for the rest of my life."

"Then what are you going to do?"

"Oh, for God's sake, Hilary, how many times do I have to tell you that I don't know!"

"Don't get angry with me, I only think that you have to have some ambition. Something to go after. That's the only thing Bruce had that I ever liked. He knew what he wanted to do and he . . ."

"Well, I'm not Bruce," he interrupted.

"I know that."

"And I'm sorry that I don't have anything that's important to me."

"But you've got to believe in *some*thing," she insisted.

"I do."

"What?"

"Us."

" 'Us'?" she asked. "What do you believe about in us? I mean, what's there to believe?"

"I believe in us."

" 'Us' meaning you and me?"

"And Hester."

"Oh, and Hester, too?"

"Is that so funny?"

"I didn't say it was funny. But you believe in all of us?"

"Isn't that enough?"

"Is it?"

"I think so," he said.

"You used to believe in the government, too. Back at Yale you wanted to go into the Foreign Service, and then all that changed. What makes you so sure you won't change your mind about us, too?"

"Oh, Hilary, I'm not going to change my mind about us. The only reason why I changed my mind about the government was because I saw how our government operates."

"Where? In Korea?"

"I saw a lot of it in Korea."

"You saw the Army, you didn't see the government. That's what governments are for—to keep armies in line."

"Oh, come on, Hilary."

"Come on, what?"

"I saw our government, too. And today. You saw it too. And last year with the CIA."

"Sure you did. You took a lie detector test, got insulted, and quit."

"I didn't quit just because of the lie detector test," P.S. said. "I just found out that I didn't want to work for the government, that's all."

"All the government?"

"The CIA."

"Then *don't* work for them! Apply for the Foreign Service school. If you really believe in doing something important, do that. That's what you wanted to do. And even if you find out that it's a disappointment, at least you'll be doing something worthwhile."

"Something as worthwhile as you taking a job at Dorcas Hardin's?"

"That's different. Girls can't get as good jobs as boys. Besides, I never finished college."

"Then go finish college."

"With Hester?"

"Other women have done it."

"Not with Hester. And besides, I'm not other women. And we're not talking about other women or about me, we were talking about you."

"Let's talk about you instead."

"No, I think you should—"

"Don't say it. You were going to say something like 'I think the best thing for you to do at this time would be to blah-blah-blah.' Why do people always have to tell me what to do?"

"Because they like you, and they worry about you."

"Bush-wah."

"It's no such thing. If you're so insistent that you believe in us, then you should want us to believe in you. And I do."

"But only if I get out of banking?"

"I don't care what you do. I just can't stand seeing you wasting your time in a bank when you'd be so much happier somewhere else."

"Like where? In the Foreign Service, in our embassy back at Seoul?"

"At least there you'd have a better chance to do all those things for Korea that you couldn't do in the Army."

"Who said I wanted to do things for Korea?"

"You did. Or at least you were concerned enough about what went on there to try to help. And if you got sent there with the government you *would* help."

"No, thanks."

"Why not? Isn't serving in Seoul one of your pretty pictures? Does it have to be the Court of St. James?"

"I'm through with pretty pictures."

"Are you? You said you were through running, too."

"Do we have to go through this all over again?"

"Philip, I don't want to go through it all over again, but don't you see I have to? I can't let myself believe that you'd be willing to work in a bank for the rest of your life—"

"What's wrong with banking?"

"Nothing. It's just not right for you. You don't have any interest in it. You're not—you're just using banking as an excuse."

"Oh, for God's sake."

"You are, Philip. You're just trying to avoid responsibility."

"Avoid responsibility?"

"Have you ever faced up to responsibility?"

"Of course I have, Hilary. My God, look at the Army. What about—"

"The Army isn't facing up to responsibility, not for you, Philip. It's too easy for you. You don't have to think. You're safe in the Army. It's a system and you're good at it, but it's too easy. And the same with banking. That's what you're doing now. You're playing it safe. Oh, Philip, you say you've stopped running . . . You haven't even begun to slow down."

"What about you and Hester? I've stopped running there."

"You haven't, Philip. Do you really think you're ready to take on the responsibility for Hester and myself?"

"Hilary, I haven't said I was ready yet."

"But it's in the back of your mind. It's one of your pretty pictures."

"And it's getting dustier and dustier."

"I don't want it to get dusty."

"You don't? You don't? Hilary, just what in the hell is it you *do* want?"

"I want to be able to—well, I guess it's as simple as wanting to respect you. And I can't. . . . You're one of the nicest persons, if not the nicest, I've ever met. But that isn't enough, you've—"

"Nice guys finish last, eh?"

"They don't *have* to, Philip!" She looked at him angrily. "That's what I'm saying. They don't have to if they stop running and start doing something important. Philip, I've met so many like you, so many nice young men in the last couple of years who just don't seem to care, and it's so sad. It's such a waste! If you don't care, then you let yourself get walked on. At least those men out at the swimming pool this afternoon cared. They cared enough so that they'd use you if necessary to keep yourself and the rest of us from getting walked on."

"Hilary, do you really think they cared? What the hell do they care about? The only thing they care about is the game. It's all some big goddam chess game to them. They plan their moves and make them, but they don't even begin to care until one of the pieces threatened is themselves. In the meantime they don't care how many pawns they lose. And, God damn it, Hilary, I'm one of those pawns! *Me.* Philip Sadler Wilkinson! You heard that little bastard, 'Call up a million Reserves' . . . a million, for Christ's sake! Do you think he *cared*? Well, you can be goddam sure *I* care. I don't like it at all. *Not one bit!*"

"Then do something about it."

"Do something abou—*what*? What, Hilary? Just *what* the hell can I do?"

"Something! Anything! Fight back. At least for the others who can't fight back, who don't know how to fight back."

"What makes you think *I* do?"

"I *have* to believe you know how to! I have to believe you're stronger than you realize. I have to believe you care what happens to you."

"Well, of *course* I care what happens to me."

"Then why can't you do something about it? Get in the government. Get yourself somewhere where you can do something. I shouldn't have to tell you that, Philip. My God, what makes me so mad, what gets me so upset, is that you've got so much! So much to give, and you just won't do it. Just—oh, Philip, Philip, if only you'd stop believing in pretty pictures, if you'd just—if you could just be strong. Be strong and still be nice. Then, then you'd be so wonderful, Philip."

P.S. squirmed uneasily.

"I mean it, you're the type of person we need in government. Not those men out at the pool. We need someone like you who *does* care. Who cares deeply not only about himself but about everybody. We need somebody strong."

"And I'm not."

"Philip, you're—"

"What makes you think *you're* so strong?"

"Me, Philip? *Me* strong? You just don't realize how weak I am." She laughed bitterly. "You think *I'm* strong . . . oh, Philip, you just don't know . . . you just don't know how weak I am. You still have this pretty picture of me and—"

"I don't think I have any more pretty pictures about you."

"Oh, Philip, let me just tell you how pretty a picture you have of me. You don't know anything about me. You think I'm strong, oh, Philip, you don't know how wrong you are. You think you had a tough year in Korea and that the CIA was so awful. You just think all I had was a tough year and survived a divorce and that made me strong again." She shook her head slowly. "Let me tell you about my abortion. Let me tell—"

"Your *what*? Abortion? No, I don't want to know about it."

"Philip, I was so weak that I—"

"Hilary, I don't want to hear about it."

"I got pregnant again. It wasn't even Bruce's chil—"

"HILARY! Stop it! *Stop it!* Be quiet! I DON'T WANT TO KNOW!"

"But you've *got* to know, Philip. If we're going to have any pretty pictures between us, then let's know what we have to start with. You've got to know exactly what I am."

"I know what you are, Hilary."

"Philip, you don't. You don't. You came trotting down here thinking nothing had changed, that we could just pick it up where we left off back at college, that nothing that happened during the past two and a half years had made any difference. You came down here thinking I had got a divorce just so I could marry you, and then—"

"I never thought that. I never said any such thing."

"Philip, please . . ."

"Hilary, what are you trying to do?" he asked anxiously. "Why do you have to destroy the only—"

"The only pretty picture you have left?"

He did not speak. He wanted to get up. He wanted to leave the house. And yet he knew that if he left he would be running. And that would be even worse than staying.

"What was I supposed to do, Philip? Philip, *look* at me. I'm not a pretty picture. I'm a person. A real honest-to-God person, Philip. And what was I supposed to do? Save myself for you? Permit Bruce to make love to me once in a while, but never let it count since I was really saving myself for you? When you never even tried to write me? Are you ashamed of me, just because I admit to myself that I needed someone? That I needed someone to love me? Let me tell you about that, Philip, so that you know what loneliness is."

"I know loneliness," he said tensely.

"No, you don't, Philip. Not really."

"I don't want to hear about it, Hilary."

"Why not? Why not, Philip?"

"Because, Hilary, because you don't need to tell me. I can remember when we first made love together. I can remember how nice it was. How tender it was. And I know we did it because we were in love with each other, and I don't want to think of you having done it for any other reason, Hilary. Not with me. And not with anybody else."

"Why? Do you feel responsible? Is that another of your pretty pictures? Am I a ruined woman because of you? You had nothing to do with it. Nothing. Nothing at all. I did it for *me*," she said. "Right in this room. Right on this bed. Right here. Right where you're sitting."

"And you weren't in love with him."

"Of course not! Of course I wasn't! I wasn't in love with anybody. Not Bruce. Not him. And, no, not even you."

"Then why, Hilary?"

"I told you. Because I was lonely."

"And that's the only reason?"

"Whatever other reason does a woman need? I did it because I was *lonely*, Philip! I was *lonely*! And when I found out I was pregnant, I didn't know what to do. So I went to—to the man and I asked him. I didn't know whether I wanted the child or not. But I had to speak to him." She told P.S. how the man had panicked and said that he couldn't marry her, and she had had to convince him that she didn't want anything more than help, and the man had said he would get in touch with her. And she had to wait a week before he called her, and during that time she thought he had run off. He told her to go out to a drugstore in Shirlington, Virginia, and stand there at six o'clock the next evening with her dark glasses in her right hand. He was sending her two hundred dollars. She went there, and a man driving a lavender Buick picked her up. There was another girl in the back of the car, and the man told them both to lie down in the back seat. Then the man drove around and around until it was dark. The man drove them to Maryland and when they came to a farm the girls were told to close their eyes so that they wouldn't recognize it. They were taken inside and led into separate bedrooms on the second floor. After a while a doctor came in who was wearing a surgical mask to cover his face, and he prodded Hilary to see how far along her pregnancy was. Then he gave her a penicillin shot and took her into another room where a nurse made her take off her dress, slip and panties. She was given a second shot and about fifteen minutes later she went into labor and the doctor scraped her out, carefully hiding what he had removed. It had not hurt so much physically as it had emotionally and she could not stop crying, and she was crying now as she told P.S. She said that she had kept asking for P.S. over and over again. And when it was over they put her to bed for several hours. Then they checked her again, and drove her back into Washington. "I kept asking for you," she said.

He brushed her tears away with his fingertips. "I wish I could have been there," he said. "I wish I could have helped you."

"And I'm weak enough to wish you could help me now. But you can't, Philip. Not yet."

"I'd like to try."

"How, Philip? By doing the right thing? By making an honest woman of me? By marrying me?"

"If necessary."

"No, Philip. . . . No, not yet. That would be too easy for both of us. Then neither one of us would have to fight. Not when you would want to devote yourself to Hester and me. I don't want that, and neither would you after a while. You're going to find something important for yourself. I know that. But I don't want it to be me. Marriage would be just another institution for you to lose yourself in. Just another pretty picture."

"Hilary, what do you *want* from me?"

"I want you to be selfish. No, maybe that isn't the right word. I guess all I want is you, really. And I want you to want me. But I don't want to be the most important thing in your life. Because—because I shouldn't be. If I were, it would mean a terrible waste of you and your talent. Because, Philip, I want something more important than that for my man."

"Hilary—"

"You've got to find it, Philip."

"And when I do I guess I'm supposed to come back? Isn't that the way this sort of thing works out?"

"This sort of thing doesn't always work out, Philip."

"I guess it doesn't," he said miserably.

There was a long moment of silence, and then P.S. said, "Hilary, would you like me to stay with you tonight?"

She looked up, almost startled, and then she smiled gently and said, "No, no, thank you, Philip, I'm all right. I think it would do us both good if we were left alone to think for a while. We've got plenty of time."

"All right," he said. He stood up and kissed her forehead. "I'll call you in the morning."

She pulled his face back to hers and kissed him on the lips. "Good night, Philip," she said. "Do call me when you wake up. We can have breakfast together."

Sunday morning, August 27, P. S. Wilkinson called room service and asked them to send up a pot of coffee, some toast, and the *New York Times*. The waiter arrived while he was shaving. He walked back into the bedroom, tipped the waiter, glanced briefly at the headlines, and returned to his shaving.

After he had dressed he spread out the newspaper on the bed and leafed through the front section while he sipped his coffee. He was turning the page when a headline caught his eye. "Holy Jesus CHRIST!" he said. He put down his coffee and leaned over the newspaper with both hands holding the page flat. "Holy Jesus Christ!" he said. "I've been . . . we've been . . . Holy Jesus Christ!"

He telephoned Hilary and asked her if she had seen the newspaper.

"No, what's wrong?"

"Under the headline 'New York Area Units to Be Mobilized,' is the 319th Military Intelligence Detachment—my unit back in New York."

"What does 'mobilized' mean?"

"It means I'm right smack back in the goddam Army, that's what the hell it means. Kennedy has had our unit put on the list to be mobilized. It means I'm going to have to get back into my goddam little green suit and play soldier again for McNamara and all those other bastards. Oh, Jesus Christ!"

"What are you going to do?"

"I don't think there's much I can do. I've had it. . . . I'm afraid I'd better get back to New York and find out what this is all about. I'm sorry, Hilary, I really am. But maybe this is only a bluff. Maybe nothing will happen."

Book Four

Book Four

23

FIRST LIEUTENANT PHILIP SADLER WILKINSON, 05 001 345, AI (QMC), leaned over the arm of his chair and felt along the coal-dust covered floor for his glasses, found them and put them on. Then he sat back staring into the gloom, cradling the back of his head in his locked hands. He had been sitting in his room in the BOQ ever since dinner at the Fort Lewis Officers' Open Mess (FLOOM) where he had watched a young lieutenant from the recently federalized National Guard division attempt to engage two Regular Army lieutenants in conversation. The RA lieutenants had turned their backs on him. It was the old game between the "Regulars" and the "militia," and it was depressing—but no more depressing and certainly far less insane than so much that had occurred during the past two months.

At the end of August the Soviet Union announced it would resume the testing of nuclear weapons. The White House stated that the Soviet decision had indicated the "complete hypocrisy of its professions about general and complete disarmament." The White House later added, "The Soviet announcement was primarily a form of atomic blackmail designed to substitute terror for reason in the present international scene." Delegates from twenty-four "non-aligned" nations began meeting in Belgrade, Yugoslavia. Some of the neutralist leaders denounced the resumption of Soviet nuclear testing as increasing the dangers of war. Others, including Tito, were tolerant of the Soviet de-

353

cision. The conference issued a second document demanding the elimination of imperialism.

A few days later President Kennedy announced: "In view of the continued testing by the Soviet government, I have today ordered the resumption of nuclear tests in the laboratory and underground with no fallout." He said that the acts of the U.S.S.R. left the United States "no other choice."

The debate over the control of access to the two Berlins continued through the middle of the month, and on September 16 the 319th MI Det (Div) received its orders calling it to active duty for a period of not more than one year at Fort Lewis in Washington State.

The Western Big Four ministers met in Washington prior to the talks between Rusk and Gromyko at the UN and agreed "that a peaceful solution to the problem of Germany and Berlin can be achieved if both sides are prepared to undertake discussions which take account of the rights and interests of all concerned." They also agreed that "an effort should be made to ascertain if there exists a reasonable basis for negotiation with the Soviet Union."

On Monday, September 18, Dag Hammarskjöld, Secretary General of the United Nations for the past eight and a half years, was killed in a plane crash in Africa. P.S.'s first thought was that he had been assassinated by the Russians. He hoped to God that it was not true. But if it was true, then he hoped the Russians had done it cleverly enough so that no one would be able to prove it. Because if the Russians had managed to assassinate the Secretary General of the UN, and the world found out about it, it might result in the same sort of crisis which had precipitated the First World War.

October had been the month of bombs. Khrushchev stated that the U.S.S.R. would probably complete its current series of nuclear weapon tests in the atmosphere with the explosion of a 50-megaton bomb. "We have a 100-megaton bomb," Khrushchev confided, "but it will not be exploded because if we did, we might break our own windows. Therefore we shall refrain. We shall explode a 50-megaton bomb and thus test the instruments for the 100-

megaton bomb. To use an old expression, May God grant that we never have to explode such a bomb over anybody's territory."

The United States immediately asked the Soviet Union to reconsider its decision. The White House stated that there was no military or technical reason for testing such a bomb.

Adlai Stevenson, U.S. Ambassador to the United Nations, told the General Assembly's political committee that the U.S. would resume atmospheric nuclear tests unless an effective test ban was signed promptly.

And on the day First Lieutenant Philip Sadler Wilkinson signed in for duty at Fort Lewis, the UN General Assembly adopted by an overwhelming vote a resolution appealing to Soviet leaders "to refrain from carrying out their intention to explode in the atmosphere a 50-megaton bomb before the end of this month." The Soviet delegate denounced the appeal as a Western "propaganda arrow."

P.S. reached over to the long flat board behind his cot and turned on his light. He yawned, stretched, and moved the chair to the desk and assembled some paper and a ballpoint and began to write:

Sunday night
29 October 1961

Dearest Hilary,

It is a little after eleven, I guess I should say a little after 2300 hours—but to hell with it. The trip out here wasn't so bad. It was a bit rough over Nebraska, at least I think the pilot said Nebraska. Come to think of it, he might have said, "Disaster!"— but those jets go so fast that by the time he finished saying "Nebraska" we would have been over the next state whatever that is . . . Kansas? Anyway, I can tell that I'm really back in the Army because on top of my bureau there are two cans of black shoe polish and a can of Brasso. And do you know something else? I miss you terribly.

Friday we started "processing," which is an Army word for standing in line until you reach a table where you fill out a form you filled out two weeks before. I had my eyes checked and the doctor told me I needed glasses which sounded sort of silly, but what he meant was I needed extra pairs. And I got shots—polio and flu, which means I have been inoculated for Polio, Influenza, Smallpox, Cholera, Typhoid, Typhus, and Tetanus. Everything but boredom. And after that a man leaned over and whispered to me. And I said,

"What?" and he said, "What did I say?" and I said, "It sounded like 'Fifteen.' " And he said, "Your hearing's fine." Another man told me my heart was beating. (Thank God!) And the next man told me to "Take this bottle, go into the next room and bring it back." So I did. I gave him the bottle and he said, "You're supposed to urinate in it." (I get my kicks.) As punishment they made me stick my warm chest against a freezing X-ray plate, and then, while I was doing that, I was to try to touch my Adam's apple with my shoulders. You will be glad to know that my blood type hasn't changed a bit—to which you are supposed to say, "Are you positive?" I had my picture taken for my new ID card, "Lick your lips, take a deep breath, honey," and I got a new set of dog tags which were different from the ones I had in Korea. They said "Episcopal" instead of "Protestant." Do you suppose we're making a new minority group here? And then I went to the PX and bought a new belt buckle and a couple of shirts, and, oh, Jesus, you can just tell what a grand fun time I've been having.

The general's speech on Saturday morning was incredible. He told us how lucky we were to be given the opportunity to serve our country, that we were the elite, and that Fort Lewis was one of the biggest Army posts in the whole wide world and I swear to God if I hear one more guy tell me to ask not what my country can do for me, I'll go berserk! Who got to ask? as the saying goes. That whole "Ask not" line drives me batty. Every time I hear it I get this picture of Sorensen and Kennedy rocking back and forth in some Georgetown living room just before the Inauguration. They're working on the Inaugural Address and Sorensen says, "How about, 'You shouldn't ask'? No, maybe, 'Please don't ask . . .'?" And then Kennedy says, "No, we need something with a little bezazz. How about, 'Ask not what your country can do for you . . .'?" And Sorensen goes wild and says, "Terrific! And for the next line all we have to do is reverse it. Something like, 'but ask what you can do for your country.' Am I right or am I right?"

After the opening speech the general introduced his staff and you'll never believe who the A/C of S, G2 is. (In fact, you probably will never even guess *what* the A/C of S, G2 is: Assistant Chief of Staff for Intelligence.) Anyway, the G2 is my old CO from Korea: Lieutenant Colonel Sturgess. He was the one I was telling you about who wanted to shave all the Korean girls' heads. Seeing him there made it like an old home week. I doubt if the feelings are mutual. But, in a funny sort of way, I was almost glad to see him because it made this whole idiotic call-up seem, for some reason, real. This whole thing is so Disneylandish that I constantly have to look at things like Brasso cans and my Army boots and ex-commanding officers to convince myself that this isn't all some sort of hideous masquerade ball. So much for all that.

The social life is all one gay tizzy whirl, dearie. We go to movies and we go to the PX and we go to the club and we go to

bed very much alone and that's it. Thank God for my friend Gene
Price and his wife. They had me to dinner last night. They have an
apartment in Tacoma, which is not too far from Fort Lewis. I think
I told you about Gene Price the last time in Washington. Well, anyway, he had to sell his business to his partner and took a very rough
loss. His partner was not the nice guy Price thought he was and so
he lost quite a lot. He has also been unable to sell his house in
Brooklyn Heights. Whenever I think I've got it bad, I think of him.
The poor guy is in trouble financially. I offered to lend him some
money, but he won't take it. I wish to God one of those guys we
saw at the pool that first time in Washington was out here to see
what's going on. But it would probably just confuse them, or more
likely, give them an amusing anecdote for when they got back. The
last straw is that Gene's wife thinks she's pregnant again.

Speaking of children . . . I hope you don't feel remorseful about
breaking our agreement not to make love. After all, we did hold out
right up to the last. God, it was so nice. Nice? Understatement. So
that's what they mean by ecstasy. Anyway, let me know if an awkward situation develops. (After reading that last line I can see what
you mean when you accuse me of being pompous.) The awkward
situation will probably be very beautiful, and if it's a son I've got
an alumnus' legacy in some of the finer prep schools on the East
Coast. Enough of that. Just let me know.

I wish I could think of something exciting to tell you. But there
isn't anything exciting doing. It's just the Army—Jesus! Ain't that
the truth!—I'd say most of the unit is taking it pretty well so far.
Morale is moderately high. Everyone is sort of thinking, "Well,
there's a job to be done, so let's do it and get it over with." We're at
about half-strength, which means in a couple of weeks we should
be getting in some new men to bring us up to strength.

I went to church this morning for the first time in God knows
how long (and believe me He does!). I went to the post chapel and
the chaplain welcomed all the new members of his flock and said that
serving your country is, in many ways, like serving God. He came
within a cat's hair of saying, "Ask not what God can do for you,"
and I'm dead certain he wanted to.

This hasn't been much of a love letter. I do love you. What more is
there to say? I wish you were here right now. Even in this wretched
cot. It would be kind of fun to try sleeping in it.

Take care of yourself and Hester, and write me: 1/Lt. P. S.
Wilkinson, 05001345, 319th MI Det (Div), Fort Lewis, Washington.

I love you—
Phil

The unit assembled at 0730 in one of the three converted
barracks assigned the 319th MI north of the airstrip. The men

sat on window ledges and crates or leaned against the walls. Lieutenant Price sat down on a box next to P.S., patted it, and said, "Early American Reservist."

The adjutant, Lieutenant Flanders, called the roll, then called the unit to attention as the major entered.

"At ease, gentlemen," the major said. "First of all, I would like to take this opportunity of welcoming you all to your first full week back on active duty—"

(Groans)

"—You have all spent enough time in the Army to—"

(Applause)

"—to know how you are expected to behave. This means, of course, you do not interrupt me when I am speaking." The major paused and looked around the room. "You also should know what you are expected to be able to do. You are all grown men . . . adults . . . you have served in the Army before . . . some of you more than once . . . you are not recruits; and therefore, I do not anticipate having to treat you as recruits. This means that during the maximum amount of the time you will be given the maximum amount of leeway and the maximum amount of opportunity to take the maximum amount of responsibility with a minimum amount of supervision for the maximum amount of your work—"

"What?" a few of the men asked. It was clear that the major had labored hard over those lines in his opening remarks, but it was equally clear that no one had any firm idea of what he meant.

"As yet," continued the major, ignoring the questioning looks, "we cannot be positively certain of the nature of the work we will be called on to do. Only one assignment has been received thus far. But," the major said, pausing, "but . . . if this assignment is any indication of the caliber of work we might be expected to produce, then I can say this much: You will be working hard, under sometimes rigorous conditions, and the results expected of you must be of a professional nature. This assignment went to Wilkinson's section."

"Sir?" Wilkinson asked.

"I'll tell you about it later," the major said.

"*We* received an assignment," Captain Willoughby said. "The CIC section was asked to investigate the sale of bootleg liquor to individuals on the National Guard troop train. The CG of the division thinks the liquor was poisoned and that it was a positive act of sabotage."

There was laughter.

"Perhaps, Captain Willoughby," said the major, "you will be kind enough to tell me why you waited until now to announce your assignment without letting me know immediately upon receipt of it?"

"Sir, I—"

"Tell me in my office after this meeting," Major Torfus ordered.

"As I was saying, the assignments will be demanding both of your talents and your time. Don't think for one minute that I am not aware of the hardships and the duress many of you have undergone in the past few weeks and by having to come out here. I know that it has not been easy. . . . And to the younger members of the unit I would like to add this: it gets harder as you get older. But . . . but, when you joined this Reserve unit you did so knowingly. You must have been aware that something like this might happen. It has happened before. Many of us were recalled for Korea. That is why there is something called a 'Reserve unit.' You have all drawn pay checks for your weekly meetings, and now you are being asked to earn it . . ."

"Ask not!" someone muttered.

". . . None of us would be here unless there was a job to do. And we do have a job: the collection, evaluation, interpretation, production, reporting, and dissemination of all intelligence information in support of the division. It should be evident from what we have seen of the division thus far that we must also add to our mission the education of the division as to what actually comprises intelligence information . . ."

(Polite laughter)

". . . For the first few weeks we will all be going through a fairly difficult period of adjustment. It is my belief that by keeping busy we will also manage to remain relatively happy. It is for this reason, then, that I have scheduled for 0930 hours this morning a five-mile hike. And this afternoon we will return to the preparation of the unit area . . . I want to see all section chiefs in my office at 0830 hours. Are there any questions?" The major paused and waited for a few moments, and he said, "That's all."

At the close of the 0830 hours staff meeting Major Torfus told Wilkinson to remain behind. When the other officers had left the major leaned across his desk toward P.S. and said, "Colonel Sturgess suggested a rather special assignment for you and Mooney. How would you like to spend some time in the desert?"

"The desert?"

"The Yakima desert. You'd be there for about three weeks as an observer attached to the division. Your assignment would be to evaluate the division's photo reconnaissance capabilities and to determine what—if anything—needs to be done to make them more effective."

"This was Colonel Sturgess' idea?"

"He suggested you for it. He thinks very highly of you."

"Sounds it." P.S. smiled. "If he thought any more highly of me, he'd probably suggest I be sent to the moon. . . . Three weeks in the desert?"

"It's not an order," the major said. "It was merely a suggestion that our detachment furnish some assistance to the division on maneuvers. However . . ." The major let the phrase linger.

"However, it would behoove me to participate."

"It would be a good thing for the unit," the major said. "A feather in the detachment's cap. It would look very good on our record to be able to show that two days after we came on active duty at Fort Lewis we were able to furnish combat support; that there was a section capable of functioning for extended periods in the field."

"General Lee used to say 'Never volunteer.' But . . . for the good of the unit, sir, I will go."

The major smiled. "I knew you'd see it my way."

"Yes, sir," P.S. said. "When am I supposed to take Mooney to the desert? And where is this desert?"

"Two days from now is when the colonel suggested you'd be there. But it would be good if you could leave tomorrow. The division is on maneuvers now."

"Tomorrow. That doesn't give us much time to gather the equipment."

"Well, what you don't have I'm sure we can borrow."

"Did Colonel Sturgess say why he wanted us in particular?"

"I didn't ask him."

"Well, then, did he say where he wanted us? Does he want us at the headquarters or with the division aviation company?"

"I'm sure he'll leave that up to you."

"Well, I think we'd probably be better off at the airstrip since there's bound to be less 'Mickey Mouse' down there, but I guess we'd be better off if we looked around once we were down there."

"Fine."

"Are we under anybody's command? Or are we sort of free-lance agents?"

"You're free-lance."

"That's nice. . . . Sir, what about the hike this morning?"

"Well, I don't think you and Mooney will need to participate in that. Use the time to round up equipment."

" 'Equipment.' . . . Our section is supposed to have a deuce-and-a-half and a three-quarter-ton truck and a jeep . . . what about vehicles? Have we gotten any yet? I think it would be best if we could take a three-quarter-ton and a trailer. If one's available."

"We'll have one this afternoon."

"Mooney will need a license for it."

"Lieutenant Flanders will arrange for him to have a test this afternoon."

"Since we're going to be observers we won't have to take too much equipment other than what we'll need to make ourselves comfortable. What about weapons? Will we have to carry them?"

"You'd better take them."

"All right, sir. . . . Why don't I just see what we'll need and try to get ready as best I can? I don't think we'll have all the equipment we need, but we'll have enough. If we can get a three-quarter-ton truck, then that will solve a lot of the problem.

We could work out of the truck and rig it for lights."

"You figure it out. Tell me what you need and we'll see what we can find for you."

"Fine, sir." P.S. stood up.

"I'm glad you're going to be on this, P.S.," the major said. "It will look good on the unit record and, who knows, you might even learn something."

P.S. went back to his building to locate Mooney, a small, balding, thirty-five-year-old man with a specialist fifth class rating. Mooney was swabbing down the latrine.

"Mooney?"

"Yes, sir?"

"How would you like to get away from all this?" P.S. asked.

"Do I get to spend three sun- and fun-filled days in gay tropical Puerto Rico?"

"Very close. You and I have been chosen for a dangerous assignment. One from which we might not return alive."

"Is this the assignment the major was talking about at the meeting?"

"That's right. We get to spend three weeks in the Yakima desert as observers."

"Aerial observers?"

"Possibly. But what we're supposed to do is to determine how effective the division is in aerial reconnaissance."

"Where's this desert?"

"Yakima."

"Where's Yakima?"

"Washington."

"There's a desert here, too?"

"Evidently," P.S. said. "The Yakima Desert, I think it's supposed to be somewhere on the other side of the mountains."

"How do we get there?"

"You drive. We're supposed to get a three-quarter-ton truck this afternoon. And you're supposed to know how to drive it and to have a license for it by tomorrow morning. We leave for Yakima tomorrow."

"In the morning?"

"As soon as we're ready. Lieutenant Flanders will help you with the license. We're going to be down there for three weeks. So you'd better start thinking about what you'll take with you."

"Water."

"What?"

"I've seen all the Foreign Legion movies," Mooney said. "If I'm going to spend three weeks in the desert I'm taking water."

"Well, make up a list of what you think you'll need and I'll make a list of what I think we'll need, and we can compare them. . . . Oh, by the way, we won't have to go on the hike. So we might as well spend as much time as we can now getting things ready."

"What about the latrine?"

"What about it?"

"It's my day to clean it."

"Then while you're cleaning it try to think of things you'll need."

"Yes, sir," Mooney said.

When Mooney had finished with the latrine he walked into Wilkinson's office and sat down on the crate opposite the crate Wilkinson was sitting on; between them was the field table.

"I thought of one thing, sir."

"What's that?"

"Toilet paper."

"Good God, you're right." P.S. laughed. "I'd forgotten about that."

"I'm a practical man."

"Okay, here's my list," P.S. said. "I've tried to divide things up into categories of living and working and night and day . . ."

By four o'clock Mooney had returned with the three-quarter-ton truck and a driver's license for it. Wilkinson had him park as close to the building as possible. There was no trailer, so they would have to carry everything in the back of the truck. This meant they would not be able to sleep in the truck. Two enlisted men from the headquarters section helped load as P.S. called off the list: "Light set; two field tables; two folding chairs; plywood board; shovel; ax; pick; field cook-set; lantern

". . . Mooney? Did you pack the extra wicks in your PI kit?"

"Yes, sir."

"Good enough. Lantern; tube; flexible nozzle; 5-gallon water can; 5-gallon gas can; two PI kits; box with maps; acetate; tracing paper; staplers; masking tape; ordnance tape; extra canvas . . ."

"All here."

"We'll leave the truck in front of Headquarters. Who's the CQ tonight?"

"I am, sir," one of the enlisted men said.

"All right, make sure you keep an eye on the truck tonight. I don't want any of that equipment taken."

"Yes, sir."

"Fine, gentlemen, thank you very much for the help," P.S. said. "And, Mooney? You come with me."

"Yes, sir," Mooney said.

Back in his office, P.S. said, "Tomorrow morning pick up your weapon from the arms room. I've made another list of things you might want to check on at the PX. They'll come in handy. Do you smoke? You do, don't you?"

"Yes, sir."

"Make sure you have plenty of cigarettes. If you want to take your lighter, throw in extra flints. Another thing that's handy are those wash-'n'-dry pads. Also small tin coffee cups, or something like that. It saves you trips. Also you might want to pick up a large jar of instant coffee or bouillon cubes. And that powdered cream. And books, what kind of books do you read?"

"You mean for relaxation?" he asked. "Mysteries."

"Yes," P.S. said. "Good, get plenty of those."

"What do you read?"

"The same. Carter Brown or Ian Fleming, anything like that which helps pass the time."

"I like Agatha Christie."

"Bring her."

"She's a little old for the desert," Mooney said.

"Make sure you have a shaving mirror, shaving cream—"

"I use an electric."

"Don't count on it."

"But if we have the light set?"

"We may not be able to hook up to a generator," Wilkinson said. "Better get yourself a safety razor."

"This *is* a hardship," Mooney said.

"War is hell. Now, remember your dog tags. Make sure your air mattress holds air. If it doesn't, borrow someone else's and turn it in later. Also make sure you have all your tent poles and pegs."

"Sir, since I'm an enlisted man, I only get a shelter-half."

"Borrow the other half. All you have to do is try to think what you'll need for three weeks in the desert and take it. We've got plenty of room in the truck, so we can carry a lot. But keep things as much together as possible. Loose gear always gets lost."

"I was thinking, sir, once we have all this stuff . . ."

"Yes?"

"Well, why don't we defect to the Mexicans?"

"Oh, for God's sake." P.S. laughed.

"Just an idea," Mooney said. "Well, sir, have we got everything?"

"I think so. . . . If you remember something tonight, write it down somewhere. I'd like to try to leave here as close to 0800 as possible."

"You know something, Lieutenant Wilkinson? You're so good at this that at times you almost make me believe you like it."

"Well, I'll tell you, Mooney, I've found a home in the Army."

It was already dark outside when P.S. crossed the unit area toward the major's office and the orderly room. A small boy was standing by the orderly room door selling newspapers. The headline was: REDS TEST SUPER BOMB. P.S. bought a paper and walked on into the building.

"Is the major in?"

"I think so, sir," the detachment sergeant said. "He's probably in his office."

"Would you ask if I might see him?"

"Go on back, sir," the sergeant said. "He'd probably like some company."

P.S. passed through the swinging gate and walked to the major's office. He paused at the door and knocked.

"Major Torfus?"

There was no answer. P.S. tried the door. It was locked. He walked back to the detachment sergeant's desk. "The major's office is locked."

"Then I guess he left, sir," the sergeant said.

"You *guess* he left, Sergeant? Isn't it part of your job to know where the commanding officer is at all times?"

The sergeant looked up at him. In civilian life he was a plant guard. P.S. knew that he was pushing fifty years old. "Lieutenant Wilkinson," the sergeant said wearily, "if the major doesn't tell me when he leaves, and if he doesn't tell me where he's going, then I don't know when he leaves and I don't know where he goes."

"All right, Sergeant," Wilkinson said. "If anyone asks for me, you tell them that I left now and that I'm going back to my BOQ."

"All right, sir," the sergeant said, and he picked up his magazine and began reading it again.

When P.S. reached his room in the Bachelor Officers' Quarters he sat down on the edge of the bed and looked at his newspaper. Under the headline was a smaller head: BOMB IN 90 MEGATON RANGE. P.S. read the article quickly. It said that that morning the Soviet Union had triggered a nuclear blast with a force greater than the 50 megatons planned. Scientists all over the world had estimated that the blast was in the range between 62 megatons and 90 megatons. The White House denounced the test, saying that it was a propaganda move in order to "incite fright and panic in the cold war."

Jesus, ninety megatons! . . . Ninety million tons of TNT . . . and Hiroshima was what? Ten KT? . . . twenty KT? . . . Call it fifteen KT, fifteen thousand tons . . . fifteen thousand goes into ninety million! fifteen into ninety thousand; fifteen into

*ninety is what? five fifteens are seventy-five, six times . . .
Jesus! That bomb was six thousand times as powerful as the
one at Hiroshima! . . . Six thousand times more powerful than
Hiroshima!* . . . P.S. lit a cigarette and tried to imagine the de-
struction caused by a bomb six thousand times more powerful
than the one dropped at Hiroshima. It was incredible. There was
no way to imagine it. It was so enormous that he couldn't even
be scared by it.

24

WILKINSON AND MOONEY passed through the Fort Lewis gates at nine in the morning and headed south on U.S. 99 and then east toward the mountains. By 11:30 they had reached a town called Morgan. It was a logging town located on a broad flat valley rimmed on the sides by almost perpendicular wooded hills. P.S. wondered whether the town was named after the Morgan horses or whether the owner of the mill was a man named Morgan. On the edge of town was a lumbermill called, appropriately enough, the Tubafor Mill. On the south side of Morgan there were farms where there was grown wheat and dandelions and Herefords and dandelions and hay and dandelions and clover and dandelions and daughters the loggers sang about. But the mill seemed shut down and the farms were still. Earlier they had passed a railroad crew who were middle-aged. They saw no young men in Morgan and P.S. wondered if they had all left to find better jobs. They passed Harry's Drive-In, BURGERS, FRIES TO GO. The building was boarded up, the paint chipped and peeling. Harry had gone long ago. And then they came to a half-broken barn, a deep red in a field of tall green grasses. The roof had fallen in, and the barn's beams were curiously like a dead man's ribs. There was something black in the barn, either rotted wood or mushrooms. As they drove on toward the mountains there was a break in the trees and they could look down at a fast-moving mountain stream.

368

"If we weren't in the Army I could really enjoy this trip," Mooney said.

"It is pretty."

"Just think of being able to pull over to the side with a picnic basket and a bottle of white wine. A busty young wench . . ."

"Drive on, Omar. As in Omar Khayyám, the *Rubáiyát* of same? . . . 'A Book of Verses underneath the Bough,/A Jug of Wine, a Loaf of Bread—and Thou/Beside me singing in the Wilderness—Oh, Wilderness were Paradise enow!'"

"Is that how it goes?"

"I think so. I'm pretty sure it is."

"I always thought it was 'A Loaf of Bread, A Jug of Wine, And Thou beside me in the Wilderness . . .'"

"A common but not grievous error," P.S. said. "I didn't spend four years as an English major at Yale for nothing."

"Were you an English major? I was, too."

"Where'd you go?"

"Fordham. I took my Master's at Columbia."

"You've got a Master's?" P.S. asked in astonishment.

"Sure, why not?" Mooney asked.

"God, I don't. I was lucky to get a Bachelor's. Maybe I should be driving. You should be the passenger."

"Not at all." Mooney laughed. "You have to have at least a Master's to drive one of these trucks."

"You know, I never asked you what you were doing before this . . . I mean what you did on the outside, so to speak."

"I'm a teacher."

"A *teacher*! Where?"

"A school in New York. High school."

"I'll be damned," P.S. said. "I never knew that."

"Taught eleventh- and twelfth-grade English."

"I'll be *damned*!" P.S. said.

They passed Dr. Rollo's Grocery Store Open on Sundays. Next came the town of Kosmos, Unincorporated, where the Lion's Club meets every Tuesday at the Palarose Café.

"'Palarose' . . . 'Palarose' . . ." P.S. said. "Isn't that the name of a knight? One of King Arthur's knights?"

"There was Pellinore."

"That's Elsinor," P.S. protested.

"No, no. I'm talking about King Pellinore in T. H. White's *Once and Future King*. You've read that, haven't you?"

"Yes . . . Wait a minute! Pellinore was the one who was after the Questing Beast."

"That's right."

"God, I loved that book," P.S. said.

"It's a nice book," Mooney said.

They drove on in silence for a few miles until P.S. said, "How are you holding up? You want to take a break?"

"No, I'm all right," Mooney said. Then, after a while he asked, "Lieutenant Wilkinson, are you married?"

"No. Are you?"

"I'm engaged. Sort of. I was going to get married next January, but this kind of changes things."

"You could still get married. Live out here."

"I don't think so."

"What's she like?"

"Well, she's much younger than me. She's only twenty-five."

I'm only twenty-five myself, P.S. thought.

"Her name is Deirdre, but everyone calls her 'Didi' . . . She's sort of a beatnik. A nonconformist . . ."

"Does she have long black hair down to her hips?"

"And she wears sandals." Mooney laughed. "But she'll grow out of it."

They passed through Randle, Unincorporated, "Gateway to Mt. Adams 3400+" and followed the signs that said WHITE PASS.

"You getting hungry?" P.S. asked.

"A little."

"There's a town up ahead where we might be able to get something to eat."

"A pronto pup?" he asked. "You see them advertised."

"We might at least be able to find out what it is."

They had hamburgers and French fries in Packwood, and by 1:30 they were on White Pass, moving up over the Cascades, Mooney shifting gears back and forth: second gear, third gear, second gear, first gear, second gear. They were in the snow line and as they rounded one corner suddenly they came upon a pond, black with ice and cold and ringed by high fir trees.

"My God, someone should be selling Salem cigarettes here," Mooney said.

Farther on was the White Pass Inn, the chair lift stilled. Inside the large heated restaurant they could see chairs piled on top of the tables. There were a few ski tracks on the slope, but they were old ones, and the snow had blown over them. They reached the peak and it was downhill from there. Mooney kept the truck in second gear. They drove beside another fast-moving mountain stream and Wilkinson watched a chunk of ice swirling down the stream as fast as their truck was moving down the hill.

"What's this all about?" Mooney asked. He pointed at a military policeman waving them to the side of the road. They pulled over and saw a large convoy parked in a rest area. The MP came around to Wilkinson's side of the truck. Wilkinson rolled down the window as the soldier saluted.

"Good afternoon, sir," the MP said.

"Afternoon," Wilkinson replied. "What's up?"

"You'll have to fall in with the convoy, sir."

"Is it going to Yakima?"

"Yes, sir."

"Well, then, it'll be our pleasure. Where do you want us? At the rear?"

"Major Bernard will have the rear position," the MP said. "You can fall in ahead of him."

"Fine," Wilkinson said. The MP saluted again, Wilkinson returned the salute. "Mooney, why don't we pull over to that last jeep?"

When they reached their position they both got out and stretched. Ahead of them was a two-and-a-half-ton truck. A major walked up to it and spoke into the darkened back of it. "If every truck in the convoy using this pass threw out as much trash as you four—"

"Five, sir."

"As you five, then, we'd have one helluva mess. First came

the milk cartons. Then came the wax paper. Next came the
orange peels. I don't want to catch any of you throwing anything
out again. If I do, I will personally see to it that you walk back
the entire way policing the area. Is that clear?"

"Yes, sir," they chorused.

The major turned back and Wilkinson walked over to him and
saluted. "Lieutenant Wilkinson, sir, from the 319th MI Detachment. The MP—"

"MI, what's that?"

"Military Intelligence, sir."

"Oh, yes," the major said.

"Anyway, the MP told us to join your convoy and I wanted to
make sure you knew who we were."

"Well, that's very thoughtful of you, Lieutenant. You're going
to Yakima?"

"Yes, sir."

"Well, that's fine. You're in the intelligence, you say?"

"Yes, sir," P.S. said. "We're supposed to check in at the
division headquarters once we get there. Would you know
where that would be located?"

"I might, Lieutenant, I might . . . But it seems to me that it
would be good practice for you intelligence people to try to find
that out on your own."

Oh, for Christ's sake . . . "Yes, sir," P.S. said. He saluted
and walked back to his truck. He closed the door and rolled up
the window, then turned to Mooney. "Did you hear that?"

"Yes, sir," Mooney said.

"Jesus!"

By three o'clock the convoy was out of the Cascade Range.
Both Mooney and Wilkinson were surprised by how swiftly the
countryside had changed. Where once they had high Douglas
fir trees, they now had soft green hills. No more mountains. An
almost parched land. A car coming slowly toward the convoy
containing a grinning driver in a plaid shirt. He gave the entire
convoy the finger.

"No sacrifice too great," Mooney said.

On either side of the road there began to be neat rows of
apple trees, and ahead of them they could see the rounded red

sandstone hills of the Yakima Firing Center. They crossed a bridge and turned left onto the large highway. After the GLEED FEED & SEED CO. and after motel after motel after motel the convoy turned off the highway, passed through the guard gates, and they were inside the Yakima Firing Center. Yakima, Washington, their home for the next three weeks.

"My God," Wilkinson said. "It looks just like the maps. It's the same color as the maps are!"

"Look at that hill," Mooney said. He was pointing at a small one shaped like a cone on their left side.

"That's called 'Squaw Tit,'" Wilkinson said. "A fairly graphic name."

"Part of the old West."

"Look, it's about quarter past four. We haven't got much daylight left. So we'd better get our tails over to the headquarters."

"If we knew where it was it would be easier."

"Follow the main road and we'll ask someone. But let's get the hell out of this convoy."

They were on a dirt road running along the edge of a wide barren plain. On their right side the ridges knuckled back into the mountains. A headquarters for a field exercise would be located between the ridges, hidden from the road, as deep within the valleys as possible. The sun had already disappeared behind them and Wilkinson knew they had no more than thirty minutes to find the headquarters.

Mooney was getting anxious. "The next man I see I swear I'm going to stop this truck and say, 'Take me to your leader' . . . and we'll end up interned in some POW camp for the duration of the exercise. How do they know who we are or what we're doing here?"

"We'll just have to tell them."

"Tell them what?"

"That we're nice guys a long way from home and buddy can you spare a dime."

"My God, look over there!" Mooney pointed at a platoon of tanks rushing across the desert and sage, dust billowing behind them. "What do you say we attack them? You take the lead tank and I'll mop up the rest."

"Slow down a minute, Mooney . . . Now, look almost straight ahead of us and about a hundred feet off the ground. It's an L-19, do you see it?"

"Yeah."

"Its flaps are down, and it's landing. So at least we know where the field is. Head for where it's going in."

"I just thought of a great line," Mooney laughed. "Follow that plane."

"Step on it, Cato."

> Operation Scrub Pine
> Yakima Firing Center
> Thursday, Nov 2, 1961

Hilary, my love:

As you can see from the above address, I have moved. Yakima is in sort of the lower right-hand corner of Washington State which, as you remember, is in the upper left-hand corner of the United States. Yakima is a desert training center for Armor. Mooney and I have been sent here for three weeks. Did I ever tell you about Mooney? He's the only other person in the Photo Intelligence Section. He's an ex-high school teacher, about 35 years old, and at Major Torfus' request we are here to observe how well the division utilizes its aerial and photo reconnaissance capabilities. So much for that.

I never realized how plush my BOQ room was before I got out here. You should see where I live now. Mooney and I live in pup tents—which, for Mooney, is fine. He's about 5'5", and he fits in one. I wish to God I did. My feet stick out the back flap.

We arrived here ("here" being a dirt airstrip) Tuesday night and spent an hour trying to find the division headquarters and finally gave up, located the airstrip and pitched our tents in near darkness. Wednesday morning we learned we had pitched our tents on the runway—well, it wasn't *really* on the runway, but our tents were close enough so that when the first plane took off at 0430 Wednesday morning I thought the damn thing had flown through one flap of my tent and out the other. Needless to say, we moved.

There has not been a thing in the air for the past 36 hours except tumbleweed and dirt. The winds have reached gusts of 40 mph and, Jesus, it's been cold! If I ever see another desert film showing the Foreign Legionnaires panting from the heat, I'll walk out. I haven't seen the sun for two days. I've been spending most of my time sitting in the front seat of our truck with Mooney trying to keep out of the wind. If I didn't know better, I'd swear it was going to snow!

This whole thing is so goddam silly! As I said, when we got here we couldn't find the headquarters. So Wednesday morning (after we moved our tents off the runway) we went looking for it again and found it hidden in a hole. We'd been told to check in with the G2, and when we found the tent a military police sergeant stopped me and said, "What kind of a 'rod' you carrying, Lieutenant?"

I thought he was trying to be cute. "A forty-five," I said.

"Don't you know the password?" he asked me.

" 'Password'?" I asked. "I had a hard enough time trying to find this place without having to learn a password."

"Well, how do I know you're not an Aggressor?"

"Sergeant," I said, "if I were an Aggressor I'd know the password."

They wanted to take me to a POW camp for interrogation, but finally I talked them into getting the G2, so I could tell him what I was here for. The G2 arrived, a fat-bellied colonel. And, of course, no one had bothered to tell him that we were coming. And when I told him why we were there, he said the division had only one camera and there wasn't any equipment down here to process the film. All the film was flown up to the Signal unit at Fort Lewis where it was interpreted and the reports sent back down here. In other words, I might as well be back at Fort Lewis.

The only excitement we have had out here is that Wednesday night Mooney found six baby rabbits. I came back from the evening repast (spaghetti in grease) to find Mooney happily stoned and clutching to his bosom two bunnies. He gave me two and kept four for himself (the pig). They spent the night in our tents. Mine kept scratching around. This morning one of Mooney's was missing. He said it was Brunhilde, though how in God's name he can tell one from another is beyond me. He found Brunhilde had been stepped on during the night. She was buried. Such is life.

I feel pretty terrible about that last letter I wrote you. I guess I sounded pretty awful. I'm sorry it didn't tell you how much I love you. I do love you, and maybe I just can't write it so it sounds it. But believe me, I do. And I miss you and I wish to God I were out of this Army and with you, and Hester.

> With all my love from the war-torn spot,
> Phil

P.S. Wilkinson sealed the letter, addressed it, and stuck it in the pocket of his field jacket. Then he leaned back against the seat of the three-quarter-ton truck and closed his eyes. There was no point in trying to get any sleep before eleven. The aviation detachment guards would be shooting off their blanks until then. P.S. heard someone walking toward the truck and he opened his eyes.

"Hi, sir," Mooney said, climbing in next to him. "Want some

of this?" He passed Wilkinson a paper cup.

"Scotch?"

"The vurrah same," Mooney said. He closed the truck door and smiled.

P.S. could tell Mooney was high. He knew that as an officer he should speak to Mooney about it; but he also knew that this trip was dismal enough without clashing with Mooney.

"Don't worry, sir," Mooney said. "I drink in the back of the truck and then I walk to my tent and that's it. Nobody knows about this."

"Good," Wilkinson said, and then after a moment he asked, "Am I that transparent?"

"Well, yes . . . And I put myself in your position, and I could see that it might bother you."

P.S. sipped the Scotch. Although he didn't particularly care for the taste, he liked its warmth and what it did for him. "Where'd you get this?"

"From my duffel bag. I got another one just like it. When you said we'd be out here for three weeks I figured I might as well bring some snake bite remedy."

"Don't talk about snakes," Wilkinson said. "I can't stand the damn things."

"I heard they like to climb into your sleeping bag to keep warm."

"Jesus," P.S. said.

"And some guy from the battle group got bitten yesterday. He's all right though. Bit him right through the boot."

"Mooney, why are you telling me all this?"

"Just bringing you the news of the day in review."

"Thanks," Wilkinson said.

"Hey, I got a newspaper!" Mooney said. "It's Wednesday's but I have it . . . you want to look at it?"

"What's in it?"

"Not much. It's got something about Khrushchev in it. What he said after that last bomb."

"What'd he say?"

"He thought it was pretty funny. . . . Listen, I'll get it. You stay here."

Wilkinson nodded.

A few minutes later Mooney was back. He slid in next to Wilkinson and shut the door. "Jesus, colder than a brass monkey!" He unfolded the newspaper and began searching for the column. "Here it is. 'Ninety megaton range . . .' Here: 'Khrushchev drew laughter from a group at the Communist Party Congress when he said that the latest blast,' and I quote, ' "proved somewhat bigger than the 50 megatons that the scientists had calculated." He said that the scientists would not be punished for their "mistake." ' "

"A million laughs, this nuclear war," Wilkinson said.

"You don't really think there is going to be one, do you?"

"God knows. . . . You mean one right away? As a result of what's been going on in Berlin?"

"Within the next six months."

"I don't think so," P.S. said. "I hope not—obviously—it just doesn't seem right. There's been too much talk. I think that's all there's going to be. It's my guess that all this stuff was so that the Soviet Union could have an excuse to resume nuclear testing."

"I think it's all political."

"Well, I think it's political, too. There's no doubt about that, but I don't think it's *all* political."

"Well, I sure as hell think our being here is political."

"You mean because it looks good on the unit record?"

"That's exactly what I mean."

"Would you rather be cleaning latrines back at Fort Lewis?"

"Well . . . at least, at least, when the day was finished there'd be some place to go instead of having to sit in a truck to keep warm."

Somewhere at the Front
Tuesday, 7 November 1961
Yakima, Washington

Dear, sweet Hilary:

Once more I have filled my tin cup with coffee, lit up a cigarette and have braced my knees against the dashboard of our sturdy truck. As I write this, the sun is sinking slowly into the purple hills behind us, I nibble a graham cracker, and ten tanks take off down the road making the most horrible noise imaginable. My God, those things are loud!

But if you really want to see how hellish this war is, today I read my last detective mystery and they were supposed to last for three weeks! Ah well, I still have Durrell's *Alexandria Quartet*.

I got a letter from Gene Price, who says everyone in the unit is sitting around on their tails waiting for work. There's nothing to do, no equipment to do it with. There still is no office furniture and the men are getting pretty restless. I wrote the major a letter telling him what was going on here (nothing) and that with his kind permission Mooney and I would like to get out of here and return to the unit. No answer yet. But, when he hears there isn't even a hand camera in the place he'll see the point in not staying around.

The desert is getting to us. Mooney and I had our first fight and we've only been here a week. I noticed Monday morning Mooney hadn't shaved and he didn't shave this morning either. After two days of wind-blown dust you get pretty dirty. So I asked him why he didn't shave. He said there wasn't any point in it. His face was chapped from the wind, he said the water never got hot enough for a good shave, and since he never went anywhere except to the mess tent and back he didn't see any point in it. Since everything he said made sense, it was even more difficult for me to tell him to shave. But it has to be done. So I told him I wanted him clean-shaven tomorrow morning. "Is that an order, Lieutenant?" Well, Jesus, what could I say but "yes"? He just sat there in the truck looking at me. He said, "Lieutenant Wilkinson, I'm thirty-five years old and I don't need to be told when to shave." So I told him if he gave me any more lip I'd make him shave his goddam rabbits, too. We're down to three now. Two escaped and the first, as I wrote before, died. They are nice little things. All the people here at the airfield bring things for them to eat. So far they seem to like my graham crackers best. Mooney took them all out for a walk this afternoon. He keeps them in his fatigue jacket pocket, then puts them down one at a time so that he can chase them. What else is there to do? There has been very little flying because of the winds. One L-19 flew into the side of a hill— pilot unhurt. A chopper flew into the side of another hill—pilot broke his leg. It's been hard on the pilots, what with the kind of weather we've been having—it rained yesterday!—the pilots are hesitant to try too much (It's murder to send a kid out in a crate like that!).

We have moved the truck next to a generator truck and so we have electric lights in the back to read by. We also have our electric hot plate cooking and things could be worse . . . I guess.

I'm glad you miss me. In a selfish sort of way, that's nice to hear. And it's even nicer for you to say you love me. Somehow when you see it in writing it means more. I never got many love letters in school. In fact, I got so few I used to pretend my sister's letters were from a "girl." I had a wonderful dream about us last night. I won't go into too much detail, but it was very pleasant. At least permit me that kind of pretty picture out here.

I send you an enormous bundle of love and a few grains of sand, write soon and love to Hester and love, love, love. One final note: I am relieved to hear about your period, period.

Phil

"Hey, Lieutenant Wilkinson?" Mooney said, "I've shaved."

"Oh, hi, Mooney, that's good." P.S. moved over in the truck to make room for Mooney.

"Listen, sir, what do you say we get out of here?"

"To go where?"

"Why don't we just pack up and go back to the unit?"

"I wish we could, Mooney, but we're here until the major tells us to come home."

"But he knows there's nothing to do," Mooney protested.

"There's nothing to do back at the unit either."

"But at least there are hot showers and dry beds and a place to go after work."

"I know . . . I know . . . but there's nothing we can do about it."

"But what if we just packed up and moved out? What if we just arrived back at the unit and said 'Here we are, gang,' what could he do about it?"

"Quite a lot, I'm afraid." Wilkinson smiled. "Maybe even get us on desertion."

"I think I'd rather take my chances back at Fort Lewis on getting shot than dying from boredom out here."

"Have you run out of books yet?"

"No, I borrowed some from another guy here."

"Any good ones?"

"A couple of Carter Browns and one Robert Dietrich."

"When you're through with them I'd like to see them, if that's okay," P.S. said. "I've been trying to read the Durrell books but find them hard going."

"Lieutenant Wilkinson, you really don't think we could just sort of get out of here? Just sort of disappear?"

"Steal away like the Arabs?"

"Pick up our toys and go home," Mooney said, and then he laughed bitterly. " *'Home!'* Achh, I should wash my mouth out with sand for saying that."

"No, I'm afraid we can't. I told you what the major's letter said. He said we had to stay here for the duration of the problem."

"But why? There's nothing to do. There's absolutely nothing to do."

"I know . . . I know . . ."

"Jesus, I'm going batty out here. I really am!" Mooney said. "I'm almost at the point where I'll start building sand castles. . . . What in God's name are we supposed to be accomplishing by staying out here?"

"We're supporting the division. We're acting as observers."

"Observed anything lately?"

"No." Wilkinson smiled. "Look, Mooney, I don't like it here any more than you do. It's just that you've got to live with it. You can't fight it."

"Why not?" Mooney asked. "If something is as ridiculous as what we're going through out here, then shouldn't you try to do something about it?"

"But we've done everything we could. I sent another message to the major telling him that we have nothing to do, that we could write our report now, make our suggestions, and finish up the work back at the post by checking what they do with the films there."

"He's going to tell us to stay out here," Mooney said.

"Probably."

"Because it looks good on some silly-assed record."

"Maybe."

War-torn Yakima
Sunday, 12 Nov 61

Dearest Hilary:

I feel as though I've been playing Lawrence of Arabia all my life! I'm tired of this desert life. Rudolph Valentino can have it. Mooney is going slowly mad . . . I keep catching him talking to himself now that all the rabbits are gone.

The days just drag by. We get up at 0630, shave (cool soapy water in the steel helmet), dress (fatigues, boots, field jacket with liner, web cartridge belt w/first aid pack, magazine pouch, bayonet, saran-wrapped .45 in holster, etc.), then we walk the 150 yards to the cook trucks for breakfast. Breakfast is a box of cold cereal, coffee, cold scrambled eggs, raw cold bacon, and great conversations: One enlisted man running finger across bottom of his mess kit, talking to second EM: "Gee, these things are still gritty." The second replies: "That ain't grit, that's *sand,* ya dumb ————!" And he says this outrageously inappropriate obscenity with such obvious relish that for some reason the entire conversation seemed designed to permit him an excuse to say that one foul word.

Mooney and I have been out here for almost two weeks now. I can't understand why the major won't let us return to Fort Lewis. God knows things are screwed up there (Price wrote me that a lot of the National Guard division men still haven't received uniforms, many of them don't have boots, and that a guy leaned against the wall in one of the barracks and his arm went through!), but there doesn't seem much point in spending three weeks in the desert just for the sake of the unit commander being able to say that he has men in the desert.

You can't imagine what it's like to spend this much time in the desert—doing nothing. Mooney has gotten himself so that he can sleep all the time. We move the truck four times each day when the wind shifts. And when we're not eating—a process we prolong for as much time as possible—we play cards for cigarettes. I've even written letters to friends I haven't seen or heard from in years—and if they don't get the letters at least they'll be returned to me and I'll have something to read. Mooney brought an American history book with him and he hasn't done any better on that than I have with the Durrell. Hilary, the thing that is really getting me down is that it's such a waste—not just Mooney and myself on the desert—but this whole silly goddam call-up!

Mooney just interrupted me to say he'd had a funny dream. He dreamt he and I were marooned in a desert for three weeks with nothing to do.

I keep thinking about your apartment and how much I enjoyed sitting with you there. . . . Maybe the desert is doing this to me . . . I find myself thinking of bright colored things, like the pillows on your daybed . . . and I think of you, dear God, how I think of you!

I wish I had more to write you. I don't have any news, really. I'm just sitting around trying to keep Mooney out of trouble. I understand that some reporters are coming out here to see how the division is doing. Maybe you'll read a story about us out here in war-torn Yakima.

God, I love you.

It was Friday evening, November 17, 1961. P. S. Wilkinson and Mooney had had their chow—tuna fish—they had made their coffee—instant—and they were sitting, as usual, in the front seat of their three-quarter-ton truck, trying to stay warm, trying to keep out of the wind. Mooney was sitting behind the steering wheel, resting his gloved hands on the crossbar, his fingers linked around his tin coffee cup. Wilkinson was sitting on the other side, leaning against the door, holding his coffee cup in his lap. Neither one had spoken since chow.

Mooney shifted his position slightly, raised his coffee cup and sipped, then he rested his hands again on the steering wheel. "Well, shit," he said.

Wilkinson said nothing.

After a few moments Mooney said again, "Shit, shit, shit."

"Umm," Wilkinson said.

"Let me ask you just one thing, sir, okay?"

"Go ahead."

"Just what, exactly, have we accomplished out here?"

"Well . . ."

"We've been here for seventeen days. We've spent two and a half weeks in this same place, in this same truck parked at the same end of the dirt airfield, and we've watched the same airplanes take off and the same airplanes land, and we've made the same trip to the same headquarters, and gotten the same answers and asked the same questions, and I just want to know what, what in the hell we've accomplished?"

Wilkinson shifted position, sliding down in the seat so that he could brace his knees against the dashboard. He took a sip of coffee and then he said, "Well, Mooney, I'll tell you. . . . You and I have found out that we can spend seventeen days together in the desert and live. Now, that's an interesting thing to know."

"Oh, screw the desert!"

There was a knock on the window next to P.S. and he turned to see who it was. *"Well, I'll be goddamed!"* he said. "Johnny Carmody! What the hell are you doing here?" P.S. opened the door and got out. He stood looking at the young man wearing an overcoat, white button-down shirt and striped tie showing between the lapels. "What are you, Special Agent Carmody of the CIA? What are you doing dressed like that in the middle of the desert, for God's sake? You lost?"

"No, no." Carmody laughed. "Business." They shook hands and Carmody stepped back to look at Wilkinson. "If you aren't the damndest sight I've ever seen. You look like a reject for Merrill's Marauders."

"Well, how are you?" P.S. asked.

"Fine. Fine."

"But what brings you here? What sort of business are you on?"

"I'm a newspaper reporter."

"My God, you mean you're one of those guys the headquarters is in such a twit about?"

"I guess so." Carmody laughed. "I'm not the only one though. The paper sent a whole bunch of us out here."

"Well, it sure is nice of you to come to see me. You're the most exciting thing that's happened to us out here since a plane cartwheeled off the runway."

"Anybody hurt?"

"No," P.S. said. "Have you got a minute? Can you sit with us for a while?"

"Us?"

"Mooney. Specialist Fifth Class Laurence Mooney, he's the other half of my section. Have you got a few minutes?"

"All the time in the world. This isn't a social call."

"It isn't? Then what is it? Surely there's no news in us."

"The hell there isn't. Haven't you read the papers? . . . No, I guess you haven't out here."

"Well, what's in the papers?"

"Army Reservists."

Wilkinson opened the truck door and motioned Carmody to slide in between Mooney and himself. "Too cold to stand outside. Here. You want me to put your briefcase in the back?"

"Hell, no. It's got my whisky in it."

"*Whisky!*" Mooney said. "Who's got whisky?"

"That's Mooney," Wilkinson said. "Mooney? This is Johnny Carmody. He was a year ahead of me at Yale. He was on the newspaper up there, and now he's on the— What paper are you with?"

Carmody told them and then he opened his briefcase and

passed the bottle around. "I suppose officers and enlisted men aren't supposed to drink together?"

Wilkinson said, "Not in front of other people anyway. But tell me, what about the Army Reservists? What's going on? Are we being released?"

"No, no, 'fraid not," Carmody said. "There've been an awful lot of gripes. Letters to congressmen, letters to newspapers, a lot of bitching and moaning."

"Go on, go on, what else?" Wilkinson asked. "What brings you here?"

"Well, some congressman came out to Fort Lewis to see what all the complaints were about. Since he might have had as many as twenty thousand votes out here, he thought he'd better listen to them. So he went around and talked to the men and it turns out they aren't too happy about being out here."

"Who is?" Mooney asked.

"Well, he went back to Washington and he said the Army wasn't prepared to handle the troops who were called up, that everything is screwed up, that there's no good reason for the call-up—you know, the whole business."

"What 'whole business'?" Wilkinson asked.

"No shoes, no uniforms, no weapons, no equipment, nothing to do but make work," Carmody said. "They feel that it's all a waste of time."

"It is," Mooney said.

"Well, maybe not," P.S. said. "What did some of them say? I mean what brought you all the way out here?"

"We're just starting here," Carmody said. "We're going to make a tour of all the posts where the Reservists and National Guardsmen are on duty. The congressman kind of touched it off though. He made a big stink about it out here and so this was a pretty good place to start."

"He probably just wanted attention, the publicity," P.S. said.

"Oh, hell, I'm sure that was most of it. But at the same time the Reservists didn't have to tell him anything," Carmody pointed out.

"They aren't Reservists," Wilkinson said. "They're National Guard."

"Well, how do you feel about it? You're a Reservist."

"What does it matter what I feel? I'm here and there isn't much I can do about it."

"But are you pleased?"

"'Pleased'? Oh, come on, Johnny, of course not! No one likes being back in the Army."

"Then you're mad. Right?"

"Look, is this between us or is this for the newspaper?"

"Whatever you like," Carmody said.

"Then let's keep it between us."

"If you feel that's necessary."

"I don't know whether it's necessary or not. I just think it's wiser," P.S. said.

"Well, then, let me read you what some of the others have said for publication," Carmody said. He opened his briefcase and began leafing through his notes.

"Say, how about another drink?" Mooney said.

"Sure," Carmody said.

"Loose lips sink ships," P.S. warned.

"Up the ruling classes," Mooney said. He drank from the bottle and passed it to P.S., who declined.

"You want some coffee, Johnny?" P.S. asked.

"Is it made?"

"In the back of the truck. As a matter of fact, why don't we sit back there? We have electric lights, and they warm it up. Besides, we can stretch out a little better."

A few minutes later they were resettled in the back of the truck. Wilkinson and Carmody sat across one of the folding field tables from Mooney. They were heating the coffee, and Carmody had spread his papers out on the tabletop.

"Okay," Carmody said. "Here's one. Question: 'Are you bitter?' Answer: 'Of course we're bitter. We read the papers. Try to figure out what the hell is happening and all we get is gobbledygook. No one in Washington tells us what we're doing this for, or why we're on active duty, or for how long. If the only purpose of this call-up is to bring publicity to the Kennedys, then there must have been others they could use.' Question: 'Who?' Answer: 'What about the unemployed? Kennedy has been making this big stink about how there are too many unemployed. Newspapers have things about White House conferences on the unemployed; there are how many unemployed youths?' My answer: '800,000 check figures.' His answer, continued: 'Okay, 800,000. Then here's an easy way to solve the unemployment problem. It must cost plenty to keep them on relief or welfare, just as it costs plenty to keep us here. Surely out of 800,000 unemployed youths they could find 156,000 fit for duty. Surely we'd be glad to stay on until they're trained. At any rate it shouldn't take a year to do it, which is how long we're supposed to stay on . . . longer if that blank McNamara has anything to do about it. . . .' "

"What was that about McNamara?" Mooney asked.

"You mean, what did McNamara do or what was he called?"

"I can guess what he was called," Mooney said. "What did he do?"

"Oh, well," Carmody said, "McNamara was interested—he was toying with the idea of having the mobilization law extended, so that the Reservists could be kept for longer than a year. But he's forgotten about that now."

"Well, thank God for small favors," Mooney said. "Read some more of the letters, they do me a lot of good."

"All right," Carmody agreed. "Here's a kind of nice one: 'If the government lets this blank continue for much longer than when the elections come up in November there'll be a few changes made. . . . If there was something to do, if there were any reason for being here, that would be one thing. But when they make you get up at 5:30 and are let off at 6 in the evening and all you did all day was scrape paint, clean latrines, pick up cigarette butts, and listen to lectures on personal hygiene all day, then the days get pretty long and you have a lot of time to think, and too much time to complain.' . . . Another guy I asked about the call-up said, 'It makes me sick. You can quote me.' And, let's see," Carmody continued, "I spoke to a few high ranking officers. . . . There was one colonel who said— Where is that thing?"

"Coffee's ready," Wilkinson said. "You want some?"

"Sure," Carmody said.

"You, Mooney?"

"If Mr. Carmody of the fourth estate doesn't mind, I'll stick to his whisky."

"Not a bit," Carmody said. "Help yourself."

"Can I use your cup, Mooney?" Wilkinson said.

"Help yourself, as the good man said."

Mooney passed the bottle over to Wilkinson and said, "Put some in your coffee. Keeps the rattlesnakes away." He leaned across the table toward Carmody and confided, "This place is crawling with snakes."

"All colors." Wilkinson laughed. "Pink ones, blue ones . . ."

Mooney snickered. "If I could get drunk enough I'd be able to enjoy this desert like our noble leader, here. He told me he liked it out here. Our noble leader said—"

"That's enough, Mooney," P.S. warned.

" 'That's enough, Mooney,' " Mooney mimicked.

"I mean it, Mooney."

"Read me some more of those things, Mr. Carmody," Mooney said.

Carmody looked over at Wilkinson and Wilkinson shrugged.

"Well," Carmody continued, "the colonel said that—and I quote, ' I tell my men that morale is like a lot of little things, it's like my belt buckle here. The belt will hold my pants up whether the buckle is shiny or not. But it won't hold up my pride unless the buckle is shined.' "

"My God," P.S. said. "Did he really say that?"

"It's right here in black and white."

"Shit," Mooney said. "Shit, shit, shit." Mooney reached again for the bottle.

"Mooney," P.S. said, "don't you think you're being a little melodramatic?"

Mooney's hand stopped in mid-air, and then it continued toward the bottle. "Well, sir, yes, yes, I guess I am being a little melodramatic." Mooney tilted the bottle again and drank. Then he put the bottle down and pushed it across the table toward Carmody. "There," he said, "that's all I want. It's enough to keep me warm tonight and possibly enough for me to sleep until noon." He turned toward Wilkinson and said, "I'm going to leave the two of you alone in a minute, but let me say this to your friend . . . And I don't give a goddam whether he puts this in his newspaper or not."

"Freedom of speech is guaranteed by the Constitution," P.S. said.

"Good . . . good," Mooney said. "Question: 'What do you think of this call-up?' Answer: 'I think it's a crock of shit.' If we're here to keep the Germans from being attacked—to save Berlin—then, then I say screw Berlin and screw the Germans. Anything that happens to the Germans is no more than what they've got coming to them. I don't see why we have to keep helping the Germans. Keep coming to their rescue. . . . For God's sake, what have the Germans ever done for us—except start two world wars. I say we've given them their chances. How many chances do you give a person to kill you before you realize he's not going to change? Let the Russians worry about the Germans. What the hell? They deserve each other. Look . . . look, this whole call-up is ridiculous. It's a waste of time. It's a meaningless gesture involving the lives of 156,000 men—not to include their wives and children and other family. And what for? What does it prove? Did you ever seen a movie called *Pork Chop Hill*? It was a book, too. It was about this hill in Korea, which is a gesture. It's during the peace talks, and nobody wants it, and more and more men are killed . . . for what? It's a gesture. And the same thing is happening here. Only it's worse. I mean it's a gesture where we don't even have the satisfaction of hitting back, of killing someone. . . . Who would we hit back at? I mean, *somebody* somewhere should be responsible. Ultimately it's the President, since he's the one named on the orders: 'By direction of the President and pursuant to authority granted in Public Law 87-117 . . .' Don't think I can't quote you that whole thing! But not even the President is totally responsible. Congress? . . . Those horses' asses. The only thing they're worried about is whether this call-up is going to help them or hurt them. If they're lucky enough to be from Washington State, then they have 25,000 new men and all this Army pay being spent in their state for the next year. . . . But Congress would rather spend the money on pork-barrel deals than provide the military with the money to be strong enough so that a call-up wouldn't be necessary."

"I think you're forgetting the Russians," Carmody said. "Aren't they the ones who made this call-up necessary?"

"Well, of course, the Russians, too. And I'm willing to bet that the majority of those Russians who were kept in the service instead of being released are just as pissed off about being there as we are here. I'll tell you, if you let some of those Russians and some of us talk this problem over, you'll see a crisis disappear pretty goddam fast."

"But you were talking—asking who you should hit back at," Carmody insisted. "Aren't the Russians the ones you should want to hit back at? Not our Congress, not the President?"

"Why not? They are the leaders," Mooney said. "Why should I kill a Russian who had nothing to do with it. Hitting back at the Russians wouldn't do any good. What would do some good is to knock around a few of those people who make them think of us as Yankees and them as Commies. No, the only real question I have to ask is, who are we trying to kid? If, as we've been told, the Russians did not release the annual draft, and kept three million men on in the service, then what good do the 156,000 of us called back into the service do? Do you think our 156,000 scare the Russians? Hell, no. Nor do the three million they kept scare me. The only thing that does scare me is the men in the position to use all these troops might just be nutty enough to do it. And they'd be doing it using *me*. And who asked me whether I'd want to go to war over Germany?"

"The Army says it needs trained men," Carmody said.

"For what? Who are we releasing? Oh, come off it, you know as well as I do that there's no military justification for this call-up," Mooney said. "This whole thing stinks of politics. It's rigged. And I don't like it. You don't see any of our NATO allies rushing to call up troops, do you? Ah, no. They're too smart for that. Let Uncle Sugar take care of the problem."

"You sound like an editorial in the New York *Daily News*." Carmody laughed.

"This whole call-up is for the benefit of our allies. We're showing them that we mean business. That when we say we'll defend Berlin we mean it. We'll honor our commitments."

"Don't you think it demonstrates the same thing to the Communists?" Carmody asked.

"Hell, Khrushchev knows it. Don't think he doesn't know we'd fight over Berlin. He's trying to make the others believe we won't help them out, then Berlin will cease to exist and so will Germany."

"Which," Carmody said, "I gather is fine with you?"

"No, it isn't," Mooney protested, "for the simple reason that I'd rather have half of Germany on our side than all of it against us again. Let's face it, we've all helped to make Germany a powerful country again. The strongest in Western Europe. And who are they out for, anyway, but themselves? No one honestly believes that if war came to Germany that East and West Germany would fight each other."

"It happened in Korea," P.S. said. "And Vietnam."

"Well, they're different," Mooney said.

"It happened here in our country, too," P.S. said.

"Yeah, well . . . I just don't think it would happen between the Germans," Mooney said. "I think they're too shrewd for that. Anyway, I've said what I wanted to say. You two talk about whatever you want, I'm going to bed."

"Don't try to change the subject," Carmody said. "I want to hear more of what you've got to say about the Reservists."

"Nope. I'm through for the night. I've done my belly-aching." He started to slide toward the rear of the truck and then stopped. "Would you mind if I took just a little one for the road?"

Carmody slid the bottle toward him. "Not at all."

Mooney took one final drink, wiped his mouth with the back of his hand, and said, "If you write about me, tell them I've got an M.A. from Columbia."

"Do you?" Carmody asked.

"Of course I do. Why should I lie to you?"

"Why should I put down you've got an M.A.?"

"Because I've earned it. Just like I earned the right to be taken seriously." Mooney opened the canvas flap and worked his way out the tailgate of the truck. When he was outside he stuck his head back through the canvas and saluted. "Good night, Lieutenant Wilkinson, sir."

There was no malice in his tone, and P.S. saluted and said, "Good night."

After a few minutes and after Wilkinson had poured out the rest of the coffee, Carmody asked, "Was he drunk?"

"No, he was a little high maybe. Look, Johnny, he's a teacher, so don't use his name on anything. There's no doubt that he meant everything he said, but as a favor leave his name out, would you? It could hurt him otherwise."

"Sure," Carmody said. "And what are your feelings about all this?"

"You mean it's my turn?"

"That's what I'm here for."

"I thought you were a reporter, not Dear Abby."

"You aren't talking, in other words?"

"I couldn't tell you anything new, Johnny. Tell me what you've been doing. How long have you been with the paper?"

"I've been with this one for about a year now. I spent two years with a small paper in North Carolina, learning the trade, so to speak."

"You've had three years' experience?" P.S. asked.

"Give or take a few months."

P.S. whistled.

"What's the matter?" Carmody asked.

"Nothing."

"Well, then, why'd you whistle?"

"It's silly, really," P.S. said. "I just find it hard to believe that anyone our age has had three years' experience at anything. Me? I've got three years' experience of treading water."

"What does that mean?"

"Well, nothing. It's just that ever since graduation I've been getting things out of the way so that I could start. I haven't even started yet, for Christ's sake. I got my Army out of the way. Two years. And then after the Army I went to work at the bank and was in their training program when I got called back in. And now, from the looks of things, I've got another year to wait before I can start again. By the time our fifth reunion rolls around, if someone says, 'What are you doing?' the only thing I'll be able to say is, 'Getting ready to start.'"

"And that makes you mad?" Carmody asked.

P.S. smiled. "Ah, no, Johnny, now I said I wasn't going to take up your time talking about the Army. I want to hear what you've been doing. What have you heard from some of the others?"

"Don't try to put me off, Phil," Carmody insisted. "I'm interested in what you have to say. After all, I've been having to talk to all these people and it's a nice change talking to someone I do know. It gives me a chance to put things in a better perspective. Now come on, admit it, the call-up does make you mad."

"I think the word 'mad' might be an understatement," P.S. said. "Look, let me try to explain this to you. All of us in the unit—with the exception of one guy who was putting in Reserve time prior to his going into the six-month program—all of us served on duty for a minimum of two years. I'd say that in most cases we did it willingly. Even with pride. It was an obligation which we met. It was our turn and we did it. We feel that it may be somebody else's turn now, that's all."

"I've got a bad knee," Carmody said. He shrugged and smiled. "I wish it were otherwise . . ."

"Well, this call-up, it isn't all that bad for me. But for some of the others it was pretty rough. There's a captain in our unit who enlisted in the Second World War. He was in in 1941 and he got out in 1946. He started a small business and zip! in 1951 he got called back in for the Korean War. So he sold out his business, at a loss, and he went to Korea, where he got himself nicely chopped up by a grenade, but he lived and when the war ended he said, 'What the hell, I've got eight years in, I'm making a decent living, I might as well stay in.' So he does and what happens? He gets rif'd when the Army goes through its Reduction in Force. He gets the back of the hand. So, he goes back out into the cold world to make a buck and—I forgot to tell you, he's a linguist. Fluent Japanese, good Mandarin Chinese—anyway, comes the Quemoy-Matsu crisis, he's back in the Army. Re-called. And when that ends he's released again. This brings him up to 1958 or thereabouts. He has a good seventeen years in the service, or in Reserves, and has three more for his twenty years and a pension. But the Reserve unit he was in doesn't want him because he's a captain and he must be promoted to major and there's no opening. So he looks around for a unit with an open-ing, and he finds ours. He joins it, he has less than three months to go on his retirement and whoopee! we get called back into the Army and off he goes again. Now, what does he say when some-one asks him what he does for a living? Does he say he's a pro-fessional soldier? Hell, no, they wouldn't take him. Now that's a guy who really has had it rough. His whole life has been screwed up because of his age and because of the Army. There's someone you ought to talk to about the call-up. He's been called up before. He knows a military call-up when he sees one."

"Meaning what?" Carmody asked.

"Meaning this is no military call-up. This is political; and the reason why all the Reservists are griping is because they're smart enough to know it. And maybe they think it's pretty contemptible of the President to think that they'd be too dumb to see what was happening, that they'd go like lambs to the slaughter. You saw what some of your boys said, you spoke to them."

"Well, let me see. I was also speaking to one of the General Staff officers about whether or not it was necessary and I can give you the answer he gave me. He said, 'The President saw a need for a partial mobilization and he should know. . . .' "

"Well, I hope he does. I mean, we can only hope to God that there was a better reason for this call-up than there appears to be on the surface. Let me make this absolutely clear: in case of war, in the case of a very real national emergency, not one of us would complain about being called back or would wish to shirk his duty. But what we have here is no national emergency, no war, only a slight variation on the same Berlin crisis that has existed ever since 1945. I think all of us are so used to accept-ing this shit the government hands out to us that everybody accepts the government as knowing best. Well, I don't think they do know best. At least I think we have the right to be told what's going on. But so far no one has taken the time to tell us why we should be carrying the load twice while so many others have never had to serve at all."

"Does my never having been in the Army really bother you that much?"

"You, Johnny? . . . No, not you. No, the ones that bother me are all the smug little bastards who found loopholes or graduate schools or some sort of tricks so that they wouldn't have to serve, and who laugh at those of us who did. I don't doubt for a minute that if you really wanted to serve, then you could have. There are ways . . . waivers, things like that."

"Well, I never really wanted to be in the Army that much. I'm afraid I'm not the military type."

"*Do you think I am?*" P.S. asked in astonishment.

"Well, I think there's more of the martinet in you than there is in me." Carmody finished his coffee and poured some whisky into his cup.

"Well . . . I'm not going to argue with you about that," P.S. said. "It's a senseless argument."

"Senseless like this call-up?" Carmody prodded.

"We don't know . . . no one tells us. Listen, Johnny, while Mooney was talking to you I was doing some thinking."

"Hold it, Phil."

"What?"

Carmody was leaning sideways in his chair.

"Something wrong?" P.S. asked.

"I want to change the reel."

"*Change the reel?* Have you got a tape recorder?"

Carmody brought up his briefcase and placed it on top of the table. "Half of this thing holds a recorder. One hour on one side. One hour on the other. We've used up an hour's worth of tape."

"When did you have it on? When did you start?" P.S. asked.

"When we first came back here," Carmody said.

"In other words, you got all of Mooney?"

Carmody nodded.

"But are you going to use that? I don't think you ought to use his name. I don't think he intended that. He just wanted you to hear what he had to say."

"He said, 'Put down that I've got an M.A. from Columbia,' didn't he?"

"Well, sure, Johnny, but you don't have to name him or name his graduate school. At least clear it with him."

"What about you?"

"I told you. This is between you and me. The only thing I'm trying to do is tell you what I think the problem is. What I think the others feel."

"Not you?" Carmody asked, smiling. "You don't feel that way?"

"Of course, I feel the same way. But I'm an officer, Johnny, and I'm not supposed to talk. But since I'm also a Reservist, I want you to understand what the problem is."

"Well, go ahead then. It's ready to roll. We can talk about whether we use the stuff later. The important thing is just to get it down."

"Still, I don't want names used. Okay?"

"Have it your way, Phil. Now what do you think is the problem?"

"Well, for instance, we want to know how long are we in for? The orders say 'for a period of twelve consecutive months unless sooner relieved.' You said McNamara wanted to extend that but changed his mind—"

"The Pentagon says that the Reservists will be released as soon as the situation permits."

"What situation?" P.S. asked. "As soon as there are replacements?"

"They also have cut the draft back from 25,000 a month to 16,000."

"When did they do *that*?"

"Recently," Carmody said. "A couple weeks ago."

"Jesus H. Christ!" P.S. said. "That took real brains. Where do they expect to get the replacements from?"

"You're asking me?" Carmody laughed. "I only work here."

"Well, that solves that question. How long are we in for? I hope to God it's not more than a year, but doesn't look like much less than that. At any rate, we would appreciate being told as soon as possible."

"I promise you, P.S., *first* thing!"

"Next question: What is our job supposed to be? Mooney and I were sent out here for three weeks to observe the division's use of aerial reconnaissance, both photo and visual. Well, they dropped and smashed their only camera the first week, so there's been no photo reconnaissance of any kind since then. But, we can't go back to the post because it looks good on our unit's record to have two men in the desert. And what about the units back at the post? A friend of mine in the unit says that all they've been doing since they got back are details and house cleaning. If there's a job for us to do, then I say let us do it. I'd even go back to Korea to work there. And the others would do it, too. Well, by God, send us where they need us. But don't have us just sitting around on our asses doing nothing."

"Some of the ones I've spoken to say the morale is pretty good. The AWOL rate is very, very low."

"The AWOL rate is an indication of the morale of recruits, Johnny. It might be a good way to tell with young kids, but these guys have been in the Army before. They may be bitter, but they're not idiots. They know going AWOL can really screw them good."

"Well, what else?"

"Ahh, yes," P.S. said. "Is this trip necessary? That's the really galling one. That's the 'Sixty-four-dollar Question.' . . . If we are being used to provide the strength behind a meaningless gesture, then, by God, look out. It'll be the Veterans' Riots all over again. No one likes being used, Johnny; and particularly being used for no reason. We've all wasted enough time by ourselves without having someone, some *deus ex machina*, waste it for us. Look at Mooney. He's a teacher. Do you honestly think that he is serving his country better by spending three weeks in the desert than he might be by spending three weeks in his classroom? Why didn't Mooney get a deferment? How come sitting in the desert is more important than teaching?"

"Well, he won't be in the desert forever."

"Of course he won't! But do you think anything that we will do out here, that Mooney will do during this period back in the Army, will be important—as important as teaching?"

"Who knows?" Carmody asked. "Maybe he's being prepared for a greater trust, a more important job."

"Ah, well, then, Johnny, if that's true, then fine. But . . . but if, as we all suspect, we're to spend our time out here doing nothing more important than picking up cigarette butts and scratching ourselves, then, by God, this country is—the government is guilty of a terrible waste. And that infuriates me, Johnny. All this crap about 'Ask not what your country can do for you,' as though our government were some sort of supreme omniscient being. I don't like them crapping around with my life when if they only did their jobs this sort of call-up wouldn't be necessary."

"Well . . . well, I don't think it's quite as simple as you put it."

"Oh, shit on that, Johnny," Wilkinson said. "Or to put it in the more articulate Mooney's words: 'Shit, shit, shit.' "

Carmody smiled. "Well, P.S., I guess I've heard enough. I've got to get out of here."

"I'd ask you to spend the night, but . . ."

"Don't bother." Carmody laughed. "I've got a hot bath and a warm bed in a motel waiting for me at Yakima." Carmody closed up his briefcase. "I had a lot of trouble finding you."

"How'd you know we were here? Someone up at Headquarters say there were two Reservists down at the airstrip?"

"Hell, no, I knew you were in the desert when I got to Fort Lewis."

"*How'd you know that?*" P.S. asked.

"A Colonel Sturgess told me. He said for me to be sure to talk to you."

25

WILKINSON AND MOONEY entered Fort Lewis at 1720 hours, Tuesday evening, the 21st of November, and ten minutes later, at 5:30 exactly, they pulled into the 319th MI Detachment's area. It was dark and there was a heavy fog, so Mooney parked as close to their section's building as possible, so that they could unload with the help of the barracks lights. Mooney backed up so that the tailgate was near the front door, stopped the three-quarter-ton truck and turned off the engine.

"Hot showers and a real bed," Mooney said.

"And latrine duty and policing up the grounds details," Wilkinson said.

"I'll never complain again," Mooney said. He opened his door and stepped out. Wilkinson gathered up the loose papers in the front seat, then got out also.

"Mooney, I'm going to check in with the major and I'll be right back. I just want him to know we're here." Wilkinson could see the major sitting at his desk, the top of his shoulders and the back of his head visible through the window. P.S. walked around to the back entrance, the entrance closest to the major's office, and paused at the door. He knocked twice and entered. "Well, sir, your desert rats have returned."

The major's head snapped up, and he looked at Wilkinson

398

standing loosely in front of him, and the major slammed his hand down on his desktop and said, "Stand at attention, Wilkinson. Have you forgotten how to enter a superior officer's office? Have you forgotten how to salute? How to announce yourself?"

Wilkinson came to attention, amazed and stunned by the major's anger. Wilkinson saluted, holding his salute and saying, "Lieutenant Wilkinson reporting in, sir."

When the major returned the salute, Wilkinson snapped his hand down to his side and remained rigidly at attention. *What the hell is going on here?* P.S. wondered.

The major remained fixedly staring at Wilkinson and P.S. tried to think if everything was proper on his uniform. He couldn't risk a glance down at himself. *We came back at the right time. He said come back at the end of the problem. The problem ended this morning. . . . Was it because of the letters I wrote him, requesting that we be returned? . . . My God, I bet that's it. He thinks I was trying to tell him how to run things.*

"Wilkinson, just who do you think gave you the right to shoot off your mouth?"

"Sir?" P.S. asked, puzzled.

"To that goddam reporter. Who told you to speak for the unit? Who told you to speak for all the Reservists and say that we think the President is contemptible?"

Wilkinson felt a hot flush creep up his neck, and through his cheeks. "Sir. I—"

"Shut up, Lieutenant! I'm not through speaking to you yet. You're at attention!"

"Yes, sir," Wilkinson said. He could see a newspaper clipping on the major's desk. He could read the upside down headline, BERLIN CRISIS ARMY: AN ANGRY ARMY, and beneath it the tag: "By John Carmody."

"Let me read you something," the major said. "This is a quote directly from the clipping I have here in my hand. Quote: 'While Lieutenant Wilkinson nodded in agreement, Mooney stated that the recent mobilization of 156,000 men was' . . . and this was Mooney's quote: 'Ridiculous . . . a waste of time . . . a meaningless gesture involving 156,000 men.' End of quote. Of Mooney's quote. And now the clipping again. 'Mooney stated that he saw no military justification for the call-up of the Army Reserves and that the mobilization,' quote, 'stinks of politics. It's rigged,' end of quote, end of that portion of the clipping." The major put the clipping back down on his desk and looked up again at Wilkinson. "Did you hear Mooney say that? Did you *nod in agreement* while Mooney said that? Do you mean to tell me that you are so stupid . . . so imbecilic . . . so—so moronic that you, an officer in the United States Army, would sit numbly—*dumbly* by, nodding in agreement, while one of your men told a reporter *that*?"

"Sir, I—"

"SHUT YOUR GODDAM MOUTH, WILKINSON!" The major was shaking with rage. "I—don't—ever . . . EVER . . . want to hear you say another WORD again. Is that clear?"

Wilkinson, braced at attention, said nothing.

"I am going to give you this clipping," the major said in measured syllables, "and I want you to take it back to your BOQ room and I don't want you to speak to another member of this unit until I tell you you can. You are to consider yourself confined to your quarters. You may go for meals, but that is *all* you may do. Is that clear?"

Looking over the major's head, through the window, Wilkinson could see Mooney looking at him curiously. *Of course! . . . He can see me. . . . He knows I'm getting my ass chewed, but he doesn't know why.*

The major handed the clipping across the desk to Wilkinson. P.S. took it, without looking at it. "Sir, my truck is still loaded. May I have permission to unload the equipment before I confine myself to my BOQ room?"

"Of course, Wilkinson."

"Thank you, sir," P.S. said. He saluted, held it until the major returned it, then took three steps backward, did an about-face,

and marched out of the office. He hurried across to the truck
and walked around it to the side hidden from the major's view.
"Let's get this truck unloaded, Mooney," he said. "The shit
has hit the fan."

"What's going on? I saw you in—"

"Apparently Carmody wrote us up, and what we said doesn't
look too good in print. I've got the clipping here, but let's get
some stuff into the building first."

P.S. helped Mooney unload the truck, and then signed in to
the orderly room and picked up his mail. There was a special
delivery letter from his father, one from the bank, one from
Charlie Merritt, and nine postmarked New York. He weighed
the letters in his hand together with the clipping and then
walked out into the darkness, past the warmly lighted Officers'
Club, between the red-brick General Officers Quarters, and cut
across the parade field toward his BOQ. Lights still burned in
the twin four-story tall headquarters buildings and a thickening
mist lent the street lights at the far end of the parade field
thick furry collars.

P.S. entered his BOQ and walked down the hallway to his
room. He unlocked the door, turned on the light, and closed the
door behind him. He was tired, filthy with three weeks of the
desert caked on him. He ran through the mail; there seemed
to be a lot—certainly a lot more than he had received before.
P.S. decided he would take a shower first, and then read the
letters. The clipping, however, he would read again. He and
Mooney had read it together while they unloaded. It was unbelievable. P.S. couldn't imagine doing to Carmody what Carmody had done to him. He couldn't understand why Carmody
had done it. They had not been close friends at Yale, that was
true; but certainly P.S. had never acted in a way toward Carmody
to have made him an enemy. P.S. unlaced his boots halfway
down the ankle, then pried them off and slid them across to
the wall. He had one stray thought—that the boots would be
a problem to clean. He shrugged and unfolded the clipping,
smoothing it against the olive-drab blanket on his bed, and he
read it again:

Some Bitter, Majority Resigned

BERLIN CRISIS ARMY: AN ANGRY ARMY

By John Carmody

FORT LEWIS, WASH.—I spent last night in the Yakima Desert with two very angry young men from New York City who, along with their fellow members in the 319th Military Intelligence Detachment, were recalled to active duty in the United States Army and were sent across this vast country to Fort Lewis, Washington, to serve what may amount to be an additional twelve months in this country's Armed Forces.

I spoke first with 35-year-old Laurence Mooney, a former Brooklyn Heights high school teacher, while his 26-year-old commanding officer, 1st Lt. Philip Sadler Wilkinson of Manhattan, looked on.

Distrusts the Germans

Mooney, a Specialist Fifth Class, distrusts the Germans and told me he would be unwilling to go to war to help them. "Anything that happens to them, they've got coming," Mooney told me. "Let the Russians worry about the Germans, they deserve each other."

Reserve Call-Up Ridiculous

While Lt. Wilkinson nodded in agreement, Mooney stated that the recent mobilization of Army Reservists and National Guardsmen was, "Ridiculous . . . a waste of time . . . a meaningless gesture involving 156,000 men." Mooney stated that he saw no military justification for the call-up of Army Reserves and that the mobilization "Stinks of politics . . . It's rigged."

Blames Congress for Woes

Ignoring the fact that the behavior of the Soviet Union in retaining on duty a combat force of 3,000,000 men necessitated a strengthening of our own Armed Forces, Mooney, the possessor of a Master's Degree from Columbia University, launched into an abusive tirade against the President of the United States and members of Congress, whom Mooney holds responsible for the mobilization. Lt. Wilkinson, obviously impressed by Mooney's intellect, offered no rebuttal when Mooney insinuated that Congress had been derelict in its duties in that, "Congress would rather spend money on pork barrel deals than provide the (Army) funds to be strong enough so that a call-up would be unnecessary."

Holds President in Contempt

When it became Wilkinson's turn to speak, the young officer who received his commission and degree from Yale reiterated what Mooney had said, emphasizing, "This is no military call-up. It is political. The reason why all the Reservists are griping is because they are smart enough to know it, and maybe it's pretty contemptible of the President to think we'd be too dumb to see what was happening."

Warns of Possible Riots

Wilkinson next warned against the possibility of riots: "If we are being used to provide the strength behind a meaningless gesture, then look out! It'll be the Veterans' Riots all over again."

Most Reservists See Need

Fortunately not all the twenty-five thousand Army Reservists feel (*See* RESERVISTS—Page 19)

The remainder of the clipping told how the majority of the Reservists at Fort Lewis saw the need for the call-up and that they recognized there was a job to do, and they were trying their best to do it. P.S. refolded the clipping and put it on the desk by his bed. The damage was done. It did not matter whether or not P.S. had agreed with what Mooney had said, his mistake had been in not shutting Mooney up. Of course, the most obvious mistake was his talking to Carmody in the first place. *But, my God, how was I to know?* P.S. thought. *How was I to know that he'd write it up that way? I never told him to write us up. I told him no names, I said I didn't want my name—oh, shit, why not? If I said it, then I should have the guts to admit it. . . .* P.S. began to undress for his shower. *I'll read the rest when I get back. . . . My God, I can imagine what Dad has to say . . . well, I deserve it, I guess . . . but, God damn it, all! God damn it, the call-up is senseless! It is a waste of time! So what's wrong with saying so? I didn't attack the President . . . I said that—what does it matter what I said? I've hung myself as usual. . . . My God, it'll be nice to get some of this dirt off. . . . What time is it? . . . Quarter to seven . . . Something to eat . . . Oh, hell, I'd have to go to the club, someone would want to say something . . . I'm not that hungry.* P.S. wrapped a towel around his waist. He was looking for his soap when there was a knock on his door. "Yes?" he said.

"Lieutenant Wilkinson, there's a phone call for you."

"Where's the phone?"

"End of the hall," the voice said.

"Right, thanks a lot, I'll be right there." P.S. put on his bathrobe and slippers and walked out of his room down the hall to the telephone. *Maybe it's Dad . . . Maybe it's the General . . .*

Maybe it's my ass! He smiled sourly to himself, as he picked up the phone. "Hello?"

"P.S.? This is Gene. Gene Price."

"Hi, Gene, how are you?"

"Fine. Listen, P.S., I know all about this—what's going on. Look, I just wanted to say that we're all behind you. All the guys in the unit think you were right. We're all behind you."

"Including the major?" P.S. asked, laughing.

"Well, he's got to play it by the book," Gene said. "I think he might agree a little with what you've said."

"But he has to be against it for the record."

"Sure, well, you can understand that."

P.S. said, "Oh, well, the hell with it. Thanks, though. . . . How's the wife?"

"She's fine. She wants you to dinner, but I told her you were confined to quarters. Little Cameron wanted to know whether you were confined because of measles."

"Tell . . . tell him it's contagious. I've got a contagious disease," P.S. said. "Well, listen, I'm standing in this cold hall in my bathrobe. I guess I'll see you tomorrow at the unit."

"Looking forward to it, old buddy."

"Same here, g'by," P.S. said. He hung up the phone and walked back down the length of the hallway to the shower.

After his shower P.S. dried himself and walked back up the hallway to his BOQ room. He dressed in an old pair of gray flannel trousers, a soft striped button-down shirt, a paisley tie, gray wool socks, loafers, and lastly his worn-out tweed jacket with the elbow patches. He opened first the letter from his father:

Dear Philip:

Your mother and I tried to bring you up properly. I had hoped that we had instilled in you a sense of values and a sense of respect for your country. Perhaps I should feel pleased that you have enough self-confidence in your opinions to speak out assured that what you have to say others eagerly await to hear. But, my God, son, a twenty-six-year-old boy should not, does not, and cannot presume to know so much that he can attack the President of the United States. Also, I don't need to remind you that as an officer in the United States Army you have an obligation to all the other men who have ever served or

will ever serve as officers in this country's military! And you do not
fulfill your obligation by permitting a man under your command to
cast aspersions upon the honor and the character of this country's
duly elected leaders.

I do not need to tell you that I have received a large amount of
letters from shocked friends, my friends, the men with whom I served
in the Second World War while you were just a baby. These men
willingly risked their lives for their country and many of them pointed
out in their letters that they did not risk their lives so that someone
(some "punk," as one put it) like you could cast aspersions upon our
government. I have tried as best I can to answer their letters. It was
a most unpleasant task and I beg of you do not put me into a position
where I may have to apologize for you again.

Sincerely,
Stewart Wilkinson

P.S. sat for a moment holding the letter in his hand. He shook
his head slowly back and forth. He knew that his father would
be upset, he knew that he might be angry, but not to understand, but not to have any inkling of what the circumstances
might have been, amazed him. P.S. was astonished that his
father would have written him that letter, felt it necessary
to write such a letter.

P.S. next opened the letter from Charlie Merritt. There was
just a short handwritten note on company stationery saying,
"You realize what the Army did to General MacArthur, don't
you? Well, fade away, fade away . . ."

The letter from the bank was from Mr. Murdoch:

Lt. Philip S. Wilkinson
319th Military Intelligence Detachment
Fort Lewis,
Washington
Dear Lt. Wilkinson:

As you are aware, we are required by law to hold your job open
for you until your return. However, in the light of your public avowal
of dissatisfaction with the government, and the irresponsible attack
you made upon our President, we feel we must suggest that you might
be happier should you find employment at another place upon the
termination of your military service.

Sincerely,
/s/Charles H. Murdoch
CHARLES H. MURDOCH
Vice-President

CHM/dd

P.S. crumpled the letter up and tossed it into the wastepaper basket. Then he thought for a moment, retrieved the letter, and put it with the others. He next turned to the letter from his brother, Carter. It said: "Give them hell. Buckle Down, Winsockie. Damn the torpedoes, full speed ahead! What fear we broadsides? Nay, let the fiend give fire. Tippecanoe and Tyler, Too! Up the Ruling Classes!"

Of the nine remaining letters, all of them were from strangers: two were obscene, four called him a Communist, one called him a homosexual, one from a little old lady said, "I am seventy-three years old and my two sons were killed in the Navy. I wish you had been killed, too," and the last one said simply, "I've always heard that if one spends enough time in the desert one loses one's head."

It was all so unreal. It didn't matter what P.S. had said to Carmody, no one had bothered to read the article closely. P.S. sat on the edge of the bed and rubbed his temples, then he took off his glasses and let his cool fingertips rest against his hot eyelids. He held his fingers to his eyelids until his fingers were warm and then he dropped his hands, opened his eyes, and since he did not have his glasses on, he did not bother to look at anything. He stared downcast at the rug. He was ashamed of himself. And, worse, he was ashamed of being ashamed of himself. What he had said, what he had done was no different, he knew, from what most of the others would have done. Gene Price had said that everyone in the unit had agreed with him. But even that was small consolation, because the newspaper clipping was a gross distortion of what he had actually said. He knew that Carmody had made it a better story, and he thought the reason why Carmody had done this to him was for the sake of a better story. He did not feel so angry at Carmody as he did at himself for not realizing that Carmody would do this, that Carmody made his living doing this. Nevertheless, P.S. was ashamed, terribly ashamed of himself, and he wished to God that he had never talked to the reporter. He knew that what he had done was wrong. As an Army officer he did have, as his father pointed out, certain responsibilities. As an Army officer he should not have permitted Mooney to speak the way he had; and he certainly should never have spoken the way he, himself, had. Instead of accomplishing any real beneficial thing, he had succeeded in embarrassing his father, infuriating his commanding officer, and humiliating himself. And for what? *Have I humiliated myself? . . . Have I? Why do I feel ashamed? . . . Because they—everyone treats me like a child . . . like I was some goddam kid back in school.* And suddenly P.S. Wilkinson knew that he had again encountered the Honor Code.

The Virginia Preparatory School lies just off the Shirley Highway between Washington, D.C., and Richmond. It is a small Southern school with dull red-brick dormitories and classroom buildings, quiet old school buildings, with quiet old Southern names—Page House, Stuart Hall, Randolph Hall, Breckenridge, Pinckney, and Coulter. The high brick wall that surrounds the school is known as the Breastworks, and the shallow pond behind the football field is the Crater. V.P.S. is an old school, with an old school's tradition. A Virginia Department of Conservation sign commemorates the use of the school by Union troops as a military hospital in 1861, and every October the school celebrates "Liberation Day" in honor of the day in 1866 when the school reopened.

Graduates of the Virginia Preparatory School who have not returned for some years are shocked by the glass-and-steel apartment houses and cinder-block ramblers that have sprung up around the school grounds, but once they have driven along the Breastworks and passed through the ornate wrought-iron East Gate, they see, with satisfaction, that the school has not changed. Neither have its customs. For example, new boys, or "toads," still must obey the Toad Code. They must be courteous to old boys and faculty. They must know the school song and cheers by the end of the second week. They must know the names of all members of the faculty and the varsity football team. They must hold doors open for old boys, and see that old boys are served first in the dining room. And they must "run relay"—meaning that they have to wake up the old boys in the morning when they wish to be wakened and see that they are not disturbed when they wish to sleep.

In 1951 Philip Sadler Wilkinson was fifteen. He was an old boy. The new boy shook him lightly. "Mr. Wilkinson? Mr. Wilkinson? It's five-thirty, sir. You asked me to wake you up."

Next year the new boy would be permitted to call Wilkinson "P.S." like the others. He watched P.S. stretch, turn over, and go back to sleep. "Sir? Hey! Wake up!"

P.S. rolled out of his metal cot, rubbed his eyes, felt around the desk behind the bed for his glasses, put them on, and looked at the new boy.

"Toad?"

"Yes, sir?"

"What is the date?"

"Thursday, the seventh of June."

"How much longer do we have until the end of the school year?"

"Seven days, twenty-three hours, and"—the new boy looked at his wristwatch—"and thirteen minutes, sir."

P.S. smiled. "Are you sure?"

"No, sir."

"Ah-hah! Ah-HAH! Toad, assume the position!"

The new boy locked his knees and grabbed his ankles.

"What is a toad, toad?" P.S. asked.

"Sir, a toad is a loathsome warty creature who eats insects and worms, sir. A toad is the lowest form of amphibian. A toad is despicable."

"Well, well, now, straighten those knees, toad." P.S. looked at the new boy and saw that his face was turning red with strain. "Toad, are you in pain?"

"No, sir," the new boy lied.

"Then you may straighten up."

The new boy massaged his calves. "Honest to God, P.S. you're a sadist."

"No, no, wait till next year. You'll be pulling the same thing on some toad yourself. I had it done to me, you had it done to

you. And did I detect you calling me by my rightful name?"

The new boy smiled.

"Ah, God, you toads will never learn. Assume the position."

The new boy started to bend over again.

"Oh, hell, go away," P.S. said. The new boy started out the door and P.S. called him back. "Hey, toad? You gonna kill the Latin exam?"

"I hope so."

"How do you conjugate the verb 'to spit'?"

"*Exspuo, exspuere, exspui—*"

"Good God, no!" P.S. laughed. "It's *spitto, spittere, ach tui, splattus!*"

The new boy groaned and left the room.

P.S. looked at his watch. It was twenty minutes to six. He could hear the new boy waking up the boy in the next room. P.S. picked up his water glass and toothbrush and tiptoed down the corridor. He stopped at Charlie Merritt's room and knocked softly.

"Who is it?"

"It's me, Charlie."

"Oh, hey, P.S. Come on in."

P.S. pushed aside the curtain of the cubicle. Charlie was sitting at his desk studying.

"Morning," P.S. whispered.

"Morning."

"Studying the Latin?"

"Yep."

"You know how to conjugate the verb 'to spit'?"

"Yep," Charlie said. "*Spitto, spittere, ach—*"

"Okay, okay!" P.S. laughed.

"You gonna kill the exam?"

"I hope so. You think you'll pass it?"

"Doubt it. I haven't passed one yet." P.S. looked over at Charlie's bureau. "Say, Charlie? Can I borrow your toothpaste? I'm out."

"Sure, but roll it from the bottom of the tube, will you?"

P.S. picked up the toothpaste and went down the hall to the

bathroom. Mabrey, the head monitor, was shaving. P.S. watched him in the mirror.

"You must have had a porcupine for a father," P.S. said. "You've got the heaviest beard in school."

Mabrey began to shave the length of his neck.

"How come you got such a heavy beard?" P.S. asked. "We all know you like little boys."

"Wilkinson, you're about as funny as a rubber crutch."

"Cut your throat! Cut your throat!" P.S. began to dance around behind Mabrey, sprinkling imaginary voodoo potions on the top of the older student's head. "Monkey dust! Monkey dust! Oh, black Pizzoola! Great Kubla of the Ancient Curse! Make this bad man cut his throat!"

Mabrey cursed and a small red stain began to seep through the lather on his throat. "P.S., will you *get out of here!*"

P.S. stared, eyes wide open at the broadening stain. "My God! My God! It worked!"

Mabrey undid the towel from around his waist and snapped P.S.'s skinny behind. P.S. yelped and jumped away. "Hey, Mr. Mabrey, sir? Hey, Mabrey? I'm sorry, I really am. I didn't know it would work."

"What would work?"

"My voodoo curse. I didn't know it would make you cut yourself."

"For God's sake, P.S., what're you talking about? I cut a pimple. Will you leave me alone before I throw you out of a closed window?"

P.S. was quiet for a moment. Then he moved over to the washbasin next to Mabrey and looked at himself in the mirror. He ran his fingers through his light-brown hair and pushed his glasses higher on his nose. "Hey, Mabrey? Do you think I'm fresh? I mean, I have great respect for you—you being the head monitor and all. I mean it. Sometimes I worry. I mean, do you think I'm too fresh?"

Mabrey finished rinsing his face. "You're a nice guy. And I'm willing to bet that if you could only learn to throw a baseball from center field to second base overhand, you might turn out to be a pretty fair little baseball player."

"*Overhand!* Whaddya mean 'overhand'? They call me 'Dead-eye Wilkinson.'" P.S. wound up with an imaginary baseball and threw it as hard as he could. Then he pantomimed being the second baseman. He crouched and caught the incoming baseball at his knees and thrust his hand down to tag out the runner. "SAFE!" he shouted. "I mean, out! *Out!* OUT!"

"Too bad," Mabrey said, and laughed. "An umpire never changes his decision."

"I meant *out*," P.S. said.

Mabrey disappeared down the hall.

P.S. brushed his teeth, being careful to squeeze the toothpaste from the bottom of the tube. He looked at himself in the mirror and chanted,"*Fuero, fueris, fuerit, fuerimus, feuritis, fuerint!*" He examined his upper lip and was disappointed. He wished that he didn't have such a young face. He wished he had a heavy beard, like Mabrey. He washed his face, wet his hair down, and walked back into Charlie's room. Charlie was P.S.'s best friend. He was very short. The other boys kidded him about being an engineer for Lionel trains. P.S. was very tall and thin, and he had not yet grown into his full height.

At fifteen he was already six feet tall, and he had a tendency to stoop to compensate. He and Charlie were known as Mutt and Jeff. When P.S. entered the room Charlie was curled up on the bed studying his Latin notes. He didn't look up and P.S. dropped the toothpaste tube on his pillow. "Rolled from the bottom," P.S. said.

"Hey, how do you expect to pass your Latin exam if you don't study? I heard you and Mabrey clowning around in the can."

"If I don't study!" P.S. said. "Do you know how long I've studied for this exam? Two years! If I flunk it again this year, I get to keep the trophy."

"What trophy?"

"For God's sake, I don't know what trophy. But I'll get something for sure. I've spent the last two weeks practically doing nothing but studying Latin. I recopied all my notes. I underlined practically the whole book. And I memorized all the irregular verbs. Come on, come on, ask me anything. God, if I don't pass it this year I've had it. Come on, ask me anything."

"Okay. What's the word for 'ridge'?"

"The word for 'ridge'?" P.S. stalled.

"Yep."

P.S. thought for a moment. "Look, I don't know. Make it two out of three."

"The word for 'ridge' is *iugum*." Charlie looked at his notes. "Okay, two out of three. What's the word for 'crowd'? And 'troop' as in 'a troop of cavalry'?"

"The word for crowd is *turba, turbae*. . . . What was the other one?"

" 'Troop of cavalry.' "

" 'Cavalry' is *equitatus* . . . I don't know. What is 'troop'?"

" 'Troop' is *turma*." Charlie laughed. "Well, you got one out of three."

"Did I get partial credit for the 'cavalry'?"

"Nope."

"Jesus, I hope Dr. Fairfax is more lenient than you are."

"He won't be," Charlie said.

"If I flunk the Latin exam again this year . . ."

"How come you flunked it last year?"

"How come anybody flunks an exam? I didn't know the answers. Boy, Charlie, I don't know what I'm going to do with you. If you weren't such a nice guy and lend me your toothpaste and things like that all the time, I'd probably feed you to the —to the what's-their-name fish. Those fish who eat people in South America all the time."

"Well, since you don't know what to do with me, as a start, why don't you let me study?"

"Sure. Sure. Okay, okay, be a grind. See if I care."

P.S. walked back to his cubicle and pulled his Ullman and Henry *Latin II* from his unpainted bookcase. First he studied the irregular verbs at the back of the book. Then he went over his vocabulary list. He concentrated for as long as he could; then he leaned out his window to look at the shadows of the trees directly below, dropped a penny out the window to see if a squirrel would pick it up, checked his window sill to see if the cookie crumbs he had left for the mockingbird were still there. He turned back to his Latin book and leafed through the Forestier illustrations of Roman soldiers.

P.S. was the fifteenth of his family to attend the Virginia Preparatory School. Among the buildings at V.P.S. there was a Wilkinson Memorial Library and a Sadler Gymnasium. When P.S. was packing to begin his first year at the school, his father had said, "Son, when your great-grandfather went off to V.P.S., his father gave him a dozen silk handkerchiefs and a pair of warm gloves. When I went off to V.P.S., your grandfather gave me a dozen silk handkerchiefs and a pair of warm gloves. And now here are a dozen silk handkerchiefs and a pair of warm gloves for you."

P.S. looked at the brightly patterned Liberty-silk handkerchiefs and the fuzzy red mittens. No thirteen-year-old ever wore red mittens, except girls. And particularly not fuzzy red mittens. And P.S. knew he would never dare to wear the silk handkerchiefs.

"Well, thank you very much, Dad," he had said.

"That's all right, Son."

P.S. left the red mittens behind when he went away to V.P.S. He used two of the silk handkerchiefs to cover the top of his bureau and his bookcase, gave one other away to a girl, and hid the rest beneath his underwear on the second shelf of his bureau. His father had done very well at the school; he had been a senior monitor, editor in chief of the yearbook, and a distance runner in winter and spring track. His father remembered all the school cheers and was shocked when P.S. didn't remember some of the words to the school song. At half time at football games his father would disappear to talk to his friends and P.S. would wander back to the field house, where the alumni tables were set up. He would locate his father and stand next to him until his father introduced him to the persons he was talking to. Then his father would say, "Run along, Son, I'll meet you back in your room." So P.S. would go back to his room and wait for his father to come by. The boy would straighten up the bed, dust the bureau, sweep the floor. And then, after a long wait, his father would come in and sit down. "Well, how are you, Son?" the conversation would always start. And P.S. would answer, "Fine, thank you, sir." His father would look around the room and remark about its not being large enough to swing a cat in, then there would be two or three anecdotes about the times when he was a boy at V.P.S., and then he would look at his watch and say, "Well, I guess I'd better be pushing off." His father would ask him if there was anything he needed, and P.S. would say that he didn't think there was anything. His father would give him a five-dollar bill, and drive away. And P.S., with enormous relief, would go look for Charlie. "Did you and your dad have a good time?" Charlie would ask. "Sure," P.S. would say. And that would be the end of the conversation.

P.S. hoped he would do as well as his father had done, but he knew he had disappointed him so far. When he flunked the Latin examination last year and tried to explain to his father that he just could not do Latin, he could see the disbelief in his father's eyes. "My God, Son, you just didn't study. 'Can't do Latin,' what nonsense!" But P.S. knew that studying had had nothing to do with it. His father said that no Wilkinson had ever flunked anything at V.P.S.; he was the first.

P.S. picked up his Latin notes and went over the translations he had completed. He wished he knew what questions would be asked. In last year's exam there were questions from all over the book, and it made the exam very difficult to study for. He pictured himself handing in the finished examination to Dr. Fairfax and saying, "Sir? Wilkinsons do not flunk. Please grade my exam accordingly."

P.S. looked at his wristwatch. The dining room would begin serving breakfast in fifteen minutes. He made his bed and put on a clean pair of khakis and a button-down shirt. He slipped into his old white bucks and broke a lace tying them, and pulled out the shorter piece and threaded what was left through the next eyelet up, as the older boys did. He tided up his room for inspection, picked up his notes, and went back to Charlie's room.

Charlie was sweeping the dust into the hall. The new boy on

duty that day would be responsible for sweeping the halls and emptying all the trash baskets. P.S. entered and sat down on the bed.

"Jesus Christ, P.S.! I just made the bed!"

"Okay, okay, I'll straighten it up when I leave." P.S. ran his fingers across the desktop. "Merritt, two demerits — dust. . . . Hey, you know what, Charlie?"

Charlie dusted the desk and then said, "What?"

"You're such a grump in the morning. I sure'd hate to be married to you."

"Well, I wouldn't worry about that. In the first place, my parents wouldn't approve."

"I'm not so sure my family would want me to marry a Merritt either. I think you'd have to take my family name. I mean, you're just not our class, you know what I mean?"

"P.S., buddy, you're in a class all by yourself."

"Well, anyway, what I mean is that you're such a grump in the morning that I can see someday your wife coming in— if you ever find a girl who's foolish enough to marry you. But I mean, she might come in some morning and give you grapefruit juice instead of orange juice and you probably bite her hand off or something."

"Or *something*." Charlie laughed.

P.S. punched Charlie in the arm. "Garbage mind! God Almighty!"

"What do you mean? I didn't say anything. You've got the dirty mind. All I said was 'or something' and you say I've got a garbage mind."

"Well, you know what I meant."

"I don't know anything at all."

P.S. looked at Charlie for a moment, then he laughed. "I'm not going to take advantage of your last remark. I'm much too good a sport to rake you over the coals when you place your ample foot in your ample mouth."

"*Ample foot!*" Charlie held up his foot. "I've got a very small foot. It's a sign of good breeding."

"Only in horses, twinkletoes, only in horses."

"Horses, *horses!* horses, my—"

"Ask me no questions and I'll tell you no lies." P.S. leafed through Charlie's notes. "Hey, the exam's at ten-thirty, isn't it?"

"Yep. If you flunk Latin again, will they make you go to summer school?"

"Probably. I really think it's archaic the way they make you pass Latin to get out of this place."

"Boy, I sure hope I pass it," Charlie said.

"You will. You will. You're the brain in the class."

"Come on. Let's go to chow."

"That's what I've been waiting for, my good buddy, my good friend, old pal of mine." P.S. jumped off the bed, scooped up his notebook, and started out of the room.

"Hey!" Charlie said. "What about the bed?"

At eight-o'clock chapel, P.S. knelt in the pew and prayed: "Dear God, I pray that I pass my Latin exam this morning. . . . If I can pass this exam, then I'll do anything you want me to . . . God, please. If I don't pass this exam, I've really had it. . . . *They must have made these pews for midgets; I never fit in them right. . . . How am I ever going to get out to Colorado this summer unless I pass that exam?* . . . Please, God, I don't want a high grade, all I want is to pass . . . and you don't have to help me on the others . . . I don't want to pass this exam for myself only. I mean, it means a lot to my family. My father will be very disappointed if I flunk the exam . . . *I wonder if Charlie will be able to go out to Colorado with me.* . . . God bless Mom, God bless Dad, God bless Grandpa Denison, God bless Grandma Denison, God bless Grandpa Wilkinson, God bless Grandma Wilkinson, God bless all the relatives I haven't mentioned . . . Amen. And . . . and, God, please, please help me to pass this exam."

At 10:15, P.S. and Charlie fell in step and walked over to Randolph Hall, where the examination was to be held.

"Well, if we don't know it now, we never will," Charlie said.

"Even if I did know it now, I wouldn't know it tomorrow." P.S. reached into his pants pocket and pulled out his lucky exam tie. It was a stained and raveled blue knit. As they walked up the path, he was careful to tie the tie backwards, the wide end next to his shirt, the seam facing out. Then he checked his watch pocket to see that his lucky silver dollar was still there.

"What's the Latin for 'then'?" Charlie asked.

"*Tum,*" P.S. answered. "Tums for your tummy."

"What's the word for 'thence' or 'from there'?"

"*Inde.*" P.S. began to sing, "*Inde* evening *byde* moonlight you could *hearde—*"

"For God's sake, P.S.!" Charlie laughed.

"You don't like my singing?"

"Not much."

"You know? I'm thinking of joining the choir and glee club next year. You know why? They've got a couple of dances next fall. One with St. Catherine's and another with St. Tim's. You wanta try out with me?"

"I don't know. I can't sing."

"Who's gonna sing?" P.S. grabbed Charlie's arm and growled, "Baby, I'm no singer, I'm a lover."

"Lover, my—"

"Ask me no questions and I'll tell you no lies."

P.S. and Charlie walked up the worn wooden steps of Randolph Hall to the third-floor study hall, where the Latin examination was to be given. They both were in the upper study hall since they were underclassmen still. P.S.'s desk was in the back corner of the study hall against the wall. He sat down and brushed the dust off the top of his desk with his palm. Someone had traced a hand into the wood. Others had traced and retraced the hand and deepened the grooves. They had added fingernails and rings. P.S. had added a tattoo. He lifted the desktop and, searching for his pencil sharpener, saw that he had some more Latin translations in his desk. He read them through quickly and decided it was too late to learn anything from them. He pulled out his pencil sharpener and closed his desk. The study hall was filling with boys, who took their places at their desks and called back and forth to each other in their slow Southern voices. It was a long narrow room with high windows on either side, and the walls were painted a dirty yellow. Between the windows were framed engravings of Roman ruins and Southern generals. The large fluorescent lights above the desks buzzed and blinked into life. A dark, curly-haired boy sat down in the desk next to P.S. and began to empty his pockets of pencils and pens.

"Hey, Jumbo?" P.S. said. "You gonna kill the exam?"

"I hope so. If I can get a good grade on it, then I don't have to worry so much about my math exam tomorrow."

"Well, if we don't know it now we never will."

"You're right."

Jumbo had played second-string tackle on the varsity this year. He was expected to be first-string next year, and by his final year, the coaches thought, he might become All-Virginia High School tackle. Jumbo was a sincere, not very bright student who came from a farm in Virginia and wanted to be a farmer when he finished college. P.S. had sat next to Jumbo all year, but they had never been particularly close friends. Jumbo lived in a different dormitory and had a tendency to stick with the other members of the football team. But P.S. liked him, and Jumbo was really the only member of the football team that he knew at all.

P.S. looked up at the engraving of General Robert E. Lee and his horse Traveller. He glanced over at Jumbo. Jumbo was cleaning his fingernails with the tip of his automatic pencil.

"Well, good luck," P.S. said.

"Good luck to you."

"I'll need it."

P.S. stood up and looked for Charlie. "Hey! Hey, Charlie?" Charlie turned around. "Yeah?"

"*Piggo, piggere, squeely, gruntum!*"

"For God's sake, P.S.!"

"Hey, P.S.?" someone shouted. "You gonna flunk it again this year?"

"No, no, I don't think so," P.S. answered in mock seriousness. "In point of fact, as the good Dr. Fairfax would say—in point of fact, I might just come out with the highest grade in the class. After all, I'm such a brain."

The noise in the study hall suddenly stopped; Dr. Fairfax had entered. The Latin instructor walked to the back of the study hall, where P.S. was sitting.

"And what was all that about, Wilkinson?"

"Sir, I was telling the others how I'm the brain in your class."

"Indeed?" Dr. Fairfax asked.

"Yes, sir. But I was only kidding."

"Indeed," the Latin instructor said, and the other students laughed.

Dr. Fairfax was a large man with a lean, aesthetic face, which he tried to disguise with a military mustache. He had taught at the Virginia Preparatory School since 1919. P.S.'s father had had Dr. Fairfax as a Latin instructor. When P.S. read *Goodbye, Mr. Chips*, he had kept thinking of Dr. Fairfax. The Latin instructor wore the same suit and vest all winter. They were always immaculate. The first day of spring was marked by Dr. Fairfax's appearance in a white linen suit, which he always wore with a small blue bachelor's-button. Before a study hall last spring, someone had placed an alarm clock set to go off in the middle of study hall in one of the tall wastepaper baskets at the rear of the room. The student had then emptied all of the pencil sharpeners and several ink bottles into the basket and covered all this with crumpled-up pad paper. When the alarm clock went off, Dr. Fairfax strode down the aisle and reached into the wastepaper basket for the clock. When he lifted it out, the sleeve of his white linen jacket was covered with ink and pencil shavings. There was a stunned silence as Dr. Fairfax looked at his sleeve. And then Dr. Fairfax began to laugh. The old man sat down on one of the desktops and laughed and laughed, until finally the students had enough nerve to join him. The next day he appeared in the same linen suit, but it was absolutely clean. Nobody was given demerits or punished in any manner. Dr. Fairfax was P.S.'s favorite instructor. P.S. watched him separate the examination papers and blue books into neat piles at the proctor's desk. Dr. Fairfax looked up at the electric clock over the study-hall door and then at his thin gold pocket watch. He cleared his throat. "Good morning, gentlemen."

"GOOD MORNING, SIR!" the students shouted.

"Gentlemen, there will be no talking during the examination. In the two hours given you, you will have ample time to complete all the necessary work. When the bell sounds signifying the end of the examination, you will cease work immediately. In point of fact, anyone found working after the bell will be looked upon most unfavorably. When you receive your examinations make certain that the print is legible. Make sure that you place your names on each of your blue books. If you have any difficulty reading the examination, hold your hand above your head and you will be given a fresh copy. The tops of your desk should be cleared of all notes, papers, and books. Are there any questions? . . . If not, will Baylor and you, Grandy, and . . . and Merritt . . . will the three of you please pass out the examinations."

P.S. watched Charlie get up and walk over to the desk.

Dr. Fairfax reached into his breast pocket and pulled out a pair of steel-rimmed spectacles. He looked out across the room. "We are nearing the end of the school year," he said. "Examinations always seem to cause students an undue amount of concern. I assure you, I can well remember when I was a student at V.P.S. In point of fact, I was not so very different from some of you. . . ."

The instructor was interrupted by a rasping Bronx cheer. He looked quickly over in the direction of the sound. "Travers, was that you?"

"No, sir."

"Brandon, was that you?"

The student hesitated, then answered, "Yes, sir."

"Brandon, I consider that marked disrespect, and it will cost you ten demerits."

"Aww, sir . . ."

"Fifteen." Dr. Fairfax cleared his throat again. "Now, if I may continue? . . . Good. There are a few important things to remember when taking an examination. First, do not get upset when you cannot at once answer all of the questions. The examination is designed . . ."

P.S. stopped listening. Charlie was walking down the aisle toward him.

"Hey, Charlie," he whispered. "Give me an easy one."

"There will be no favoritism on my part."

"How does it look?"

"Tough."

"Oh, God."

"Merritt and Wilkinson?" Dr. Fairfax said. "That last little bit of conversation will cost you each five demerits."

The Latin instructor looked up at the electric clock again. "When you receive your examinations, you may begin. Are there any questions? . . . If not, gentlemen, it might be well for us to remember this ancient Latin proverb: '*Abusus non tollit usum.*'" Dr. Fairfax waited for the laugh. There was none. He cleared his throat again. "Perhaps . . . perhaps we had better ask the class brain what the proverb means. Wilkinson?"

P.S. stood up. "'*Abusus non tollit usum,*' sir?"

"That's right."

"Something like 'Abuse does not tolerate the use,' sir?"

"What does the verb *tollo, tollere, sustuli, sublatus* mean?"

"To take away, sir."

"That's right. The proverb, then, is 'Abuse does not take away the use,' or, in the context I was referring to, just because you gentlemen cannot do Latin properly does not mean that it should not be done at all."

"Yes, sir," P.S. said, and he sat down.

Dr. Fairfax unfolded his newspaper, and P.S. began to read the examination. He picked up his pencil and printed in large letters on the cover of his blue book:

PHILIP SADLER WILKINSON
LATIN EXAMINATION
LATIN 11—DR. FAIRFAX
VIRGINIA PREPARATORY SCHOOL
7 JUNE 1951—BOOK ONE (1)

Then he put down his pencil, stretched, and began to work.

P.S. read the examination carefully. He saw that he would be able to do very little of it from memory, and he felt the first surge of panic moisten his palms. He tried to translate the first Latin-to-English passage. He remembered that it fell on the right-hand side of the page in his Ullman and Henry, opposite the picture of the Roman galley. The picture was a still taken from the silent-movie version of *Ben Hur*. He recognized some of the verbs, more of the nouns, and finally he began to be able to translate. It was about the Venetian ships, which were more efficient than the Roman galleys because they had high prows and flat keels. He translated the entire passage, put down his pencil, and stretched again.

An hour later P.S. knew he was in trouble. The first translation and the vocabulary section were the only parts of the exam he had been able to do without too much difficulty. He was able to give the rule and examples for the datives of "agent" and "possession." The English-to-Latin sentences were the most difficult. He had been able to do only one of those. For the question, "How do you determine the tense of the infinitive on indirect statement?" he wrote, "You can determine the tense by the construction of the sentence and by the word endings," and hoped he might get some credit. The two Latin-to-English passages counted twenty points apiece. If he could only do that second translation, he stood a chance of passing the examination. He recognized the adverb *inde* but saw that it didn't help him very much. The examination was halfway over. He tried to count how many points he had made so far on the examination. He thought he might have somewhere between fifty and fifty-five. Passing was seventy. If he could just translate that second passage, he would have the points he needed to pass. Dr. Fairfax never scaled the grades. P.S. had heard that one year the Latin instructor had flunked everybody but two.

He glanced over at Jumbo. Then he looked back down at his own examination and swore under his breath. Jumbo looked over at him and smiled. P.S. pantomimed that he could not answer the questions, and Jumbo smiled again. P.S. slid his glasses off and rubbed his eyes. He fought down the panic and wiped his hands on his pants legs, and looked at the passage again. He couldn't make any sense out of the blur of words.

He squinted, looked at them, put on his glasses again, and knew that he was really in trouble.

He leaned over his desk and closed his eyes. *Dear God, please help me on this examination . . . please, God, please . . . I must pass this examination.* He opened his eyes and looked carefully around to see if anyone had seen him praying. The others were all working hard on the examination. P.S. looked up again at the engraving on the wall above his desk. Beneath the portrait was the legend "Soon after the close of the War Between the States, General Robert E. Lee became the head of a school for young men. General Lee made this statement when he met with his students for the first time: 'We have but one rule in this school, and that is that every student must be a gentleman.'" *They left out that other rule,* P.S. thought. *They left out the one that says you have to have Latin to graduate! . . . Or is that part of being a gentleman, too?*

He read the Latin-to-English passage through twice, then he read it through backward. He knew he had seen the passage before. He even remembered seeing it recently. But where? He knew that the passage dealt with the difficulties the Romans were having in fortifying their positions, but there were so many technical words that he could not get more than five of the twenty points from the translation, and he needed at least fifteen to pass. . . . He was going to flunk. *But I can't flunk! I've got to pass!*

P.S. knew if he flunked he wouldn't be able to face his father. No matter what excuse his father gave, his father would not believe he hadn't loafed all term.

He looked at the passage and tried to remember where he had seen it. And then his mouth went dry. He felt the flush burn into the back of his neck and spread to his cheeks. He swallowed hard. *The translation's in my desk! . . . It's in my desk! . . . Jesus . . . oh, Jesus! . . . It's the translation on top of the stack in my desk . . . in my desk!*

All he would have to do would be to slip the translation out of his desk, copy it, put it away, and he would pass the examination. All of his worries would be over. His father would be happy that he passed the examination. He wouldn't have to go to summer school. He and Charlie could go out to Colorado together to work on that dude ranch. He would be through with Latin forever. His Latin grade would never pull his average down again. Everything would be all right. Everything would be fine. All he would have to do would be to copy that one paragraph. Everyone cheated. Maybe not at V.P.S. But in other schools they bragged about it. . . . Everyone cheated in one way or another. Why should that one passage ruin everything? Who cared what problems the Romans had!

P.S. glanced over at Jumbo. Jumbo was chewing on his pencil eraser as he worked on the examination. Dr. Fairfax was still reading his newspaper. P.S. felt his heart beat faster. It began beating so hard that he was certain Jumbo could hear it. P.S. gently raised his desktop and pretended to feel around for a pencil. He let his blue book slide halfway off his desk so it leaned on his lap. Then he slid the translation under his blue book and slid the blue book and notes back onto his desk. He was certain that everyone had seen him—that everyone knew he was about to cheat. He slowly raised his eyes to look at Dr. Fairfax, who went on reading. P.S. covered part of the notes with his examination and began to copy the rest into his blue book. He could feel the heat in his cheeks, the dryness in his mouth. *Dear God . . . God, please don't let them catch me! . . . Please!*

He changed the smooth translation into a rough one as he copied, so that it would match his other translations.

From these things the army was taught the nature of the place and how the slope of the hill and the necessity of the time demanded more than one plan and order for the art of war. Different legions, some in one part, others in another, fought the enemy. And the view was obstructed by very thick hedges. Sure support could not be placed, nor could it be seen what work would be necessary in which part, nor could all the commands be administered by one man. Therefore, against so much unfairness of things, various consequences ensued.

He put down his pencil and looked around the study hall. No one was watching. P.S. carefully slid the translation back into his desk. He looked to see if the translation had given him any words that might help him on the rest of the examination. His heart was still beating wildly in his chest, and his hands shook. He licked his lips, and concentrated on behaving normally. *It's over . . . it's over . . . I've cheated, but it's all over and no one said anything!*

He began to relax.

Fifteen minutes later Dr. Fairfax stood up at his desk, looked at the electric clock, then down at his pocket watch. He cleared his throat and said, "Stop!"

Several students groaned. The rest gathered up their pencils and pens.

"Make certain you have written out the pledge in full and signed it," Dr. Fairfax said.

P.S. felt the physical pain of fear again. He opened his blue book and wrote, "I pledge on my honor as a gentleman that I have neither given nor received unauthorized assistance on this examination." He hesitated, then he signed his name.

"Place your examinations inside your blue book," Dr. Fairfax continued. "Make certain that you put your name on your blue book. . . . Baylor? If you and, uh, Ferguson and Showalter will be good enough to pick up the examinations, the rest of you may go. And, um, gentlemen, your grades will be posted on the front door of my office no sooner than forty-eight hours from now. In point of fact, any attempt to solicit your grade any sooner will result in bad temper on my part and greater severity in the marking of papers. Are there any questions? . . . If not, gentlemen, dismissed."

The students stood up and stretched. An immediate, excited hum of voices filled the study hall. P.S. looked down at his exam paper. He slid it into his blue book and left it on his desk.

Charlie was waiting at the door of the study hall. "Well, P.S., how'd the brain do?"

"You know it's bad luck to talk about an exam before the grades are posted."

"I know, I'm just asking you how you did."

"I don't know," P.S. said.

"Well, well, I mean, do you think you passed?"

"I don't know!"

"Whooey!" Charlie whistled. "And you called *me* a grump!"

They walked down the stairs together. At the bottom Charlie asked P.S. if he was going to lunch.

"No, I don't think so," P.S. said. "I'm not feeling so well. I think I'll lie down for a while. I'll see ya."

"Sure," Charlie said. "See ya."

In his cubicle in Memorial Hall, P.S. took off his lucky exam tie. He put his silver dollar back onto his bookcase. He reached inside the hollow copy of *Gulliver's Travels* for the pack of cigarettes he kept there. Then he walked down the corridor to the bathroom, stepped into one of the stalls, and locked the door. He lit the cigarette and leaned his forehead against the cool green marble divider. He was sick with fear and dread. *It's over! It's all over!* he said, trying to calm himself. He did not like the new knowledge he had of himself. He was a cheater. He rolled his forehead back and forth against the stone, pressing into it, hurting himself. P.S. had broken the Honor Code of the school, and he was scared.

I shouldn't have cheated! What if someone had seen me! I shouldn't have cheated! . . . Maybe somebody did see me . . . Maybe Dr. Fairfax will know I cheated when he sees my exam . . . Maybe somebody will check my desk after the exam and find the copy of the translation. . . . I cheated. Jesus, I cheated! . . . Stupid goddam fool. . . . What if somebody finds out! . . . Maybe I should turn myself in . . . it would prove that I really am honest, I just made a mistake, that's all. . . . I'll tell them I couldn't help it. . . . Maybe they'll just give me a reprimand.

But P.S. knew that if he turned himself in, they would still tell his parents he had cheated, so what good would that do? His father would be just as angry. Even more so, since Wilkinsons don't cheat either. P.S. knew how ashamed his father would make him feel. His father would have to tell others that P.S. had cheated. It was a part of the Southern tradition. "My son has disgraced me. It is better that you hear it from me than somebody else." His father would do something like that. And having other people know he had cheated would be too much shame to bear. And even if he did turn himself in, the school would make him take another exam . . . and he'd flunk that one, too . . . he knew it. . . . *Oh, God, what am I going to do?*

If he didn't turn himself in and no one had seen him, then who would know? He would never cheat again. If he could just get away with it this one time. Then everything would be O.K. Nobody need ever know—except himself. And P.S. knew that he would never be able to forget that he had cheated. Maybe if he turned himself in, it would be better in the long run. *What long run? What the hell kind of long run will I have if I turn myself in? Everybody in the school will know I cheated, no matter whether I turn myself in or not. . . . They won't remember me for turning myself in . . . they'll remember that I cheated in the first place.*

P.S. wanted to cry, but he couldn't. He dropped the cigarette into the toilet and flushed it down. Then he went over to the sink and rinsed his mouth. He had some chewing gum in his room; that would cover the smell of his smoking. He looked at himself in the mirror. He couldn't see any change since this morning, and yet he felt so different. He looked at his eyes to see if there were wrinkles under them now. *What shall I do?* he asked his reflection. *What, what the hell shall I do?* He turned on the cold water and rinsed his face. He dried himself on a towel someone had left behind, and walked back down the corridor to his room. He brushed aside the curtain, entered the cubicle and stopped, frozen with fear. Mabrey, the head monitor, was sitting on P.S.'s bed.

"Wilkinson," Mabrey said, "would you mind coming with me?"

He called me Wilkinson, not P.S. . . . not P.S.! "Where do you want to go?"

"Just outside for a few minutes."

"What about?"

Mabrey got up from the bed. "Come on, P.S."

"What . . . what do you want me for?"

"We want to talk to you."

We! WE! P.S. picked up his jacket and started to put it on.

"You won't need your coat," Mabrey said.

"It doesn't matter, I'll wear it anyway."

P.S. followed Mabrey out of the dormitory. *I didn't have a chance to turn myself in,* he thought. *I didn't have a chance to choose. . . . Oh, God damn it . . . God damn it!*

"You think you'll make the varsity baseball team next year?" Mabrey asked.

"I don't know," P.S. said. *What is he talking about baseball for?*

The new boy who had wakened P.S. passed them on the walk. He said hello to both Mabrey and P.S. He received no answer and shrugged.

Mabrey and P.S. took the path to the headmaster's office. P.S. could feel the enormous weight of the fear building up inside him again. Mabrey opened the door for P.S. and ushered him into the headmaster's waiting room. Nelson, a pale, fat-faced senior, was sitting there alone. He was the secretary of the Honor Committee. P.S. had always hated him. The other members of the committee were Mabrey, the vice-president; Linus Hendricks, the president; Mr. Seaton, the headmaster; and Dr. Fairfax, who served as faculty adviser. Mabrey motioned that P.S. was to sit down in the chair facing the others—the only straight-backed wooden chair in the room. Every now and then Nelson would look up at P.S. and shake his head. The door to the headmaster's office opened and Mr. Seaton came out, followed by Linus Hendricks, Dr. Fairfax and— *My God, what is Jumbo doing here! Don't tell me he cheated, too! He was sitting right next to me!* Jumbo walked out of the room without looking at P.S.

Linus Hendricks waited for the others to seat themselves, then he sat down himself and faced P.S. "Well, P.S., I imagine you know why you're here."

P.S. looked at Hendricks. Hendricks was the captain of the football team. He and Mabrey were the two most important undergraduates in the school.

"Well, P.S.?" Hendricks repeated.

"Yes, sir," P.S. said.

He could feel them all staring at him. He looked down at his hands folded in his lap. He could see clearly every line in his thumb knuckle. He could see the dirt caught under the corner of his fingernail, and the small blue vein running across the knuckle.

He looked up at Dr. Fairfax. He wanted to tell him not to worry. He wanted to tell him he was sorry, so very sorry.

The headmaster, Mr. Seaton, was a young man. He had just become the headmaster of V.P.S. this year. He liked the students, and the students liked him. He was prematurely bald, and smiled a lot. He had a very young and pretty wife and some of the students were in love with her and fought to sit at her table in the dining room. Mr. Seaton liked to play tennis. He would play the students and bet his dessert that he would win. And most of the time he would lose, and the students were enormously pleased to see the headmaster of the school have to get up from the table and pay his bets. Mr. Seaton would walk very quickly across the dining hall, his bald head bent to hide his smile. He would swoop up to the table, drop the dessert, and depart, like a bombing airplane. P.S. could tell that the headmaster was distressed he had cheated.

Linus Hendricks crossed his legs and sank back into the deep leather armchair, Mabrey and Nelson leaned forward as though they were going to charge P.S.

"P.S.," Hendricks said, "you're here this afternoon because the Honor Committee has reason to suspect that you may have cheated on the Latin exam this morning. We must ask you whether or not this is true."

P.S. raised his head and looked at Hendricks. Hendricks was wearing a bright striped tie. P.S. concentrated on the stripes. Thick black, thin white, medium green, thin white, and thick black.

"P.S., did you or did you not cheat on the Latin examination?"

P.S. nodded.

"Yes or no, P.S.?" Hendricks asked.

P.S. no longer felt anything. He was numb with misery. "Yes," he said, in a small tired voice. "Yes, I cheated on the examination. But I was going to turn myself in. I was going to turn myself in. I swear I was."

"If you were going to turn yourself in, why didn't you?" Nelson asked.

"I couldn't . . . I couldn't yet . . ." P.S. looked at Dr. Fairfax. "I'm sorry, sir. I'm terribly sorry." P.S. began to cry. "I'm so ashamed . . . Oh, God . . ." P.S. tried to stop crying. He couldn't. The tears stung his eyes. One tear slipped into the inside of his glasses and puddled across the bottom of the lens. He reached into his back pocket for a handkerchief, but he had forgotten to bring one. He started to pull out his shirt tail, and decided he'd better not. He wiped his face with the side of his hand.

Mr. Seaton walked over to P.S. and gave him his handkerchief. The headmaster rested his hand on P.S.'s shoulder. "Why, P.S.? Why did you cheat?"

P.S. couldn't answer.

"P.S., you were the last boy I expected this of. Why did you feel you had to cheat on this exam?"

"I don't know, sir."

"But, P.S., you must have had some reason."

Nelson said, "Answer the headmaster when he's asking you a question, Wilkinson."

P.S. looked up at him with such loathing that Nelson turned away.

Mr. Seaton crouched down next to P.S. "You must have been aware of the penalty for cheating."

P.S. nodded.

"Then why, in God's name, did you risk expulsion, just to pass the Latin examination?"

"Sir—sir, I flunked Latin last year, sir. I knew I'd flunk it this year, too. I—I knew I couldn't pass the Latin exam ever."

"But why did you *cheat*?"

"Because . . . because, sir, I had to pass the exam."

The headmaster ran his hand across his forehead. "P.S., I'm not trying to trick you, I'm only trying to understand why you did this thing. Why did you bring the notes into the exam with you?"

"Sir, Mr. Seaton, I didn't bring the notes in, they were in my desk. If they hadn't been, I wouldn't be here. I didn't want to cheat. I didn't mean to cheat. I—It was just the only way I could pass the exam."

Nelson rested his pudgy arms on the sides of his leather armchair and looked at the headmaster and then back to P.S. Then he said, "Wilkinson, you have been in V.P.S. for two years. You must be familiar, I imagine, with the Honor Code. In fact, in your study hall, there is a small wooden plaque above the proctor's desk. On it are carved the four points of the Honor Code: 'I will not lie. I will not steal. I will not cheat. I will report anyone I see doing so.' You are familiar with them, aren't you?"

"Of course I'm familiar with them," P.S. said impatiently.

"Why did you think you were so much better than everyone else that you could ignore it?"

"I don't think I'm better than everyone else, Nelson," P.S. said.

"Well, you sure aren't! The others don't cheat." Nelson sat back again, very satisfied with himself.

Dr. Fairfax came from behind the chairs and stood next to P.S. "Unless you hold your tongue, Nelson—unless you hold your tongue, I shall personally escort you out of here."

"But, sir," Nelson whined, "I'm only trying to—"

"SHUT UP!" Dr. Fairfax roared. He returned to the back of the room.

Mr. Seaton spoke again. "P.S., if you had flunked this exam, you would have been able to take another. Perhaps you would have passed the re-examination. Most boys do."

"I wouldn't have, sir," P.S. said. "I just cannot do Latin. You could have given me fifty examinations, sir. And I don't mean any disrespect but I would have flunked them all."

Mabrey asked the headmaster if he could speak, then he turned to P.S. "P.S., we—all of us—have been tempted at some time or another to cheat. All of us have either resisted that temptation or, perhaps, we were lucky enough to get away with it. I think that what we want to know is what *made* you cheat? Just having to pass the exam isn't enough. I know you, P.S. I may know you better than anyone else in this room, because

I've shared the same floor in the dorm with you this year. And we were on the same floor when you were a toad. You're not the kind who cheats unless he has a damn good—" Mabrey glanced over at the headmaster. "Excuse me, sir, I didn't mean to swear."

The headmaster nodded and indicated that Mabrey was to continue.

"What I mean is this, P.S. I know you don't care how high your grade is, just so long as you keep out of trouble. . . . You're one of the most popular boys in your class. Everybody likes you. Why would you throw all of this over, just to pass a Latin exam?"

"I don't know. I don't know. . . . I had to pass the exam. If I flunked it again, my father would kill me."

"What do you mean he would kill you?" Mr. Seaton asked.

"Oh, nothing, sir. I mean—I don't mean he would hurt me. He would just— Oh, God, sir, I don't know how to explain it to you. If I flunked the exam again, he'd just make me feel so, I don't know . . . *ashamed* . . . so terrible. I just couldn't take it again."

There was a moment of silence in the room. P.S. began to cry again. He could tell the headmaster still didn't understand why he had cheated. He looked down at his hands again. With his index finger he traced the veins that crossed the back of his hand. He looked over at the wooden arm of his straight-backed chair. He could see the little drops of moisture where his hand had squeezed the arm of the chair. He could make out every grain of wood, every worn spot. He took off his glasses and rubbed his eyes. He tried taking deep breaths, but each time his breath would be choked off.

Hendricks cleared his throat and recrossed his legs. "P.S.," he said, "we have your examination here. You signed your name to the pledge at the end of the exam. You swore on your honor that you had not cheated." Hendricks paused. P.S. knew what he was driving at.

"If I hadn't signed my name to the pledge, you would have known I had cheated right away," P.S. explained. "I didn't *want* to break my honor again, I was going to turn myself in, honest I was."

"You didn't though," Nelson said.

"I would have!" P.S. said. But he still wasn't sure whether he would have or not. He knew he never would be certain.

"So, we've got you on lying and cheating," Nelson said. "How do we know you haven't stolen, too?"

Dr. Fairfax grabbed the lapels of Nelson's jacket, pulled him out of the chair and pushed him out of the room. The old man closed the door and leaned against it. He wiped his brow and said, "Mr. Seaton, sir, I trust you won't find fault with my actions. That young Nelson has a tendency to bother me. In point of fact, he irritates me intensely."

P.S. looked gratefully at Dr. Fairfax. The old man smiled sadly. Mabrey was talking quietly to Hendricks. Mr. Seaton sat down in Nelson's chair and turned to P.S. "I know this is a difficult question. Would you—would you have turned Jumbo in had you seen him cheating?"

P.S. felt the blood drain from his face, *So Jumbo turned me in! . . . Jumbo saw me! . . . Sitting next to me all year! . . . Jumbo turned me in! Why, in God's name?*

He looked up at the others. They were all waiting for his answer. He had the most curious feeling of aloofness, of coldness. If he said yes, that he would have turned Jumbo in, it would be a lie, and he knew it. If he answered yes, it would please the headmaster though. Because it would mean that P.S. still had faith in the school system. If he said no, he wouldn't have turned Jumbo in, it would be as good as admitting that he wouldn't obey the fourth part of the Honor Code—"I will report anyone I see doing so." He waited a moment and then answered, "I don't know. I don't know whether I would have turned Jumbo in or not."

"Thank you very much, P.S.," the headmaster said.

P.S. could tell that Mr. Seaton was disappointed in his answer.

"Gentlemen, do you have any further questions you would like to ask Wilkinson?"

"Nothing, sir," Hendricks answered.

The headmaster looked over at Dr. Fairfax, who shook his head. "Well, then, P.S., if you don't mind, we'd like you to sit in my office until we call for you."

P.S. got up and started for the door.

"Have you had any lunch?" Dr. Fairfax asked.

"No, sir. But I'm not very hungry."

"I'll have Mrs. Burdick bring in some milk and cookies."

"Thank you, sir."

The door opened and P.S. stood up as Mr. Seaton walked over to his desk and eased himself into the swivel chair. P.S. had been sitting alone in the headmaster's office for several hours.

"Sit down, please," the headmaster said. He picked up a wooden pencil and began to roll it back and forth between his palms. P.S. could hear the click of the pencil as it rolled across the headmaster's ring. Mr. Seaton laid the pencil aside and rubbed his cheek. His hand moved up the side of his face and began to massage his temple. Then he looked up at P.S. and said, "The Honor Committee has decided that you must leave the school. The penalty for cheating at V.P.S. is immediate expulsion. There cannot be any exceptions."

P.S. took a deep breath and pushed himself back into the soft leather seat. Then he dropped his hands into his lap and slumped. He was beyond crying; there was nothing left to cry about.

"We were able to reach your father before he left Washington and he is waiting for you in the other room," Mr. Seaton said. "I've asked him to wait outside for a few minutes, because I want to speak to you alone. I want you to understand why the school had to make the decision to expel you. The school—this school—is only as good as its honor system. And the honor system is only as good as the students who live by it."

P.S. cleared his throat and looked down at his fingernails. He wished the headmaster wouldn't talk about it. He knew why the school had to expel him. It was done. It was over with. What good would it do to talk about it?

"The honor system, since it is based on mutual trust and confidence, no doubt makes it easier for some students to cheat," the headmaster said. "I am not so naïve as to believe that there aren't any boys who cheat here. Unfortunately, our honor system makes it easier for them to do so. These boys have not been caught. Perhaps they will never be caught. But I feel that it was far better for you to have been caught right away, P.S., because you are not a cheater. Notice that I said you *are* not a cheater instead of you *were* not a cheater. . . . Yes, you cheated this one time. I do not need to ask whether you cheated before. I know you haven't. I know also that you will not cheat again. You were the last boy I would have expected to cheat. I am still not entirely satisfied by the reasons you gave for cheating. I suppose a person never is. Maybe it is impossible to give reasons for such an act." Mr. Seaton began massaging his temples again. "P.S., the most difficult thing that you must try to understand is that Jumbo did the right thing. Jumbo was correct in turning you in."

P.S. stiffened in the chair. "Yes, sir," he said.

"If no one reported infractions, we would have no Honor Code. The code would be obeyed only when it was convenient to obey it. It would be given lip service. The whole system would break down. The school would become just another private school, instead of the respected and loved institution it now is. Put yourself in Jumbo's shoes for a moment. You and Jumbo are friends—*believe me,* you are friends. If you had heard what Jumbo said about you in here, and how it hurt him to turn you in, you would know what a good friend Jumbo is. You have been expelled for cheating. You will not be here next fall. But Jumbo will be. Jumbo will stay on at V.P.S., and the other students will know that he was the one who turned you in. When I asked you whether you would have turned Jumbo in, you said that you didn't know. You and I both know from your answer that you wouldn't have turned Jumbo in. Perhaps the schoolboy code is still stronger in you than the Honor Code. No one likes to turn in a friend. A lot of boys who don't know any better, a lot of your friends, will never forgive Jumbo. It will be plenty tough for him. Just as it is tough on anybody who does his duty. I think—I honestly think that Jumbo has done you a favor. I'm not going to suggest that you be grateful to him. Not yet. That would be as ridiculous as my saying something as trite as 'Someday you will be able to look back on this and laugh.' . . . P.S., you will never be able to look back on this and laugh. But you may be able to understand." The headmaster looked at his wristwatch and then said, "I'm going to leave you alone with your father for a few minutes; then I suggest that you go back to your room and pack. The other students won't be back in the dormitories yet, so you can be alone." He got up from behind his desk. P.S. rose also. He looked down at the milk and cookies Mrs. Burdick had left him. There was half a glass of milk and three cookies remaining.

The headmaster looked at P.S. for a moment and then he said, "I'm sorry you have been expelled, P.S. You were a good student here. One of the most popular boys in your class. You will leave behind a great many good friends."

"Thank you, sir," P.S. said.

"I'll see you before you and your father leave?"

"Yes, sir."

The headmaster walked into the waiting room. P.S. could hear Dr. Fairfax talking, and then his father. The door closed, and P.S. sat down to wait for his father. He could feel the fear building up inside him again. He did not know what to say to his father. What could he say? He sipped the last of the milk as the door opened. P.S. put down the glass and stood up.

Stewart Wilkinson closed the door behind him and looked at his son. P.S. tried to meet his father's look, and then both their glances wavered, and P.S. saw his father looking down at the plate of cookies and the empty milk glass. "Where did you get the milk and cookies, Son?"

"Mrs. Burdick brought them to me, sir."

"Did you thank her?"

"Yes, sir."

Stewart Wilkinson walked over to the couch and sat down

next to his son. The boy remained standing.

"Phil, Son, sit down, please."

"Yes, sir."

P.S. looked down at his hands again. Neither one spoke until P.S. took a deep breath and said, "I'm sorry, sir."

"Yes . . . yes, Son, I know you are. . . . I'm terribly sorry myself. Sorry for you. Mr. Seaton told me that another boy turned you in, is that right?"

P.S. nodded.

"He also told me that he believes you would have turned yourself in had you been given enough time."

"I don't know whether I would have or not. I never had the chance to find out."

"I think you would have. I think you would have."

He waited for his son to say something; but there was nothing P.S. could say.

"I was talking to Dr. Fairfax outside—you knew he was my Latin teacher, too?"

"Yes, sir."

"We always used to be able to tell when the first day of spring came because Dr. Fairfax would put on his white linen suit."

"Yes, sir."

"At any rate, that man thinks very highly of you, Phil. He is very upset that you had to be expelled. I hope you will speak to him before you go. He's a good man to have on your side."

"I want to speak to him."

"Phil . . . Phil . . ." Stewart Wilkinson paused, then spoke again. "Phil, I know I am partly responsible for what has happened. I must have in some way pressured you into it. I wanted your marks to be high. I wanted you to get the best education that you could. V.P.S. isn't the best school in the country, but it's a very fine one. It's a school that has meant a lot to our family. But that doesn't matter so much. I mean that part of it is all over with. I'm sorry that you cheated, because I know you're not the cheating kind. I'm also sorry because you're going to have to face the family and get it over with. This is going to be tough. But they'll all understand. I doubt that there is any of us who has never cheated in one way or another. But it will make them very proud of you if you can go see them and look them in the eye."

Stewart Wilkinson picked up one of the cookies and began to bite little pieces out of the edge. Then he shook his head sadly in the gesture P.S. knew so well. "Ah, God, Son, it's so terrible that you have to learn these lessons when you are so young. . . . I know that you don't want me to feel sorry for you, but I can't help it. I'm not angry with you. I'm a little disappointed, perhaps, but I can understand it, I think. I suppose I must appear as an ogre to you at times. But, Phil—I— If I'm tough to you, it's just because I'm trying to help you . . . maybe I'm too tough."

They were both quiet, and P.S. wondered whether his father wanted a denial. He was about to speak when his father said, "I'll go speak with Mr. Seaton for a while, Phil, and then I'll come on over and help you pack. If you'd like, I'll pack for you and you can sit in the car."

"No, that's all right, sir, I'll pack. I mean most of the stuff is packed up already. I'll meet you over there."

They rose together and stood looking at each other. There was one brief moment when they could have reached out to each other, touched each other, comforted each other, but as soon as they recognized the moment they knew also that the moment had passed.

"I'll be through packing in a few minutes. I'll meet you in my room," P.S. said.

"Fine, Son."

Together, they carried the footlocker down the staircase of Memorial Hall. P.S. stopped at the door, balanced the footlocker with one hand, then pulled the heavy door open. The door swung back before they could both get through. P.S. felt his father stumble and the boy said, "I'm sorry."

They carried the footlocker across the small patch of lawn between Memorial Hall and the main drive and slid it into the back of the station wagon.

"How much more is there, Son?"

"A couple of small boxes, some books, and a couple of pictures."

Stewart Wilkinson pulled a silk handkerchief out of his back pocket and wiped his brow. "You think we can get all of them in one more trip?"

"I think so, sir. At least, we can try."

They turned back toward the dormitory. Stewart Wilkinson placed his hand on his son's shoulder as they crossed the lawn. "Phil, Mr. Seaton told me that he thinks he might be able to get you into Hotchkiss. How does that sound to you?"

"It's a funny name for a school."

"Hotchkiss, funny? Why?"

"I don't know, it just sounds funny."

"Well, do you think you'd like to go there?"

"Sure. I mean I don't know. I haven't given it much thought."

Stewart Wilkinson laughed. "I guess you haven't."

P.S. looked worriedly at his father for a moment. He wondered whether his father was making fun of him. And then he saw the humor in his remark and laughed too.

They brought the last of the boxes down from the room and slid them into the car and closed the tailgate.

"Did you get a chance to talk to Dr. Fairfax?"

"Yes, sir. He came by my room while I was packing."

"What did he say?"

"I don't know. I mean he was sorry I was going and all that, but he said I'd get along fine anywhere and that it wasn't the end of the world."

"Did he say 'in point of fact'?"

"Yeah." P.S. laughed. "He said. 'Well, boy, you'll do all right. In point of fact, you have nothing to worry about.' I really like old Doc Fairfax."

They went around the side of the car and climbed in.

"Anything you've forgotten? Books out of the library, equipment in the gym? Anybody special you want to see before we go home?"

"No, thanks, that's all— Hey, wait a minute, could you,

Dad?" P.S. got out of the car. "It's Charlie—Charlie Merritt. I'd like to say good-by to him."

"Sure, Son, take your time."

The two boys spoke together for a moment, standing in the road; then they shook hands. Stewart Wilkinson turned off the engine and watched as the boys walked back up the road toward him. As they drew near, he got out of the station wagon.

"Dad, this is Charlie Merritt. Charlie, you remember my father."

"Yes, sir. How are you, sir?"

"Fine, thank you, Charlie."

"Sir, Mr. Wilkinson. I'm sorry about P.S. getting kicked out and all."

Stewart Wilkinson nodded.

"He's just sorry because I won't be around to borrow his toothpaste any more. He likes to lend it to me because I always roll it from the top and lose the cap."

P.S. and Charlie laughed.

"Hey, P.S.?" Charlie said. "Does this mean you're not going to have to work off the five demerits Doc Fairfax gave us this morning?"

"What did you two get five demerits for?" Stewart Wilkinson asked.

"We were talking before the exam," P.S. said.

Father and son looked at each other, and then P.S. turned away. P.S. took a deep breath and tried to smile. "You know? It's funny," he said. "I mean, it seems that that exam took place so long ago. . . . Well, Charlie?" P.S. stuck out his hand and Charlie took it. "Well, I guess we'd better get going. I'll see you around, okay?"

"Sure, P.S.," Charlie said.

The two boys shook hands again solemnly. Then Charlie shook hands with P.S.'s father. P.S. and Stewart Wilkinson got back into the station wagon.

Charlie walked around to P.S.'s window. "Hey, P.S.! Make sure you let me hear from you this summer, okay?"

"Sure, Charlie. Take care of yourself."

They drove around the school drive, past the Wilkinson Memorial Library and the Sadler Gymnasium, and then they turned down the slight hill toward the Breastworks, and as they passed through the ornate, wrought-iron gate P.S. began to cry.

It was cold now in his BOQ room. P.S. Wilkinson pushed himself up from his Army cot and walked stiffly to his desk. He pulled out a piece of writing paper and looked at it for a moment, letting it flap gently in his hand. And then he sat down.

"Dear Hilary," he wrote. "I don't know how to write this except in the most simple form. Will you marry me?"